INDEX

	Page
FOREWORD	
Satan Comes to Cedar Springs	7
A Twist of Tea	15
Good Help is Hard to Find	21
Small Town Sweethearts	26
Stillborn	32
What George Would Have Wanted	36
The Burying Trade	42
Zeke and Hannah	48
Timmy's Picture	51
Scrimping and Saving	55
Billy Goat Bold, Billy Goat Sold!	59
An Obligation	64
May Your Name Never Prosper	72
Bright Lights, Big City	84
Fox in the Hen Pen	109
House on Old Bark Road	114
Election Time	118
Suicide	121
Old Friends	125
Widow Woman	131
I Remember Anna	146
Fly Dope and Whisky	158
The Gift	162
Covered Bridge Secret	167
The Journey	174
Culver's Last Ride	187
Mothers Day	196
Cell Phone	208
The Lawson House	214
A Life for Lilian	224

FOREWORD

Welcome to Cedar Springs, population 750. Like many small villages in central New Brunswick, it has schools, stores, garages and gas bars. It has a restaurant, post office, library and a variety of churches. There are some fine old gingerbread houses, a few salt boxes decked out with porches, several post-war storey-and-a-halves, lots of rambling ranchers with patios and swimming pools, three clusters of mobile homes squatting on concrete pads, and a few ancient, bulging, dilapidated paint-chipped pock-marked eyesores waiting for Halloween pranksters to set them afire.

The people of Cedar Springs are mainly descendants of English, Irish, Scottish, German, Danish and Dutch immigrants. Graveyards in and around Cedar Springs tell their stories of birth, marriage, children, epidemics, military service and death. For generations people have intermarried to the point that what passes as family history is really a stew of fact, gossip and myth. Still, folks can often guess which rock pile the snake is under. Now and then we like to dust off the skeletons in closets and rattle the bones.

Cedar Springs is no better and no worse than other local villages. The Cedar Springs Weekly reports two or three unlawful incidents a week, a drunk driving charge, a forged cheque, an altercation which occurred after a dance, or a charge of poaching. Some Saturday nights, young men make nuisances of themselves after they have a few drinks, by getting in their cars and then burning rubber up and down the road. Apart from those exceptions its citizens are generally law-abiding, content to go peaceably about their lives.

The nearest town of any size is Woodstock. Industry in the St. John River valley centres around potato farming. Those who don't farm or work at the major processing plant earn a living through satellite and subsidiary industries--machine shops, garages, fertilizer plants, co-ops, farm and feed outlets, farm machinery dealers and transportation companies. Then there are those with government jobs: people who work on the roads, teach in the schools, nurse in the hospitals.

Children in rural areas surrounding Cedar Springs have, since the 1950s, been bussed to regional schools more than 20 miles from home. Old one-room schools--except for one in Armond--have been turned into sheds, barns, granaries, private homes and Women's Institute halls. Some left vacant have been allowed to collapse back into the earth.

In the early 1990s Premier Frank McKenna touted the Information Highway. Every school is now connected to the Internet so most children from six on are computer-literate. The parents are a little slower getting on line but many are learning from their kids. In fact, some of the first adults to latch on to computer technology were farmers, those with computerized machinery, computerized cooling and drying systems for potato and grain storage facilities, where a difference of a degree in air temperature could cause disaster costing thousands of dollars. And, of course, there are those who balk like mules against learning anything new. These are the people who stand in long line-ups for the one harried teller at the bank, instead of using the banking machine, the same people who bought VCRs and never programmed the clock.

Although welfare rolls are swollen with the seasonally employed, single-parent families and plain old doggers born with their hand out, expecting and getting the world to give them a living, the area around Cedar Springs is thriving and construction goes ahead when the weather is fine. Large new homes spring up near the water, or high on the hills. Vinyl siding, and government grants for insulating old homes, have given the countryside a prosperous look. Many who had left the area in the 1950s, 60s and 70s to work in Ontario or further west have been selling their city homes, returning to New Brunswick and rebuilding along the river. Foundation builders, well-drillers, plumbers, electricians, and contractors are booked for months in advance.

In earlier times there were only a few ways to classify the population. There were Protestants and Catholics. There were those who went to the Legion and drank and those who didn't. Now the distinctions are more subtle.

Despite some people falling away from the church, religion seems more profitable than ever. For a scattered population there are literally dozens of churches and more being built all the time. Catholics, Baptists, Presbyterians, Wesleyans, and a variety of evangelical splinter groups work and live side by side with Mormons, Mennonites, and folks who ignore religion altogether--until there is occasion to call a minister for a death or a marriage.

Along the St. John River is some of the world's pleasing scenery. Throughout the summer and fall tourists jam the roads, motels, hotels, lodges, cabins, and campgrounds.

Winters are harsh and long. The more hardy take advantage of the snow to snowmobile and ski. Those who can afford it grab a month or two of sunshine in Florida, Hawaii, Honolulu or the Cayman Islands. The rest go to the local malls to find someone to complain to.

Still, times have changed. Community life isn't what it once was. The Women's Institute is dying out. The Red Cross has shut down in many areas. You don't see farmers holding running- board meetings or standing around the mill spinning yarns. Small farms where farmers kept several kinds of livestock and grew a variety of produce have given way to agri-industry, agri-business and aggravation. Many small and middle-sized farms went bust in the 1960s and 1970s. The farmers that remain are not only the best businessmen, but also the most alert opportunists. They are the ones who know how to stretch a dollar, who know which government official to romance, and who are always on the spot when government goodies in the way of subsidies, grants, crop advances and low-interest loans are handed out. Many are also smart enough to marry nurses and school teachers to see them through the lean years.

It has been 60 or more years since the cheese factory, the woollen mill, the old cedar and grist mills shut down. Lately village grocery stores have closed, their trade going to the Fredericton malls or the Superstores. People drive to work, some 30 to 40 miles to the pulp mill at Nackawic. General

Finally he had all the meat in the back of the pickup hidden under the tarp he'd tied snugly to the bed. He climbed into the cab. To celebrate a job well done he reached under the seat for his bottle of Seagram's and took a good belt. Soon the whisky began to warm his belly. The window of the truck cab was open and just as he was recapping the bottle, he heard a car pull off the road ahead and stop. Looking through the trees, Ralph could just make out the shape of a vehicle. Mounties? Rangers? He couldn't tell. He decided to sit tight. Within a few minutes, the hard work of packing the moose out, the waiting and the whisky made him sleepy and he nodded off.

The vehicle which had pulled in ahead of Ralph was a 1988 4-wheel-drive Blazer with a fold-down seat that belonged to Lance McElvy, local pharmacist, town councillor and member of the Benevolent Order of Elks. For several months Lance had been carrying on with Mary Lou Pritchard, whose husband Murray at that precise moment was sitting in the Legion mulling over someone he'd seen on the Oprah Winfrey Show who had a penchant for cross-dressing. Although the Blazer offered little in the way of room or ambience, Lance and Mary Lou's mutual ardour more than made up for any inconvenience.

The woods and the pasture beside where Ralph had parked his truck was owned by Marlin Shaw. Marlin, now in his 70s, has an old horse he uses to twitch logs out for his winter wood, and he always keeps a bag of oats in the passenger seat of his farm truck as a lure for his horse, so that he doesn't have to tramp all over the pasture to catch it.

Bye and bye the horse, which had been grazing away at the lower end of the pasture, made its way up over the hill and came alongside Ralph's truck. Then it stuck its head through the open window on the driver's side and reached across Ralph to look for oats. In its search for a treat the horse snorted a couple of times and Ralph came to.

The head and neck of the grizzled old gelding almost filled the cab. Ralph let out a shrill bleat, surprising the horse which, trying to withdraw its head, caught the ring of its halter in the horn on the steering wheel, causing the horn to blare sharply. The startled horse bolted. Over the fence it went. It leapt the ditch, galloped through the trees and sideswiped the Blazer, cooling off its occupants, I bet, before taking off back across the field at a rapid pace.

Ralph waited until the Blazer was out of sight before starting the pickup and leaving for home. He was passing sedately through town when he met the weaving Camaro, driven by Murray Pritchard, that had come from the Legion. The Camaro was being pursued by a cruiser, lights flashing, siren wailing, and all this was being watched with great delight by a bevy of elves and witches and ghosts and goblins, standing on the corner sampling the spoils of their night of trick-or-treating. The blood, which had been seeping out of the moose quarters, ran out of the back of the truck when Ralph yanked the wheel to the right and then left again to miss the Camaro, and as he turned the corner the blood shot out and spattered the gremlins on the corner. Of course, when he came into the shop Saturday morning, Ralph had to tell someone about his moose. He'd already washed out the bed of the pick-up, unaware that the blood had splashed the kids. Little did either of us know that the blood from the moose meat was going to turn Cedar Springs on its ear.

The next thing that happened involved Willis Bull. I've known Willis since he was born. Nice fellow. Shy, though. Never married. Anyway he told me the next part...

The day following Halloween Willis was back working at the garage. Oil and grease had already covered the cuts and scratches on his hands. Now and then he would shudder violently. Once he dropped the wrench he was working with. Another time he upset a whole litre of oil down over a customer's car engine. At 9:45 he decided to take a coffee break at the restaurant next door.

In the restaurant he found his usual window seat and ordered two whole-wheat doughnuts and coffee, double cream, double sugar. When the order came he concentrated on his food. It was the first time he had eaten since yesterday noon.

Almost diagonally across from the restaurant is the Cedar Springs Cemetery. Nearest the road, the graves are more recent. Most of the markers are modern black rectangles, seated in granite blocks. Further back the stones date from the early 1800s and lean in every direction. There are tall six-sided monuments, book-shaped slabs of white marble sculpted with doves and cherubs, and cold gray stone crosses.

Separating the old and the new graves is a narrow roadway wide enough to allow a hearse access. Just a few feet off this roadway into the newer section of the cemetery, several men were gathered. One, arriving about an hour earlier to deliver the rough box and prepare the site for a burial, discovered that the edges of the grave had been torn away, and a lot of topsoil and rocks were in the bottom of the hole. He had called the funeral director Kevin Ryan at Catelle's Funeral Home and the local detachment of the Royal Canadian Mounted Police, both of whom appeared on the scene at about the same time.

After some speculation, they agreed that something had indeed been going on there. In fact the whole place was a mess. But there were no real clues as to what had caused it. One of the RCMP privately wondered if it had been some sort of pagan ritual, but not wishing to draw ridicule, he kept his mouth shut. While his partner walked around with a measuring tape, he took out his notebook and began jotting notes. In the end they decided it was likely some of the town's teenagers out hell-raising on

Halloween and after a while the Mounties told the men from the funeral parlour to go ahead with their work.

Inside the restaurant Willis watched the Mounties drive up to the cemetery, and felt the two doughnuts turn to acid as his stomach lurched sideways. His heart continued to beat rapidly, and when Charlie Owens, the owner of the hardware store, slipped unnoticed into the booth opposite him, it threatened to stop completely.

"I don't know what this world is coming to," Charlie began. "Kids today. There's nothing they won't do. Hung the cat on the door of the shop. Looked like the cat might have been run over, but I couldn't tell for sure. Then downtown they started fires in the garbage cans and rolled them out into the street. Then a gang of them broke into the school. Why, before supper last night the phone rang and it was a bunch of them brats acting out. Scared the wife almost out of her wits. I'd like to get a chance to take one of them across my knee. That's the trouble with kids these days. There's no discipline any more. Nobody makes them mind. They get away with murder. Oh, I blame television. Why, you should hear some of the things they say to the teachers, and the teacher's just got to stand there and take it. If the teacher ever laid a hand on one of these precious little brats, why they'd have her arrested for assault. I just don't know...."

Charlie often delivered a similar monologue. He considered himself an expert in child psychology, even though the only living creature he and his nervous bird-like wife ever raised was the fat old neutered tomcat, whose one regular activity, outside eating, was shedding hair. Grace, who worked behind the counter in the restaurant, and who happened to be raising teenage twin boys with little paternal influence or financial support, stifled a strong urge to tell Charlie where to get off. Her fine handsome boys were into sports, music and all kinds of school activities, and they gave her very little trouble. Yes, she really wished Charlie would shut up, especially since he ate like a warthog and never once left a tip. Instead, she said, "More coffee, Charlie?" Then she went back to clearing up.

Just then the door opened and Nola Wickins, commonly known as Newsbag Nola, bustled in all excited. When she wasn't gathering news, she was usually collecting for the Heart Fund, the Cancer Society, the Red Cross or Cystic Fibrosis. Already out putting the bite on her neighbours for this week's charity, Nola had visited several homes picking up bits of scandal along the way, which she now laid on the folks in the restaurant.

"You'll never believe this," she said, "but last night someone got in the graveyard and made a mess of one of the graves there. You know that grave they dug yesterday morning. Old Norman Hiller, he'd been at Della's nursing home for years. Anyways, just before supper, he'd been watching football on television, and Della happened to look in. He was always nodding off as he sat there, you know. Well, when she looked in again half an hour later, he still hadn't moved. So something made her look a little closer. Dead as a doornail. He'd been dead all the time."

" Of course, it would be hard to tell with Norman," Charlie said. Ignoring the interruption, Nola continued.

"Anyways, somebody tore up the graveyard last night. The RCMP are out there right now. I hope they get to the bottom of this. You imagine! Halloween tricks are one thing, but that is just plain wilful damage. A desecration! Why, there's no telling what those young hoodlums will think of next. It's dreadful, I tell you."

Willis listened to all this. One of his hands began to throb. He noticed another long scratch on his inside wrist, and pulled the cuff of his coveralls further down. Nobody paid him any attention.

Without stopping for breath, but dropping her voice to a stage whisper, Nola leaned across the counter towards Grace and launched into a whole new subject: "You'll never believe this but they say Jean Fowler is having an affair. Last night her husband almost caught her. He came home unexpected, but whoever she was with ran through the patio doors and out the back. Jean's husband has vowed to kill the man Jean's playing footsie with. Well, it would serve the culprit right, for messing with a married woman! I wouldn't want to be in that guy's shoes."

Nola paused for emphasis and looked around the restaurant, "Now, who do you suppose she has been seeing? Well, I'm not one to gossip, but I've got a good idea. You mark my words. We'll find out soon enough. A secret around this town doesn't last long."

When Nola was gone, Willis looked out again to the cemetery and noticed that the RCMP were just leaving. He waited a few minutes, then stood up, fished in his pocket for a couple of loonies, dropped them on the counter, and went back to work.

Over the next few hours everyone who came into his garage had a different theory on who had messed up the grave that was soon to be Norman Hiller's final resting place.

The rest of Willis's day was busy, four grease jobs and oil changes, eight tire punctures, and a steady stream of customers at the gas pumps. Around three o'clock, he glanced up to see a hearse lead a large procession past the garage towards the cemetery. Most of those in the procession had to be curiosity-seekers, since Norman, a mean and cantankerous old spit at the best of times, had had no family and no friends to speak of.

Finally around 5:30 business began to slack off and Willis took time to give thought to the events that led up to what happened last night.

He had met Jean right there at the garage. In her mid-thirties, Jean was a lively, attractive woman with a good figure. Her husband drove transport, taking long hauls, sometimes being gone for weeks at a time, and she was lonely. She had let Willis know that she was available. One thing led to another. Although he became totally obsessed with her, he was always very careful not to be seen coming or going. To reduce the risk of discovery he always left his pickup at the garage and went to her house on foot.

The night before, they had intended to begin their evening with a candle-lit supper but, in planning their night together, Willis had not taken into account Halloween. He had forgotten that the tricksters, ghosts and goblins would be out and about. Finally, when he felt he could wait no longer, he took a chance and walked up the road. No other person or vehicle met or passed him.

He arrived at Jean's without being seen and slipped inside. Willis was still a little nervous so they decided to have a cocktail before dinner to relax a bit. Lucky for Willis, they were still in the living room, when the lights of her husband's 18-wheeler unexpectedly swept the yard.

Jean pushed Willis towards the patio doors at the back. Since Willis had always had other things on his mind when he visited Jean, they had never discussed a swimming pool and, since he had never been there in the daytime, he was not even aware that one existed. Before his eyes could adjust to the dark, he pitched forward into the ice-encrusted water.

As it happened the hum of the truck's reefer and the squealing of the brakes on the turning 18-wheeler covered the sounds of Willis's thrashing about in the pool and in a few minutes he had scrambled out, scaled the fence, and dropped to the other side, from where he took off across an empty lot.

Just as he reached the road several cars turned the corner. Willis ducked down out of sight. Dripping, he listened as rock music, blaring from the open windows of the cars full of teenagers, slowly faded into the night. Once again he got up and started running, unmindful of the squelching sounds of his water-filled shoes. When he reached the graveyard access road another car came along, lighting the whole cemetery. Willis crouched behind an old tombstone and waited. When that car had passed he leapt up and, with lowered head, he again began to run. Unfortunately he was not paying enough attention and did not see the open grave, into which he fell headlong.

When Willis came to, his first thought was that he had fallen into a grave that was already occupied.

Now Willis is not a tall man. Stretched to full height, he would measure around five feet seven, and he was carrying more weight than was healthy. Likely he could have swung himself up out of the hole but he couldn't get hold of anything solid to haul himself out by. Instead he clawed frantically. The grass gave away, and damp soil thudded around him. He caught his fingers on the rocks. Finally, with terror giving him superhuman strength, he literally tore his way out of the grave, and ran for home.

Once inside, he had a shower and went to bed, but he was too wound up to sleep. He got up again and spent the rest of the night in front of the television set, finally falling asleep in a chair.

So it had felt like a really long day at the garage and quitting time couldn't come too soon. Every muscle in his body ached with exhaustion.

The way he figured it, there was no one who could actually pin the grave desecration on him. I mean, he was the last person in the world to even think of such a thing. Except for his affair with Jean, he'd always minded his own business and taken few chances. All he had to do now was be calm, keep his mouth shut, and stay away from other men's wives. In fact, it might not be a bad idea to start going to church once in a while.

When Jean and her husband pulled in at the pumps just before closing, his heart did its now familiar Texas two-step. There was nothing for it but to walk out and face them. The husband leaned out the window, and said "Fill'er up--regular."

Willis nodded, filled the tank and made change, but he ignored Jean altogether.

Then as the car left, he saw Jean drop a balled up potato-chip package out the window of the passenger door. Always one to leave the premises neat and tidy before closing up for the night, Willis bent to pick up the wrapper. It felt heavier than it should have. He unrolled the ball and inside he found his watch band. The watch itself, which had his initials etched on the back, could be anywhere.

Well, Willis came into the barber shop Saturday morning. There was no one else in the shop at the time. I saw his hands all scratched up, and noticed a lump on the top of his head. Just joking, like, I asked him if his girlfriend did that to him. And that's when he told me the business about the grave.

As for the dead tomcat that showed up on the door of Charlie Owens hardware store, it got hit by the milk truck and died instantly. I guess it was kind of mean of Grace's boys to hang the dang thing on the door Charlie Owens' hardware store. But he'd never liked kids much, and kids can sense that, don't you know. And besides, the cat was already dead.

So, there you have it. Cedar Springs is no better and no worse than any other small town in the county. In fact, the next time Rev. Freddie comes in for a hair-cut, I ought to set him straight about this Satanic Cult thing. On the other hand, it's a lot more fun to listen to that than him ranting about drinking, fornicating and video gambling.

A TWIST OF TEA

In Cedar Springs in the 1940s Beulah Taggert and her children heard the wolf howling at the door many times. Only the growling of their empty stomachs turned that wolf away.

Beulah was not immoral, nor was she lazy, dull or stupid. Her mistake was to fall in love with Jim Taggert and marry him.

Jim Taggert was a fine-looking man, tall, with reddish blond hair and a pleasant manner. He never struck Beulah or the children. He didn't blaspheme. He did not smoke or chew snuff. He never took a drink of liquor. For Jim Taggert, religion was his drug of choice.

The first few years of their marriage were good for Beulah. Jim worked wherever and whenever work was available--for farmers during planting and harvest, and in the logging camps in the winter. Eleven months after their wedding their first boy was born, and 13 months later, another. And regularly, thereafter, usually in dead of winter, the babies came. By the early Spring of 1946 Jim and Beulah Taggert had seven children, four boys and three girls.

Their nearest neighbours were Emily and Eldridge March, whose immense and imposing home was one of the first in Cedar Springs to have electricity, indoor plumbing and a bathroom. Eldridge March was a mild-mannered man. He always wore a suit with a vest and pocket watch. He would nod if he met you on the street but he preferred to remain apart from most neighbourhood activity. His father, Cleaver March, had owned two prosperous mills during the late 1800s and early 1900s. Eldridge himself had taken a bit of a fall during the 1930s, but he and Emily were still comfortably off. Because of the gasoline shortage, they had put their Packard up on blocks for the duration of the war, but they always had a smart buggy and drove a fine pair of matched horses. In short the Marches were the cream of the neighbourhood, financially speaking.

Conscious of her place on the social register, Emily March knew the background of everyone in the community. She decided who was acceptable and who was not. She counted the months after marriage when each new couple's first child was born. When a young girl was sent off to Boston to live with an aunt for a year Emily somehow made it known that the girl was likely pregnant and was probably giving the baby up for adoption. No sir, you couldn't fool Emily March.

Mindful of the duty that accompanied her position in the community, Emily served as president of both the Red Cross and the Women's Institute. She chose members of the executive in both organizations and made sure those who did not meet her standards were not included. Beulah Taggert was definitely not asked to join.

The old wood frame storey-and-a-half house where Beulah Taggert and her children lived was falling to ruin. The sun poured in through the undraped windows and the board walls in summer, turning it into a fly-infested sauna. In the winter the wind wailed through the cracks. Beulah struggled to feed and care for her children, often foregoing food herself so there would be more for the young ones. Her only indulgence, her single luxury, was to brew a small pot of tea and to sit for a few minutes to rest and watch a sunset.

Almost every year after planting was done, local church leaders announced upcoming revival services. It was camp meeting time, a time when several Southern Baptist ministers would arrive in the community to Spread the Word and Harvest Souls for Christ. Children living nearby watched with fascination as circus-sized tents were erected on a flat stretch of pasture just above the creek. A long railing was affixed on which to tether horses. Trestle tables were set up and women baked chickens, hams, rolls, cakes and pies. They prepared salads and dusted off their best jars of jellies, pickles and preserves to be eaten during breaks in the services.

The camp meetings usually lasted about three days. People were seduced by the drawling speech of the Southern Baptist ministers. Alternately whispering, howling, begging, weeping, they were pitchmen of the first degree. They pranced up and down the platform as they detailed their own sins and how God had forgiven them and made them whole. Collection plates were passed often and the money collected turned over to them to help them further Spread the Word.

The music was lively. There were lots of fine singers in Cedar Springs who welcomed an opportunity to show off their talents. Old revival hymns took on new life and power in the harmony provided by duets, trios and quartets. To stand in the centre of the tent, with nearly the whole community singing in one voice, was to feel the chills ripple up and down one's back. And when the altar call came, people rose from their seats and stepped forward to kneel at the foot of the platform. With tears and prayers and a heavy arm around their shoulders, they admitted they were sinners seeking salvation and offered their lives to Christ.

On the last Sunday afternoon of the camp meetings, there would be a baptism and new converts would be dipped into the creek by a minister and his team of assistants. On the shore young boys watched with fascination as the young women emerged from the water, their dripping white dresses clinging to their nubile bodies.

When the camp meetings ended, most people went back about their business, the women to housekeeping and child care, the men to farming, building or sawing wood. Jim Taggert was the exception. For him the camp meetings caused an emotional overload. He became a Revival groupie. Each year, Jim would get saved, find the Lord, put all his money in the collection plate, and then go off with the Southern Baptist preachers to spread the word.

Meanwhile Beulah and the children struggled along on their own. A few potatoes, a little buckwheat and lard, berries the children picked or a few trout the boys caught were what they lived on. Rarely was there milk. Beulah drank her tea black--until the tea caddy was empty.

Worn out by child-bearing and malnutrition, Beulah had no energy left for home decorating; the house stayed bare. The kitchen and living room area was all one room with a small bedroom at the back. The kitchen table was covered with oilcloth worn through on the edges. The open shelves held a few plates and some battered crockery. Behind the table was a long bench next to the wall. In front were three or four rickety chairs, two without backs. Upstairs were two tiny bedrooms, one for the girls and one for the boys. The toilet was an outhouse out back of the lilac bushes.

The only heat in the whole house was from the wood stove in the kitchen. The oldest boys carried water from the springs and Beulah washed by hand, hanging the diapers outside in good weather or, when it rained, on a long string above the stove.

Folks said that Jim Taggert was crazy religious to leave his family and many clucked their tongues disapprovingly.

One day, driving home from the mill where he'd had grain ground to flour and grist, Dean Booker was passing the Taggert place when he noticed that the woodpile was gone. Further on he spotted the two oldest boys, 11 and 12, struggling to cut alder bushes with a small dull hatchet.

Dean Booker, a returned man from World War I, earned his living with mixed farming. He was grateful to live in Cedar Springs with his pretty wife Janet, his growing family, his healthy livestock, his own strong capable hands and his land to work. But driving home he couldn't get the Taggerts out of his mind. It was still early spring and cold. No telling when Jim Taggert would be back, whether he'd followed the revival meetings or gone to the woods. How could Beulah manage by herself, Dean wondered.

When he got home, Dean watered and fed the horses and went inside. While he was eating dinner he mentioned what he'd seen to his wife. Janet Booker, a community nurse, was aware of the state of the Taggerts' home, having been there to assist in the delivery of the last five of their children.

At the time the Bookers had little cash in hand, but owning a woodlot and a farm with cattle, pigs, sheep, hens and horses, meant they had ample food and firewood. They sold cream to the creamery, and each spring the sheep were sheared, the wool cleaned and carded and sent to Briggs' Woollen Mills to be made into blankets. Janet and Dean's sister both sewed for the family. In short Dean and Janet considered themselves well off.

"We'll have to do something, Dean," Janet said.

"Guess we will," he agreed.

After their meal was over, Dean went back out and hooked the horses to the double wagon. Then he threw on a cord of dried maple and birch stove wood and some cedar kindling. Using a plank for a ramp, he rolled on a barrel of potatoes and a barrel of Pippins and Alexanders gathered from the apple orchard the previous fall. He added a box of eggs, and half a side of pork that had been hanging in the smokehouse. Meanwhile Janet filled an Oxydol soap box with new flannel diapers she and her daughters had sewn to donate to the Red Cross. Scanning the cellar shelves, she found bottles of pickles and preserves, which she wrapped in newspaper and placed in the box. Then, almost as an afterthought, she added a pound of King Cole tea. Dean drove his wagon of provisions back to the Taggert's.

Beulah, when she saw the firewood, began to cry. Then she apologized that she could only offer him hot water to drink, because there was no tea in the house.

"Hot water's just fine," he said. "Just had dinner. Stomach's been a little touchy."

As soon as he and the two older children had unloaded the sled, Dean stepped into the kitchen and Beulah set a cup before him. It was cracked and chipped but it still had a handle. Her cup did not. The children lined up silently on the bench by the wall and listened to the conversation.

"When do you expect Jim back?"

"Can't say, for sure," said Beulah. "You know, when Jim gets the call, he's bound to spread the Good Word."

Dean gazed into the tired face of the forlorn woman. He had little use for a man who shirked responsibility--for whatever reason--and there were lots of things he could say about a man who would walk off and leave his family to starve or freeze to death, but pity silenced him. No doubt she'd already had enough sermons on the subject. She set down her cup and pulled her ratty sweater together for warmth.

"Weather's got to let up any day now," he said. "Bound to get warmer pretty soon."

"Yes," said Beulah. "I do so look forward to Spring."

"You got some fine lads, there, Beulah. Hard workers, too, I see.

Beulah smiled.

Dean finished his cup of hot water, picked up his leather mittens from where they had fallen on the floor, and said, "Well, I must be going. Janet's waiting for me."

"Thank you again," Beulah said. "You and Janet have always been so kind. I don't know what we would have done."

But Spring was a long time warming that year. Jim Taggert still did not return and the Taggert family barely made it through. Meanwhile life in the community went on. Men looked after their livestock, women wrapped turbans around their hair, carried out their spring cleaning and planned what to plant in the garden patch and flower beds. Weekly church services and monthly trips to the general store for supplies provided the social life. Many of the wives also attended Red Cross and Women's Institute meetings. That year, they made six quilts to be raffled to raise money for foreign missions. Of course, Emily March had the last word on the worthiness of any project, and since the rest of the farm women had all they could do to keep their own homes together, they usually let her take the reins.

A highlight of the monthly Women's Institute meeting was the social time, where food, recipes, and gossip were passed around. They discussed Euphemia Walker's wild daughter, the shameless one that stayed right there in Cedar Springs and had a baby--no telling who the father was--then ran off and left it for Euphemia to look after. Then somebody remarked that Jim Taggert had still not returned.

"Must have spread the Word clear back to Jerusalem by now," said someone else.

"Tsk, tsk, tsk!" said Emily March, disapproving of the younger member's flippant remark.

"Well, I don't care what you say. The Taggerts are nothing but trash," added a woman from the crossroad. "All those children running around in rags! Whatever can that Beulah be thinking of?"

"That old house they live in is a blot on the neighbourhood," said the secretary-treasurer of the WI, who was at that moment unaware that her husband had already received notice the bank foreclosing on their farm.

"Always begging," said Emily March. "Always coming around begging for something. No manners at all. You'd think she'd have more pride."

An older member seated by the quilt frame threaded her needle, then deftly nipped the thread and knotted it before picking up her quilt stitches. "'Pon my word, I don't know what they live on," she said.

"Well, I'll tell you, I finally fixed her," said Emily March. "I just got sick and tired of her sending those kids over all the time for tea. Always have runny noses, and they'd stand there big as life and tell me, "Ma wants to borrow a twist of tea."

"A twist of tea." Well, I ask you. I suppose she just expected me to hand out a pound of tea any old time, as if Eldridge and I had nothing better to do than feed half the neighbourhood.

"It took me a while to wise up, but I did, I can tell you. After she'd sent those children over for about the third time in a month to borrow--borrow, nothing!--to beg more tea--I thought to myself, I'll give her a 'twist of tea'.

"So every day that week when Eldridge and I finished our meals, I always let the pot cool. Then after I poured the remaining liquid on the ferns--cold tea is very good for ferns, you know--I scooped the tea leaves out of the bottom of the pot, set them in a pan in the warming oven and let them dry.

"Well, the very next time those brats showed up at the door, I was ready. I tore off a quarter of a page of newspaper and I shook out the old tea leaves from the warming oven, twisted them up in the newspaper and sent them over.

"I tell you, I'd like to have seen Beulah's face when she drank that tea."

The women around the quilt listened silently to Emily's report. Finally Janet Booker jumped up saying, "Oh my goodness. Look at the time. We must be getting home. Dean will be wondering what ever happened to me."

Who could have guessed that the middle Taggert boy would become a minister and 20 years later, would lead the funeral service for Emily March?

GOOD HELP IS HARD TO FIND

If you had happened to see Ron Goodall on his way out with a roller to roll a field of wheat he was planting one evening last June, it's likely you wouldn't have noticed anything different, unless you got up real close. Then you would have known that he was furious. His jaws locked his lips into a thin line. The scowl he wore was black as the night which would soon close in on him.

But by the time he had finished rolling the field, and shut down the machinery, his anger had worn off. He had said some really nasty things to his wife Marie earlier in the day, and she hadn't spoken to him throughout supper. When he finally came in to the house she had already gone to bed.

Ron and Marie Goodall operate a 300-acre farm out on the Chisholm Road near Cedar Springs. A young couple with two school age children, they keep beef cattle and raise grain, peas and potatoes. Ron is the fourth generation to operate the Chisholm Road farm since his ancestors arrived from England in the late 1800s. Marie, whom he had met at the Nova Scotia Agriculture College in 1980, grew up on a farm in the Annapolis Valley.

The Goodalls are well suited. Both are used to farm life with all its joys and disappointments. Strong and fit, they rarely begrudge the long hours and the back-breaking labour. They are accustomed to living at the whim of weather and market conditions and, in spite of occasional setbacks, they believe it is the only place to raise a family. The Goodalls get along as well as most young couples. But on the rare occasions when they do spat, long-eared mules would be more yielding.

When the children were small Marie spent most of her time in the house, and Ron worked with the part-time assistance of a hired man. But, as they say, good help is hard to find and when in the middle of planting their hired man decided to quit and go driving truck, the Goodalls were left in a bind. Few part-time workers were willing to give up their unemployment insurance cheques for a few weeks of farm labour. They were having too good a ride and it took too long to get back on the U.I. benefits, so unless it was all "under the table" it wasn't worth it for them to actually work. And Ron's experience was that when these people were finally forced to get a job, things got broken or neglected, so they were more of a nuisance than a help.

In the end Ron worked harder and longer, far past the point when many a lesser man would have called it quits. But one man can only do so much and Ron was stretched to the limit. Marie couldn't stand to see him kill himself, so she called her mother to come over and sit with the kids, and went out to help Ron. The next day she put on a second pair of jeans and woollen socks, and stepped into her barn boots. Ron was working back of the barn that morning, disking a field that had had two years of timothy.

When Marie asked him what she could do, he told her to take the John Deere, hook on the vibra-shank (sort of a cross between a harrow and a cultivator) and work on the west field.

Marie backed the tractor up, hooked onto the vibra-shank and moved into the field in which they had had potatoes the previous year. She stayed right with it all through the morning. Just before noon, when Ron drove up, she looked over and gave him a friendly wave.

Instead of waving back, he jumped down from his tractor and started yelling. He was jumping-up-and-down-mad. He said words she'd never heard him use before. He questioned her intelligence, and made slurs about her heritage. He gave his opinion on the only things women were fit for, and where she should be spending her time, i.e., in the kitchen, where she belonged. With that Marie climbed out of the John Deere and strode to the house, saying, among other more colourful things, "That's it. Go get yourself another hired man. Or do it yourself!"

Well, it turned out that Marie had accidentally vibra-shanked the wrong field, the only field that Ron, working on his own, had been able to get sowed and rolled. Marie didn't talk to him for three days.

Ron was able to get another hired man for the summer. Bruce Shaw, fresh from Carleton University, showed up one morning, anxious to earn some extra money and build up some of the muscle he'd lost sitting in lecture halls.

After the planting came the haying, and with the weather we've had this last year, getting the hay in wasn't easy. Everything seemed to go wrong for Ron. The machinery broke down and they sent the wrong parts. When he turned the cows into a new pasture, several of them overfed on the young clover and swelled up like balloons. Naturally the vet was away when it happened. Ron was standing in the pasture, thinking about some of the old farmers and the way they would push a dart into the cow's stomach to let the gas out, when Anna Walker came along. (Anna Walker, first and foremost an herbalist, is one of the area's characters. Ruggedly individual, she follows her own drummer and some times even hums along. There are those in Cedar Springs who say she's a witch, but that's nonsense.) Anna stopped and looked at Ron and at the cows and then she crouched down on the ground and crawled under the fence. "Before you do anything else," she said, "why don't you try giving each of them a teaspoon of Sunlight dishwashing liquid in a quart of water. I think that will work."

Anna stayed in the pasture while Ron ran to the house and returned with the dishwashing liquid and a couple of two-litre pop bottles. While Ron held the cows' heads up, Anna managed to get the water and soap down their throats. After one or two major burps, the cows got up and walked away.

"Well, I never heard of that before," he said to Anna, grinning happily. "I thought I was going to lose them there for a while. Thank you. Thank you so very much." Anna smiled, crawled back out from under the fence, picked up her basket and walked on down the road. Ron just shook his head in wonder.

Bruce Shaw was working out well. When Ron assigned him a job he went ahead and did it. One day he had mowed and raked the lower field while Ron was mending pasture fences. And the next decent day, Ron sent him out to mow again, pointing towards the upper field in the distance. Marie, meanwhile, was baking. Six dozen cookies and two pans of date squares were cooling at the back of the counter. At half past eleven, she was putting bread in the pans when the back door opened. One glance at Ron's face, and she knew something had gone haywire. He shut the door quietly, walked over to the rocking chair beside the stove and sat down.

"Ah, oh," said Marie. "What's happened now?"

"Well, it's mostly my fault," Ron began.

"What is? What's gone wrong this time?"

"Well, it's the young fellow."

"Oh Lord, Bruce isn't hurt?"

"No, no. He isn't hurt."

Now there is a slight jog in the road at the north end of the farm, and Ron had neglected to tell Bruce precisely that it was the piece on the right side of the road past the maple grove that needed cutting. Where Ron had been pointing was actually across the road, on a hay field belonging to the neighbours.

"I sent him out to mow," Ron said. "I wasn't a bit worried. He's so good with machinery. I could hear the mower start with a nice steady purr, and I figured he knew what he was doing.

"Just after 10:30 I got the baler running, hooked it up to the John Deere, and thought I'd take a couple of swipes around the lower field to make sure everything was working right, before stopping for dinner.

"Well, I was headed off down the lane, kinda shaking hands with myself for getting the baler working, when I looked over to see how the young fellow was coming along. There was the field I'd sent him to, all just ripe for mowing, and not a blade of grass was cut. I could hardly believe my eyes.

"I followed the sounds of the mower and, be darned if Bruce hadn't gone across to the other side of the road and mowed the neighbour's hay. Could you credit that? What in the dickens had possessed him to go across the road? Any darn fool would know I meant the upper field, the other side of the maple grove."

Marie finished putting the bread in the pans, set them up on the warming oven, and folded a tea towel across the top. "Then what?"

"For a minute or two I wondered why they didn't go out and stop him," Ron said, "but just then a car drove up--the neighbour's daughter--and she told me her Mother had had to take her Dad to the hospital. He had had some kind of spell or something. Well, that explained why they didn't stop my hired man."

"So, maybe they don't know about it yet?"

"Doubtful."

Ron spent the next few hours trying to figure out how he was going to resolve that one. The young fellow had done a real good job on that field--corners just as neat, not a spear left. When he came in for lunch Ron had cooled down.

In the afternoon Bruce baled the hay Ron had mown and hauled it in to the barn. Since it was Friday night and Bruce had a big date on, Ron told him he'd better take off early.

Finishing the chores for the night, Ron came in to sit before the fire. Still worried, he turned on the TV news and heard the weather forecast. They were calling for rain. He stood up, shut off the set, and put his coat back on.

"Where are you going now," Marie said.

"I'm going to rake that hay."

It was two in the morning when Marie heard him fall into bed.

First thing Saturday morning as soon as the dew was off, Ron went down to his neighbour's field again and baled the hay Bruce had cut. Marie called her mother to come over and sit with the kids, while she took the trailer down to the field. With Marie driving the tractor, Ron loaded the bales and they had the whole thing in the neighbour's barn by midnight.

Several days later the neighbour's wife stopped in. Her husband was going to be all right, she said. He'd suffered a ruptured appendix. "All he could do was lay there in the hospital and worry that he wouldn't get his hay in," she told the Goodalls. "You can't imagine how happy he was when I told him you'd looked after the hay. The doctor said he wasn't supposed to be lifting anything. I don't know what we would have done without you."

"T'wasn't much," Ron mumbled. "What are neighbours for? Glad we could help."

Ron excused himself and headed for the barn, leaving her talking to Marie and Marie blowing on what a good man he was. "That Marie," he thought. "Giving me a reputation to live up to, like always."

Well the rain held off. Ron got his own hay in. There was plenty for their own stock and he had a few hundred bales to sell. Things were looking so good, he began thinking about buying more land. He'd had his eye on some land near Brookside. A visit to the records office showed him that it belonged to Anna Walker. He'd driven out there a couple of times to talk to her, but she never seemed to be around. He'd have to keep after it.

"You want to know something," he said to Marie one night just after they'd gone to bed.

"What?"

"You know that field you vibra-shanked about two weeks after I'd had it all planted and rolled? Well, it's the best looking field on the farm."

Marie laughed and held him close. "As they say, good help is hard to find."

SMALL TOWN SWEETHEARTS

It was love at first sight when Mavis Shaw and Clayton Anderson met at the Carleton Liberals Salmon Fry a few years ago. But as they were both by nature reticent it would be several months before Clay got up the nerve to ask Mavis out.

Mavis had grown up in Cedar Springs. After graduating from high school, she had taken a business course at Community College and had gone to work for the Province of New Brunswick in the Department of Transportation. Clay's family had moved to Bowmanville, Ontario in the mid-1950s and he had been born there. Old enough to remember the 1960s, Clay was far too bashful to "let it all hang out," either then or later. And until he met Mavis during a trip to the Maritimes to visit his grandparents, his relationships with women had been limited. For one thing, as a stockroom clerk at Eaton's catalog store, he didn't have that many opportunities to meet girls. For another, his shyness rendered him a near mute if a girl made any move in his direction.

Once he had seen Mavis, he knew she was the one meant for him. Before his vacation was over he'd found work here at a Home Hardware store, and returned to Bowmanville just long enough to give notice at Eaton's, collect his belongings and say goodbye to his folks.

Of course he knew about sex. He'd heard stories in the locker rooms and he read a lot. And, Lord knows, he thought about it.

Well, they did go out eventually and soon began keeping regular company. Weeks later when Clay first attempted to kiss her goodnight, they accidentally locked noses. Clay reared back and then when he darted at her face again in the dark his lips skidded sideways and he almost inhaled one of her new pearl clip-on ear rings. Even so, raised into soaring flights of fancy by the bungled kiss, he didn't come down for three days.

Mavis's ardour, already fanned by chapters and chapters of Harlequin Romances, burned just as brightly. When not with Clay, she spent her time alternately humming and sighing.

Mavis's knowledge of carnal matters was as meagre as Clay's. She had enough basic information, but no practical experience. For a while that didn't matter. Being in each other's company was enough. They walked through parks arm in arm. They lingered in the local diner, gazing deeply into each other's eyes, while their french-fries stiffened and dried. They went to the movies, and saw so little of what was happening on the screen that they might as well have saved their money. (For years after, the smell of buttered popcorn would cause Mavis to smile and Clay to cross his legs and pull his jacket down.)

After more months of courtship, they began to consider marriage. They talked about where they would live, how they would finance a home, and whether they should both work. In fact they talked about everything but that issue uppermost on both their minds, sex.

They decided on a June wedding with all the trimmings--bridesmaids, a best man, flower girls, ring bearers, etc. etc. They talked about ministers and whom to invite, and where to hold the reception, and if they could afford a band. Each gave a lot of thought to the matter of birth control but they didn't talk about it to each other. Mavis, after reading everything in *New Woman* and *Cosmopolitan* and Red Book on the subject, began to consider various methods. As it happened that particular month's issues all talked about the dangers and unpleasant side affects of birth control pills. IUD's were reported to have caused bleeding and nasty infections. Diaphragms, if properly fitted, and condoms, if carefully applied, were touted as being the safest and least dangerous devices for both parties. But even the thought of talking to Clay about using condoms sent Mavis into fits of anxiety. She worried for months.

Then in one of the next issues of *Cosmopolitan* Mavis came across a quiz..."Are You and Your Mate Sexually Compatible?" She read it over and wondered, and wondered.

Maybe, she decided, it was time to find out. Mavis made an appointment to see a gynaecologist--in Fredericton--where she managed to weather the agonizingly embarrassing ordeal of being fitted with a diaphragm. That way at least, she figured, she wouldn't have to ruin a romantic interlude by having to deal with such a personal and disconcerting matter as birth control.

She carried her prescription for the diaphragm and spermicidal jelly to the nearest pharmacy and passed it to the druggist. As her order was being filled, she moved over to the greeting card rack, and began skimming the messages. She had given her name as Mrs. Mavis Anderson, and the druggist called out, "Mrs. Anderson, Mrs. Anderson," several times before Mavis realized he was talking to her. She ran back to the prescription counter, paid for her purchases and, turning to leave, walked straight into Nola Wickins, whose sole occupation was worrying about who in Cedar Springs was doing what and with which and to whom. Fortunately for Mavis, Nola was suffering from a bad ear infection and didn't hear the name Mavis answered to. Then as the druggist caught Nola's attention, she began searching her bag for her prescription. Mavis took advantage of this distraction. "Nice to see you Nola, gotta run."

Luckily for Mavis, when Nola called Mavis's mother, to find out what Mavis was doing in Fredericton, she didn't get a chance to ask. Mavis's mom was on her way to prayer meeting--she wanted to be there early because she was directing the program that night.

Later that evening when Mavis and Clay were snuggled together in the car at their favourite parking spot near the river, she suggested they go away for a weekend together. Clay agreed.

"Why don't we go to Chatham?" Mavis said, thinking no one knew them there.

"Sure," said Clay. "What about the Fisherman's Inn? You see that advertised all the time. And we could take in the Miramachi Festival."

With appropriate fibs to all concerned, they slipped away the following Friday at noon. The weekend started out fine. They held hands as they hummed along the Renous Highway.

A few miles out of Newcastle, it struck Clay that he should have bought some condoms--just in case.

Mavis, on the other hand, smiled, secretly thinking how clever she was to have obtained the diaphragm and spermicidal jelly. As she recalled the tasteful pink-flowered cosmetics case she had bought to keep it in, she realized it was still at home in her lower dresser drawer. She had forgotten to pack it.

What to do? What to do? "Clay," she said. "I'd like to stop at the shopping mall and run in to the drug store. There are a few things I've forgotten."

"Sure, Mave baby, we can do that little thing," Clay said. "Tell you what. I'll drop you off at the mall and while you are in there I'll stop at a service station, make sure we don't run out of gas or anything. Then I'll meet you back at the mall."

Clay carried on into town, found a service station and, as luck would have it, spotted a drug store half a block up. Bracing his shoulders, he strode purposefully towards the drug store, opened the door and went in. There were a few other shoppers, but they seemed bent on their own business, so he walked up and down several aisles until he found the condom display. He quickly chose a box, then grabbed some razor blades and a bottle of mouthwash and walked to the check-out counter. There were two customers ahead of him. He picked up the Mirimachi Herald from the rack and placed it over the other things. Behind him was a young mother with a toddler, squirming in her shopping basket. The baby suddenly reached out, pushed his paper to the floor, grabbed the box of condoms and began chewing on the corner of the package. After what seemed an eternity, the mother saw the baby chewing on the box, took it from him, and set it on the counter. The babe began to howl.

Clay again pushed his purchases along the counter. The cashier didn't bother to look up as she rang through his paper, his blades and his mouthwash. But when she came to the package of condoms, she happened to pick up the wet sticky chewed corner, stopped, looked at it, then looked up at Clay as if she blamed him for doing it. Gingerly she reached for Clay's $20, and holding it with her thumb and forefinger, she placed the bill on her cash register and made change.

The lineup was getting longer. The clerk snapped a plastic bag open, tossed in Clay's purchases, pushed it across to him and turned to the next customer. Clay reached for the bag, caught one handle, and dumped everything out over the counter. The package of condoms struck the candy rack and bounced onto the floor. As he struggled in the enclosed space to collect his stuff, a customer at the back of the line picked up the package of condoms and passed it forward to him, while the other shoppers studied him with interest.

Sweating by now, Clay ran outside, jumped in the car and headed back to Mavis at the shopping mall.

Meanwhile, Mavis had entered the mall and gone straight to Shoppers Drug Mart. It was fortunate that she could remember her diaphragm size and that it was in stock. She walked down the aisle to the birth control products and found what she needed. Then she saw some tissues and some shampoo which she placed in her basket. Rounding the front of the aisle, she noticed that aromatic candles and candle holders were on sale. Thinking these would add to a romantic evening in their hotel room, she bought them as well.

Again there was a lineup at the checkout counter. The clerk had to send someone off to find a price. Then she had to change the cash register tape. Then there was a long wait while someone's credit card limit was approved, and finally it was Mavis's turn. When she was almost at the counter she turned around to see Clay enter the store and wave. "Oh no," she thought, "I hope he isn't going to stand there and watch me." But Clay was watching. Unconcerned, the clerk checked through Mavis's purchases until she got to the box containing the diaphragm. Holding it high in the air, and waving it back and forth, she yelled to a clerk at the back, "How much is this?"

"What is it?" said the clerk.

"Diaphragm, Ortho, number 811-44."

Face crimson with embarrassment, Mavis glanced over to Clay who was intently studying the camera display. His ears were beet red.

They rode to the hotel in silence.

"Well, I guess we'd better check in," said Clay. "You hungry?"

"Yes, I think so. Yes I am," said Mavis. Over a long leisurely meal they began to relax. Then they went for a walk along the quay. Then they stopped into a tavern and listened to some music. And then they went back to their hotel.

While Mavis was in the bathroom, Clay undressed. Realizing he wouldn't need the condoms, he put them away in his case. To pass the time he studied the pictures on the wall. Above the bed was a 3'x4' seascape with the figure of a man in the foreground, gazing out to sea. In profile the figure bore a strong resemblance to Marlin Shaw, Mavis's Dad. Clay was glad the man in the picture was facing the waves.

At last Mavis, dressed in her peach negligee and matching peignoir, came back in the room and got into bed.

They turned towards each other and began their first sexual experience. Alas, in the exuberant performance of their coupling, the bed and headboard were set in motion and bumped against the wall. This caused the hook holding the seascape to jiggle out of the wall and the picture came crashing down on Clay's head. Not only did it bring their romantic interlude to an abrupt halt, it opened a nasty cut in the back of Clay's head which began bleeding profusely.

After a few moments, during which Mavis feared the worst, Clay regained consciousness enough to get dressed and let Mavis take him to the Hospital Emergency.

By the time they had located a doctor and the doctor had placed six stitches in Clay's scalp, it was 3 a.m. They returned to the hotel room and fell asleep with exhaustion.

Except for a slight headache Clay felt good as new the following morning. After breakfast they explored the town. In the afternoon they went to the festival. The music was great. They then decided to buy some wine and some Chinese take-out and go back to their hotel room.

Clay opened their wine. Mavis lit the candles. They found music on the radio/TV and they sat on the floor and made a picnic. By the time the wine was finished they could not keep their hands off each other any longer. They flung the covers back and climbed into bed.

As noted, Clay had read all the books, and listened to all the talk and began real slow. Everything was wonderful. Better than wonderful. It was ecstasy. It was heavenly. It was the best. Then suddenly, Mavis began to shriek and thrash. Slightly disconcerted but game nevertheless, Clay attempted to hang on–bent on giving Mavis the best he had to offer. Mavis screamed and, raising her knees, flung him to the side. Momentarily confused, he searched her face for some explanation and noticed light flickering around the room. He turned to see flames leaping up the side of the bed, where the covers had fallen onto one of the candles. The fire alarm went off.

Clay scrambled to his feet, grabbed their picnic blanket and quickly smothered the fire. The alarm continued to sound. Mavis ran to the window and lifted the sash to let the smoke out. Then she opened the door to create a cross breeze. That was a mistake, the air current drew the smoke into the corridor which set off every alarm up and down the hall. Heads poked out of every room. One woman ran down the hall in her nightgown, hair in curlers, holding three fur coats and a cat in a carry crate. Two young, scantily clad women ran out of a room ahead of a tipsy middle-aged man in a business suit. Fire trucks could be heard in the distance.

Once again Mavis and Clay hastily dressed, and shamefaced Clay went out to the lobby to speak to the fire chief. The fire chief insisted on coming back to their room to see for himself that everything was okay. As he surveyed the damage, he took in the wine glasses, the burned sheets, the sorry remains of their picnic, and the bandage on Clay's head.

"Don't you think you'd better be a little more careful from here on in, son?" he said.

Sheepishly Clay agreed. On Sunday morning, after Clay had generously tipped the maid for having to clean up the mess in their room, they paid their bill and checked out.

And still they hadn't finished what they'd started. In the end they took care of that on a car blanket in a secluded corner of a hayfield on their way home. Alas, Mavis had removed her diaphragm when she got up Sunday morning. According to the directions, she had rinsed it, dusted it carefully and returned it to its small pink case inside her cosmetics bag. Clay, thinking that Mavis had taken care of things, had tossed the condoms in the waste basket before he left the hotel.

Well, the wedding went off as arranged. The bride was lovely, the groom was handsome, the bridesmaids' dresses blended beautifully. Parents and grandparents sniffled and smiled. They went to Niagara Falls on their honeymoon.

And despite all the concern over birth control, nine months and two days later Mavis and Clay became the proud parents of twin boys. Which all goes to prove that despite fumbling, fire, falling pictures and family planning, nature has a way of taking care of things.

STILLBORN

What with long hours at the Green Lantern restaurant and keeping an eye on two active teens, Grace Avery felt she had been neglecting her mother Martha since they moved her to Forest Glen Manor. She made up her mind that the next Sunday she would go to Forest Glen and spend the whole afternoon.

By the time she got to the Manor her mother already had a visitor, Janet Booker. Janet had served as a community nurse throughout Cedar Springs and the surrounding area in the 1930s and 40s. Martha and Janet had known each other all their lives and since they were into reminiscing, Grace sat back and put her feet up.

Martha was sitting up, with one leg tucked under her as she always did, and Janet was facing her.

"Janet, do you remember the time you brought the dead baby into our bedroom? Why, I thought I'd die of fright."

Janet laughed: "Why, Martha, now you know that dead baby couldn't hurt you."

"That's what you said at the time."

Grace, who had listened silently to that point, said: "So, what was the story?"

"Oh, it's such a long, long time ago," Martha said, "but I remember it better than yesterday. Janet was out there at Boucher's--you know, who lived out there on the hill, in an old house set back from the road?"

"Can't say as I do," said Grace. "But go on."

"Well, Janet was busy with Myra Boucher who was having her fourth or fifth child. I don't know now, she had so many..how many did she have Janet?"

"Counting still-births and miscarriages....maybe 15."

"Good God," said Grace. "Fifteen pregnancies. That means she was pregnant over ten years altogether."

"Big families were common back then, dear," said Martha to Grace. "No such thing as birth control...."

"Not much," Janet agreed then picked up the story.

It was the dead of winter. The moon was in its first quarter begrudging the little light that filtered through the clouds. At nine o'clock

Janet and Dean Booker and their children settled down for the night. Awakened about 11:00 p.m. by a banging on the door, Janet got up to see one of the Boucher children standing there. He'd walked over three miles through the woods alone in the dark. "Ma says for you to come. Her water's broke."

"Come in and get warm," said Janet, "while I get ready." The road, what road there was back then, was almost impassable, but Dean Booker got up and harnessed the horse and hitched it to the closed in sleigh while Janet gathered her things. Janet and the Boucher boy set off and Dean, after adding a couple of sticks to the fire, closed the dampers and went back to bed. Two miles up the road, Martha Avery happened to be up stoking the stove when she heard Janet's horse and the bells on the sleigh. Martha ran out to the road and hailed her. Janet said: "I'm off to tend Myra Boucher. Come with me. I can use your company."

"Just give me a minute." Martha ran into the house, grabbed a basket and filled it with fresh bread, pickles and preserves, a pound of butter and a jar of cream. Then, writing a note and leaving it on the table, she pulled her hat and gloves on and hurried out to the road where Janet waited with the horse. Steam rose from the horse dung which had dropped during the wait.

As soon as Martha was snuggled under the robe, with the Boucher boy between them, away they went. There were huge drifts of snow to be crossed and several times they had to get out and walk along, attempting to keep the sleigh upright, but they made it to the Boucher house.

When they got there, they found a bleak situation. There was a fire in the kitchen stove and several solemn frightened children were gathered around. The husband was nowhere to be seen. "Gone to the woods, likely" thought Martha, stirring up the fire and filling the kettle from the hand pump at the kitchen sink.

Janet first looked in on the mother. Myra lay in the middle of a sagging bed. The room smelled and the covers were filthy. But Janet had expected as much. She'd brought along fresh towels and sterilized cotton sheets and rags. As Myra's contractions allowed, Janet bathed her and attempted to comfort her while Myra strained for the birth. Several hours passed. Martha had the children settled down and had made up a bed for herself and Janet.

But Myra's labour was taking too long. Janet had a feeling something was wrong. She opened the door and spoke to Martha, telling her to take the horse and go for the doctor. Martha bundled up and set off just as dawn was breaking.

There was little to be done but wait. Janet made porridge for the children, then got them bundled up to go outside and play. Martha meanwhile drove three miles to the nearest phone. When she got the doctor on the phone he refused to come. The Bouchers had never paid a bill, and besides he disapproved of the way Myra lived. Martha turned around and headed back out to the Boucher place.

Meanwhile Myra was losing ground. Exhausted from the long labour, she did little more than groan but Janet kept encouraging her and at last one tiny foot appeared. A breach, exactly what Janet feared. Janet worked against the contractions to turn the baby and was finally successful. Alas, by the time the baby came out, it was obvious that the umbilical cord had become wrapped around its neck and it had strangled.

Myra rose up in bed. "Dead ain't it?"

"Yes. I'm so sorry."

Myra said nothing, but lay back.

Janet tied the cord and set the small, still, blue and bloody corpse in a basin on the dresser and covered it with a towel. Then she went to work massaging Myra's abdomen to make sure the placenta was expelled. When that was done she packed the birth canal, changed the bloody sheets and left Myra to rest. Then she carried the stillborn child to the spare room where she bathed it and wrapped it in a towel. Martha and the horse and pung were just coming into view.

"The doctor wouldn't come," Martha reported.

"Well, it wouldn't have made any difference," Janet said. "It was already too late."

"Oh, dear God! What can I do?"

"First you will have a cup of tea and then if you could stand it, maybe stay with the children while I go down and get Dean to make a casket."

"No, you stay here," said Martha quickly. "I'll drive down and check on my house and get the horse fed and watered while I'm at it."

Dean Booker listened while Martha told him what had happened. Then he hitched a fresh horse to the pung, sent Martha on her way and went straight to his workshop. There was a small box, about the size of an orange crate, which he had made with the intent of using it for a tool chest. He found two fresh pine boards, measured them and with the handsaw shaped them to fit the box.

Following the instructions in Janet's note, he went into the house and in the drawer of the chest in the spare bedroom he pulled out a bolt of white cotton and a baby blanket, carried it out and placed it in the long-sled beside the hand-made coffin. In the barn he harnessed a team and hooked it to the long sled and set out.

When Dean arrived at the Bouchers, Janet and Martha had things fairly well under control. Janet swaddled the tiny corpse in white cotton. Although Myra knew the baby was dead, she asked to see it and Janet handed it to her. Keening softly, Myra rocked back and forth. After a while she handed the baby back to Janet who placed it in the box, which she had padded with white cotton, and tucked the baby blanket around it. Janet set the small coffin on two chairs in the front room of the house and went to the kitchen where she told the children if they wanted to pay their respects to the unborn, now was the time to do so. All the solemn-faced children walked quietly into the front parlour and gathered around the small pine box.

Dean went home but Martha and Janet stayed. That night was as cold as the previous one. So after getting Myra and the children settled down, Martha and Janet climbed into a small bed in the north room.

Janet lay there for a while. Unable to rest, she got up, pulled her shoes on over her bare feet, and in her flannel nightgown she traipsed downstairs, picked up the box with the baby in it and brought it back to the room. Martha jumped upright.

"Janet! Whatever are you doing?"

Janet found a chair and drew it up beside the bed and placed the baby in the box on the chair.

"I feel it isn't right to leave the baby in the room alone," she said.

Martha was horrified. She thought Janet had gone mad. "I can't sleep in a room with a dead baby." She was all for striking right out for home in the middle of the night.

"Come on, Martha. That little baby isn't going to hurt anyone."

Neither got much sleep, as it turned out. Janet got up every hour to check on Myra. Martha got up to put wood in the kitchen stove.

Dawn arrived at last, cold and gray. By afternoon the baby's father and Myra's oldest son had returned from the woods. Janet and Martha prepared supper for them while they took care of their animals and harnessed Janet's team. Then Janet and Martha left for home.

Sixty years later, while Janet and Martha were reminiscing, Janet said: "Now Martha, as I said that night, what harm could come to us from that little baby? It couldn't hurt you. But the rats!"

"The rats?"

"The rats. I was so worried that the rats would get in and chew on that small still corpse. That's why I wanted to keep an eye on it during the night."

"Was there a funeral or anything?" said Grace.

"I don't think so," said Martha. Grace looked at Janet.

"No. No funeral. In the morning the men carried the small box to the back of the farm, and buried it."

"Not even in the church yard?" said Grace.

"No." Martha replied. "Lots of families buried their dead on a corner of their own land. Sometimes there's a marker. Most times not."

WHAT GEORGE WOULD HAVE WANTED

Father Patrick Ryan hurried towards Forest Glen Manor nursing home where his mother, diagnosed with Alzheimer's disease, lay dying. Although she hadn't spoken for several months now, he continued his weekly visits, and tonight he planned to use the time spent by her bedside planning his hectic schedule of community work. But no sooner had he opened his calendar than the woman who shared a room with his mother returned by wheelchair from the dining room. Father Ryan greeted her more warmly than he felt.

"I am not a Catholic," she announced abruptly.

"Is that so?" he said graciously.

"No, not Catholic. I have sometimes wished I was Catholic. Just go and confess your sins and then go right on doing what you always do. But I think priests should be able to marry. It's not natural, this celibacy stuff. (Father Ryan smiled. He'd heard it all before.)

"You know, I have always felt sorry for people who never got married. Especially women. Take my younger sister, Mary. Her having to get on all alone without a husband to look after her. And not a chick nor a child to care for. Me, well I had George and the boys."

With an inaudible sigh, the priest laid aside his calendar and prepared to give this old woman his attention. As his mother slept on, the old lady slowly climbed out of her wheelchair, and settling herself on her bed, she began to ramble.....

"George was a good man," she began. "He never drank nor smoked, and he never looked at another woman. My sister Mary ran around with a lot of different men, but none of them ever seemed to suit her. Just too independent, I guess.

"It wasn't easy at first, me being married to George. I was used to a big family with a lot of noise, people coming and going, but George couldn't stand any confusion. "Can't a man come home and get some peace and quiet?" he'd say. I used to like to play the piano and sing, but George would say, "Listen, the dickybirds are out." Then I realized how common it was to sing to myself, so I stopped.

"Well, of course, I was looking forward to having our own home and fixing it up all special like, but George said there was lots of room at his folk's place, and there was no sense in having two houses. And, if that was what George wanted, why it was all right with me.

"The old house was out on the ridge, north of Cedar Springs, not far from the Anna Walker place. We slept up over the kitchen those first years. I could hear his mother downstairs rattling pans from about 5 in the morning. I got up and came down to help her, but she said she didn't want any help. His mother had her own ways of doing, and wanted things just so. George told me to leave her be.

"George had one sister, Liza, but Liza wasn't quite right. I don't know. The things they have today, medical advances, special training and all that, it might have been different for Liza today. But it was awful back then. She'd run away, and George would be sent to get her. He'd get so mad when he had to stop what he was doing and go look for Liza, he'd slap her silly.

"If she was a calf that jumped fences, I'd knock her on the head and throw her on the manure pile," he'd say. At first I used to stay out of her way, but then I saw she really wouldn't hurt anybody, so I used to let her come in our room. She would walk around, touching this or that on the dresser, sort of humming and singing. "Quit that racket," George would say. "She ought to be locked up somewhere." George's Ma and Pa just let him talk. In the end Liza got pneumonia and only lingered a few days after she got sick. "Best thing that ever happened," said George. I guess he was right, but you know, I kind of missed her.

"One time, I went off on my own to visit one of our neighbours. She seemed glad that I came, brought out china cups, and put the tea pot right on. We had a lovely afternoon, talking about this and that, I can't remember what all. She showed me the quilt she was making, and a sweater she was crocheting. I told her how much I admired her geraniums, and when I was about to leave, she pulled a slip from one of the plants, wrapped it in waxed paper and gave it to me. I couldn't wait to get home and put it in water to root. When I told George about it, he said he thought his wife could find something better to do than go traipsing all over the neighbourhood, bothering busy folks. I hadn't thought of that. Anyhow that geranium slip took root, and grew like anything. In no time, I had a whole row of flowers coming along. But then, George backed over them with the tractor when he was putting wood in the cellar. "Flowers are just a waste of time," he said.

"Well, soon after I found out I was pregnant, and didn't feel much like going anywhere. Besides, George thought pregnant women should keep themselves out of sight.

"When the baby was born, George said we would name him Frank. I didn't care. Frank was the perfect baby. He cooed and laughed. I loved to hold him and play with him but George said I was just spoiling him, and when he cried I ought just to leave him be, not let him think I would run every time he whimpered. But when George left the house, I used to go in and hug Frank so hard he almost cried.

"Our next baby was another boy. We called him Arthur, after George's Dad. Arthur was a colicky baby and never seemed to sleep more than ten minutes at a time. Sometimes I thought I would tear my hair out if I didn't get some sleep. A lot of nights I walked the floors with him. George grumbled about it, so I would take Arthur down to the kitchen at night, and rock and rock him. Sometimes I would wake up cold and realize that Arthur had finally gone to sleep, and I had dropped off myself. Then I would really have to hurry to get the fire going, the kettle hot, and breakfast started. George always wanted a hot breakfast when he sat down at the table.

"That next Christmas George's dad died. I'd grown quite fond of the old man. We hadn't talked much, but he had been comfortable around. All through it, George was a brick, never shed a tear. I asked him to take his mother's arm at the service, but he said, 'Let her be.' As soon as the funeral was over he just went back to work. He was strong, my George.

"Not long after that his mother had a little spell. A stroke, the doctor said. Then she had another. She had been ironing and suddenly fell over backwards. I had to help her to bed. One side of her face was paralysed so I had to be careful when I fed her. The boys didn't know what to make of her at first, but you know, kids can get used to anything. George said why did this stuff always happen to him.

"When she had the stroke it also affected her legs and one arm. She soiled the bed. Of course, she couldn't help it, but that meant a lot of washing and changing.

"In a few weeks, she got a little better. I managed to get her up to sit in the rocking chair by the window, there next to the stove. After a while, it got quite peaceful, with her sitting there by the fire, rocking back and forth, kinda company, like. I always kept a towel handy to wipe her face if I saw someone coming in.

"Poor George. He couldn't look at her at all. So in the evening I would help her to her room off the kitchen where I could keep an eye on her and see if she wanted anything.

"I used to get the children ready for Sunday School, I looked forward to that. We'd get all dressed and go out. Except George; he said it was a waste of time and that he was tired after a whole week of hard work, and for us to go on and just leave him be.

"Well, I would sit in the church and look over at my boys, all clean and shining, their hair all neat, and I was proud about to burst. I guess I did dote on my kids too much. I always wanted to surprise them with little things I made, or thought they wanted. Sometimes it wasn't easy to buy things because George thought I was extravagant and that he should handle the money.

"But I would bake them gingerbread cookies. I made them potato dolls. I remember one day Arthur came home from school with a drawing he had made. The wind had whipped it out of his hand and it had gotten wet. I put it by the stove to dry. Well, it crinkled up a bit, so I took a flat iron and smoothed it out.

"Some of the ink and colours had run but that didn't matter to me. It was my boy's work and I tacked it up by the calendar. George wanted to know how I could put such a mess up on the wall.

The next morning, I showed Arthur how I had put the painting in my scrap book for safekeeping, along with a baby curl and a few other things. Arthur just nodded and went on to school.

"We had some good times. George didn't believe in taking vacations. Said we couldn't afford it, so just the kids and I went. We'd take a bus to Pocologan on the Bay of Fundy and set up a tent. After a few days, I always called George to see how he was doing or if he had changed his mind and he'd just tell me to leave him be. The kids and I would spend the whole week on the beach just playing in the sun. My oh my, those were good times! But I think George was glad to see us home though he never really said so.

"The years pass quickly, don't they? Yes, the years pass so quickly. George wasn't much for remembering anniversaries and birthdays. Before you knew it, the kids were grown. One night I was worrying about them staying out late, and the next, they'd finished school and gone. Frank went west, Vancouver first and then further north. Arthur went to Toronto, to the Ontario College of Art. Neither one was much for writing home, but they used to phone once in a while.

"Over the years I had a lot of letters from my sister Mary. She travelled all over and did a lot of different things, but she never stayed with anything or anybody very long. She worked at photography, mostly. She joined women's groups, protested this or that. She told me about her friends, but at times I know she was lonely.

"Still, Mary didn't come to see us very often. Actually, I was secretly relieved because George didn't like her at all. 'She's just too smart for her own good, tearing here and there, talking all the time, asking questions,' George said. 'Why can't she find herself a husband, and let us be?'

"George's mother died in her sleep. One morning when I took in her breakfast, I found her. She was lying on her side with her hands under her face, looking peaceful as could be. I had taken care of her 15 years after her stroke.

"Then there was just George and me. Oh my, the place was so quiet. Sometimes I turned on the television just to hear the sound of voices.

"One day right out of the blue, I said, 'George, why is it that you never talk to me?' He grunted and said, 'Why would I? You're always here. What's there to talk about? Why can't you leave it be?' Then he went on reading the paper. So I stopped talking too. That was what George wanted.

"I often wondered what Mary was doing. The last I had heard she had moved to Calgary, she had given up photography and was managing a dress shop. She would be good at that. She always did have a flair for clothes. She had her own style.

"Well, one day I was in the middle of spring cleaning when George didn't come in for dinner. I found him in the barn, where he had fallen down while cleaning the manure stable. He'd had a stroke. I knew it in a minute. I recognized the signs from all the years I looked after his mother.

"I was so shocked that I hardly knew what to do at first. I dragged him into the house and up onto the couch. The smell of manure was terrible. And he'd soiled himself as well. I got his dirty clothes off and bathed him. I thought of calling the doctor but I knew George would just tell me to leave it be. I sat with him the rest of the afternoon. His eyes were open but his face was twisted this awful way–all squinty like, and half grinning, just like when he was slapping poor Liza, beating the boys, or giving me what for. Once I tried to turn him over so he could rest his back, but when I did his arm came crashing down across my head. I left him then, put on my coat and went to the barn where I finished cleaning the stable. After that I fed and watered the animals. George lingered through the night, his breathing rough and raspy. At 5:30 a.m. the room suddenly went quiet. George was dead.

"Then I tried to get hold of the boys and tell them to come home but Arthur was travelling somewhere in Europe. Frank couldn't be reached by radio phone. I left messages but he didn't get them, or something. Then I called Mary, and she was here the next morning. It was Mary who went with me to the funeral parlour, and helped me pick out a casket, make arrangements with the minister and so forth. I didn't know what to do about paying for this, but Mary said not to worry. She'd help me get a lawyer and straighten things out. George always believed in keeping his finances to himself.

"Well, when I sat down with the lawyer and he told me what George had left, you could have knocked me over with a feather. Who would have guessed that there would be so much money? Of course he never spent anything and neither did his folks before him, so there was all that, too. And then there was that big house we lived in.

"Well, the cattle were sold. At first I considered selling the place. But then I got to thinking about all the work I had put into it, about all the memories, all the wonderful times when the boys were small.

"Instead I decided to have the place redone. New paint, new paper, new furniture, new drapes. I planted flowers all around the house. I had the piano tuned, and started taking lessons. I went to a quilting, and I had such a good time that I put one on myself. I learned to drive the car, so I could take myself to the store and to the library. In fact, I became a regular old gadabout.

"Life was pretty good after that. And then the house got too much for me, so the boys helped me find this place. It's nice here. Your mother is always quiet, doesn't talk much. But I'm used to that. She's still company. And she isn't suffering."

"No," said Father Ryan. "Just waiting for God to take her."

"Yes, waiting for the end, just like the rest of us.

"No, I'm not Catholic. Sometimes I wish I was, but what has an old lady like me got to confess about? I've been a widow now 33 years.

"I didn't go to the cemetery where George is buried. I just let him be. It's what George would have wanted."

THE BURYING TRADE

I've been working around the Catelle Funeral Home for close to 40 years now. I guess you could call me a handyman. There's always some job to keep me going. Things need filling or emptying. Things need opening and closing. Things need to be got ready and put away afterwards. It's pretty good work.

Yes, I've been around a while. I'm 68 past. Why I remember when there was a horse-drawn hearse. I could tell you just about everyone that's been buried up and down the river here. If I was a mind to, I could tell you some of the secrets buried with them.

The Catelles were good to work for. When Kevin Ryan took over the business, things didn't change much. Never had a problem with him either. But, I got to tell you there were some funny times. Don't suppose you'd remember young Lewis Avery? He assisted Mr. Ryan for a while. Folks says I made this up, but it's true, I swear.

Well, anyway, a couple of weeks after the end of World War II, they were sent to Saint John to pick up a body and bring it back to Woodstock.

An outgoing chap who liked to hear himself talk, 19-year-old Lewis had only been working at the funeral home for a couple of weeks. Lewis was a good hard worker and he had a fine voice, which came in handy when there was no one to sing at the funeral of the deceased. Kevin liked the boy well enough but found his incessant chatter tended to get on his nerves. Still, he could not think of a way to head Lewis off without hurting his feelings, so he put up with it.

The road to Saint John in those days was not great. There were long stretches of gravel to get through, and it took them a good part of the day to drive down. Neither had been there before and they were awhile finding the loading docks. Then it took two more hours to get the paper work sorted out and the coffin containing the deceased transferred to the hearse.

All this effort gave Kevin an awful thirst, so he parked the hearse in a church yard and sent Lewis back down the street to the liquor store. When Lewis returned Kevin took a couple of good swigs to make sure he had the right stuff, then proceeded on up the highway.

Bye and bye Kevin began to get sleepy, so he turned the wheel over to Lewis. On his way around to the passenger's seat he downed another snort or two and settled back.

Lewis drove carefully, gently guiding the large, elegant, smooth-running vehicle around the turns and twists of the road as he made small talk and read the road signs aloud. Kevin was not listening. He was asleep.

Just north of Fredericton, Kevin stirred and asked Lewis if he was tired. Lewis said no, but he sure could use something to eat, then launched into what his family had for Sunday dinner.

"Well," said Kevin, who was getting thirsty again, but didn't want the young fellow to see him take another drink, "there's a place just along here where we can gas up. I'm not too hungry, so why don't you go in and have a bite, while I stay with the vehicle."

Lewis drove up to the gas pump and had the tank filled, watched to see that the tank cover was in place and, while waiting for his change, gave the chrome cap an extra wipe. Then he pulled over to the restaurant, got out, and went inside.

Kevin finished his pint, and was just settling down for another nap when a soldier in uniform walked over to the window of the hearse.

"Say, you couldn't find room for passenger?" the soldier asked. "I'm trying to get home to Peel."

It was late and it was getting cold, and the soldier looked about done in. Kevin said: "Well, I'll tell you, we have a body back there in the casket which we are returning to Woodstock. My assistant is in the restaurant having supper so I can't let you have his seat, but there's probably room in the back, if you don't mind riding alongside the casket."

The soldier hadn't had any sleep for several days. He was bone-weary and anxious to get home, and he knew there wasn't much chance of another ride coming along that time of night. Besides, after what he had seen and experienced in the four years he had spent overseas, the casket and its contents didn't bother him. He threw in his kit bag and climbed in after it. Then he wrapped himself in his blanket, and settled down. In minutes he, too, was fast asleep.

Lewis, meanwhile, tucked into a hot chicken sandwich with lots of mashed potatoes and gravy, and topped that off with a large chunk of blueberry pie with ice cream, which he washed down with two glasses of milk, while he talked to the waitress. Feeling better, he paid for his meal, thanked her, and went outside. Seeing Kevin sprawled on the passenger's side, Lewis climbed into the driver's seat, started the motor, and eased the hearse out onto the road.

Lewis had been driving for about an hour when he started getting drowsy and thought he would sing a little to keep himself company. He ran through the *Old Lamp Lighter,* one of the popular songs of the time. Kevin slept on. Then Lewis sang *My Grandfather's Clock* and *White Cliffs of Dover,* and, now in full voice, was just moving into *Till We Meet Again,* when the soldier in the back awoke.

After a minute or two the soldier pulled aside the curtains that separated the front seat from the back, and said: "Is it okay if I have a smoke back here?"

Lewis's hair stood on end. He swung around fast and he pulled the steering wheel with him, thus aiming the new hearse, which only had 430 miles on its speedometer, straight into an alder swamp.

Kevin awoke with a grunt, saying, "What in tarnation is going on?"

For once Lewis was as quiet as the corpse. Nobody moved a muscle.

After a few seconds the soldier, who had served in the front lines and had often seen terrified men do strange things, immediately realized what had happened. "I guess the young fellow turned out for a moose," he said. "Let's see if we can get this thing back on the road. I've just got to get home tonight."

Lewis was still trying to live down the accident when, a few weeks later, they had a call to go out to Pool Hill and prepare a woman for burial. Lucy Lambert had died suddenly on the way home from the local dance hall.

In those days, Lucy was what was known as loose. She had given birth to nine children, fathered by a variety of local males including the tax collector, a politician, two deacons, three potato pickers and a pulp cutter from the North Shore.

As Lucy's charms started to fade and cash gifts from admirers grew scarce, she began making home brew, the illegal proceeds from which she rounded out her budget. And though Lucy's mothering instincts were somewhat spotty, her family grew and thrived and, in time, each of them found homes of their own nearby.

It was early winter by then and this particular Saturday night some of the fellows who had been drinking her home brew offered to take Lucy to the dance. So Lucy got all gussied up, and off they went.

They had been at the dance for about an hour and Lucy, who had been dancing with first one and then the other, was getting warm. She began taking off her clothes. Nobody at her table was paying any attention, so she stripped to her high heels and went out on the dance floor alone. That was the moment the musicians stopped for intermission.

Well Lucy's nudie stroll caught everybody's attention, including the bouncer's, and he took it as a personal affront. He was having none of that kind of behaviour. No. So he set out to catch her. But the floor was slippery and Lucy was fast. Then, just as the bouncer closed in on her, one of the young fellows stuck a foot out and tripped him. The bouncer bumped into someone else, knocking him off his feet, and they all sprawled on the floor in a big heap. Someone yelled "Fight" and the fun was on.

Fists were flying, chairs were breaking, women were screaming, bottles were smashing on the floor. Just then a space at the back cleared and the fellows who had brought Lucy to the dance saw their chance, grabbed her and ran for the door. They made it. As soon as they had the 1939 Chevrolet headed towards home, they hooted with glee. Lucy, high as a kite, joined in the laughter, then suddenly stopped. "I'm going to be sick," she said. "Roll down the window."

While they waited for Lucy to finish tossing her cookies, the men in the car were passing the bottle back and forth, and when she slid down in the seat, they just thought she had passed out, so they continued on home. Only when the light came on as they opened the door to get out, did they realize Lucy was not breathing. Lucy, while vomiting, had burst a blood vessel in her throat and choked to death.

By the time Lewis Avery and Kevin Ryan got there from the Catelle Funeral Home, all the men whom Lucy had been with were cold sober. Lucy's body was stretched out on her bed. When they started to take the body to the funeral parlour, her son stepped forward and demanded that she remain in her own home until burial. "Ma don't like them places," he told them. "She said we was never to put her in a funeral parlour. She's going to stay here."

Kevin sent Lewis back to the funeral parlour to pick up a low-priced coffin and the various equipment they would need to lay out the body and, while waiting, asked if any of Lucy's home brew was left. Someone produced a glass, and Kevin helped himself. Bye and bye, Lewis returned and they carefully prepared the body. One of her daughters-in-law had brought over a nice blue dress, and when their work was finished, Lucy in her blue dress, with her hair all combed, looked quite fine.

After Kevin and Lewis left, everyone sat around wondering what to do next. It was just afternoon and there was a long night ahead. They might as well have a little drink, they agreed, a little drink in Lucy's honour. Well, one drink led to another and by evening they were all three sheets to the wind. Then someone thought it would be a good idea to sit Lucy up so she could join the party. Then another took the body out of the coffin, and began dancing it around the floor. And so they partied throughout the night.

But one after another the home brew claimed the mourners and by daybreak when the first of them started to come around, they realized they were in trouble. In the middle of the floor was Lucy's body, the hair all down, the blue dress a shambles. Further it was stiff and they could not get it back in the casket. Once again somebody went for the undertaker and Kevin sent Lewis out to see what was going on.

When Lewis stepped into the room, he couldn't believe his eyes. He turned around and went back to town for Kevin. Kevin wasn't too happy about being called out again that early in the morning, and Lewis was babbling even more than usual. After a while Kevin figured out what had been going on.

"All right," said Kevin. "We'll go out and fix her up again. But I want you to keep your mouth shut about this. Otherwise, we'd have to drive clear out to Glassville and get the sheriff and sign a lot of papers and a whole bunch of stuff. Besides they were just having a party. And I don't think Lucy would have minded. Think you can keep quiet about this?"

"Well, sure, but..."

"No buts, just promise me you are not going to noise this around. Can you do that?"

"Yes, I guess so," agreed Lewis, and they carried on to the Lambert place.

Kevin walked in and looked around. "Okay," he told them, "the party is over. This is a disgrace. You know what you have done is against the law. Now I am going to fix up this body once more, and if anyone so much as goes near it, I'll call the sheriff, and you'll all go to jail, every manjack of you."

On the following day the pallbearers, contrite and doleful, sat in the front row of the nearly empty church and waited to carry Lucy to her final resting place. Of course, Lucy hadn't been much of a churchgoer, and nobody had offered to provide music for her funeral. But after a quick word from the minister, Lewis stepped up to the front of the chapel and, in his clear, strong voice, sang *Amazing Grace, Shall We Gather at the River,* and *I Will Meet You in the Morning.*

And so in the end, Lucy Lambert had as good a sendoff as any in the county.

The whole incident shook Lewis up badly. He couldn't believe that people would do such a thing as get a corpse up and dance with it. He began to wonder if he was cut out for this kind of work after all. Still it was a job, and he was saving a little money and had his eye on a fine horn he had seen in a music shop across the border in Houlton.

Four more funerals took place that winter but these were of the traditional kind. Old people whose time had come, and two of them had died quietly in their sleep. For three of the funerals, Lewis was asked to sing, which he did. About February there was a thaw and a freeze-up again, which left the roads as treacherous as they can be in this part of the country.

One morning, they got a call to go to Grafton and pick up the body of a man in his fifties who had died of a heart attack. The man's house was high on a hill at the end of a long driveway, and half way up the hill Kevin got the hearse stuck. Lewis kept offering advice. Kevin got out and handed him a shovel. And so they shovelled and pushed and spun the wheels and, with each try, the hearse settled even lower to the ground.

About then along came a man from Newburg driving a team of horses, hauling a long sled. Lewis ran down and hailed him and the man agreed to help them out of the ditch. He unhooked the sled and fastened a chain to the hearse, hooked his team to the chain and pulled the hearse out backwards. After all that effort, Kevin decided it would be best to leave the hearse on the road, and try to carry the body down the hill.

They removed the basket in which they usually transported bodies from the hearse and carrying it between them, they made their way up the hill. The man who had died weighed over 250, and when Lewis saw the body, he wondered aloud how they were ever going to carry it back down the hill. Kevin meanwhile had spotted an eight-foot toboggan standing by the shed door, and turning to Lewis, he said: "We'll ask them if we can borrow that for a few minutes."

After offering his sympathies to the grieving family, Kevin quietly explained that he couldn't get the hearse up the hill, and asked if it would be okay to use the toboggan. They said yes.

It was all Lewis and Kevin could do to lift the 250 pound body into the basket and carry it through to the front door, but they managed and in a few minutes had it placed squarely on the toboggan.

Kevin said: "Lewis, now I'll take the lead, you get behind and hold it steady."

Together they proceeded down the hill. Just as they rounded the driveway out of sight of the house, Lewis's feet went out from under him. On his back he slid past the toboggan, and kicked the legs out from under Kevin. Kevin fell backwards on top of the basket and away they went down the hill, straight into the back of the hearse. The basket went up in the air and broke into a dozen pieces. The body fell out. Kevin skinned both knees and cracked his shoulder and Lewis was knocked out cold.

By the time Kevin got his breath, Lewis was beginning to come around. "Well," said Kevin, "if that big sonofabitch wasn't dead before, he sure is now. Let's get him loaded."

When spring came that year Lewis decided he's had enough. The horn he had been wanting went on sale. He bought it and still had about $80 in his pocket, and on the way home he decided it was time to change careers. He quit the funeral directing business, packed a suitcase and took a train to Toronto, where he soon found work as a night club singer at the Brass Rail, on Yonge Street.

The young man who took Lewis's place was a sombre, self-important type, and Kevin never really warmed to him. I can't say as I did either.

Now and then when Kevin was in his cups, he was surprised to realize he missed young Avery. He missed his humour and his sunny disposition and yes, he even missed Lewis's singing and his conversation.

ZEKE AND HANNAH

You couldn't call Zeke Hardlow a good-looking man. Grizzled, dirty, toothless, he had a face like a junkyard dog. His clothes were lashed together with board-nails and binder twine, and he smelled like a hen-pen on a hot day.

As negligible as his comeliness were his charm, wit and personality. Every now and then, he would haul off and cuff Hannah, his wife, just to show her who was boss. Numerous times over the 20 years they'd been together he had blacked her eye and Hannah, never a fighter, had simply put up with it. In fact she really cared for Zeke, and usually managed to find ways to overlook his abuse.

Zeke Hardlow had only two things going for him. He could play the fiddle, and he could fix things. Though not overly endowed with gumption, he managed to odd-job his way through life and could do almost anything you asked him to in the way of repairs. When he fixed something, folks would say, "Now, how much is your bill?" And Zeke would say, "Oh, I don't know, whatever you think it's worth."

The folks of Cedar Springs were usually pretty good about it. They'd reach in their pockets and pull out a $10 or a $20, and Zeke would turn and spit, and say, "Yep. That'll do."

A mountain of a woman, Hannah waddled through her days, watching soap operas and baking. Tasty soups and stews she made for her Zeke, hot biscuits, doughnuts, filled cookies and butterscotch pies with meringue four inches high. You could tell by her girth that she sampled her products.

The house out on the Chisholm Road where Zeke and Hannah lived was fairly old, and mirrored their individual eccentricities. The fridge was a 1948 GE, and it opened with the door handle off a '54 Dodge. Half a sheet of plywood laid over a cable spool served as their table, and each of the chairs, which had been rescued from a land-fill, had different coloured pieces where Zeke had replaced a leg or rung, but had never gotten around to painting them. There were a couple of scraggly plants in the kitchen window.

On a shelf Hannah had her own collection of mementos. Scattered in among the rocks and driftwood were a jar of kidney stones from an earlier operation, a post card mailed in Toronto from their son Herman, Herman's baby tooth, Zeke's black toenail from the time he dropped an anvil on his foot and, finally, Dear Brother Alf's ashes, which they planned to bury when Zeke got time.

One thing Zeke always seemed to have time for was playing the fiddle, and he played with unexpected skill; that's what got him into the kind of trouble with Hannah that almost became their undoing. Hannah had asked him to go to the corner store to pick up some 6-49 tickets and two litres of Baxter's Heavenly Hash ice cream.

It was a clear night, a cool night, and there was a full moon with a ring around it. Zeke was restless. In the store he ran into a banjo player called Archie Fox who said he had a little party going on at his house and that Zeke ought to stop by. Zeke agreed to go along for half an hour or so, but first he had to take home the ice cream and get his fiddle.

Leaving Hannah eating ice cream, reading the Cedar Springs Weekly and watching Wheel of Fortune on TV, Zeke picked up his fiddle and drove over to Archie's.

Stella, Archie's woman, with her accordion already strapped on, let him in and introduced him to a friend of hers called Babs, who was sitting on the couch tuning a guitar. Zeke sat down at a chair by the kitchen door, opened the case and drew out his fiddle. Archie set four Labatt's Blue on the kitchen table and picked up his banjo.

Babs wasn't too impressed with Zeke and his little Mona Lisa smile when she first saw him, but when Zeke drew the bow across the catgut, she changed her mind. He didn't just play, he transcended. Warming up, he would tease out a few little notes, stop and listen and look at the fiddle, as if he expected to find a mouse in it, then he would cuddle it into his neck and draw the bow across the strings. Strange sounds he made, eerie. You began to hear birds chirping, a kitten mewing, then the long-drawn-out wail of the coyote. Then some more low notes would chase the whine, and you heard a locomotive picking up speed. Suddenly you were tapping your foot to a laughing jig. Whippoorwills and waterfalls and whistling winds were heard. In his repertoire Zeke had ragtime, blues, rock and roll. He played polkas, waltzes and all the old hymns, and after a few drinks, Zeke was good for the night.

Around one in the morning, Zeke happened to look across at Babs, who was keeping up to him as if they had been practising for years. She gave him a little grin, and Zeke grinned back. Zeke was flying high.

Meanwhile, just after the eleven o'clock news, Hannah matched her tickets with the 6-49 numbers on TV and discovered she had a winner. Not just a piddly little $10 or $50 or $5,000 ticket, but a big one. All six numbers matched.

She threw on her coat and, thinking she would likely meet Zeke on the road, she started walking towards Archie and Stella's. Although Hannah wasn't used to walking any distance, with the excitement and all, two hours later she found herself at the Fox's. She was just rounding the corner when she looked in the window to see Zeke and Babs sitting there grinning at each other.

Although it took a lot for Hannah to get her dander up normally, when she saw her Zeke sitting there leering at a strange young woman, Hannah got riled. She turned around and stomped all the way back home.

To make a long story short, time got away from Zeke and his friends. First one then the other would take the lead, and they played everything from *Irishman's Shanty* to *The Old Rugged Cross*. The next thing Zeke knew the beer was gone and it was daybreak. He stood up, shut the fiddle in its case, said 'so long' and headed for the Chevy.

After he pulled in his driveway, he climbed down out of the cab and walked quietly in the back door. From the kitchen Hannah called out, "That you Zeke?" He said, "Well, it ain't the Easter Bunny!"

That was all she needed. She waited until he put the violin case down. Then she came out swinging. She clipped Zeke on the side of the jaw and knocked him over backwards. When he got up, she flung him against the wall. He crumpled and she stood over him yelling until he got to his feet, and then she hit him again. Meanwhile, caught completely off guard, Zeke couldn't believe what Hannah was doing. Never had he seen her act like that. All he could think of to say was, "Hannah, baby, don't! Don't! Now quit that. What's got into you, Hannah? Ow, ow, ow."

Suddenly, between the excitement of winning the lottery, her long walk to the Fox's and back, and giving Zeke a trimming, Hannah ran out of steam. She righted a kitchen chair and sat down with a thud. Zeke gingerly slid into a chair across the table from her, glancing at her in amazement as he checked for broken bones.

After a while, out of years and years of habit, Hannah got up and made a pot of tea, cut two hefty wedges of blueberry pie, added double dollops of ice cream to each plate and set one in front of Zeke. They ate in silence, but Hannah was thinking hard. She ought to leave Zeke. That would teach him. She could buy a brand new car and go. She could go and stay at Herman's in Toronto. But she didn't much care for Herman's wife and they had no spare room and she didn't know anybody there, and in a big city she would be scared to go out anywhere. And besides she didn't drive. Or she could move out and have a place of her own. But then, she thought, what would I do alone? Zeke's all I have. There would be no one to cook for. No one coming in and out. Ah, it was all too much to figure right now.

Taking the 6-49 ticket out of her apron pocket, she stuck it up on the mantle behind Herman's postcard, the jar of kidney stones and Brother Alf's ashes, and promised herself to deal with everything later. Meanwhile, she would lie down for a nap. After 10 minutes or so when she appeared to be safely sleeping, Zeke crawled in beside her, and together they snored the morning away.

TIMMY'S PICTURE

There aren't too many in church today. It's getting near the holiday season and I guess people are busy with so much going on. The pew where I sit is about half way back. I like to sit by the window. I can't hear so well from here, but I like to see who all is around.

They have chosen a hymn I don't know--and I have been coming to the Cedar Springs United Church for 50 years. I do wish they would stay with the hymnal. But I think it's this new minister. He trained somewhere in the States I've heard. Right full of himself, I'd say. And he could do with a haircut. Still he can sing and, if he can preach as well as he can sing, the service won't take too long.

It's good to get out to church today. That nice Smith girl with Extra-mural came in to sit with Ben. I warned her if he gets out of control, not to try to stop him. He will strike out at the least little thing. Just watch he doesn't hurt himself or burn the house down. Watch where he goes and we'll get him back somehow. I feel a little guilty leaving Ben with that slip of a girl, but she told me she worked in Centracare for six years, so I'm sure she can handle things. Yes it's good to get out to church.

The sermon today is about forgiveness. Forgiveness. Well, I like to think I am a forgiving type of person. I can forgive all right. But forgetting, now that's something else again. And, yes, I will admit I carry grudges. I wish I didn't but I do.

I wonder how Ben is doing. He was a good husband, the best a woman could want--until he got Alzheimers. No one knows how it is dealing with a person with Alzheimers. Not unless they have had the experience. It's like living with a dozen different people at once, none of whom you know. The Ben that I grew to trust and love is gone. I don't know what inhabits his body these days.

Forgiveness. That's the sermon. It seems hard, though, to forgive God for what has happened to Ben. Certainly he didn't deserve this. But then, nobody ever gets what they deserve, do they?

On the other hand, maybe they do. Over there next to the aisle is Fiona Jenkins, sitting with her husband and their mentally handicapped son. They have a big family, but the others, the smart good-looking ones, have all flown the nest. Before Ben got sick, we used to eat at Walmers, and I learned that one of Fiona's sons worked there. There was no mistaking his looks. Just like his father. I've heard since that he has AIDs. And then someone told me he's an alcoholic and suffers from an eating disorder.

Well, what next!

Fiona and I went to school together. I remember the year we were in Grade nine. That was the year the regional high school opened. And I had the biggest crush on Timmy McDonigal. I think Timmy was about fifteen at the time, beautiful teeth, a bright smile, dark red curly hair, freckles, and the light of the Irish imps dancing in his eyes. Twice we had gone for long walks along the railroad tracks. I was crazy about him.

That fall, with my potato-picking money I bought a Brownie Hawkeye camera for $12. I took it to school and snapped pictures of everything and everyone. I took pictures of Fiona and of Judy McWaid (who later stood up with me when Ben and I were married). And, among these pictures was one of Timmy.

It was one of those lucky accidents that inspire all amateur photographers. By chance the lighting was perfect. I remember the day. It was slightly overcast. Timmy is standing on the railway tracks, hands in the pockets of his bomber jacket. Behind him the creek swerves in among the trees. Timmy is wearing a big smile, hamming it up for the camera. Later that afternoon he kissed me. We would skip down the tracks a ways, and then we would stop and hold each other and kiss again. Timmy was a laughing person. And even though I was thrilled to my toes, I had to laugh too. Oh, what a time that was. I didn't get home until after dark, and my mother was furious. But I was in love, the way a schoolgirl falls in love that first time. I think I must have shook something loose when I went head over heels, because I couldn't think of anything else but him for the rest of that year.

Well, of course I had to show my snapshots around. But what I didn't know at the time was that Fiona Jenkins also had a crush on Timmy. Anyway, one day I went to look at my pictures and the one of Timmy was missing. I went through them again and again. I checked my desk and my bookbag and I asked Judy and Fiona if they had seen it, and they both looked me straight in the eye and said no.

Time went on. In February Timmy McDonigal dropped out of Grade 10 and joined the army. He was sent to Germany, I believe. I never heard from him again and I didn't see him for several years.

After finishing vocational school, I went to work in the telephone office and it was there I met Ben. He was a lineman. We dated for two years, and then got married. And then the children came along. And the grandchildren. And my life has been full. Oh, we had our ups and downs, the same as everyone else, but there was nothing we couldn't handle together. Until now.

Once when the children were small, Ben and I took a trip to Toronto. While they went to the Riverdale zoo, I went shopping. And who should I meet in the Eaton Centre but Ivy, Timmy McDonigal's older sister. I hadn't seen her in years. We went to the food plaza and had a cup of coffee. Of course I asked her about her brother and she told me Timmy was dead. He had got out of the army, moved to Ontario, married and had a daughter, Nancy. He and his wife were later divorced and after that he began drinking heavily. In the end he died of a heart attack.

While Ivy was telling me all this, she was rummaging around in her purse and came out with some pictures. The first one she showed me was the one of Timmy on the railroad tracks by the creek. She told me that when Timmy died, Fiona, who had kept it all those years, had sent the photo to her. The next photo was one of Timmy in the coffin. I can never understand why someone would want to take a photo of a person in the coffin, or why they would want to carry it with them. But there was Timmy's corpse, eyes closed, hands folded over a dark suit, red curly hair resting on a satin cushion. It was a good clear photo. You could even see the dusting of freckles on his nose.

It was as if someone had punched me in the stomach, not once but several times. I felt anger, despair, revulsion all at once. Fiona's thieving treachery and her great big lies. And Judy must have known about the picture, too. Maybe she even had a hand in stealing it from me. Maybe Timmy knew as well. "Well," I said evenly as I handed Ivy back the photos, "one mystery solved. I always wondered what became of that picture. I took it, you know."

I left Ivy after a while and went on with my shopping, then met Ben and the kids at McDonald's. The kids had loved the zoo and were full of all the exciting things they had seen. I tucked the business about Timmy way into the back of my mind. But that night in my dreams Timmy was rubbing his freckled nose against my cheek and we were running along the railway tracks, hand in hand, kissing, laughing, until we came to the overpass and his hand slipped from mine.

Forgiveness. Oh yes. Forgetting? Now, that's hard.

Fiona had trained as a nurse. Then she got married around the same time Ben and I did. She had four children, three daughters and a son, and was expecting another when I got news of her again. I had heard her husband was one for gallivanting. In a small place like this it's hard to keep secrets. Then, can you believe this, her husband started fooling around with her sister and got her pregnant as well.

Both women had their babies, and I later heard that Fiona's husband got religion and started going straight. However, their last baby was born mentally handicapped. My soul! I suppose he would be around 40 now, and she has had to feed and diaper him all those years. But no one has ever heard her complain, that I know of. There's no reason for me to know. We have never really spoken since high school and I guess that's my fault. I have been too wrapped up in my own life.

We had just celebrated our 35th wedding anniversary when I noticed a change in Ben. One morning he left the house to go to work. As a habit I always watched through the pantry window to see him drive up the road. I glanced out a few times and didn't see him. Then I realized that I hadn't heard the truck start. I wiped my hands on my apron and went out to see what was going on. Ben was sitting in the driver's seat with the keys in his hand and a strange and rueful look on his face. "I don't know what to do," he said. "I don't know what I am supposed to do."

Within months he no longer knew me nor our children. And it has grown progressively worse. I have to dress and undress him too, now. Just like Fiona and her boy. I wonder if her husband helps out. You know, it must have taken a big heart for her to forgive him for sleeping with her sister. I don't think I could forgive either one of them. Especially since the sister's child is now a renowned surgeon.

But my, it's nice to get out this morning. I like the way the sun slants through the stained glass windows. Forgiveness, the minister is saying. "Drop your grudges. While you're home holding a grudge against someone, they're out dancing."

And I think to myself. "Oh, no, they are not, young man. The person I hold a grudge against is sitting over there next to the aisle, hanging on tightly to her grown-up son, who will always be five years old, at least mentally." I glance back at Fiona and her family. He would be a nice-looking young man if he had been born right. She's had it hard all these years. No doubt she has paid for her sins more times than enough. I guess it's time to let the past go. It was only a photograph. We were just children. And Timmy has been dead for twenty-five years. Timmy with the big smile and the impish laughter. I doubt if he would ever have made the husband Ben did.

As we are leaving the church, Fiona moved into the line in front of me. "Good morning, Fiona," I said. "How do you like our new minister?"

"Oh, good morning, Ellen," she said with a smile. Then, tugging her son back into the line in front of her, she added. "He preaches a good sermon. He just seems so very young."

"Yes," I replied.

"How is Ben these days."

"Failing," I said. "Every day it is a little worse. Every day he loses a little more. It's hard."

"I know," she said. "It's hard."

SCRIMPING AND SAVING

I've just come from the Dr. White's office. It was cold and smelled of disinfectant. Dettol, I think. It seems kind of funny having a doctor so young. He went to school with our children. Anyway, he wants me to see a specialist about this pain in my stomach. But the specialist is in Saint John and I'd have to go down there and stay overnight. I could take the bus, but I don't know my way around, so I'd have to take taxis once I get there. And I'd have to find a place to stay. My soul, that would cost a lot of money. Maybe I'll put it off for a few days.

I don't go to the doctor very often. I'm not one of these people who can sit around a doctor's waiting room every other day of the week just for something to do, demanding prescriptions for every little sneeze. I had to wait quite a while. There was a young woman in the waiting room, stranger to me. She spoke to me nice enough, but I'm not one for small talk. At last the receptionist called me. "Isabel Boughan?" I stood up. "Come this way," she said.

I've always been careful with money. You never know when something will come up. I've always managed to tuck some away for a rainy day. When Ellis and I were married I told him right away that I would look after our finances. At the time Ellis was working at the plant and spending money faster than he made it. He wanted to go out every Saturday night. They had a dance at the Cedar Springs Legion Hall and he liked to have a few beers during the evening. But I said, "Ellis, one or two beers are enough. We need to watch our pennies." Ellis just laughed, saying, "This woman knows how to stretch a dollar."

I scrimped and saved, and it wasn't long before we had a down payment on some land. We bought a few head of cattle and did quite well with them. Ellis was wonderful with the animals. He'd stay up all night with a sick calf, and we never lost one.

Prices were good and we made a little money and I always put something by. Our son and daughter were born 14 months apart. They were both healthy and strong, thanks be. And for a while, when they were small, Joanne was able to use the clothes Allison grew out of. My, my, children's clothes are so expensive today. I don't know how these young couples do it. And today the kids have to have everything they see on television. There is so much waste!

As I was saying, we bought a little more land, and the farm began to prosper. Ellis found a second-hand tractor. He got a real good deal on it and of course he was handy around machinery and that gave him something to work with.

One thing I can say is that Ellis and the children had good nutritious meals. There was no junk food in our house. I planned the menu very carefully. Oh, I can tell you, we didn't eat steak at every meal, like some. But I always managed to save a little out of the food budget. And I never wasted a thing. Ellis didn't like leftovers, so I ate them. If a tray of cookies got singed, I put the rest out for company and ate the burned ones myself.

Ellis was a hard worker. All those years, Ellis he never complained. He worked from sunup to sundown. Every day but Sunday. Once in a while he would say to me. "Isabel, let's go out to dinner, see what other people look like. Maybe take in a movie."

"That sounds nice," I'd say. "But we have to remember Allison will be going to college in a couple of years, and we need to start saving for his tuition. And then there's Joanne's graduation coming up. It all takes so much."

And I remember him saying, "Isabel, why don't you buy yourself a new dress and a new pair of stockings. Seems like you've worn that same dress every day for five years. And you can't go around in this weather with nothing on your legs."

"It isn't the same dress," I'd tell him. "I have three house dresses, which I made out of the same cloth. It's good durable material that will stand lots of wear and it was on sale at a very good price. And I can't just go running out spending money all over the place. I hear there is talk of the government raising taxes. We need every cent." Ellis would shake his head and go back to work.

New dress, indeed! I had a perfectly good dress for Sundays. It had belonged to my older sister. And she always bought the best. Of course it wasn't in the latest style, but I was never one to be bothered by that. I was too tall and I'd never have felt comfortable in lace or frills and furbelows. I didn't much care for the colour, sort of a bilious green. Avocado, I guess they call it. But there was lots of wear left in it yet, and it suited me just fine.

I always had it in the back of my mind that Ellis and I would take a little trip one day. Maybe drive to Niagara and have a honeymoon. We didn't take a honeymoon when we were married. I told Ellis at the time, "Why waste time driving half way across Canada to look at the falls, when you can see the same thing on the shredded wheat box?" (Of course, once we were married, I didn't buy shredded wheat very often. So expensive. It was much cheaper to buy oatmeal and that was a lot better for your digestion.

The pain in my stomach seems to be moving, sort of higher up, almost like a cramp. Maybe I need a purgative. Then I suppose I should keep that appointment with the specialist. But I don't know. Even with Medicare there is always an expense. I'll just wait and see.

Ellis and I had a good life. We didn't go out much. We stopped going to the Saturday night dances before the children were born. Baby sitters were hard to find, and we didn't like to leave the animals. And working as hard as Ellis did, come Saturday night he was too tired to go out and hop around a dance floor.

We bought a new television set. Not one of those big ones that take up half a wall, but a 14-inch. Ellis set it up in the kitchen, since that's where he sat in the evenings. There was a good carpet for the living room, and he didn't want to mark it up with his boots. So he used to sit there by the window of an evening, reading the papers or watching the television. I had a little desk in the kitchen and I'd look after our books and accounts and look for ways to cut corners.

If Ellis had lived, we would have celebrated our 30th anniversary last fall. He was a good man. And we had a solid marriage although I must say I had hopes the children would get an education and go on to good paying careers. We had enough money saved for their education--and I can tell you there were years when it was hard to save--but Allison dropped out in his first year of university and went off to take pictures in the Amazon, then came back here to farm. And Joanne put herself through on scholarships. She refused our help. She was determined to show us she could do it on her own. She knew how hard we had scrimped and saved for Allison's education. But she's never done anything with her degree. Right now she's working as a receptionist in town.

It's funny how things happen. About six months before Ellis died a flyer came in the mail about pre-arranged funerals. And I said to Ellis, "this looks like a pretty good deal." It made sense to look after things now instead of waiting until after you retire when there might not be an income.

"Whatever you want," he said. But for some reason I put it off.

Well, who would have guessed Ellis would drop dead right in his tracks walking from the barn to the house! He was only 53. Never had a sick day in his life. Never missed a day of work. He didn't smoke and he didn't drink any more than those few beers before we were married. It just goes to show. The doctor said he suffered a massive heart attack.

I was flabbergasted. I didn't know where to turn. I didn't know what to do. I couldn't imagine life without Ellis. But for once, I thought, Ellis would have the best. I dug into our savings and I bought him a polished oak casket, lead-lined with a lovely cream-coloured interior. There were white lilies on the material. There was a matching satin pillow and on the outside was a magnificent brass name-plate. Then I bought a new black dress and hat, with gloves and purse to match. I never wanted anyone being able to say I stinted on Ellis's funeral.

Last week I sold the cattle and the farm machinery went up for auction. Even with prices being down at the moment, I did rather well. Certainly I won't have to worry about being a burden on the children.

Sometimes the pain isn't that bad. Maybe I'll just go home and try some bicarb and a heating pad.

BILLY GOAT BOLD, BILLY GOAT SOLD!

Coming home to Cedar Springs from the airport, after seeing their youngest son on a plane to Toronto where he would be attending university, Louise realized that she and her husband Ernest would be alone in the old farm-house for the first time in 26 years.

As Ernest concentrated on the highway busy with a Sunday crowd and tourists, Louise thought about the work and worry and joy and confusion that went with raising three strapping sons. All that laundry, the endless cooking, the racket. The many sleepless nights of wondering if they would all survive the hi-jinks of their teen years.

Well, it was behind them now. The two oldest boys were married and settled down, with nice wives and good jobs, and now the youngest was on his way. She felt a moment's panic that the mothering years had swept so swiftly by. Then, right on the heels of that thought, Louise decided it would be great to have time for herself, time to slow down, time to maybe take a course at the Community College, to sit on the front porch and read, to work in the garden, to enjoy the lovely late summer weather. The possibilities were endless.

Meanwhile as Ernest drove along carefully following the speed limit, he was considering whether or not he should fence in the lower field that didn't get hayed during the recent long wet spell; this would give the cows a little more pasture. Or whether he should take the cows up to the sale and be done with farming altogether. But right now the price was so bad you could hardly give them away. And he might as well keep them since he had the feed and the barn space. By the time they got home, Ernest had pretty well made up his mind he wouldn't do anything for a while, but he'd probably go up to the sale and see for himself how the market was going.

Bright and early Monday morning Louise decided she'd give the place a thorough cleaning, beginning right after breakfast. Ernest was already up and gone out to do the chores, so she stripped the beds, grabbed the laundry basket, threw in the towels and bath mats and came downstairs. Before starting the coffee and mixing pancakes, she had the laundry sorted and one load in the washer.

After breakfast Ernest lingered long enough to hear the 8 a.m. news, then he put on his cap and jacket, checked for his keys to the pickup and took off for Florenceville. The pickup had a four-wheel drive, heavy springs, and a high cap on the back, large enough to transport a cow or anything smaller, if the need arose.

There was a good-sized crowd gathered at the show barn. The auction was just starting. Something different today--the auction of exotic birds, emus and ostriches.

While at the sale he got talking to some of the fellows who were raising emus, and he stopped to look them over. But the more he thought about the price and about all the things that could go wrong with them, the more he decided that he didn't need any long-necked nasty birds around the place, especially birds that were bigger than he was.

But Ernest, with a few extra dollars in his pocket from selling the old seeder, was in a buying mood. He had enough cows. Didn't have any use for a horse. He looked over the pygmy goats, cute little things, with their long ears and delicate feet. Too small, he decided. Then he looked at the sheep. But shearing was a hard job, and the price for wool wasn't that great either. Still, Ernest had it in his mind to find something in the livestock line. In the end he wound up buying a goat, a 10-month old ram.

Although they kept a joint checking account for food, clothing, utilities and farm supplies, and a joint savings and retirement fund, Louise and Ernest each had personal accounts. Ernest paid the $42 for the goat out of his own account, knowing he had no justification whatsoever for buying the ram. When Louise asked him what he planned to do with it, he said he had some ideas. Louise backed off. He would talk when he felt like it.

In fact Ernest did not want to discuss the goat with Louise, and found himself feeling defensive as he tethered it in the barnyard, away from the fence and near enough to the apple tree so that it could get shade, but wouldn't get tangled up in the chain. He didn't ask her how she spent her money, or why she bought material by the bolt, just so she could cut it up and make quilt patterns, so why should he have to tell her what he was doing with his? If he wanted a goat, he'd darn well have a goat, and that was that.

Tethered in the yard, the billy goat seemed happy enough as he munched away on the weedy grass, now and then flicking his short tail and wriggling his hide to move the flies. Ernest went on with the fencing. Louise cleaned the upstairs and then worked her way downstairs. Windows, walls and woodwork were scrubbed and shined, rugs vacuumed, cobwebs whisked away. She also found time to concoct a stew, and at 10 to 12 put the dumplings in.

When Ernest came in to dinner at noon, they both were ready for a good meal. They finished off with blueberry pie and Ernest went back to his fencing.

After she finished the dinner dishes Louise stepped out on the sun porch to hang out the dish-towels. Then she glanced across the yard near the barn and looked at the goat. The goat stopped chewing and stared back at her.

What an odd-looking animal, she thought. Just like something out of Greek mythology. Strange.

After that every time she went out into the yard, the billy goat would stop chewing and watch her.

It was a very ordinary goat with a long face, nobby horns and a scraggy beard, but as days passed, it seemed to Louise to be wearing a permanent smirk. After a while, the goat's knowing looks began to bother her. It got so bad that she wouldn't bend over to take laundry out of the basket in front of the goat. Even when she backed around the other side of the line, she could feel him leering. So she began going out the front door and leaving the car in the driveway, thus avoiding the back yard altogether.

Well, the goat wasn't all that concerned. He munched. He flicked flies. He lay down with his legs tucked under him and ruminated, enjoying the summer air, unaware that his countenance was anything less than pleasing.

Louise, however, was uneasy just knowing the goat was in the yard. She had wanted to get the garden turned over and ready for winter, but she couldn't face it. Different times she asked Ernest to move the goat out back of the barn. She didn't dare tell him the cursed goat was leering at her, in case he thought she was losing her stitches. So she made a point about the goat defecating in the yard and the possibility of tracking the stuff into the house. Ernest heard her, but didn't reply. "Women!", he said to himself, "always moaning about something. There's nothing wrong with that goat and that's as good a place as any to tether it. And that goat is doing a fine job of trimming the grass, even if I do say so myself."

Turning to Louise he said: "Did you know that goats were domesticated as early as 7000 BC? You can see them pictured in ancient Egyptian art."

"Humph," said Louise.

"Goats are found all over the world. They are even mentioned in the Bible. Why their milk has twice as much cream in it as cows' milk."

Louise, knowing from experience that Ernest would never admit to having made a mistake, dropped the subject. But after that she simply stopped going outside the house. She also stayed away from the windows and closed the curtains in the kitchen. Her reaction to the goat, she knew, was ridiculous, but she couldn't help her feelings. She felt humiliated by the goat. Her plants were dying on the front porch. The goat made her self-conscious. Ernest made her cross.

One night she couldn't sleep, so she flounced out of bed leaving Ernest snoring soundly while she padded down stairs for a glass of milk. After warming the milk and drinking it, she went back upstairs but instead of climbing in beside Ernest, she went into the spare room and stretched out on that bed, where there was a cool breeze coming from the north window.

Suddenly, she sat up with a jerk and let a squall out of her that could be heard half way around Cedar Springs. For there in the window was the goat, peering and leering, shaking his beard and grinning at her. He had climbed up the woodpile and onto the shed roof, which brought him to eye level with the window.

"Ernest," she screamed. "Ernest. Come quick."

"What? What?" Ernest awoke with his heart pounding, squeezing his chest like a vise.

"The goat! It's on the roof. It's looking at me." Ernest grunted and swung his legs over the side. For a few seconds, he sat on the side of the bed, waiting for his head to clear. Then Louise yelled again and the few hairs he had left reached for the sky. Ernest traced the sound to the spare room.

Meanwhile all of Louise's hollering had startled the goat which slid back off the roof, down over the wood pile and onto the ground. It hesitated for a few seconds, and then trotted back over to the tethering stake.

"Now, now, Louise. Settle down," said Ernest, as he peered out the window to see the goat quietly munching on grass behind the shed.
"What in tarnation's the matter with you, woman? There's nothing out there." Of course, if he'd looked closer, he would have seen the goat tracks in the dew on the roof, but he was too sleepy to notice. Absent-mindedly he patted Louise on the bottom, and stumbled back to bed.

"You've got to do something about that goat, I tell you," said Louise, while turning pancakes the next morning. "There is something about that goat. I don't know what it is, but that goat it is too knowing. It is driving me nuts. It has an evil grin. It's always watching me. I don't trust that goat for one minute. And I don't want it around here."

"Ah, it's all in your head, woman. Pass the syrup," said Ernest wondering to himself if she were maybe going through the 'change.'

"I'm telling you, Ernest. You mark my words. That goat is trouble."

Polishing off the last of the hot pancakes and sausage, he leaned back from the table and slurped his coffee, while considering which job needed doing around the place first.

Actually, the first thing he had to do was fix the car engine. He loved their new Plymouth Sundance. It was the first new one they had had in years. It was only three months old, so it had to be something to do with the timing.

When he finished his breakfast, he got up and went outside, where he opened the hood on the car and began tinkering underneath. He thought he saw what the problem was, but he needed another wrench which was in the toolbox on the tractor.

While he went off to find the wrench the goat, which was still loose from its tether, rounded the corner, balanced for a second and then hopped onto the hood and then onto the roof of his new precious Plymouth Sundance. The goat stood there, looked towards the house, and then casually jumped down and walked over to the woodpile. Ernest, coming back with the wrench in his hand, heard the clatter. He walked around to the back of the car and stopped; his astonishment turned to fury when he saw goat tracks and a big dent in the roof.

With that he threw down his tools, grabbed the goat's chain and led it over to his pick-up. "Mr. Goat, you're going for a ride," he said.

The last Louise saw of the goat, it was heading up to another livestock sale in Florenceville. Now she can be heard singing to herself almost every day as she hangs clothes on the line, or paints the lawn furniture, or works in her garden. Ernest is through stringing fence posts and has started mending the shed roof. As he waits for a new windshield for the Plymouth Sundance he wonders if a man could make any money on those emus.

AN OBLIGATION

After the flurry of morning baths, beds, breakfasts, most of the elderly who lived at Forest Glen were either napping on their made beds or sitting in the sunroom. Some were strapped into their chairs to keep them from falling forward. Others stared into space. And still others mumbled or talked to one another.

Nola Wickins, filling in for one of the RNAs who was home on maternity leave, had had a rough morning. In the night, one of more recently arrived ambulatory patients, a young man who suffered brain damage in a motor accident out on the Chisholm road, had taken it upon himself to collect all the dentures from their containers on the night stands and stored them in a plastic bag in the laundry room, among the soiled laundry. Fortunately, the bag hadn't been tossed into the incinerator chute with the garbage. But Nola had the job of cleaning the various dentures and finding the proper owners.

Since a similar event had taken place at Forest Glen a few years ago, all dentures were marked and numbered. The problem was, one woman's upper denture was still missing.

"Just listen to that!" said Nola, scrubbing and nodding towards room 206 where Jenny Baxter could be heard, shouting, singing or talking to herself.

"What does she want now?" said the other staff member.

"I don't know. I'm busy with this mess!"

"Well, it can't be too serious," said another worker. "I'm going for coffee. Anybody want anything?"

Meanwhile the voice from Room 206 continued...

Once I was Prom Princess. Once I was the belle of the ball.
Once I was voted "the girl most likely."
I was a June bride. Queen of the May.
And once I was even "the other woman."

Now I no longer dazzle with beauty and youth.
I creak and mutter and sigh and glare.
Waiting for death and watching life pass
by my chrome geriatric chair.

"What a metamorphosis! How did the years reduce me from Princess to Grandmother of the year to a Sunday obligation to my children? Yesterday they brought birthday cards and a cake to mark my 80th birthday. They are good kids, take care of their obligations. Good kids? Why, they're already grown-ups, parents, grandparents, already.

"Eighty years on this planet. Imagine. Where did the time go? How did I get to be this old? How did I get to be so alone? I was the one that should have gone first.

"What about all those married years, Sam? The promises that we would be together always. And, then you left. Died. Left me here, by myself. Alone. Diminished to a case, a number, a recipient, an obligation."

When I was a young woman, I related.
I donated, I made pies, flattered the guys,
I joined the clubs and played the fool,
Took my turn teaching Sunday School.
I wore gowns and pearls and basic suits
When I led the Women's Institute.

"And then the war came and the young men left. Which war, you ask? Well, there is always a war. A war to end all wars. Men seem to crave war, see it as a pissing contest. They never learn that war, like grass fire, creates the fuel of its own power, that it obliterates everything in its path. And it is always the innocent who are caught in the flames: children, women, animals.

"Oh yes. And the strong and the adventurous young men left. My Samuel couldn't wait to go, afraid at 25 he was already too old. They left their home towns and we women were left with the frail, the foolish, the flat-footed. And we wrote air-letters and waited and read the casualty lists in front of the post office. Oh yes. I see war cemeteries today and think of those boys, 17, 18, 19 years old and my soul weeps anew. Why, they were hardly old enough to shave.

"And then the war was over. And Sam came back. And we got married. We settled down, Sam and me. Settled down. For a while."

I chauffeured the kids in the family car,
Handled a booth at the spring bazaar.
Stood all day long in the scorching sun,
Cooking and caring for every one.
I cooked for Thanksgiving,
giving thanks when it was over.

"I bought presents, made preserves, put my best foot forward, put others first and waited my turn. And then after 40 years, you left. Died. Lying there in the coffin, eyes shut, hands folded. You looked so peaceful, Sam, except for that wisp of a smirk I knew so well. A little surprise you left me, never explaining the joke to me, your wife. You shared that with eternity. But we had some good years, Sam, didn't we?

"Now I am left, left over. Left behind. Dreams have dwindled. I am reduced from a mother and a matron to obligation."

There doesn't seem to be a place for me,
No one wants to see the face of me.
No one wants me on their knee.
I am nothing.

"I am nothing, less than nothing, less than a tiny speck of an iota. A zero, a nilly, a zilch, so silly, I don't even know why I'm here. I have become an obligation."

I feel worthless and second-rate.
I don't want to participate.
I feel neglected, rejected
Subjected to self-pity,
A lamentable waste of space.

"Well, would you look at that. Here comes the nurse. She says, 'And how are we today, dearie? Have your bowels moved?' How's that for a greeting. 'Did your bowels move?' But I am too slow-witted these days for repartee. I mean how would she like it if I asked her in front of everyone if she got over that dose of herpes.

"Oh, shame on me. She doesn't mean anything by it. She doesn't know any better.

Oh, I feel no-good, misunderstood,
outcast from life's neighbourhood.
I feel wasted, saddened, useless, ancient
And sorry I am in the way. I worry.

"Now here comes Dr. White. 'Don't patronize me, you pipsqueak. Keep your hands off me. I intend to go in the box the way I am.' A few years ago, he wouldn't have dared to talk to me like that.

"But I am still a person. I deserve respect. Well, if not respect, at least acknowledgement that I am still breathing in and breathing out. That means I am alive.

"I am a Canadian. Although my ancestors came to this country from Ireland, England, Germany and Holland, I am a Canadian. I was born in Cedar Springs where my father was born, where my grandfather was born and where my great grandfather settled as a young man.

"In a one-room school just down the road, we learned to sing *O Canada*, and took pride in lines of gold stars.

"I have travelled by car, bus, train and plane, by boat, by ferry, on foot and on thumb. I remember, heh, heh, heh, when Shirley and I were hitch-hiking around the country just after the war, why we had all the time in the world. We would sit around and wait for a convertible and let all the closed in cars go by, or we'd watch for one with two good-looking guys and an aerial. Then we'd have music. Remember the nickelodeons? Ah, of course you wouldn't. Music...how I loved music. *Zena, Zena, Zena.* My late great father said once, that when I sang I sounded like a pig caught under a gate. Well. I still wanted to hear music and I still wanted to dance. Then it was five songs for a quarter. Do they still have those things? Not quarters, nickelodeons? From Zeballos to Peggy's Cove, from the Niagara Escarpment to Hay River, North West Territories, from the Klondike to the Cabot Trail, it is my country. I travelled it all.

"I have climbed Mount Royal, strolled through Stanley Park, picnicked by the Bow River, stayed at the Lord Beaverbrook, danced at the Harbour Castle and wandered the cobblestone streets of old Quebec. I have swum in the Atlantic, in the Pacific, in Lake Ontario, Erie and Superior. I have been enchanted with this majestic Dominion from the Rockies to Prince Edward Island, from the Saskatchewan wheat fields to the Annapolis orchards, from Niagara Falls to the Bay of Fundy to Twillingate, Newfoundland.

"I have always loved Canada, so proud to be a Canadian. I mean, where else can you travel from sea to sea and never have to produce a passport. Well, yes, the United States of America--I've been there, too. That was when I was young and vigorous, when I could still do 'jaunty.'

"But jaunty I don't do much any more."

I feel down and unwanted,
A dunce, an encumbrance,
Not like I was once,
When I was young and soaring,
With juices that were roaring and flowing,
Back then I knew where I was going,
Not like now, when I sit, wondering
If I can move across the floor to the door
Of the bathroom before I wet myself.

"Oh, where is that nurse? I need her now. Somebody. Help. I have to go to the bathroom.

"The bathroom, the bathroom. For so many years the only room I could walk into and close the door, close out needs and wants and demands of others. The bathroom, where life's landmarks were announced and pain was flushed, was flushed away. In the bathroom I beheld that first bright round red spot of blood that marked the end of childhood, the bathroom where I studied my face in the mirror, wondering if others could tell that I had just washed away the stains of lost virginity. In the bathroom where I carried out the rituals of tubes and jellies and disks of birth control. And checked my pregnant belly for signs of growth and later watched the angry red swirl of the miscarriage, and cringed from the sharp darts of loss for the child that never was. I rocked and moaned and hugged my grief tight to my aching heart. Years later in that same bathroom I palpated my breasts for lumps. In the mirror, year after year, I watched the smooth skin parch, and the dark hair grey. The bathroom where I could grunt and sigh and cry and wipe my eyes and numb my grief with cold water and a smile."

Oh, this old wrinkled body has had its day, I tell you.
There was a time when I turned young men's heads.
Oh I had the pick of the swains, I tell you.
And now, all those old swains are dead.
But I am still here.

"Who knows, maybe I'll have the answer one day. Maybe I'll know what it all means. Maybe I will find out what happened back there and where I went wrong and if anything really matters. Meanwhile I am still breathing. Inhaling, exhaling, impaling thoughts with small darts of memory. I have opinions too, and if I have larger dentures than I have debentures, what of it?

"You can't take it with you, so they say. Who would want to, I ask you? I would rather soar on a different plane where there will be no aching ankles and swollen joints. Who would want to come back as this wrinkled sack when there is a chance to have wings of gossamer, custom-tailored, streamlined, wings guaranteed to repel acid rain?

"But right now I feel a draft in the noon heat. Where is that nurse?

"I have given some thought to 'what I think' about the here and the hereafter. There is a lot of that kind of time in here. I have been considering whether I have a creed or doctrine.

"The idea of a male deity that claims obeisance of men and every other creature including women, that demands human and animal sacrifices, that has his son killed so that we may live, is repugnant to me.

"I can't put much stock in an omnipotent, omniscient bearded god, a mongrel cross between Moses and Santa Claus with the politics of Idi

Amin. Nor can I put much faith in some kind of fertility statue or ritual. When I see the goddesses with their painted faces, standing in a circle, holding hands and chanting something about Mother Earth, I feel no urge to join the circle.

"The world was made in seven days, we learned at our mother's knee. Then I grew up and knew first-hand how to churn butter and decided that somebody's calculations were out by a few billion years. Somehow the 'Big Bang' theory seems silly to me when I study the perfection of a fiddlehead fern or experience the four seasons. The patterns and cycles of life, the way so many plants and animals live, strive, feed off each other...tells me there is a master plan, maybe a divine design.

"Considering that a tiny germ or virus can outsmart any antibiotic over time and that the human body will often heal itself despite the snipping and hacking surgeons get up to, it is difficult to have a lot of faith in the experts. I well remember one of our highly respected doctors got wealthy performing tonsillectomies. Taking out tonsils, convincing reasonably intelligent, God-protected folk they didn't need them, and might cause trouble down the line. When he got tired of looking down throats, he snapped out appendices. He didn't get mine. Then the next generation went after wombs. You'd be hard pressed to find a womb inside any woman 50 or older in Cedar Springs. The younger doctors built swimming pools, joined country clubs and took European vacations on wombs. That time, they got mine too, but I no longer had any use for it.

"No I don't know exactly what I believe about the 'hereafter.' I am still working hard on the 'here.' My times of spiritual ease and--infrequently, awareness--happened when, with an old dog, I had daily walks through the woods. I felt most grounded and alive in among the trees--the saplings, the spruce stands, the ancient maples, many of which are now in their decline, or already felled by gale winds. Older even than me. At those times I became aware and satisfied that I, too, would one day become food for birds and insects--the same as the living trees that were here before Confederation.

"I'm not so sure I want a hererafter. With my luck I would have to spend eternity re-reading my own bad poetry. Contemplating, yet again, my sins. (To be truthful, I'd rather like to contemplate some of them right now--if only I could remember them.) Yes. I recall the loving, the smell of the pines, the rough blanket under my ass and the fragments of moon shining through the trees. I remember the song, *Sail Along Silvery Moon*. But what was my lover's name? Oh, never mind.

"Gore Vidal said : 'Why is it so important to continue after death? We never question the demonstrable fact that before birth we did not exist, so why should we fear becoming once more what we were to begin with?'

"What do I believe in? I do believe in the power of love. As an example I recall the love that surrounded my family in this neighbourhood when my father and mother died, when my Sammy died, as people came to shovel snow and plough the driveways, people who brought food and the strength and comfort of their presence.

"Given the rest of the cycles and patterns displayed throughout the earth and all of its creatures, it seems wasteful that the knowledge and insights for which one strives a lifetime end with death.

"Well, as I started to say, I really don't know anything much for sure, and I know less as I grow older. Except for one thing: those folks who told me 'wisdom comes with age' lied.

"It was James Baldwin who said: 'I think all theories are suspect, that the finest principles may have to be modified, or may even be pulverized by the demands of life. And that one must find, therefore, one's own moral centre and move through the world in the hope that this centre will guide one aright.' I like that.

I wish there was more I could contribute.
But the world has changed.
My hard gained skills are no longer needed.
My knowledge no longer applies.
My truths have grown into future lies.
No one wants to hear how
To make soap, or shoe-laces,
Or grow tomatoes in vegetable cans
In kitchen windows scrubbed with newspaper and Bon Ami.

"Would you like to hear how I harnessed a team of horses and with the children bundled down in hay under a buffalo robe in the sled box, drove to Woodstock to be with my mother when she died? Only 53, she was. It shouldn't have happened.

"But I am still here, like you and you and you. I have a right to be here, like politicians and preachers and parsons and such. I have a right to be here. Like soldiers, and carvers and blacksmiths and music teachers and poets, I have a right to be here just as much, standing here as I clutch my handbag with notes and names and bottles of pills and tissues and snapshots to remind me that I have a life.

"Excuse me, I'll just take that rocker, if you'll move the cat..

"Black power, grey power, higher power, horse power. What does it all matter? Some days only memory truly warms me. What a flower I am in my mind! In my memory, I can dance through the garden, I can smell the lilac and can taste the honey and never feel a sting. I can sing with the voices of angels, in my memory, and in my mind. In my thoughts I can have a romantic liaison with Clark Gable and Harry Belafonte and Robin Chetwynd or Kelly Bull. Say what? You've never heard of Robin Chetwynd? The most beautiful man in Canada, without a doubt. I only saw him once.

There's something I should do today
Instead I think I'd rather stay
And dream of times that used to be
When I was young and strong and free
Of pains and aches that build a cage
And keep one prisoner of age.

I'll ramble over grassy hills
Until my soul with sunlight fills
I'll walk in fields 'neath azure skies,
In clover, kissed by butterflies,
Or make wet footprints in the sand
A smooth round pebble in my hand.

I'll taste the spray upon my face.
Recall again a warm embrace.
I'll hear the songs we used to sing
And sip my coffee, savouring
Each memory of tenderness
The shape of every happiness.

WE CLEAVE IN THIS LIFE AS WE NEAR DEATH TO ALL THE GOOD MEMORIES THAT HAVE COME OUR WAY. OUR LIVES ARE AS A STORY TOLD AND WE HAVE THE CHOICE TO DETERMINE HOW IT ENDS. IT CAN END IN FAITH TOWARD GOD'S SALVATION THROUGH CHRIST OR DIE IN UNBELIEF. GOD OFFERS US ETERNAL LIFE WHERE THERE IS NO PAIN, SORROW, SICKNESS, OR DEATH. THERE IS A PLACE AFTER DEATH GOD HAS PREPARED FOR BELIEVERS.

"And then there was Kelly, ah his hair was raven black. His smile was wide and warm as the night. His skin like brown velvet. Kelly. Dead now. Ashes and compost.

"BUT AS IT IS WRITTEN, EYE HATH NOT SEEN, NOR THE EAR HEARD, NEITHER HAVE ENTERED INTO THE HEART OF MAN, THE THINGS WHICH GOD HATH PREPARED FOR THEM THAT LOVE HIM." I CORINTHIANS 2:9

I think I'll take an hour or two
To ponder of things we used to do
And why we went our separate ways
And wasted all those summer days,
Although we knew it couldn't last
Our time so swiftly passed.

I WRITE THIS AT 80 YEARS OF AGE.

"Yes, life is still good in patches, when I can get it together and if I take a chance. In my head I can dance, I can dance. I can dance. But I think I will sit this one out."

"HAVE FAITH IN GOD"

MAY YOUR NAME NEVER PROSPER

"I curse you all for what your son did," said the ancient brown crone. "May your name never prosper."

Well, the whole Fletcher family is gone now. They are all dead. There is nothing left to see but the names on a tombstone. Just outside Cedar Springs, the red granite Fletcher monument, by far the largest in the cemetery, sits high above the valley which includes 1200 acres of prime farm land once owned by the Fletchers. The graves are untended. The individual foot-markers are sunken into the earth. The Fletcher plots are bare. There are no plastic flowers, no wreaths, no military crosses, no willow trees.

FLETCHER
Albert Fletcher 1886-1963
His beloved wife Louise 1895-1950
Son Clyde 1919-1942
Daughter Doris 1920-1948
Son Jack 1921-1945
Infant son Ralph January 1-May 1, 1923
Infant son Randolph January 1-May 2, 1923
Daughter Bonnie 1928 -
Son Blair 1930-1972

I see Bonnie's date of death is not on the stone, but she is long gone, found dead in her apartment. Married Bill Cook right out of high school. They moved to Oshawa in 1950 where he worked for General Motors.

Blair died in the fire. A terrible way to go but he likely would have drunk himself to death sooner or later anyway.

Clyde, I remember, married at the beginning of the war. Clyde only had one son, Blake his name was. But he didn't spend much time around here. Blake died in 1990. Now that made the newspapers. Half of San Francisco's gay community attended his memorial, and they released some 2000 white balloons out over the Pacific. I'll bet that set old Fletcher spinning in his grave. And Blake was the last of them. Gone and forgotten.

What? You've never heard of the Fletcher curse? I thought everybody knew about that. It was an old Indian woman, Aggie, who put the curse on the Fletchers. She was a Micmac. I don't think I ever knew her last name. But I remember well the day it happened. I had just gone there to work, cleaning, scrubbing, doing the dishes, kitchen work, you know. It was a fine sunny day in early summer. The roses were beginning to come out--Mrs. Fletcher always had such a lovely garden--and I stopped by the corner of the house to admire them as I was going down to the back garden to cut some rhubarb for pies. And that's how come I heard it. Funny thing, there was not much commotion. The dogs didn't even bark and those pesky things would bark if they heard a sparrow sneeze three miles away. Aggie must have walked right past them and they didn't even budge. Anyway when I saw her, she was bent over the front step shaking out a little bag of dirt. Then the door opened and Albert himself came out with Louise right behind him. And that's when she said it: "May your name never prosper."

The funny thing is, I never figured out why Aggie cursed Albert. After all it was his son Jack who caused all the trouble. As far as I know old Albert and Louise treated everyone fairly, even the Indians. In fact, they found work for the Indians when most people wouldn't have them around the place.

When Aggie, tormented with grief and rage over the death of her granddaughter, spoke the ancient curse, the Fletchers were the most wealthy and powerful family in the county.

Before things started going downhill the Fletchers had amassed four farms into the 1200-acre spread along the river. They operated a sawmill, a woollen mill and a foundry and they bred some of the finest coach horses in the province. They had survived the Depression through a lucrative contract with the war department to manufacture pins for hand grenades in their foundry.

To go back even further...As I heard it Albert Fletcher came from coal mining town near Birmingham, England. On his 13th birthday, he entered the mines for the first and last time. There was an accident that day. Four miners were lost and Albert himself was trapped. He wept. He screamed. He choked. He froze with fear. Then suddenly there was a pinhole of light and he was rescued.

Albert was born in the middle of nine children in a poor family where every crust was needed, where there was no place for a boy who could not earn his keep. Yet he knew after that first day he would never be able to go back underground.

The following morning, at dawn's first light, he wrote a note for his mother and left it on the kitchen table. Saying goodbye to no one, he put on his coat and walked out the door and closed it behind him.

A mannerly boy, Albert had a pleasing way about him. However, his sunny face and his innocent mien hid a native cunning and powerful strength of will. He walked most of the way to Liverpool, living on stolen apples and bread.

Albert was a survivor. He would take many chances, but he always carefully calculated the risks. The first thing he needed was a nest egg. To get a start, he acquired money in any way he could. He begged. He pandered. He stole. He ran errands. And he hoarded. At fifteen he got work on a ship bound for Halifax. Although he was only a boy and vulnerable, he was adept at talking his way out of tight places. Aboard ship, after helping them with their steamer trunks, Albert attached himself to a family which included the father, a university professor, the mother and their three daughters. When Louise, the youngest of the three daughters, smiled shyly at Albert, he tripped over his own feet.

Albert could have stayed in Halifax. The professor even offered to send him to school, but Albert had other plans. He knew he wanted to work with animals. He wanted to work outdoors. He wanted to be his own boss. In short he wanted to be a farmer. He could already read and write and what he needed, he'd decided, couldn't be learned in a classroom. Instead he found work in the apple orchards, and made himself useful in any way he could. He learned everything he could about fruit trees.

Just under six feet tall, Albert built strength daily as he laboured for a living. He worked on the stream drive and learned the lumber business. He worked on the railroad where he impressed the bosses and earned the trust of his fellow workers. He helped on farms with the lambing, the planting, the harvest, all the while carefully studying the methods used. He thought of shortcuts, ways to speed things up. He considered the kinds of machinery that would be needed to do a better job. He drew up an overall plan. He thought about it. He obsessed about it. He hoarded and he schemed. In 1907 he bought his first piece of land here in Cedar Springs through a bank sale. He was 21 years old.

Not only had Albert watched and learned, Albert had the right instincts. He intuitively knew what to plant and when to plant it. More than that, he knew how to market what he produced. He knew about living soil and rotating crops and pasture land, long before agriculturalists started teaching these methods.

Albert had a gentle way with animals, and they served him well. Within a few years, he bought his second farm.

He had a new house built. Fourteen rooms on two levels, the house overlooked the valley. The clapboards were painted white. Why, it was almost as grand as the Marches' place. A verandah ran around three sides, which would later be glassed in. Then he proposed to Louise. And in 1918 Albert and Louise were married.

Their first son, Clyde, was born a year later. Then 11 months later Doris came along and 14 months after that Jack arrived. Having three kids in diapers, along with trying to keep that big house up, meant a lot of work for Louise. And, of course, Albert wasn't any help to her, busy as he was building up his businesses.

Then infant sons Ralph and Randolph were born New Year's Day 1923. Born prematurely, when they were only four months old they came down with diptheria and died, just a day apart.

For the next two years, Louise hardly came out of her room. Albert had a woman come in and look after the meals and another to do the housekeeping. Then he hired a nurse for the children. Meanwhile the doctor came and went. Louise wept endlessly. The doctor prescribed a narcotic to help Louise rest. I suppose nobody really understood what was going on at the time, but I would imagine Louise became addicted to whatever it was the doctor gave her. She would sit for hours and hours and stare out the window just looking down the road. When Clyde, Dorothy and Jack were allowed into her room, she hardly glanced at them. Cautioned not to upset Mommy, the children tiptoed in and out, and after a while spent less and less time with her.

Well, I don't know what would have happened to Louise but after a while Albert had to admit she wasn't getting any better, so he took her to a specialist in Boston. It didn't take the specialist long to discover Louise's drug dependency. Instead of weaning her off gradually, they took her off the stuff completely and Louise nearly died. She had violent seizures and they had to strap her down. It's a wonder she survived. For a while she even lost her mind. After a couple of months, Albert went down and brought her home and soon she began to pick up again. Meanwhile Clyde, Jack and Dorothy went their own way. Dorothy turned out fine, but Clyde and Jack needed a firmer hand. Today, I suppose some psychologist would explain how they felt rejected by their mother and neglected by their father. Who knows? Maybe they were just born rotten.

When Bonnie was born in 1928 and Blair in 1930, Louise came through all right. She always had hard births, and in those days they kept the new mother in bed for at least two weeks which, as we now know, isn't a good thing, since the woman loses her strength and muscle just lying around. But that's just 20-20 hindsight, eh?

Albert had branched out. In the early 1920s he couldn't seem to go wrong. He had made contacts and was friendly with many who had power and political clout. He had excellent crops. He made a name as a coach horse breeder. He built up the harness shop and the foundry.

From the Indian reservation down the river several families used to show up regularly to provide cheap labour during seed-cutting and planting and in the fall.

Meanwhile, unable to enjoy marital relations with Louise, Albert had a quiet affair with a woman in the village. But when Louise got better, Albert ended it. He and Louise started going to church. He became a deacon, served on the school board and on county council.

When Albert and Louise's sons Clyde and Jack were small they spent many hours with the Indian children who freely moved between the farm and the reserve. Clyde and Jack were expected to work on the farm and they did, understanding that it would all be theirs one day.

However, during their teen years they seemed to go off course. Jack had a mean streak. He was abusive to the animals. When Albert caught him beating a horse one day he chastised Jack severely. After that, there was bad feeling between Albert and his second son.

Clyde didn't do much better. Clyde was a bully and a sneak. He liked to fight, and on a Saturday night both boys were as like as not to return home drunk and bloody. Louise despaired. Albert raged, but nothing seemed to register with the boys.

Doris, a pliant and dutiful child, grew into a young woman. They sent her to Netherwood, an elite girls' school. Then she went to teacher's college–Normal School, they called it back then.

Each spring and fall the Indians appeared. Brown and wrinkled, with wisps of yellowing hair, old Aggie looked like one of those apple dolls you see at a craft fair. Too frail for field work on Albert's farm, Aggie kept an eye on the children while the rest of her family helped with the planting, the lambing, the shearing, and the harvest.

Aggie's life was devoted to serving her family, her two sons and her grandsons, but her granddaughter Carol was her favourite. I can't tell you what happened to Carol's mother. I suppose I never thought much about it, but Aggie always had Carol with her when I saw her.

Carol brought sunshine into the old woman's life. She was a merry child, always smiling and singing. At night Aggie held her in her lap, sitting in an old rocker crooning away until it was time for bed.

Carol never went to school. Instead Aggie taught her the songs and the lore of her people. She taught Carol the art of basket making, of tanning hides to the softness of flannel, of mixing dyes and designing beadwork. Aggie forgot her own aches and pains as she watched the child grow into young womanhood.

Then, the fall before Blair was born, Louise asked Albert if they could get Carol to come in to the house and help with Bonnie and the baby. They could always use extra help in the house during the harvest.

Carol showed up the next morning at the kitchen door. Louise explained how the washer worked and where to find things in the house. Carol was quick to grasp what needed to be done. She also had a way with animals: horses, dogs, cats, sheep--she seemed to speak their language and could walk among even the wildest of them unafraid.

A few days after Carol started working at the Fletchers, Jack fell off the ladder in the tannery and broke his leg. He was laid up all that fall.

Idleness didn't improve his character or his morals. He watched Carol as she went about her chores.

"Carol, how'd you like to bring me a cup of coffee," Jack asked one morning. In a few minutes a steaming cup was placed in his hands.

"Thanks."

Carol, eyes downcast, continued with her cleaning. Jack watched her, noting her attractive figure, her glossy blue-black hair and her smooth bronze skin.

"Don't you ever talk?" he asked.

"Not much," she answered shyly. Jack drifted off to sleep. The following morning he was sitting in the shadows as she stepped out the back door to throw the dishwater onto the flower garden. Then she lifted her face to the sun, and Jack felt a powerful stirring. He wanted this girl.

"How old are you, Carol?" he said a few days later.

"Fourteen."

"Got a boyfriend?"

"No." She giggled.

Louise spent nearly a month in bed after Blair was born. Eventually she did recover, but it was a long while before she got her strength back. So Carol stayed on to help out around the house.

One evening, when Louise was feeling stronger, she and Albert went to a prayer meeting. Carol put the baby to sleep and went back to the kitchen to clean up the supper dishes.

Now Jack may not have had a way with animals, but he was smooth with the women. He took his time, teasing, beginning gently, but before the evening was out he had Carol in bed. Over the next three weeks, he took her every chance he had.

Then harvest finished. Albert paid off the Indians and they disappeared back to the reservation. All except Carol. Louise kept her on to care for baby Blair and look after the housework.

When Jack's leg was healed he began going out in the evenings with Clyde and their friends, spending time in town, hitting the dances, the bars, the whorehouses. He bought a Studebaker. One night just before Christmas, as Jack was finishing the barn chores, Carol stepped into the light.

"Carol," he said, surprised. "What the hell are you doing out here in the cold?"

"I had to talk to you."

"What about?"

"I am going to have a baby."

"You're what?"

"A baby." Jack felt a jolt of fear. His father would kill him. His father had warned and warned him not to get involved with the Indians.

His father might even cut him off completely. Jack's mind whirled. Then he got that crafty look in his eye.

"Whose is it?'"

"Yours."

"How do I know that for sure? You could be sleeping with every young buck on the reservation for all I know."

"It's yours. I haven't been back to the reservation."

"Oh yeah. Well, I've got to think about this. Go on in now. I'll see what I can do." Carol turned and walked away into the darkness.

That night on the way to town he told Clyde. They had stopped at the Enterprise Hotel.

"Jesus H. Christ, Jack. What'd you bother her for? She's just a kid."

"I know. I know," said Jack grinning sheepishly. "But, she was ripe. She was willing."

"Willing. For Christ sake, Jack. She's under sixteen. That's statutory rape."

"But she's only an Indian. She wanted to. And you know, until you've tried that smoked meat, you don't know what you're missin'."

"You silly born bastard. You had your pick of half the women and all the whores in this town, and you have to go screwing a 14-year-old!"

"What am I going to do, Clyde?"

"Order another drink." Clyde turned the matter over in his mind. "How far along is she?"

"I don't know, maybe three, maybe four months."

"We could see if we could get her an abortion."

"Yeah, I thought about that, but even some old whore abortionist isn't going to frig around with an Indian."

"I don't suppose."

"Well, drink up, I gotta get out of here. I gotta get up early in the morning."

"Yea, okay. Where are you going?"

"I'm signing up."

"Signing up?"

"The army. I'm joining the army."

With Clyde gone, Jack was on his own. Something had to be done about Carol, but what? There was no way he could have a papoose kid running around. Of course, the idea of marrying Carol and becoming a father to the child never even came into his head. Instead he nosed around to find out what other men did when they found themselves in that kind of situation. They told him he should try giving her turpentine and quinine and then get a coat hanger or a knitting needle and push it up through her cervix. Well, the upshot of it all was Jack got Carol to meet him in the tack room one night after everyone else had gone to bed. He gave her enough whisky to get her drunk. Then he mixed the quinine and turpentine and got her to drink most of that before she passed out.

Jack, of course, had been drinking along with her but as soon as she was unconscious, he laid her across the bench and took her panties off. Reaching for the long knitting needle he had stashed beneath the saddle blankets he went to work. His hand was shaking and the light was dim and it took him a couple of jabs before he got the needle inserted into the cervix and then it slid on in, easy as pie. When he pulled the needle out, there was a little bit of blood, but not much. He waited for twenty minutes or so, but she was still sleeping soundly. He got her underwear back on her, covered her with one of the horse blankets and left her there while he walked up to the house and went to bed.

After several hours Carol awoke. Her mouth was dry. She had violent cramps and had to urinate. She got up and went outside and squatted down behind the barn. Another cramp bent her almost double, and she became sick to her stomach. Still drunk and disoriented, Carol turned towards the road and started walking.

Well, some kids out sliding found her the next day on the side of the road, half way down the hill, not half a mile from the reserve. How she got that far in the shape she was in, I can't imagine. But she was still alive and the kids got her on the sled and took her to Aggie.

Albert had little to say when Clyde signed up. Somehow he had been expecting it. He even felt a little pride that Clyde wanted to serve. When Jack came home and said he had signed up, too, Albert just nodded. He figured it was more the thrill of adventure than dedication to king and country that made Jack join the army. It would be rough without their help around the place, but he'd manage. The war would make men of them. Just before he went overseas, Clyde came home with a woman on his arm, saying they'd had got married.

With the boys gone, with Doris in boarding school, and Louise back on her feet, life at the Fletcher household settled down.

Aggie got Carol in bed and had her drink some hot sweet tea. Carol was shaking like a leaf. After a while they got her warmed up and she went to sleep. All night Aggie pondered. Her experienced eye told her Carol was somewhere between four or five months along, and yet Carol's underwear had been stained with blood.

When Carol awoke finally, Aggie smiled and hugged her. "Women have babies." she said. "That is the way of nature." Carol wept and slept.

A little later when Carol awoke again Aggie asked her who the father was. "Jack Fletcher," Carol said, and then drifted off to sleep.

Aggie worked at her crafts and waited. She worried about the bloodstains on Carol's underwear. If she had known Carol was pregnant earlier, she could have prepared a tea of ragwort, rue, partridge berry, mugwort and lovage as an emmenagogue to cause what could pass as a spontaneous abortion. And that would have been all there was to it. Now there was nothing to be done.

In the early evening Carol began showing a fever. Aggie felt Carol's forehead, she was burning up. Carol began thrashing around. Then she drew her legs up nearly to her chin and began to groan. Suddenly a warm burst of blood poured forth. Aggie found rags to catch it, along with dark liverish chunks of matter. After a while it stopped and Aggie packed the birth canal with dried alumroot and bloodwort and Carol went back to sleep. For a while it looked as if Carol was going to be okay, but then she began to haemorrhage. Aggie tried everything in her power to stop the flow of blood, but between the fever and the hypothermia, Carol had no resources left. As Aggie prayed, the blood slowed to a trickle, and then Carol stopped breathing.

Aggie sat by the dead girl all day and into the night, keening softly. In the morning, she bathed Carol's body and wrapped it securely. She dug a hole near the root of a maple tree and buried the bloody rags and sheets. Then she took the bloody water and poured it onto the ground. After that she called the women of the reserve. And together they carried out the burial ritual.

It was almost spring before the Fletchers heard of Carol's death. None of the Indians worked at the farm during the winter. When Carol disappeared, Louise figured she had just got lonesome and had gone off home. She had muttered a little about how undependable Indians could be and decided she was well enough by then to look after Bonnie and the baby by herself. She was saddened to learn of Carol's death. Had it been anybody but an Indian Louise would have prepared a basket of food and gone to visit, but in the end, with Bonnie and Blair taking up every waking moment, she did nothing about it at all.

Aggie's grief turned to despair, then into a terrible rage. This loss was unbearable. Finally, one morning she went to the base of the maple tree where Carol's blood had been poured. The earth was dry now, the blood through the winds and the rain had become part of the soil. Aggie scooped a handful of dirt into a small leather pouch, and placed it in her apron pocket.

It took her two days to walk the six miles to the Fletcher house. Nobody knew her age for sure, but she was already in her nineties by then. Things being as they were, nobody paid any attention to the old Indian woman shuffling along.

When she reached the Fletchers, she walked through the gate, stopped, raised her head and looked around. She saw the hills and the fertile fields. She saw the coach horses. She took in the new cars around the foundry. She looked at the white pillars that marched across the front of the portico. She thought of all the years her people had worked for the Fletchers, and she thought how little they had in comparison. And now, without Carol, she had nothing.

Suddenly she bent down, and taking the small pouch of earth from her pocket, she began sprinkling it around the front step. Just then Albert opened the door and he and Louise stepped through. They were on their way to church.

"What are you doing, Aggie?" asked Albert.

Aggie gave the pouch a final shake and placed it in her pocket. Then she straightened and looked at them both, from one to the other.

"Carol is dead," she said. "For this I curse you. I curse you. May your name never prosper."

Louise looked to Albert. "What is she talking about?"

"I don't know. She's crazy maybe. And to Aggie, he said. "Go on home now. Go on."

"May your name never prosper," said Aggie. Then she turned and left, shuffling back the way she came.

Life for the Fletchers continued. Louise missed her sons. But almost all the young men in their community had gone to the war. She spent time working with the Red Cross and the Women's Institute. She made meals and took care of her small son Blair. Doris got through Netherwood, applied for and found a job teaching in Toronto. Albert looked after the farm and his business.

Then the first telegram came: Clyde died on June 6, 1944. He was shot before he stepped onto the beach of Normandy. Several weeks later the second telegram arrived. Jack was also killed in France. What the telegram didn't say was that Jack's tank unit had been accidentally bombed near Caen by a squadron of American B-24s.

After the war things were changing rapidly. There were many more cars on the streets. There were paved roads. Few people drove horses any more. The harness shop closed. The last of Albert's horses were sold for fox meat. The sheep they kept. But with the boys gone, and with the Indians from the reserve refusing to help with the shearing, it made too much work for him and Blair and a hired man.

In 1948 Doris died suddenly of a brain tumour.

By then Albert was 60 years old. Blair didn't seem to have much interest in the farm. A year after the war ended, they got rid of the sheep.

Albert bought a tractor and then a second one. They concentrated on potatoes. Then they had five years of straight bad luck. The first year there was a drought and the yield was miserably small. The next year there were torrential rains, which washed a lot of the seed out. Then there was blight. The last two years, although the Fletchers had a reasonable crop, so did everybody else and the price fell off.

Still Albert struggled. Then one night after supper, when they were fighting to get the last of the crop in, Blair got the Farmall tractor mired. Albert went out with chains and helped to drag him out. In a hurry he hooked the chain too high. The tractor bucked, shivered for a few seconds in mid air, then flipped over backwards, pinning Albert underneath. Blair couldn't get Albert out by himself so he went for help. When they got back Albert was unconscious, but they were able to raise the tractor far enough to pull Albert out from underneath. They took him to the hospital, where they brought him around. But Albert's legs had been crushed. It would be two years before he would walk again.

Without Albert's direction and drive, Blair foundered. Half the crop stayed in the ground that year. Those potatoes brought in had been bruised and frozen, and by spring, most of them were running out under the door.

Blair began drinking, quietly, unobtrusively. Meanwhile Louise carried on, looking after Albert and running the household. One day she found a lump in her breast, but she said nothing of it. Within a year she was dead of cancer. That was 1950.

Albert was devastated. The loss of his sons Clyde and Jack had been hard, but he had always had Louise to lean on. He saw nothing of Clyde's son Blake. His daughter-in-law had moved back to Maine to be with her family when Clyde went in the army. She had sent a couple of pictures, and sporadically kept in touch with Louise by mail, but that was all.

Bonnie married right out of high school. Pregnant, they said. That first one was a girl, a mongoloid. She died when she was five.

Blair never married. He stayed around and looked after his father. Then a chance came to sell the farms and they took it, retaining just five acres around the house.

In 1963 Albert Fletcher died quietly in his sleep. Bonnie came down from Oshawa for the funeral. Bonnie's second child had died a crib death. She and her husband were split up by then. Clyde's son Blake wired flowers from San Francisco.

For the next nine years Blair lived alone in the Fletcher house. He read the newspapers. He sold farm equipment. He visited the tavern. He lost his driver's license several times and could often be seen weaving drunkenly home.

Meanwhile the settlement continued to change. A processing factory opened, providing a market for those people still farming. Other industries grew up around the processors.

One night Blair came home drunk, and lay down on the chesterfield with a lighted cigarette in his hand.

Everyone in the community stopped what they were doing to go and watch the Fletcher house burn. It didn't take long. Several fire trucks arrived but there was not enough water to do any good. Within a few hours the house was levelled except for the fireplaces and chimneys. It took three days to find Blair's body.

None of the family attended Blair's funeral. Neither the neighbours nor the police could find Bonnie. His nephew Blake sent flowers from San Francisco.

Well, now, nobody really believes in curses any more, do they? I mean, death comes in every family. You couldn't exactly say there was anything that strange or odd about any of their deaths. Ralph and Randolph died as infants, diphtheria likely. Albert died of old age. Louise died of cancer. Clyde and Jack died in the war. Doris had a brain tumour. Blair died in the fire. All except Bonnie: she was found dead in her apartment in Toronto. Died of natural causes, so they say. But she wasn't found for a week, and who could really say by then? Anything could have happened. She could have been murdered. Who knows? But one thing is for sure, the Fletcher family is all gone now.

I wonder where old Aggie is buried.

BRIGHT LIGHTS, BIG CITY

When Sheila Belyea arrived in Toronto, with her Grade 12 diploma and a certificate of excellence praising her shorthand, typing and bookkeeping skills, she wasn't long landing a job at Simmond's Real Estate on Queen Street, working in the secretarial pool. She carried out her duties cheerfully and competently, grateful to have a job which paid $33 a week. This was enough to afford a bright sunny furnished room on Palmerston Avenue, a 25-minute walk to the office.

Sheila left Cedar Springs September 3, 1953. After waving goodbye to her parents she climbed on a bus that would take her to Edmundston, where she would change for a bus to Montreal. All the way, her excitement was so powerful that she could hardly sort her hopes from her fears. For so long she had dreamed of this time, when she would be on her own, where she was no longer distracted by her mother's querulous voice or woken by her father's cursing. In Montreal she caught another bus for Toronto, arriving at Dundas and Bay Street in the early afternoon.

Hugging her purse tight to her side, she lifted her suitcase and walked several blocks to the YWCA, where she took a room for two nights. She paid for her lodging with $6 from the $20 she carried in her purse. Her other $100 was in a small pocket carefully stitched to the inside of her bra, where it comforted her with its scratchy bulk. After she booked in, she went out and walked around until evening. Her walk took her through Queen's Park and into the Annex, up to Bloor, east to Yonge and south to College. She bought a city map and three newspapers, the *Star*, the *Telegram* and the *Globe & Mail*. Before she went back to her room she picked up a box of Graham crackers, two apples, a small container of peanut butter, a piece of cheese and chocolate milk. That night she scanned the ads, studied her map and checked the phone book, looking at the prefixes of telephone numbers in order to place the offered jobs on the city map.

Although the YWCA was clean, comfortable and safe, she found the noise and bustle of sharing the bathrooms with strangers disconcerting. The following morning, a Tuesday, she arose early, showered and dressed and, after carefully locking her room, she walked down to the lobby where she began making telephone calls. On her third interview she was hired to start work on the following Monday. (The office on University Avenue, gone now, has been replaced by the Mt. Sinai Hospital.)

Hardly able to contain her delight at landing a job so quickly, she walked to Queen's Park, sat down on a bench and took out her city map. She unfolded the "classified" sections of the newspapers and looked at rooms for rent in the Annex. She visited several places offered before choosing a bright sunny room on the third floor of a house on Palmerston. The room was spacious and its French windows looked out on a back garden lush with roses and shrubs. From there she could also see into the gardens of the houses to the north and south and those which faced the next street east. She had her own tiny bathroom, which contained a sink, shower and toilet. For years afterwards, when she tried to quiet her mind for meditation, she thought of that first room on Palmerston.

As soon as Sheila had secured her room she looked for the nearest bank, which turned out to be the Bank of Nova Scotia. There she opened an account and deposited $80 of the money she had brought with her, carefully saved from three seasons of picking potatoes in Cedar Springs while going to high school. The rest she kept in her purse.

Over the next few weeks, she learned her way around the new job. With a dictionary and her street map she checked her spelling, always turning in clean, attractive, error-free correspondence. By the time she received her first pay cheque, the money in her purse had dwindled to $6. She cashed her cheque, kept $10 out for expenses and banked the remaining $12. Three months later she was moved out of the secretarial pool to a corner desk of her own, just outside the office of a new partner, and given a raise. She was 19 years old.

From the time she was 12, Sheila had been making her own clothes-- aprons, blouses, dirndl and circular skirts --having learned to sew on her mother's old treadle sewing machine. The first major purchase Sheila made after she had been working four months was a portable electric Singer sewing machine, $119.00. At the time it seemed an outlandish expense, but it would pay for itself within a year, and she would still be using that same sewing machine 50 years later.

Sheila studied the frocks worn by the women around her and spent several lunch hours perusing the pattern books at Eaton's and Simpson's. She compared materials and prices. She walked through the finer dress shops and carefully inspected the needle work. Then with part of her next pay cheque she bought a measuring tape, needles, thread, scissors, pinking shears, pins and tailor's chalk.

A couple of weeks later she purchased four yards of navy wool gabardine, pellum, lining, a zipper and buttons. Then working evenings on her knees with the material laid out on the floor, she cut material for a suit. The shoulders and lapels gave her no trouble, but the inset button holes took a lot of time. She made three button holes on waste material before she got it right. Carefully pressing each seam as she went, she finished that suit four nights later. Then she created three simple cotton blouses, two white and one pale blue, to go with it.

In time she made six suits, differing only in trim and detail. Each was exquisitely tailored and fit perfectly. She bought a string of pearls, earrings, matching purses, shoes and gloves. Being 5'10" tall, Sheila's decision to dress in the classic fashion was the right one. She carried herself well. Her dark brown hair, cut short, had enough natural curl to soften her strong features. In all she had a look of competence and quiet elegance.

Meanwhile Sheila got to know the city through long, rambling walks on weekends, from Eglinton to the Lakeshore, west to Parkdale, north to High Park, back along Bloor, and down Palmerston. She gazed at store windows and explored residential streets. She spotted signs for houses for sale. She studied areas of commercial development. From what she was learning through her work she began to understand how to set a sales price on a building, how much money would be needed for renovation. She learned how to write a contract, who were the competent contractors, how to deal with unions.

Although Sheila was career-oriented, that didn't stop her thinking about marriage and family. She had listened to the other secretaries discussing parties and boyfriends. She had even gone on a couple of blind dates, but these turned out to be disastrous. The first date was with a man who was 5'6" tall. They had, at his insistence, gone dancing at the Masonic Temple on Yonge street, where he attempted to fling her through several Latin American dances. Sheila had never learned to dance well, and the experience was humiliating. The second blind date, which occurred a week later, was with a good-looking, well-spoken man who turned out to be a car salesman. They went to dinner at a restaurant on the Queensway. His table manners were atrocious and on the way home, he drove down to the Lakeshore in Mimico and turned in at the first motel. Sheila asked him to take her home. He began calling her names. Sheila got out of the car and he sped off, showering her with gravel. The half hour she spent finding a phone booth and calling a taxi gave her plenty of time to make up her mind that there would be no more blind dates.

Sheila decided she wouldn't wait for the right man to come along. She would make her own life. Having studied the marital relationships of her aunts and uncles, she knew early on she didn't want anything like theirs. And she certainly did not want a relationship like that of her parents, full of bitterness, recriminations and rage. There were worse things than being an old maid. So she concentrated on her career.

Once a month she went to the movies where she watched Rock Hudson and Elizabeth Taylor, Marilyn Monroe and Cary Grant and all the other beautiful people, and lost herself in the frivolous romances. She went to Rogers and Hammerstein musicals and left the theatres humming the tunes.

Sheila continued her weekend walks until she knew the city well. She studied the people she saw on the street and wondered what their lives were like. Now and then she grew wistful, but with work, movies, concerts and visits to the Art Gallery of Ontario, she had lots of activity to occupy her time. Mrs Meizner, her landlady, spoke little English but she was delighted to have a clean quiet young lady like Sheila in her upper room. Mrs. Meizner cut flowers and left them in a vase on the table beside Sheila's door. Sometimes when she made pirogies she would listen for Sheila's key in the front door. A little while later Sheila would hear a knock and when she answered, there would be a beaming Mrs. Meizner holding a steaming plate out to her, saying "eat, eat." Sheila thanked her and tried the food. It was delicious.

On the second floor of the house were three male boarders. Now and then Sheila could hear a radio or record player playing classical music. She listened, getting her first taste of Mozart, Vivaldi and Beethoven. How delightful. How different from the whining of Kitty Wells or the drone of Wilf Carter, the drivel from Carl Smith, or Hank Snow, with his *Husky, Dusky Maiden of the Arctic*, which her mother had listened to on CFNB Saturday Hit Parade back in Cedar Springs.

At age 21, after two years with Simmond's Real Estate, Sheila had saved nearly $1,500. Her boss, married with two small children, was spending much of the time when he was supposed to be handling real estate deals in bed with one young woman or another. He had made one half-hearted pass at Sheila, but she pretended it didn't happen. Instead she covered for him and did what she could to complete his sales. Then it came to her that there was no reason to continue to complete his sales and secure his commissions when she could do it for herself. She applied for and received her license to sell real estate. He was decent about it. He admired her ambition and passed on some of the smaller residential stuff he didn't want to waste time on. Sheila was grateful.

Despite her diffident nature, Sheila could sell houses. She learned to drive, acquired a driver's license and bought a used car, a Comet, for $600. She knew the city. She knew her way around City Hall. She knew what the taxes would be, and what bylaws governed which area. When she took a buyer, whether a single person or a young couple, to a view a property, she looked at it and talked about it as if she were buying it herself. If the house had graceful lines, French windows, closet space, she pointed that out. If the wiring or plumbing looked like it needed work, she pointed that out, too. She also knew the schools, churches, and shopping areas in the vicinity. She didn't push, but she worked very hard and closed deal after deal. She was honest, she kept her word. She was always on time. The word spread. In fact she was so good that she sold one couple a new house every two years as they moved up in the world. Clients came by word of mouth. Her savings grew. She kept her expenses to a minimum. She bought a second-hand Underwood typewriter and had a phone installed in her room. When she wasn't showing houses, she looked after her own books and correspondence. She became very fond of Mrs. Meizner and exchanged pleasantries with the other tenants.

Then Mrs. Meizner became ill. Sheila rescheduled her appointments and took time off to nurse her. She called the doctor who told her that Mrs. Meizner should go to the hospital. "No. No hospital," Mrs. Meizner begged. "No die in hospital. No." Sheila put in a call to Mrs. Meizner's son Philip, a mining engineer at Cold Lake, about his mother's condition. He thanked her for calling and asked her to keep him informed.

After many more hours on the phone Sheila found a doctor who would come to the house. He diagnosed heart trouble and prescribed pills to ease the pain. Mrs. Meizner then suffered a stroke. Three days later, around 9:00 a.m. after Sheila had bathed her patient, changed the bed and fed her, she was gathering the soiled linens to take to the laundry room in the basement when Mrs. Meizner uttered a long sigh and was still. Sheila made a second call to Philip, informed him of his mother's death and, on his instructions, made arrangements for Mrs. Meizner's funeral and burial. Philip arrived back in the city in time for the reception following the funeral.

To Sheila, Philip appeared a cold and distant man. She had come to love Mrs. Meizner, but she couldn't squelch a feeling of being used by him. As soon as everyone left, he requested that she join him in the sunroom. He stood with his back to the window.

"I have been giving this situation some thought," he began, "and I have a proposition to make to you. As you may or may not know, my work is considered essential by the Canadian government. It is also time-consuming, which means that I don't have time to take care of Mother's affairs, mostly giving the tenants notice, selling the house and so on. Now, it's obvious Mother trusted you. So I am proposing that you stay on, take care of the house and look after the tenants. For that, you would live on the premises rent free."

Sheila listened in silence. Unable to see his face with the light from the window behind him, she could not read his expression. His tone was all business. She replied in kind.

"Thank you for your expression of faith in my character, and thank you for the offer. However, I have my own business to run, and I need to give my time to my clients."

"Clients? I understood that you were employed as a secretary."

Sheila smiled. "Oh, I certainly carry out secretarial tasks. However

I am also a real estate agent. That work, too, is time-consuming. I have been merely reorganizing my work around your mother's illness."

"I see. Very well. I'll have to make other arrangements. And, what do I owe you for taking care of Mother?"

"Nothing. It was my gift to her for all her many kindnesses. However, if you like I can handle the sale of the house."

"That won't be necessary. My lawyer will see to it. You will be leaving when?"

"My rent is paid to the end of the month."

"And the others?"

"To the end of the month."

"Very well."

Sheila excused herself and went to the front parlour where she cleared the dishes and put the food away. There was a small house on Brunswick Avenue north of Bloor. $18,000 was the asking price. If she could somehow swing a loan...she had $9,000 in savings, but what did she have for collateral? Just her wits and her track record. That evening she prepared a proposal for the bank loans officer.

During the next two days, she went to the Bank of Montreal, the Toronto Dominion, the Bank of Commerce and the Bank of Nova Scotia. She chose the bank which gave her the best interest on the shortest mortgage.

Two days before end of the month the deal was finalized. After six years in the city Sheila owned her first house. She said her goodbyes to the remaining boarders at Palmerston, piled her typewriter, her Rolodex. her sewing machine, her clothes and papers into the Comet and moved the few blocks northeast, where she celebrated her 25th birthday with two girlfriends, Polly, a high school teacher, and Liz who worked as a secretary at Queen's Park.

As soon as she had a telephone installed in her new home she went to a printer and had letterhead and business cards made: Cedar Springs Real Estate. Sheila Belyea -- AV8-6474. Then she sat down and wrote to all those she had done business with in the past, thanking them for their business and informing them of her new address. She sent one to her former employers at Simmond's Real Estate. And, just as a reminder to Philip Meizner, she sent a letter and a card to him. Perhaps in future he wouldn't be so quick to underestimate people.

The Palmerston house was sold. Sheila had made enquiries and discovered it had gone for $32,000. Not a bad price, she thought, but she could have done better.

It was 1959. When not showing properties, Sheila renovated her house. After making sure the wiring and plumbing were up to snuff, she hired a contractor to put in a new kitchen, which she designed herself, and two new bathrooms. While he worked, she stripped walls, scraped floors, repainted and papered. She measured the windows and sewed drapes. She shopped for rugs and good second-hand furniture. In fact some of her best buys included two chairs and a sofa she purchased at the Salvation Army store and a chest of drawers and armoire from Crippled Civilians. She bought bedroom sets and restored them.

As soon as the renovations were finished, Sheila rented out the two top floors, which more than covered the house payments, taxes, insurance and repairs. In 1960 the house was worth more than $25,000. She thought of selling it, but she liked the area, liked the cosmopolitan hustle and bustle of nearby Bloor Street and the proximity of the university where she sometimes attended concerts and lectures, so she remained on Brunswick. She considered setting up a separate office, but then wondered what the advantage would be. Merely more expense. She had all the business she could handle on the phone. She kept in touch with her former boss at Simmond's. She passed on information on commercial properties. They threw most residential business her way.

By the time Sheila Belyea reached her 30th birthday, as well as having her own home free and clear, she owned $150,000 in stocks, bonds and savings. She celebrated by buying a new car, a Ford Thunderbird. It was outrageously expensive and absolutely gorgeous.

All during the time she lived in Toronto, Sheila had returned once a year to Cedar Springs to visit with her parents. Her two brothers had long since moved to British Columbia. Always she brought gifts which were received with less enthusiasm than she would have liked. Her mother asked her if she planned to stay an old maid all her life. The year she drove home in the Thunderbird, her father asked her if she'd borrowed it from a boyfriend. It was always a relief to return to the city. She once told Polly and Liz that her biggest nightmare was to land in Cedar Springs and lose her purse and her return ticket. It was a silly nightmare, because she rarely flew, and she could always have money wired.

In 1964 Toronto was changing. Coffee and folk music clubs were opening in Yorkville. Times were more free and open. Sheila was beginning to feel that her own life was a treadmill. She could take life a little easier, but what would she do with herself? "Not a chick nor a child," as her mother would say. Then one day she received a letter from Philip Meizner, post-marked Toronto. The letter explained that his head office had been transferred to Toronto and that he would be living there in future. He wished to take her to dinner, if she was agreeable, and would call her when he arrived in town to set a time. The letter was more formal than personal.

They met at the Park Plaza Hotel where they had drinks at the roof garden before going down to the dining room. Philip, lean and tan, wore a charcoal gray business suit. His hair was short and he was clean shaven.

He was also wearing glasses. Myopic, Sheila guessed. Sheila looked stunning in a light green raw-silk gown with a white jacket of the same material. She had learned the best use of make-up, which emphasized her eyes and mouth.

The first thing Philip did after their drinks arrived was to upset his own. She realized he was nervous. So she began talking about changes in the city. But conversation was halting. He knew nothing about real estate. She knew nothing about engineering. Three times they started talking at the same time. Then he said: "You first. Tell me what you do here in the city besides work." Sheila talked about a gallery she'd recently visited and then steered the conversation back to him.

His work was connected to the Department of National Defense, he told her, supposedly classified but mostly dull routine. His interest and fascination was with minerals--nickel, copper, etc.

"And you're married," Sheila said. "Do you have a family?"

"No. And no," Philip said. "You?"

"No. Too busy getting the business established."

"Not even close?"

"No. You?"

"Well, I did ask a young lady to marry me but she wasn't interested in living in Cold Lake at the time."

"And you're here permanently now?"

"Yes. I will still be doing a lot of travelling. But I will be based here."

"You said you were thinking of an apartment to live in?"

"Yes."

"Well, there are some very nice places at Bloor and Church Streets. Isn't that where you said your office was located?"

"Bloor and Bay."

"Actually I've never lived in an apartment. I've thought about it. Neat, clean, lights, heat, parking, everything taken care of. In fact I haven't made it too far from your own home on Palmerston. That was such a lovely house."

"Yes, I guess. But I couldn't handle it from Cold Lake."

"That house has tripled in price since you sold it."

"No kidding? I guess I should have let you handle the sale in the first place."

"Well, I did offer, if you remember."

"Yes, you did. That's true. However, I was so embarrassed that I had made an officious boor of myself in your eyes, that I passed the whole thing over to my lawyer. Incidentally, he is currently in trouble for embezzlement."

Sheila laughed. Philip liked the sound.

After dinner it was still only 8:30 p.m. Philip asked Sheila if she'd like to take in a show. "It's a beautiful night," she said. "Why don't we walk a bit."

"A good idea."

They left the Park Plaza and strolled down University Avenue. They didn't talk much but soon discovered they were both comfortable with the silence. At the feet of the statue of Sir Adam Beck they stopped. "Every time I look at that statue, I swear he is going to step down and walk up the street," Sheila said.

"It is rather good, isn't it? Wasn't he the founder of Ontario Hydro?"

"Yes."

"What would it be like, do you suppose, if we didn't have electric power?"

"I can't imagine. Yet I grew up with lamplight. Studied at the kitchen table with light from an Aladdin lamp. We had a pump with cold water in the house. The only hot water was in a tank on the side of the kitchen stove. I had my first shower at the YWCA when I arrived in Toronto. It was a thrill!"

"Were your parents very poor?"

"No. No more than anybody else in the neighbourhood. It was just that the hydro line was only built in Cedar Springs in 1953, which was the year I came to Toronto."

"You never thought of going to university?"

"No. My only wish was to get out of Cedar Springs and be on my own."

"What made you choose Toronto?"

"You know, I don't remember. I think I heard somebody saying there were lots of secretarial jobs in Toronto. Maybe from the school library... I do recall that almost everybody else who left Cedar Springs went to Oshawa to work in General Motors or to Detroit to work for Ford."

"Why were you in such a rush to leave Cedar Springs?"

"I wanted to get out from under the authority of my parents. Also, I didn't see any future for myself there. I didn't want to teach, to nurse or marry a farmer. I guess I had to try my wings. But that's enough about me. You went to university, obviously."

"Oh yes. There was no question about that. It was expected of me."

"What about your father?"

"My father was a minister."

"Oh yes, I recall your mother mentioning that. He was a Baptist minister?"

"Yes, a Baptist minister. He died three years after we arrived in Canada, which was right after the war. They'd bought the Palmerston house. I think there was insurance, so with the boarding house my mother was able to manage."

By the time they had reached her house on Brunswick, Sheila had learned that Philip had had a rather lonely childhood. School kids made fun of his accent. He wasn't good at sports. He was good at design and engineering. His mother had insisted on top grades, and he achieved them with ease. Sheila also intuited that he felt there was a lot missing from his life.

On Sheila's doorstep, he turned to her, saying:
"This has been very pleasant."
"Yes, I've enjoyed it."
"Would you mind if I called you again?"
"I'd like that."

Philip and Sheila dated for six months before he asked her to marry him. After they got over their initial shyness and awkwardness, they found they were well suited. Under Philip's cold manner was a delightful sense of humour which Sheila treasured. He discovered in her a warmth and softness that enchanted him. They were married in the Bloor Street United Church in a small ceremony, attended by a handful of close friends. A reception was held later at the Park Plaza.

During the next year they bought a house on Russell Hill Road. With Philip spending long hours at the office, Sheila managed the repairs and renovations and created a garden. She learned to cook. One by one the rooms were redone. Sheila continued selling real estate but Philip became the centre of her existence. They attended concerts and lectures at Massey Hall. They attended shows at the Imperial Room of the Royal York. They enjoyed productions by the National Ballet. They spent weekends at Stratford where they saw *Timon of Athens* and *As You Like It*. They took a holiday in Europe. They entertained friends. They had been married three years. Then Sheila became pregnant. She did not tell Philip right away. Instead she made an appointment with a doctor, just to be sure.

The next week passed slowly. Philip had to return to Cold Lake and was gone for several days.

The night he came home, Sheila had planned a little celebration. When he arrived they hugged and kissed. Then he took his bags upstairs. He showered, shaved, and put on casual clothes, before returning to the kitchen for ice cubes to go with his Scotch and soda.

"What are we having?" he asked.
"Pirogies."
"Pirogies. Oh boy, that brings back memories." Philip carried his drink into the sunroom.

Sheila set a pretty table and opened a bottle of red wine. She turned on the new stereo record player and placed Acker Bilk's *Stranger on the*

Shore on the turntable. When all was ready she went to the sunroom and found Philip sitting with his drink untouched, the unopened paper in his lap and tears pouring down his face. She sat down on the arm of his chair and cradled his head in her arms.

"Oh, my darling. Whatever is the matter?" Philip did not answer but continued to sob for several more minutes then said:

"I'm sorry. I'm so sorry. I have no idea what came over me."

"Did something happen at work?"

"No. Nothing. I think I'll lie down a while."

"Well, sure." said Sheila, trying to hide her disappointment. "That's a good idea. You must be tired after the long drive."

Philip walked into the master bedroom and sat on the side of the bed. When Sheila looked in half an hour later, he was lying on top of the bed fully clothed and sound asleep. She pulled a blanket over him. At midnight she checked again and he was still sleeping. At that point she woke him and encouraged him to get into his pajamas. Uneasy and restless, Sheila decided not to disturb him. She went to sleep on a cot in the dressing room. When she awoke in the morning he was gone. Since he usually left before 7:00 a.m. Sheila was not alarmed. She had two clients that day and would be showing houses up until seven-thirty in the evening. From time to time while driving around, she thought of Philip's behaviour the previous night. She also thought about her reaction to it. She had never seen a man cry in her life. Her first feeling had been one of distaste, as if his behaviour was an aberration. But that soon passed. She loved him dearly.

She spent her day delighting in the idea of being a mother, planning changes to accommodate a new baby.

Philip did not go to work that day. Instead he drove down to Sunnyside and parked the car, not facing the water but the Gardiner Expressway. And sat there. Around 6:30 p.m. Philip left Sunnyside and drove home, parked the car in the garage and went into the house. Since Sheila was out showing a house he went straight to the bedroom. He took off his suit jacket and hung it in the closet, then he stretched out on the bed where he remained until Sheila returned at 10:30 p.m. He got up and they sat together watching the late news. Although he seemed a little distracted, Sheila felt that demanding an explanation was not a good idea. Instead, she stayed close to him, held his hand and hoped her physical presence would comfort him. They went upstairs to bed at 11:45. Sheila had been going to tell him about her possible pregnancy, but it didn't seem the right time. She would wait until after her doctor's appointment and see what the tests said. In the morning when she awoke, Philip was gone, presumably to work.

But Philip hadn't gone to work. He hadn't even showered or shaved. Again Sheila didn't notice. He had a separate dressing room with its own bathroom. Even if she had gone in there, there would have been nothing to alert her. The bathroom would be clean and tidy. A soiled towel would have been tossed down the laundry chute. Apart from a few anonymous toiletries, his suits in the closet, his shirts, socks, underwear, etc. in the chest of drawers, there was little evidence of a man's presence in the house.

Before Sheila left for her doctor's appointment she went into her office to go over some contracts. She had just opened the first file folder when Philip's secretary called to remind him of his 11:00 a.m. meeting with the CEO. Sheila thanked her for calling and told her that Philip had already left, then joked that there would have to be a major calamity for Philip to miss an appointment. His secretary chuckled and agreed. She did not mention that Philip had missed the whole previous day. She had been in the secretarial world long enough to know that where husbands and their wives were concerned, it was tactful to keep her mouth shut or plead ignorance.

The doctor confirmed what Sheila already suspected. She was approximately eight weeks pregnant. Sent home with a prescription for iron tablets to guard against anaemia, Sheila felt quietly delighted. After all the years of struggle she had a husband to love, a beautiful home, a career she enjoyed and now she would become a mother. On her way home she bought ingredients for a special meal.

That evening when Philip came in, she poured a drink for him, and sat down with him in the sunroom.

"I've been to the doctor today, Philip."

"You have?"

"Yes."

"Not sick, are you?"

"No. I'm pregnant."

His reaction was not what she expected. For a second he sat motionless, and then a look of someone hunted, assaulted, or even terrified flashed across his face.

"You don't seem very pleased," she said.

"Oh, well. Yes. It's just...fatherhood...it's such a big responsibility, I don't know whether I...."

"Well, Philip! Really," Sheila laughed. "You'll be a wonderful father. I just know it."

"But we don't even have a cat. Or a goldfish."

"What on earth do cats and goldfish have to do with anything?"

"I wouldn't know what to do with a baby. Do they come with directions?"

Sheila laughed, relieved. Sheila had already had time to consider parenthood. All he needed was some time to think about it.

The rest of the evening they discussed plans for the expected child. Sheila, excited and joyful, was aware that Philip seemed to be only half-listening, but she bubbled on anyway.

The next morning she came down stairs just as Philip was leaving. As she kissed him goodbye she noticed that he hadn't shaved. She knew he kept a razor at the office. Even so, that was not like him.

For the third day in a row, Philip did not go to work. He drove around for a while and then parked the car near the Humber River, got out and walked away. That night he didn't come home for supper. He wasn't home at midnight. Sheila was worried, but she couldn't think of anybody to call at that time of night. She walked the floor and waited. He did not return. At 9:00 a.m. she called his office, and his secretary said that he hadn't arrived yet. She promised to have him call when he came in. At noon Sheila called again. That time she was told he wasn't available. Sheila decided to wait to see if he came home for supper, but he did not. At 9 p.m. that evening, she called one of the other engineers in his firm and asked if he knew how she could reach Philip. He said he did not know, that he had been out of the office and hadn't seen Philip for several days. Sheila walked the floor until midnight.

Just as she was about to start calling hospital emergency departments, Sheila heard a car pull up outside. A uniformed police officer got out of the cruiser and walked up to the front door. He asked for Philip. Sheila said he hadn't been home for several days. Then he told her that Philip's car had been found near the Humber. The keys were still in the ignition. A suit jacket which contained his wallet was draped over the passenger seat. There were no signs of a struggle, no evidence of foul play. However the car would have to be moved or it would be impounded. Then, since he had several more hours to kill on his shift, he offered to drive her out to pick it up. Sheila grabbed her jacket and purse.

On the way out to pick up the car, Sheila asked questions, but the officer had no information for her. They would file a missing persons report, but he wasn't sure it would be of much help. He asked her if there had been any problems.

"Not really," Sheila said. "But he did seem a little distracted. And extremely tired. Two nights in a row he came home and went straight to sleep. Which is not like him."

"Has he ever done this kind of thing before?"

"No. That's just it. It's so unlike him. I mean, if ever there was a person of regular habits, it was Philip."

They listened to the crackle of the police radio.

"Anything else?"

"Well, the only other thing is the last night he was here I told him that we're expecting a baby."

"How did he react?"

"Shocked...well that isn't the right word. He worried that he wouldn't be a good father."

"What did you say to that?"

"I said, that was nonsense. Philip would be a wonderful father."

"Any financial worries?"

"No. I mean, we're not millionaires but he has been an engineer in the same company for years and years and I've had my own real estate business. We're comfortable. I thought the timing would be perfect for us to have a baby."

"Well, it's a pretty big thing becoming a father. We've got five kids. It sure changes your life."

"Yes. I know that. But Philip is the most tender, the most thoughtful..." and then Sheila became aware of the tears pouring down her face.

The police officer pulled in next to Philip's car and turned over Philip's car keys to her. "Well, sometimes people just have to go off by themselves for a while," he said.

"But when he left he hadn't shaved. It's just so unlike him."

"Oh, one other thing, do you happen to have a picture of your husband?"

"No I don't. A friend of ours took snapshots at our wedding. I planned to have some enlarged. But in our move to Russell Hill Road they were mislaid."

"That's too bad. I'll take a description but it doesn't give us much to go on."

Sheila thanked the police officer, got in Philip's car, adjusted the seat and the mirror and drove home.

Over the next week she called the station twice a day, until they began putting her off. No, there had been no progress on the missing person's report, every avenue was being explored. And finally, no, the officer in charge of that case is not in. Someone would call her if they had anything.

One morning just as she was leaving for an appointment, she opened the door to find two men standing there. Both were medium height. One was dark-haired and strong-featured. The other was fair and slightly bald. The one with the fair hair greeted her and asked for Philip.

"He isn't here," Sheila said. "He's been away for several days." She noticed an accent, European. But she couldn't pinpoint it. The dark-haired man stood, silent, watching her.

"Where did he go?"

"I'm not sure. He doesn't discuss his work with me."

"When do you expect him to return?"

"Sorry. I can't help you with that either. He didn't say. Look, I'm on my way out, but if you'll leave your name, I'll tell him you called."

"That won't be necessary."

As well as calling the police, Sheila drove out to the place where Philip's car had been parked. It was April and the water level had lowered. She walked along the banks. All she saw were ducks and debris. She walked up and down the nearest streets.

After two weeks she called Philip's office and made an appointment with his supervisor. This proved futile. The supervisor seemed to be exercising extreme care not to say anything about Philip in any way. He quickly pointed out that personnel records were confidential and that even he did not have access to them. Sheila asked what Philip had been working on when he disappeared. Again the supervisor was not forthcoming.

During week three she put ads in the "Personals" column of the Toronto Star and Telegram, simply saying, "Come home Philip. We need you."

The weeks passed with no sign of Philip. Sheila began showing physical signs of her pregnancy. There was no morning sickness, no real discomfort of any kind. She kept as busy as possible. The real estate market was bright. Houses were bought and sold before they were built. All of Cabbagetown was changing hands as people bought up dilapidated edifices and restored them. Bare white walls were the fashion, and parts of Cabbage Town became known as the white paint district.

Months passed. Sheila talked to Philip's personal physician who assured her that his health was fine. She saw a psychiatrist and spent two sessions with her, explaining the situation. She mentioned finding Philip in tears, how he had slept for 12 and 14 hours straight in his clothes, and that he hadn't shaved the last day before he disappeared. He hadn't taken anything from the house. In fact his wallet was in his jacket thrown over the seat of the car which still had the keys in the ignition when the police found it. The psychiatrist suggested a number of possibilities, that he had been suffering from depression, that he could have had a schizophrenia episode, but she couldn't really make any proper diagnosis without seeing Philip. More time wasted, Sheila thought. Still, she would try everything she could think of.

Night after night she went over the possibilities. Had Philip simply been frightened off by the thought of fatherhood? Did the European men who'd turned up at her door have anything to do with Philip's disappearance? Had he been robbed or murdered? If so, why were his jacket and wallet left in the car? Had he faked a suicide? Despair, rage, fear and ever diminishing hope filled her nights.

Then it was November. A week before her due date, Sheila was talking to her friend Polly.

"Aren't you worried going into labour with no one there?" Polly asked.

"A little. But, what am I to do? Besides I'm only five minutes from the hospital."

"I'm going to be taking a special education course at the university, or I'd come up and stay with you. What about asking Liz?"

"Liz. Isn't she still at Queen's Park. What about her husband?"

"No. The man she married turned out to be a five-star brute. He broke her nose on their honeymoon. She stayed three years, hoping he'd change. All she got for her effort was two more black eyes and some broken ribs."

"Oh Lord, I had no idea."

"Well, she didn't want anybody to know. I only found out by accident when I stopped by there one day. She was supposed to meet me for lunch at Eaton's, but she didn't show up. After my last class I drove out to her home. The back door was open, so I went inside. I found her just sitting in a chair. Her mouth was bleeding. One eye was nearly swollen shut. I wanted to take her straight to the doctor, but she wouldn't go."

"Doesn't she have a daughter?"

"Yes. Jenny. Eighteen months old now."

"Where was she?"

"At the sitter's. I called my office and said I had an emergency, that I would be gone for the day. I stayed with Liz until 5:30. Then she said she would be fine. But of course she wasn't. Things would go smoothly for several weeks and then there would be another episode.

"Well, one night he complained about the napkins. Her linen napkins were in the laundry, so she had set the table with paper napkins. Liz started to explain that she hadn't had time to iron them when he reached over and slapped her across the face. Jenny started screaming. He turned to Jenny, pulled her out of the high chair, carried her to her room, threw her on the bed and closed the door. Then he came back and sat down at the table as if nothing had happened and went on eating dinner. Liz could hear Jenny sobbing but she waited until he'd finished the main course. Then she got up to clear the plates and serve dessert and coffee. While the coffee perked she looked in on Jenny and saw that she had cried herself to sleep.

"Liz waited until the next morning when her husband left for work, packed a few things for Jenny and herself and cleared out. That night he showed up here looking for her, but she hadn't been in touch with me at that point. Not that I would have told the bastard anyway. But she called Friday morning just as I was leaving for school. She has been holed up at a motel in Sunnyside but she is nearly out of money. I was just thinking she needs a safe place and you need some help right now."

"I'll call her. What's the number there? I'll go pick her up."

"There's no phone in the room. But it's No. 9. Listen, give me ten minutes and I'll go with you."

At the motel, Polly walked up to No. 9, rapped on the door. Then, leaning in close, she said. "It's me, Polly, and Sheila."

Liz opened the door and they went in. Sheila could hardly believe this was the same vivacious dark-haired beauty she had known. Liz's face was green and brown mottled. Her hair was lank and unclean. Jenny was sitting silently in the middle of the bed sucking her thumb.

"You're coming home with me," said Sheila. "Heaven knows, I've lots of room. In fact there is a suite on the second floor which looks out over the garden. It even has a separate entrance. You'll be safe there."

It took only a few minutes for Liz to bundle Jenny up and get in the car. As they neared Russell Hill Road, Sheila explained that they would drive in the lane, park behind the house and walk the few steps to the kitchen. If Liz wanted, she could get down out of sight until they were safely in. The extra precaution was hardly necessary. It was 9:30 p.m. The street was empty of cars and people. The dog-walkers wouldn't be out until 11:00 p.m. to midnight.

Sheila took Liz and Jenny up to their suite. Jenny fussed a little but soon settled down. Sheila made cocoa for Polly, Liz and herself. They talked until midnight about plans and pain and fear and disillusion, and also hope.

"Good grief!" said Polly. "It's midnight. I've got early classes tomorrow. I'll call a cab."

"I can drive you home," Sheila said.

"No, stay with Liz and Jenny."

After Polly left, Sheila turned to Liz. "Well, what can we do but go on? Look at it this way. You have a bright and beautiful daughter. I am fine financially. This is as safe a place as you're going to find in the city. Together we'll manage. Now, let's get to bed. I also have an early appointment. Everything will work out, you'll see."

But as she got into bed, Sheila felt an overwhelming sense of loss. This was the time she looked forward to all day, the time when she and Philip would prepare for bed, and then snuggle like two spoons in a drawer. "Where, oh where are you, Philip?" she moaned. "Will I ever see you again?"

Sheila's and Philip's son was born December 1. After an arduous labour, Sheila rested while a nurse took the baby away to be examined, weighed, cleaned, diapered and dressed in a tiny shirt. After a while the nurse returned, placed the baby in Sheila's arms, and positioned him at a breast. Immediately he began sucking. Sheila studied his little round face with delight. "What shall I name you?" Then she thought of Mrs. Meizner.

Her name had been Mattie.

"Yes," said Sheila. "You're name is Matthew. Matthew Philip Meizner. Now, my son, did you come with directions?"

Between Liz and Sheila they worked out a plan whereby Liz would look after the house and the children and Sheila would continue selling real estate. The plan worked well for a year, then Liz became restless. They talked it over; Liz would go back to university during the day and Sheila would look after Jenny and Matthew. Then in the evenings Sheila would show houses.

They managed for another few months. Then Liz joined the women's liberation movement, which fit her like a glove. Liz discovered she had a taste for politics. Remembering the abuse she had taken from her husband, she was fist-shaking angry. She became strident. She cut her hair short, threw her bra away and took a course in the martial arts. She began attending marches and protests. After Liz had appeared on a TV news program, her husband caught up with her. He was waiting for her one afternoon when she was leaving the university grounds and heading for the subway. He pulled up beside her, saying, "Hello Liz. I've been looking for you."

"Go away. Leave me alone." Liz replied.

"Get in the car."

"Come near me and I'll scream."

"Okay, scream." With that he lifted a hand gun out of his shirt and aimed it at her. Liz froze.

Seeing her face, he chuckled. "Maybe another time," he said as he sped away down the street.

Liz found a phone and called Sheila. "He'll kill me," Liz said. "Sooner or later, he's going to kill me."

"Do you think he knows you're living here?"

"I don't know. Probably. I have to get out of here."

"What does he drive?"

"A red Pontiac Firebird."

"Ah, oh. It's just pulled up across the street. Look, get on the streetcar and go to the bus station. I'll meet you there as soon as I can. It will take me a few minutes to get the kids ready."

"Okay."

Sheila put a call in to the nearest police station, explained that her roommate was being stalked by her abusive husband, and that he was now outside Sheila's house waiting for her to come home. Then she scooped Liz's toiletries into a bag and packed a small suitcase. When she looked out again, the Firebird was nowhere in sight. Just then a cruiser pulled up. Sheila ran out to tell them that the Firebird was gone. "He just passed us," said the female officer. "Is everything all right here?"

"Yes, we're fine, but I have to go out now."

"Well, we'll check back later and make sure everything is okay."

"Thank you so much. I appreciate it."

Sheila opened her small office safe, removed $1,000 and slipped it into her bag. With rush-hour traffic, it took her nearly an hour to get to the bus terminal. When she pulled up Liz ran out and grabbed Jenny.

"Thank God," Liz said. "There's a bus leaving in five minutes. I've got our tickets."

Sheila passed Liz the suitcase, then took the money out of her purse. "Here, take this."

"Thank you. Oh thank you. I'll pay you back as soon as I can."

Sheila leaned down and planted a kiss on Jenny's cheek. "Take care of your mom. Now run, you two."

Sheila got back in the car where Matthew sat chortling, unaware of any problem. She was going to show a house this evening, but she would have to cancel. She drove down Bay Street and out the Gardiner to Sunnyside. Then she parked the car, put Matthew in the carrier, and off they walked along by the lake. But crises comes in twos and threes. When they returned home, Sheila bathed and fed Matthew and put him to bed. No sooner did she have him settled than the phone rang. It was her father calling from Cedar Springs. Her mother had taken a fall off a step stool while washing down the front stairs. She was in the hospital in serious condition. She had cracked ribs and a ruptured spleen.

"I'll be there as soon as I can get a flight," Sheila said.

"I'd go to Fredericton and pick you up, but I don't like to leave her."

"That won't be necessary. I'll rent a car."

Sheila called the airport and learned that there was a flight at 7:30 which would get her to Fredericton by 10:00 p.m. With luck she could just make it. She called and ordered a cab, then packed a diaper bag for Matthew and an overnight case for herself. With Matthew in the carrier that was all she could handle. After a quick shower, she dressed in her new pantsuit. Then, carrying a sleeping Matthew still in his pyjamas, she collected her bags and was at the front door just as the cab pulled up. The driver reached around and opened the door for her. She slid the bag across the seat and climbed in behind it. Then they headed for the airport. Had Sheila not had so much on her mind she would have spotted the red Firebird across the street from her house.

As soon as the cab pulled away, Liz's husband drove down the lane and parked in behind. Then he took a tire iron out, smashed a window and gained entrance to the kitchen. When he discovered that Liz was not there, he began trashing the place. He found her and Jenny's suite and took the tire iron to everything that could be broken. He ripped the clothes in the closet to shreds. He uncapped nail polish and poured it all over the new rug. Drawers were pulled out, their contents strewn around. He went from room to room, smashing, slashing, until he'd laid waste the whole upstairs and then he came down to the kitchen again. He found Javel and cleaning fluids under the sink. He poured those over the living room furniture. He smashed the television set and the record player. He took LPs out of their jackets and jumped on them. Lastly, he went into Sheila's office and dumped all the files out onto the middle of the floor. He lit a match and set a fire in the trash basket. Then he calmly walked through to the kitchen and out the back door, climbed into his Firebird and drove off. He was at Davenport and Dupont by the time the police cruiser passed the house on Russell Hill, but there was nothing to be seen from the street. Sheila had pulled the curtains in her office and the other downstairs rooms before leaving for the airport.

Fortunately Sheila had been able to get a direct flight, and Matthew slept until they were coming in for the landing. Then the air pressure hurt his ears and he began fussing, but he stopped as soon as Sheila lifted him into the carrier. The stewardess helped them off the plane first. As she was attempting to hire a car another passenger heard her say that she was going to Cedar Springs.

"Excuse me," she said, "but my husband I live in Cedar Springs. You'd be welcome to come with us. Save you trying to get a car this time of night. He's just collecting my luggage."

"That's awfully kind of you," said Sheila. "I don't want to put you out."

"Not putting us out a bit. By the way, I'm Louise Grant. This is my husband Ernest."

"I'm Sheila Meizner. This is my son Matthew."

"How do, Mrs Meizner," Ernest replied. "Car's right outside."

On the way up river, Louise discovered that Sheila's maiden name was Belyea.

"Well, now," said Ernest. "You'd be Dan Belyea's daughter, went off to Ontario a few years ago."

"Nearly 20 years ago," Sheila agreed. Then she explained that her mother had taken a fall and she was on her way to the hospital.

"And where is your husband?"

"We're separated."

"Oh," said Louise. "I see. Well, it's happening more and more these days. How long will you be in Cedar Springs?"

"I'm not sure. Depends on how mother gets on."

At the hospital Sheila went to the front desk and asked for her mother's room.

"She is in ICU," said the attendant. "But you can't take the baby in there. Let me call the nurse. What's your name?"

In a few minutes the nurse returned along with Sheila's father. He looked frightened and out of place. Diminished somehow. Sheila gave him half a hug with one arm and asked about her mother.

He shook his head. "Not good. They'll only let you stay about five minutes." Then reaching for Matthew, he said, "Here, I'll take him. You go on in." Sheila hesitated, wondering if Matthew would start to howl. Then she lifted him out of the carrier and handed him to her father. Matthew awoke, then beamed at his grandfather. Sheila rushed down the hall. Her mother opened her eyes briefly, smiled wearily, and said, "Sheila, you came. Good."

Mrs. Belyea did not recover, but lingered long enough for Sheila's brothers to return from the west. Meanwhile Sheila caught her sleep in bits and pieces. Surprisingly, her father took over Matthew's care--even diapering him, allowing Sheila an extra few hours rest between trips to the hospital. Matthew gurgled happily as he was lifted from one set of arms to another. He was a hit with Sheila's brothers as well. It was the first time the family were all together in one place since 1953. Since none of them were letter-writers, there was lots to catch up on. They discussed Philip's disappearance, but could shed no light.

Sheila stayed a week after the funeral. She washed and cooked and cleaned and hoped her father would be able to manage. He drove her and Matthew to the airport, helped carry their bags, then stood silently with tears pouring down his face as he handed Matthew over to her. That was when Matthew began crying, and he fussed all the way back in the plane.

A limousine from the airport dropped them at Russell Hill Road around 3:00 p.m. Overwhelmed by emotional and physical exhaustion, for the first time Sheila did not admire the well-kept grounds of her lovely home. Instead she unlocked the front door, stepped over the pile of mail, then stopped still. Every thing in the hallway was ruined. She opened the door of her office, to find that a fire had burned itself out, but not before destroying a lot of her papers. Pictures had been slashed. Her real estate catalogues were strewn over the floor. Miraculously, the telephone had survived. She called the police. Then sat down to wait.

"Do you know who might have done this?" asked the officer.

"No." said Sheila, explaining that she had been in New Brunswick for the past three weeks, attending her mother and the funeral following her death.

"Can't think of anybody who might have had a grudge?"

"Oh, God. My former roommate, Liz. Her husband threatened to shoot her the day I left. His car was on the street that day."

"Where is your roommate now?"

"I can't tell you. After she called I went to meet her at the bus station. She caught a bus. That's all I know."

"Why didn't you report the incident?"

"Well, I had called earlier, and the police cruised up and down the street, but the Firebird wasn't there by then. And I'd no sooner returned from the bus station when I got the call from my father, telling me my mother was in the hospital."

"Okay, why don't you stay in a hotel for a couple of days, just to be on the safe side. Call us when you're settled. You should also get in touch with your insurance agent."

Sheila and Matthew spent the next month at the Seaway Hotel, while the police and the insurance company assessed the damage and various specialists went over her home for clues. Although most of Sheila's legal papers had been destroyed, she found an untouched file in her basement, which contained invoices for her artwork and most of the fine pieces of furniture. The insurance company was slow, but in the end, co-operative. She received the full amount for which her house and contents were covered.

In the disorder of the vandalism she missed something that occurred to her much later. Philip's suits and shirts were gone.

While at the Seaway Hotel, Sheila called her father every night. Considering his recent loss, she hadn't planned to mention the destruction of her house but broke down and told him. He listened quietly as she sobbed out her story, then he said:

"I don't suppose you'd consider coming back to Cedar Springs."

"Oh, I don't know. There's my business to consider, not that I've given it much attention lately."

"Hard to know what to do," he said. "I've been thinking about getting rid of the farm. Don't seem to have the heart for it, now that your mother's gone."

"Well, Dad, the experts say one shouldn't make major changes for at least two years after a death."

"That what they say, eh? So, what about you?"

"See, the thing is, since the break-in I'm afraid to let Matthew out of my sight. I have taken him to a daycare centre, but he came home half sick. They told me he'd cried for a solid hour after I left. I love my work, but Matthew comes first."

"Maybe you could set up shop down here..." her father said.

"It's a thought. Anyhow, I'll talk to you tomorrow."

After Matthew had settled down, Sheila considered their future. Without Liz's help, she couldn't look after Matthew and run all over the city, too. She was uneasy about leaving him in daycare. Her father could use her help. A man's presence would be good for Matthew. In the end, she decided to have the Russell Hill house repainted and new carpets laid.

Then since she couldn't sell it without Philip's consent, she rented it to a an English professor, his wife and their two children. She did, however, sell her Thunderbird, and drove home in Philip's Buick. Matthew travelled well. As they pulled in to the farm house in Cedar springs, her father came out to meet them. Matthew smiled, then said his first word: "Gump."

"What's that, young man?" asked her father, swinging Matthew in the air.

"Gump," said Matthew pointing at his grandfather. "Gump."

"Well, Dad, that's his first word, Gump."

"Ho, ho. Maybe he's callin' me grump."

"I'm sure he means grampa," said Sheila.

"Gump," Matthew repeated, patting his grandfather's cheek.

In the 20 years Sheila had been away, there had been many changes in Cedar Springs. Everybody had a fridge, a freezer and TV. Houses, once drab and gray, were covered with vinyl siding. There was an air of prosperity. But the biggest change was in the relationship between Sheila and her father. Sometimes he seemed a little wary of her, but grateful for her presence. Matthew became the centre of his life. He carried Matthew to see the cows. He walked him through the fields, pointing out buttercups and clover. As soon as Matthew learned the word dog, her father brought home a small puppy. To see them play was worth cleaning up after the initial puppy leaks. The next winter, her father built Matthew a small sled, with sides on it.

Meanwhile Sheila renovated the house, room by room, starting with the kitchen. She sorted her mother's things, throwing some out and keeping others. As she laboured, she pondered this woman who had given her life and realized that they had never really had an intimate conversation. She knew nothing of her mother's girlhood and very little of her mother's family. Her mother had been given to complaining, and that was what Sheila remembered. In fact, Sheila had been surprised at how much her father had been pained at her mother's death. To have seen the two together, one would think that they had hated each other. But obviously not so.

Even after putting money aside for Matthew's education, Sheila had done very well financially. She had the income from the house on Russell Hill Road. Her father insisted on buying the groceries and paying the bills at the farm. And every time she turned around he was buying something new for Matthew.

"Dad," she'd say. "You're spoiling him."

"Aw shoot. The boy needs a little spoiling. When you and your brothers were his age, I didn't have the money for anything. We were paying off the mortgage and the farm was barely paying for the feed and seed. Then you and the boys got away before we could do anything for you. I've always felt bad about that."

"What's to feel bad about? Both of them have good paying jobs and smart wives. I'm okay, at least financially."

"That's true enough. You've done well, girl. A lot better than your old man."

"Oh, I wouldn't say that..."

"You know, when I was overseas during the war, all I dreamed about was getting the farm. When I got back I sank everything I had into this place. Next to your mother it was all I ever wanted. Lots of returned men struck out for Ontario, got jobs in General Motors. Others went to college on government money and carved out big careers. But I didn't have time for all that. I just had to get on the land. And I stayed with it.

"It was a struggle keeping the mortgage paid up. Crops failed. Markets changed. I made mistakes. And always the worry over money. It soured your mother.

"See, I always had the idea that I was building up something for the boys. I figured you'd go off and get married. Turned out, neither one of your brothers was the slightest bit interested in the farm.

"Every summer other men my age would come back here on vacation. They'd be driving big cars, talking about golf and throwing money around. Now, I didn't give a damn about golf. But I'll admit I was envious. Then you came home in the Thunderbird. Kind'a showed me up."

"Oh, God, Dad. I'm so sorry."

"Not your fault. I've been a pig-headed fool. Can't blame you."

"I guess things never turn out as we planned."

"No, no they don't. Which brings me to ask what you plan to do about Philip? It ain't likely he'll show up at this stage of the game."

"Well, there's really nothing I can do. After seven years I can have him declared dead, sell the house, car and so on. I keep getting statements from his bank, so his savings are drawing interest, which will likely come to me.

"Funny, when I left home I had two things in mind. Making money and gaining my own independence. I used to lie upstairs in my room and pray for it."

"Well girl, you've shown you can make it on your own."

"Yes. But I have no husband and Matthew has never seen his father."

"I guess it proves we should be careful what we pray for. Sometimes that's exactly what we get."

FOX IN THE HEN PEN

Ron Harley had been barbering in Cedar Springs since 1953. He'd gone to barbering school in Montreal, came back and set up shop on Main Street. Classed 4-F because of a heart murmur, he didn't get in the military and held a secret shame that he hadn't done his part in the war effort. He kept a bottle of vodka under the counter which he treated himself to now and then. On slow days, he treated himself fairly steadily.

Customers liked coming in to Ron Harley's barber shop for a variety of reasons. He gave a good haircut and he kept his price reasonable. Second, the barbershop was a great source of gossip. And then there was the fact that when they got Ron Harley laughing, it was hard to get him stopped.

Over the years he had heard every joke and every story and sometimes a dozen different versions of almost everything that happened in Cedar Springs. Sometimes he made up a few tales himself just to stir the pot. It was hard to know where truth left off and fiction began. Local legends abounded, told and retold as fact to each new and gullible generation.

Before Nat Freewater died over at Della's nursing home, he spent quite a bit of time in the barber shop. One morning he was sitting there waiting for his turn when Marlin Shaw came in.

"Hear there was some shootin' out at your place, Marlin."

"Where'd ya hear that?"

"Can't just remember now."

"Shouldn't believe everything you hear, you know. T'wasn't my place anyways. It was Will Cranston's."

"So what happened?" said Ron.

Nat thought for a while, then he told his version of the story...

"Will Cranston, now 83 past, doesn't hold much truck with the newfangled clothes the young fellers are sporting these days. As far as he's concerned you can take all your high-tops, your nylon Tex-made magic-fill jackets and your thermal jogging underwear, stick 'em in your hat and pull the eartabs down. He, Will Cranston, has been wearing woollen union suits, overalls and gum rubbers for nigh on 80 years, and he doesn't intend to change now--even if they are harder to find than hen's teeth sometimes. He says as much to his wife Tildy, and he says it fairly often.

"When their grandson Kenny arrived with three friends from college to spend the last part of their winter holidays in the country, Will found something new to gripe about. Kenny, the apple of his eye--though he'd never be soft enough to say so--had had his ear pierced and was wearing an earring.

"'Now, Will,' said Tildy. 'Just never you mind. That's the latest style, that's what all the boys are wearing these days. And that earring isn't hurting you one durn bit.' Will shook his head in disgust.

"Over the next few days Will did a lot of jawing. He had strong opinions on a variety of issues and made them known to anyone who would listen. He didn't believe in smoking. He wouldn't have liquor in the house. He wouldn't go for dancing. He did not allow foul language. He didn't like them calling him Gramps. He thought young folks should have more respect for their elders. He didn't like them leaving half the food on their plates or not coming to meals on time. He didn't like them ramming all over the fields with snowmobiles--trying to kill themselves. He didn't believe that young men should sit around of an evening playing cards and tempting the devil. He didn't like them teasing Tag, Will's old black and tan mongrel dog, and he especially did not like those foolish lookin' earrings.

"But Will had more on his mind than the boys' shenanigans. Something was sneaking into the henhouse at night and stealing his hens. A fox, likely. And he planned to do something about it.

"This particular night Will went to bed early. Tildy followed him upstairs half an hour later. Then the boys got out the playing cards.

"In the night it turned real cold and about 2 a.m. Will decided he'd better go down and stoke the fire. The boys, still up playing stud poker in the living room, heard the old man start down the stairs and quickly switched off the light. While sitting in the darkness, they heard Will go to the woodbox and back, fill the stove and turn the damper. They listened some more for him to go back to bed. But he didn't. Instead he rummaged around in the cupboard, found his shot gun shells and loaded his shotgun. Then he stretched out on the wooden couch by the window, pulled a patchwork quilt over his union suit, and waited.

"Just now Will heard a noise outside and came awake with a start. Something was in the henhouse. He jumped up, pushed his feet into his gum rubbers, grabbed his shotgun and took off out the door. Kenny and his friends tiptoed into the kitchen to find out what was going on. They couldn't see anything through the frosted window, so they opened the door and stepped out onto the porch.

"The dog, Tag, about 14 years old, was both blind and arthritic. But he sensed something out of the ordinary going on and rose stiffly from behind the stove. When the boys opened the front door Tag slipped out and hobbled off to investigate.

"After a few minutes the boys spotted Will at the henhouse door. They saw him cock his rifle and raise it to his shoulder. Then they saw the wind catch the back flap of Will's union suit where the button was missing. As Will stepped back to take aim, Tag, who had been trotting up behind him came forward and just as Will pulled the trigger, Tag's cold nose made contact with Will's bare skin.

"Will leapt in the air. His shot went wild. The fox was so surprised by the bang, it dropped the hen it was stealing and skittered out past Will and Tag to disappear into the night. Tag then began to bark.

"Leaning his gun by the side of the hen house, Will reached inside and turned on the light. When he saw the remains of five of his best laying hens lying on the floor in a heap of feathers, he was fit to be tied. He roared and he bellowed. He cursed and he swore. He ranted and he raved. He seethed and he stomped. He said words that made the college boys blush and their ears turn red, earrings and all. Some words Will shouted, they never would have guessed he even knew.

"Tildy, alarmed by all the noise, got up, put on her robe and came downstairs. She could see the boys on the porch staggering around, bent in half, slapping each other on the back and howling with glee. 'What in tarnation's going on?' she asked. They pointed to Will out by the henhouse.

"'Come in out of that, you old fool,' she yelled across the yard. 'You'll catch your death of cold.' And then she instructed the boys: 'Stop that right now. Go put those cards away out of sight and get on up to bed.'

"Will didn't have much to say when he came in for breakfast after doing his morning chores. As he sat down to his pancakes and bacon Tildy noticed that his face was as long as a daisy churn, but she knew better than to comment.

"Will was still mad about the hens. But that wasn't the worst of it. Somehow he had also managed to flatten a rear tire on the tractor and shoot the headlights out of his pickup which he'd parked behind the henhouse so the boys wouldn't run into it with the snowmobiles. And still he didn't get the fox.

"Will was almost through his breakfast when the boys came to the table. Kenny was the last to sit down. 'How ya doin' this morning, Gramps? Sleep well?' Will glared at him.

"'You just watch your smart mouth, sonny,' Will replied. 'And when are you going to take that durn lookin' thing out of your ear?'"

Listening to Nat's story, Ron Harley laughed until the tears flowed.

Then he whisked the hairs from around Nat Freewater's neck, dusted it with talcum and removed the apron from Nat's shoulders. Nat got to his feet, dropped three dollars into the cigar box where Ron kept his change, said 'so long' and walked off up the street.

After Nat Freewater left, Ron picked Marlin Shaw a little. "How old would you say Nat was?"

"Has to be gettin' on for 90."

"Jeez, I wouldn't mind being in that good a shape when I'm 90."

"Nat was quite a scout when he was a young feller..."

"Yes?"

"Had the busiest pecker in the county at one time. His wife had a whole slew of kids and still he found time to get out and around. He used to sell for one of them companies, Raleigh's, I think it was. Everything from horse liniment to Lydia Pinkham's. They used to say about Lydia Pinkham's, it was a tonic for women, that there was 'a baby in every bottle.' Nat must a sold a hell of a lot of it. Of course, he did some pretty good advertising for it. At one time or another he put half a dozen women around here up the stump."

"How did you find out?"

"No trouble finding out. The kids looked jest like him. Blue-green eyes, black hair, square jaw. They always said the kid fathers itself. And in Nat's case that was sure true."

"Husbands must have been delighted when they found out."

"You know, that's the funny thing. I don't recall one woman being thrown out when the new kid didn't match the others. Maybe it was pride, or the husband just didn't want to know. Or maybe he just accepted the kid and went along."

"That would take some doing."

"I don't know about that. Men came back from the war. They'd had their fun overseas. Couldn't say much if they came home and found a family addition, now could they? Anyway, there was one case I heard about, that was a little different. Seems one of Nat's daughters went away to work and she hooked up with this young feller from the next county. They went for each other in a big way. When she brought him home to introduce him to Nat and his wife, Nat nearly had a heart attack. He'd fathered the boy on one of his many trips when he was a salesman. He tried to talk the girl out of marrying this young fellow, but she wouldn't listen. Nat went to see old Doc Bartley, and told him the problem. I don't know what Nat had on the old Doc--but I hear tell the Doc did abortions for the upper crust. Maybe it was that. Anyways, he gave Nat something to give the girl, something that made her vomit and gave her a hell of a pain in the stomach. When she complained of dizziness, Nat took her straight to Doc

Bartley. Doc said it was appendicitis and he'd have to operate. Well, he might have given her an abortion, but it's for sure he tied her tubes. Fixed it so she would never have children."

"Why didn't he just tell her she couldn't marry him?"

"Guess he figured they'd probably already been together that way. Like father, like son, you know..."

"Did the daughter ever find out?"

"Don't know. They went off to live in the States, somewhere in California, I think."

HOUSE ON OLD BARK ROAD

Fitzhenry White, 102, lived with his grandson Clayton Anderson and Clay's wife Mavis. This day he had a visitor. Dean Booker had dropped by. Mavis served tea and date squares to the two old men and left them to talk. Fitzhenry's hearing was poor, so Dean spoke up. After general comments about weather, crops and politics, they began reminiscing about the old days.

"Fitz, do you recall ever hearing about the haunted house out on the old Bark Road?" said Dean.

"I do," said Fitz. "It was the young folk who first learned that the house was haunted. It was around 1913. The place had only been abandoned a few months when a bunch of us boys decided to sneak in and have a look around." Dean sat back and listened as Fitz told the story:

The house was two-storey wooden structure, with gable windows on the west side. At one time it had been painted white but it had weathered to a soft gray. It sat back from the road, down a long lane lined by maple trees. In the yard was a huge lilac bush and a cherry tree. On one side, between the house and the road, was an orchard which yielded a variety of apples. On the other side was a vegetable garden all grown over with weeds.

What we noticed first was that nothing had been taken when the people who owned it had left. There were curtains at the windows. Plates and cups were on the kitchen table. The kindling was laid in the stove. A couple of coats still hung on a nail behind the scullery door. Patchwork quilts covered the beds. Yet over all was the musty smell of damp and mildew.

We weren't inside the house for more than a few minutes when the wailing began, followed by scuffling noises that ended in the sound of something falling. We took off like scalded cats.

As time went on, rumours got around. Hoboes passing through talked of this place as they built fires for warmth near the railway siding. Children on their way to school were frightened out of their wits by the yelling and the screams of pain emanating from the empty house. In the silence that would follow, the children said they felt that the house was watching them as they ran towards the safety of the school.

Word continued to spread. Around 1922, Nat Freewater and his wife and another young couple went there on a Sunday ride and stopped to see the house. With a team of horses and the rubber-tired wagon, the trip took a couple of hours.

They drove in the Old Bark Road, left the wagon and the team of horses tied to a fence near the rock pile just south of the house, and walked up the path to the door. It was already ajar, so they stepped inside. Nat was leading the way with the other couple following and Nat's wife--I forget her name now--bringing up the rear.

On the left side of the front hall was a living-room, on the right side, a smaller room which could have been a bedroom and, further to the back, a kitchen and pantry and a shed. Upstairs, there was ....

Well, nobody ever really found out, because as soon as she stepped inside the front hall, Nat's wife happened to glance up. Over the stairwell above her head was an open trap door. Something there was watching her. Whatever it was moved and suddenly there was a great commotion up there for just a few seconds. Her screams pierced the air.

Nat told me about it later. He said: "You know, during the First Great War, I survived the battle fields of Ypes, Mons, and Vimy Ridge with whiz-bangs whistling through the air and men falling all around me, and I thought I'd learned to control fear. But when the wife shrieked, I jerked around, grabbed her, and leaped for the door. The other couple were fast on our heels."

Nat always said he didn't believe in ghosts and, after everyone's heart stopped pounding, he told his wife she had probably seen a bird or something through the trap door. In any event, they got back in the wagon, drove home, and never went back.

But there's always the curious. Through the years, when families drove by that house, even babes in arms would shudder and cry uncontrollably and older children huddled close together.

Well, the Depression of the Dirty Thirties came and, one by one, houses in that area were abandoned as folks searched for work across the country. Forest began to reclaim the meadows.

After the Second War, there were still a few open fields. The ruins of those old houses, the remnants of old barns and outbuildings, were still standing, but the only people who went near them were hunters and trappers. Occasionally hunters would report that from one of the ruins on the Old Bark Road, moans and screams could be heard, and when you went near there, you always felt eyes watching you.

Now, this is all hearsay, but around 1850, there was a village of about ten families near the Gibson Stream. People first came into the area around 1783 and it was settled by the soldiers of Delancy's Brigade when they were given land grants along the valley.

I've heard it told that one of the first families to move there arrived in dead of winter, armed only with an axe and a buck saw. They cleaned the snow away from a space, cut trees, and using the banked snow as a ramp, they rolled the logs into place to build a cabin in which they survived that first bitter season. Later they cut window holes and covered them with deer hides.

Before the First World War, thousands of orphaned children came here from Great Britain, and they were parcelled out by the welfare office to people around the area. Whoever wanted two or three could have them. They were called the home children. Most of the children were 10, 12 or 14. Some were a little older. A lot of the families who took the children just took them in as unpaid labourers. The children were put to work washing dishes, scrubbing floors, milking cows, cleaning stables, carrying wood, or whatever chores had to be done. They were used like slaves, many reported later. All sorts of abuse occurred. Whippings were commonplace. And worst of all, I'd guess, was the psychological pain they endured, for the home children were looked down on by the members of the families who took them in.

In those days people got away with anything, especially with children. Because these children had no one to complain to, many looked on them as little more than domestic animals, one of the home children told me many years later. Dreadful things went on. Some had no proper clothing and lived in appalling conditions. The occasional child was given decent clothes and sent to school, but most were not.

At the head of the Gibson Stream, Doc Bartley had a hunting camp, and each fall he took a few people out with him to go camping. One year I went along just for the hell of it. Hunting season started September 15. Since we always did a lot of tramping, each of us carried a blanket and a ground sheet and if night fell when we were a distance from the camp, we slept right on the ground.

We went up across this field this night, and lay down on the ground beside the remnants of the old house. There was an old barn still standing. You could see shafts of moonlight through the boards on the walls, as the moon rose in the sky.

We were always looking for deer's eyes and during the night, one of the other hunters gave me a nudge and said, "I saw a set of eyes over there, right over those rocks." I looked over and said, "that's a rock pile." Doc Bartley said, "Yes, but under that is an old well." Then Doc Bartley told us about the haunted house.

The story was that the woman who lived in that house took in orphaned children, and she used to beat them unmercifully. In a fit of rage one day, she picked up a club and beat one boy to death. She and her husband then threw the body down the well and before the day was out, they filled the well with rocks. The next morning, they hauled more rocks and made a pile on top, and after that they got their water from the spring where they watered the cattle. However, within two weeks they sold their cattle and left. No one saw them go.

The sheriff was the law in those days, and months would pass before he made his circuit. Those who had suspicions of what happened didn't want to get involved and they kept their mouths shut. Nobody really thought anything about it. After all it was only one of the home children. They looked on beating about the same as someone shooting a moose out of season. By the time the sheriff got around to asking questions, no one would tell him anything.

Why did no one ever dig up the well, and see what was under it? Nobody knows. It has been over 90 years since the boy went in the well, so it is doubtful any evidence could be found today. Those who perpetrated the crime disappeared, and everyone who ever set foot in the house has since passed on--of natural causes, as far as I know.

Dean Booker glanced at the clock. "Say, look at the time. I must be getting home. Janet will be wondering what ever happened to me."

"Come in again, Dean. It's kind a nice to reminisce a little."

"I'll do that. So long, now."

ELECTION TIME

It was election time in Cedar Springs. The polls were being held at the Women's Institute Hall. It was past six o'clock and farmers who had been in the fields all day had had an early supper and come to the hall to vote. Standing around outside smoking and talking were Marlin Shaw, Dean Booker, Zeke Hardlow, Archie Fox, John Webster, Will Cranston, Ron Goodall, Roy Potter and Allison Boughan. The men exchanged remarks on the lateness of the season and their prospects for a decent crop. They talked about the price of cattle and they talked about the recent firearms regulations.

All of the men standing around kept guns on their property, usually three--a 12-gauge shotgun, a 30-30 rifle and a .22. They'd learned to shoot from their own fathers and most of them applied for a moose license in the fall just to get an excuse to go hunting.

Moose, bear and deer hunting stories were told and retold at these events. They talked of the danger in handling guns, and that you had to know what you were doing. You also have to know what you are shooting at.

"Lotsa moose around these days," said Marlin Shaw.

"Darn things are a hazard on the road at night," said Dean Booker. "You really have to watch for them."

"That's right," said Ron Goodall. "I read that there had been 235 accidents in New Brunswick alone where people had run into moose. I've seen a couple of the cars afterwards. Totalled."

John Webster glanced over at Roy Potter and then cleared his throat: "Well, I guess it's pretty safe to tell a little moose story on Will here." All the men went silent. Will Cranston turned and looked at John, grinning a little and wondering what was coming next.

"This is going back a bit, oh, maybe 60 years. At that time moose weren't that plentiful around here and it was against the law to shoot one out of season, same as it is now. Anyway, one morning I was sitting at the breakfast table and the wife was standing at the stove cooking pancakes. She looked up across the field and there was a moose right out in plain sight. She hollered and I jumped up, and I grabbed the .303, loaded it and ran out the back door. I crouched down and watched. The moose strolled along, but I couldn't get a good shot at it because it was right in line with the Potters' barn. After a little, it started walking again. The first shot went wild. The next one hit it just under the ear. Well sir, the moose dropped right there. I stepped up to it and slit its throat.

"I figured the Potters had to have heard the shot so I emptied the shells and went back into the house and put the rifle away. Then I walked across the field. Roy was just finished milking. I said, Roy, I got a moose down there in the field. Half of it is yours, if you'll give me a hand dressing her out.

"Now the thing is, it was a few days before moose season. and I didn't know how far the sound of those shots had gone. Anyway, Roy grabbed his hunting knife and down he came. I'd hauled the moose in onto the barn floor. Well, it didn't take us long. We skinned and cleaned it and buried the guts. Then we shared it up. Now I don't know what Roy did with his share. Meanwhile my wife packed our moose meat in sealer jars and set it on to simmer. Took all day to process it. But by suppertime it was finished.

"Well, sir, that evening a neighbour from down the road showed up and told us that the word was out, somebody had shot a moose. I never let on a thing, but after he left I went to bed and got to thinking. Somehow I had to get rid of the moose meat.

"The next morning, right after breakfast, I went out to the barn and scattered new straw around the barn floor. I'd salted the hide the day before and put it out of sight. Then I hooked up the team and dragged the plow around. I'd been meaning to plow that north field anyway. Well, I plowed a furrow and went back to the house. And while I turned the furrow, my wife laid those sealer jars of moose meat end to end right under the furrow.

"I worked away until the sun was almost overhead and it was comin' on to noon. By then I was gettin' a little gant.

"I unhooked the plow, walked the horses back to the barn, watered them and then, just as I was going in to dinner, the sheriff drove in. "Good day, Sir," I says. "Just in time for dinner." Then I called in to my wife. "We got company. Put another plate on for the sheriff."

"She put another plate on. Then we all sat down to eat. When he was finishing his pie, the Sheriff said, 'John, you never heard anything about some shots being fired out this way recently?'

"Don't recall that I did, exactly." I said. "But then I likely wouldn't have paid much attention. Young fellows shooting porcupines, maybe. Good bounty on them these days. Why, the young fellows have cleaned up on the porcupine around here. Darn nuisance that they are. Quills in the dog's noses. Quills in the cattle. Chew up the harnesses. Darn nuisance, porcupines."

"After a while the sheriff got away and the wife and I kind of shook hands with ourselves.

"Two weeks went by. I finished plowing that north field and set to work on the one next to the pasture. And then we got an early snowfall. Early and heavy, lasted about three days.

"About the second morning after the snow fell the wife was cooking dinner and she happened to look out to see a team coming. It was Will Cranston. He was driving that lovely pair of bays and he had them hooked to the long sled and he was after grain for his hens. I got up and looked out the window and there came Will, one runner of the long sled jammed right down in that one furrow where the moose meat was buried. Well, the wife was fit to be tied. I cussed and swore and went out to the barn. Anyway, she invited Will in for coffee and doughnuts and by that time I'd cooled down and got philosophical. I helped Will load the grain and said, 'so long.' Well, by crikey, that time Will drove out around the road. After a while I went up to the field just to see if he might have missed one or two jars of moose meat. But, nosiree. Every jar was mashed to smithereens."

Roy Potter laughed at the story, shook his head and said, "I had no idea you lost your moose meat, John. My soul, we had moose meat all winter long. Didn't even bother to kill a beef. Now, I'm feeling that I was kind of unneighbourly."

"John, John," said Will Cranston. "Ya' should a' shot me. I guess I figured it was easier going straight from the Potters' yard to yours instead of going out around the road. Yes, sir, you should've shot me. I'd understood."

SUICIDE

William and Mathilda Cranston were heartbroken. Their grandson Kenny, age 22, the apple of their eye, the joy of their old age, their hope for the future, was dead. A suicide.

Kenny had been attending the Halifax Art College. He was in his final year and just days away from graduation when he took his own life. The last time Kenny had been in Cedar Springs was during the winter holidays when he and three college friends had stayed with the Cranstons.

"Oh Lord, Tildy," said Will, holding onto his wife after hearing the news. "Oh Lord, and all the time he was here I jawed about that durned earring he was wearing. Should have kept my mouth shut." Mathilda was too stunned to reply.

"What happened, do you think? He seemed in good spirits while he was here. Didn't seem to have a care in the world. In fact, that kind of worried me, that he just didn't seem to care about anything. Was he doing okay in college? Was that the problem? Can't have been. Why Kenny had the whole world in front of him."

Mathilda spoke: "Such a pretty baby. Of all the grandchildren he was my favourite. I could only admit that to you Will, but you know he spent more time with us in those early years than he did with his mom and dad."

"Do you think I was too hard on him, Tildy? Not allowing smoking in the house. Asking him to show a little respect for his elders. Did I treat him like a kid?"

"Oh Will. He knew you loved him. He thought the world of you. It had to have been something else. I can't imagine what."

As word of their grandson's death circulated through Cedar Springs, the women in the community started cooking. Before the day was out the kitchen and pantry of the Cranston house was filled with baking. Brown bread, lemon and coconut pies, date-nut squares and more. One neighbour had even sent over a large roasting pan full of steaming cabbage rolls.

Tildy was a basket case. Everything confused her. She couldn't remember what she was supposed to do and was grateful when Nola Wickens arrived to help. Nola Wickins, who worked as a homemaker, had no regular jobs lined up for the day, so as soon as she heard the news she drove to the Cranstons, rolled up her sleeves and got things organized.

Nola greeted the callers, found room on the counter or in the fridge for the offerings and made tea. Tildy and Will accepted condolences, Will sometimes weeping unashamedly while Tildy nodded and thanked people for coming. Nola made a list of all the food brought in, and by whom, and wrote down a description of each plate, Pyrex pan or Tupperware dish, so that those could be returned later.

Kenneth Cranston was found dead Sunday morning, August 7, in the house he shared with three other students in Dartmouth. He had hanged himself.

That weekend Kenny's roommates were all away. One went home to his folks in Saint John. One stayed the weekend with his girlfriend and the third went on a hiking expedition. The owner of the rooming house lived near Citadel Hill. Thinking the boys would be away for the weekend, he decided to go in, look around and see if any repairs were needed. Finding Kenny's body almost stopped his heart. He called the police. The smell was vile.

One by one, as Kenny's roommates returned to the rooming house, they were questioned by police. Everybody that remotely knew Kenny was questioned, but no explanation for the suicide could be found.

The coroner's inquest said death by asphyxiation. An autopsy revealed a lethal amount of drugs and alcohol in Kenny's system. Where he got the drugs was not known. He wasn't under doctor's care and took no prescriptions that anybody had been aware of. From what the landlord told reporters Kenny had obviously planned his suicide in advance and set it up so it could not fail. In the rooming house was a wet bar in one end of the rec room. The wet bar was hidden by a sheet of fake cherrywood on the frame that reached from the counter top to the ceiling. It was designed to lift from the bottom and attach to a hook in the ceiling. Kenny used the hook for a second purpose. He attached a strong nylon cord to the hook on the ceiling. He lined up several bottles of Lithium, Xanax, Seconal and something else. He placed two bottles of scotch on the counter. Then he turned on the stereo system to a rock station and sat down on a bar stool. He tied the bottom end of the cord around his neck and began washing the pills down with Scotch. When his landlord found him, all the pills were gone. "He'd finished the first 26 oz. bottle of Scotch and was half way through the second," said the landlord, "when he passed out. The weight of his head falling tightened the rope until he slid sideways and the stool went out from under him. He must have died Friday night."

At the barber shop in Cedar Springs everybody had an opinion on Kenny's death and on suicide in general.

"Obviously he didn't intend to fail," said Ron Harley the barber, as he gave the pharmacist Lance McElvy a trim.

"No, so many would-be suicides are failures," McElvy agreed.

"Remember a few years ago there was this guy shot this woman, then stuck a gun in his mouth and shot off half his face, but continued to live?"

"Yes," said Marlin Shaw. "I just forget her name now, but there was that Fredericton woman, Marlene somebody, who rammed her car into a cement bridge abutment and lived. But she is paralysed. Has to have everything done for her."

"And there are many others who take drug overdoses and live," said McElvy, "brain damaged, little more than walking corpses. No, this Kenny Cranston knew exactly what he was doing."

"Well, you hear about suicide on the Indian reserves all the time. Every time you pick up a paper you read where another Indian kid takes his life."

"A guy came in here the other day for a haircut, a Torontonian, he was holidaying with some local folks," said Ron Harley. "A man in his early sixties, I'd guess. He was a talker. He told me he did a lot of dope when he was younger, all kinds including snorting cocaine and mainlining heroine. Occasionally he would freak out, topple over the edge of sanity, become violent, and wind up in psychiatric wards."

"Sounds like he could have been dangerous," said McElvy.

"Oh, he was clean, hadn't taken anything in years, but he told me that one time in the Sixties he went to California. Travelled all around there. Hung out at Haight-Ashbury. Didn't have much money but he was bunking with some other fellows in a fleabag hotel on the second floor, drinking 75-cent magnums of California wine, and playing poker. The hotel, instead of a fire escape, had a long rope tied to the heat radiator in case of fire. They'd been drinking for several days. And then one of the men quit playing, and sat making hanging knots in the rope while the rest of them continued playing poker. He said he suddenly heard a flub, flub, flub, as the rope went out the window. And his first thoughts were: 'Shit. Now we will have to get the police in and I am here without a passport. And I had a pair of jacks, too.'

"And then they all trooped down stairs to investigate. They found the man still standing on his broken heels, with the rope still around his neck. He had tied it too long."

Ron's story had got Lance McElvy laughing so hard he was shaking. Ron had to hold up with the clippers until he got himself under control. Marlin Shaw started chuckling. But Lance's laugh was so infectious that Ron, in fits of laughter, was bent almost double.

"The poor simple son-of-a-bitch," said Marlin Shaw. "Couldn't do anything right, now could he?" Marlin's remark made the other men laugh even harder. Marlin pulled out his handkerchief and mopped the tears from his face. That was the point where Will Cranston opened the door and stepped inside. All three men were startled into silence. Soberly, Ron

Harley finished Lance McElvy's hair, whisked the trimmings off his neck and removed the apron.

McElvy paid Ron for the haircut, nodded at Marlin and Will and went back to the pharmacy.

"This must be a real bad time for you Will," said Marlin Shaw. "Kenny was a fine boy. You must have been proud of him."

"Yes," said Will. "There ain't no rhyme or reason. That's the thing. Nobody knows why. He never left a note. He was popular with the girls as far as I know and the College says he was a good student, would have graduated in two weeks, even had a job lined up. What the hell happened?"

Listening to the old man's grief, it struck Ron Harley that in all the 40 or more years he had known Will Cranston, that was the first time he'd ever heard him swear.

"Thought I'd better get a haircut," said Will. "Kenny's funeral is tomorrow."

OLD FRIENDS

Nola Wickins liked being married. Her husband, Basil Wickens, was a salesman for Cressman Bearings and spent his days on the road. This gave Nola plenty of time to look after the house and do some volunteer work. By 11 a.m. most days her house was spic and span. Nola's cookie jar was always full, her larder laden with peach, strawberry, raspberry, apple preserves, Lady Ashburnham and sweet mixed pickles and various other goods which she canned in season.

Then one morning she woke and all her children were gone; two were already in university and the youngest, a computer nut from the time he was four, had left to take advance computer technology at Radio College and Arts in Toronto. That same evening her husband came home and, instead of sitting down to dinner, poured himself a scotch and soda. Then he said: "Nola. I want a divorce."

Nola felt she had been broadsided. She hadn't seen this coming. She'd always kept a clean house, prepared good nutritious meals. Their sex life had been sporadic but adequate as far as she was concerned. She'd never turned him away. Now she was speechless.

"Did you hear me?" her husband said again. "I want a divorce."

"Why?"

"I'm not happy here. I haven't been happy for a long time. I found someone else and we fell in love. And I want out."

"Just like that?"

"Just like that."

"What will we tell the children?"

"The truth. They are old enough to be on their own. But right now I am going to pack and leave." In less than a quarter of an hour Nola was alone in her beautiful home with its fresh drapes, clean windows, full larder, polished tables, and cupboards full of carefully folded linens. She got up, turned off the warming oven, put her coat on and went outside to the back garden. Her mind felt numb. She noticed that the roses needed work. So she slipped her gardening gloves on, took the shears and nipped off the dead roses. In a few minutes she heard her husband close the trunk of his car. Then she heard the car door slam.

The rest of the summer Nola alternated between rage, jealousy, despair, disappointment and fear. Fear of the future. How would she spend her time? All she'd ever done was housework. Her husband had been fair as far as money went, sharing what they had and leaving her the house. But university and college for the three children had taken a big chunk out of their savings and Nola felt she could use some extra income. She made up her mind to get a job. Housework she was good at, and housework she could surely find.

In her usual fashion she forged ahead with her plans. Soon she was looking after three houses and working part-time at the Forest Glen Manor. Each of her housekeeping jobs was different. One couple ran a family business, and two days a week the wife went in to look after the books. They had school-age children. Nola would go to work at 7 a.m., get the kids off to school, change the beds and start bread. By the end of the school day the kids came home to a sandwich or cookies and milk and she supervised their activities until the parents got home. Another house belonged to school teachers. No children. But the house really needed thorough weekly cleaning. Her third house belonged to John Webster whose wife had died a year previously.

This day, as always, she went in early and prepared breakfast. Mr. Webster finished his toast and bacon, set his coffee cup aside and, pushing his chair back from the table, inquired what plans Nola had for the day.

"Housekeeping, errands, some book-work," she said. "Why do you ask?"

"I've got a hankering to see Adam Craig, my old neighbour who's down at Forest Glen Manor."

"Oh yes, I know Mr. Craig," said Nola. "His wife's been dead, what? A year? She had a stroke six years ago. He did his best to look after her. But all those years of bathing, dressing, feeding, lifting, and pushing her wheelchair wore him out. And he's what? 85?"

"Thereabouts."

At that stage of his life John Webster rarely suggested an outing in the car, preferring to sit in the big chair on the sun porch where he could read, look out over his orchard, fields and woodlot, see the passing traffic on the road, or watch for visitors entering the driveway. Throughout the day, when he wasn't in the sun porch, he often napped on the kitchen couch with the cat curled up on his chest. As Nola stacked the dishes and carried them to the pantry, she mentally revised her schedule.

"Well, I was planning to run a few errands in Woodstock anyway," Nola said. "What time would you like to go?"

"What time do they have visiting hours?"

"Oh, I think any time after breakfast. They are pretty flexible."

"Then let's go now. We'll take my car."

Nola shut the drafts and checked the dampers on the wood stove, returned the milk to the fridge, ran a damp cloth over her face, put on her jacket, gathered her purse and car keys and went out to the garage. The

Webster's old brown Dodge started easily. She let it warm up for a few minutes, then backed out towards the house and opened the passenger door. Meanwhile John Webster was still struggling with the buttons on his cardigan. "Ah, these old fingers are stiff," he remarked.

"Let me do that," Nola offered. She quickly did up the buttons and helped him into his coat. Then she found his hat and gloves and steadied him down the steps and into the car.

The roads were good and John Webster commented on this one and that one who had once lived in various houses along the way. People whom Nola vaguely remembered and some who were before her time were often at the front of his memory these days. Half listening, she planned her route. She would drop Mr. Webster off at the nursing home and while he was visiting with Adam Craig she could get the shopping done.

They were lucky when they arrived at Forest Glen to find a parking space near the entrance. Remembering that the door of the manor was kept locked for the safety of the residents, Nola took Mr. Webster's arm, accompanied him to the front door, read the code directions, pressed the appropriate buttons, and heard the lock click open. They passed through a common room, where several residents, strapped to their chairs, hunched over their trays. One or two gazed up at them as they passed. Nola smiled at them. John Webster nodded. A woman with tangled hair and missing dentures was busy disrobing, exposing flaps of old yellow breast, and yelling, "Get me out of here. Where is my daughter? I want to go home. Won't someone help me?"

On the other side of the room, a man turned from the window and, addressing the shouting woman, said: "Ah shaddup, ya old fool. Yer annoying everybody." Another resident watched the half-naked woman, shook her finger and snapped: "Dirty. Dirty old thing!"

When John Webster and Nola entered Adam Craig's room, they found him sleeping. His cheeks were sunken. The skin of his face, shaped by skull beneath, was pink and paper thin, with veins visibly tracing across his forehead and temples. John sat down in the chair, saying, "I won't disturb him, I'll just sit here and rest a while. You go on ahead and I'll wait here."

"Well, if you're sure you'll be okay," Nola said. "I'll try not to be too long."

Back in the car Nola hurried to the bank and to the post office, dropped the prescriptions at the drug store and hiked on out to Sobey's where she purchased the items on her list. She also picked up a small box of chocolate, which she thought John could leave on Adam's table. She doubted Adam would have much appetite for chocolate, but he might like to pass it around to his favourite nurses.

All in all Nola was gone less than an hour and pulled back into the same parking space she'd used previously. She locked the car and hurried into the manor.

When she came to Adam's room, she could see that John had moved his chair over close to Adam's bed. Someone had lowered Adam's bed and rolled up the head so that he was at eye-level with John. They were deep in conversation. Nola took the opportunity to scamper down the hall and speak to residents Nellie Crabbe and Joyce Antworth, old friends whom she'd too long neglected. After short visits with them, Nola walked back to the lounge, picked up a Reader's Digest, and returned to a chair just inside Adam's door.

Both men were deaf, John more so than Adam. After a few moments Nola heard Adam say: "John, we've known each other for over 80 years."

"Yes, Adam," said John. "Do you remember the ball games we played in Strong's field? I could always hit pretty good, but you were fast. You could catch anything."

"Yes, baseball. A long, long time ago... You were always the better dancer."

"Oh, I liked to shake a leg," John said, obviously enjoying the compliment. Then rubbing a hand over his bald head, he grinned, saying, "but, Adam, the girls all went for you...that fine head of hair. And you still have it. Me, I've got more face to wash, less hair to comb..."

"You raised a big family, John."

"Six of them. May and I were lucky, I guess. Times were hard, especially after the fire, but they were all healthy. They're all married now, except the youngest. Fourteen grandchildren, at last count."

"Blanche and I weren't blessed with children. But Edwin, Blanche's nephew, lived with us all his life, you know. Guess you could say we raised him. Did his best to look after us and his wife, too. Then Edwin had that heart attack. Two years ago, now. Who'd have thought God would take him before me?"

"You always drove a nice car, Adam. I always admired the fine cars you had over the years. Never felt I could afford anything too fancy."

"Yes, Blanche wanted the best. She played the church organ for 36 years, you know."

"Yes, yes she did," John agreed. "You, Will Cranston, Nat Freewater and I made up a pretty good choir along with the women. Sang at a lot of funerals. And Blanche always played."

"Yes, a lot of funerals over the years. Most all our friends are gone now, John. God has taken them home."

"That's so. But, I still can hear those women singing *Beulah Land*. Two of them were altos and yet they could hit those high notes just as true. And Nat, remember Nat?... couldn't he warble?"

Both men were silent as they remembered.

Adam Craig was a devout man, a professed Christian who lived by the golden rule. John Webster was an honest man, a kind man, and as good a living man as any around but John harboured doubts about the Old Testament God and he didn't put much stock in an afterlife. Still, John respected Adam's beliefs, and would do nothing to shake his faith. As if reading his mind Adam said: "You've been a good living man, John."

"Oh, 'bout average. Always tried to keep my word, be a decent citizen."

"Your promise has always been gold, John. You and May never turned anyone away. She must have fed half the people in this community."

"Yes, she did that all right. I chose her well."

"Have you made it right with the Lord, John?"

"As right as I can, Adam," John replied.

The two men went on to talk of matched horses they had both owned, community events 60 years past, house parties they had attended, church suppers and basket socials. As Nola eavesdropped on their conversation she picked up the Reader's Digest and read "Campus Humour" and "Life's Like That," and attempted to increase her "word power."

Then she heard Adam say, "John, you know we've been friends since we were boys."

"Yes, Adam, that's right."

"We've been neighbours all our lives, went to the same church, lived through the hard times and the good."

"Yes, Adam, we share a lot of memories."

There was a short silence, then Nola heard Adam say: "You know, John....in all the years we have been neighbours, there's never been a cross word between us."

"No, Adam. There hasn't."

Adam leaned back into his pillows. John, seeing that Adam was tiring, began to struggle to his feet. Nola dropped the magazine, and gave John a hand up.

"Thanks for coming in, John," Adam said. "I'll see you again--if not in this life, then in the next."

"So long, old friend." The men shook hands and John Webster turned to go.

"Ready?" Nola said.

"Ready."

They made their way back to the parking lot. Nola buckled them in and started the car. At home John took off his hat and coat and hung them over the woodbox. Then he made for the couch where the old black and white cat waited. Nola carried in the bags of shopping and, as she put the food away, she came across the chocolate she had meant to leave with Adam. She set it aside and went on getting lunch prepared. After a short nap, John Webster got up, washed his hands and sat down to eat.

"This is good, Nola. I don't know what I'd do without you these days. How you manage to get this old house shipshape and get good meals too, I don't know."

"Oh, it's nothing, really," said Nola, obviously pleased with the compliment. "I enjoy housework. I know that sounds crazy in this day and age when most women want to go out and have a big high-powered career. But I like housekeeping and I need the exercise."

"Well, I want you to know that your efforts are appreciated." Nola positively beamed.

As soon as Nola had John Webster settled in his favourite chair, she got busy with the washing and ironing. She was just pulling a casserole out of the oven when the phone rang. "Want me to answer that, Mr. Webster?"

"Yes, Nola. If you would."

Nola said hello and identified herself. Then said, "Oh dear. Oh dear. Is that right? Oh dear. Well, I'll tell him. Thank you for calling. Goodbye."

Turning to John Webster she said that Adam Craig had just passed away. The funeral would be held Friday at 2 p.m. from the Catelle Funeral Home.

John Webster nodded, then sat silently in his chair for a while. After that he picked up his paper and began to read.

As Nola told Grace in the Green Lantern later, John Webster didn't react to the news at all, like she figured he would. "It was almost as if he already knew," she said.

WIDOW WOMAN

At 11: p.m. the dog barked. Alice Grauhman awoke from a sound sleep, sat up and looked out her bedroom window to see Art Elliot's pickup in the yard. She shoved her feet into her slippers, pulled on her house coat, walked downstairs and opened the door. As Art's huge frame filled the doorway, the smell of booze hit her in the face.

It wasn't smart of Alice to let Art in, but she'd had a hard week, starting with the death of her husband Earl in a snowmobile accident, followed by a police investigation, a house full of people, a wake and funeral. Then earlier in the day, after committing the sin of having her hair cut, she had been shunned at the church she had attended for 18 years.

"Art? What's the matter?" said Alice. Earl and Art had been buddies since Earl got out of the army. Automatically she turned to the sink, filled the tea kettle and set it on the stove. As she took cups down from the cupboard, Art stepped up to her from the back, put his arms around her and groped for her breasts, Surprised, she spun to face him, still holding the cups above her head.

"What are you doing?"

"I thought you might like a little company, seein' as how Earl's gone." Alice looked at this leering lout, his face flushed with alcohol, his gut hanging out over his belt, and she started to laugh.

"What's so funny 'bout that? I could use a little lovin' and you pro'lly need some, so here I am." Art reached for her again, but this time Alice dodged him. She put the cups back in the cupboard, tightened the belt of her house-coat and said:

"I think you'd better leave." The dog, hearing, anger in her voice, growled low in its throat.

"Aw, come on, Alice. Be a sport."

"Leave now, or I'll set the dog on you," said Alice opening the front door.

Art pulled himself together and walked out the door. "S'OK. You ain't a natural woman anyway. Earl told me. 'S why he always had a girlfriend."

Alice banged the door shut and locked it. She was furious and yet felt sullied to find that Earl's best friend would think she was available to anybody. And then to say that Earl had had a girlfriend. He was bastard in many ways, she knew that, but she'd never thought he was unfaithful. She walked back up the stairs and got into bed. Wide awake now, she let her thoughts wander back over the past week.

She had been walking through the hall on her way upstairs to bed when a police cruiser had pulled into her yard. Two RCMP officers, a man and a woman, had come to the door.
"Mrs. Grauhman?"
"Yes?"
"I'm sorry to disturb you this late. But we have to tell you: your husband has had an accident." Alice looked from one to the other.
Then the female officer said, "Mrs. Grauhman, could we come in for a few minutes?"
"Yes, of course. What happened?"
"We haven't been able to complete our investigation but as far as we know, your husband lost control of his snowmobile and was thrown."
"He just bought the snowmobile yesterday," said Alice. "Is he hurt? Where is he?"
"He's dead, ma'am. Killed instantly. Struck a tree. Looks like his neck was broken."
"Oh."
"The body is at the Woodstock hospital. Think you are up to going down there? We'll drive you and bring you back."

The hospital was busy, with a skeleton staff running to and fro. Lights flashed on and off. Codes barked from the intercom. There'd been two traffic accidents within hours of each other. In one the "Jaws of Life" had been needed to remove one of the victims. Due to a recent cutback, one whole ward of the hospital was closed down, but Earl's body on a gurney had been covered with a sheet and placed in the first room of the empty ward.
Alice walked over to the gurney. Except for his eyes being slightly open, Alice could see no marks on his face. She wondered if he was really dead.
As if hearing her thoughts, the female police officer said, "Yes, Mrs. Grauhman. It's hard to believe. He was pronounced DOA the minute he arrived at the hospital. But he died instantly when he struck the tree. Is this your husband?"
"That's Earl. But I don't see, I mean how do you...?
"The body has been kept cold, Mrs. Grauhman. He was found by the driver of a transport, who saw the snowmobile cross the TransCanada ahead of him. The snowmobile was going very fast. It's likely that your

husband lost control. It fishtailed and turned over, throwing him against a tree. The trucker contacted us. We were at the scene with minutes, but your husband was already dead."

"Oh."

"Now, how do you want to handle the funeral? Perhaps I can call a funeral director for you."

"Well, I ...yes, I guess....Cedar Springs." The male RCMP said to the other officer, "I'll handle that. You help Mrs. Grauhman back to the cruiser. Here is his wallet. The rest of his clothes are in the bag right there."

Alice put the wallet in her purse. The officer picked up the green garbage bags containing the rest of Earl's things.

At home, Alice declined the policewoman's offer to stay with her until her family arrived. It was already three in the morning. Alice waited until 6:00 a.m. to call the children.

After the police officer left, Alice opened the garbage bag. His snowmobile outfit, his woollen sweater, shirt, pants, long underwear, socks were all there, as were his boots, mitts and goggles. Only his helmet was missing. Alice held up his trousers and felt a ring of keys jangle. She looked at the keys--one to the house, one to the pick-up, and three she had never seen before. She then took his wallet out of her handbag. In all the 28 years they had been married, she had never opened his wallet, and felt slightly furtive as she flipped through it. There were cards, kid's school pictures and a number of receipts, mainly for items purchased in the Framingham, Massachussetts area. There was also close to $6,583 in cash, including $5,000 in US funds. Alice sat staring at the money. She had never seen any denomination higher than a $100 bill and she had always handled the $5s and $10s Earl gave her for grocery money with great care, counting each penny and stretching every dollar as far as it would go. She got up, took the wallet and placed it in the cedar chest, about halfway down. She went to the bathroom and, thinking that she would have to make up beds for her children when they arrived tomorrow, she took the wallet out of the cedar chest. She then wrapped it in an old pillow case and shoved it through a hole the cat had made up under the box springs of her own bed, wedging it securely into a corner under the mattress.

For two afternoons and two evenings Alice stood at the foot of the plush gray open casket where Earl's embalmed corpse lay still, cold and unreal. It reminded her of the mannequins she'd seen at the Eaton's store in Toronto a few years ago. For most of the time Alice's son Trevor stood next to her, with her daughters Rita, Sonja and Lois, making up the receiving line. Alice accepted sympathy, nods and handshakes, as she was sniffed at, hugged and patted. Her back ached. Her legs ached. Her teeth ached. Her glasses kept slipping down her nose. Faces moved in and out of her vision like tides, while the smell of carnations and mums clogged her throat. She also noted the astonishing number of people who gushed vile halitosis. Now and then she glanced at the waxy countenance of her late husband, then stood a little straighter. People, in an attempt to be kind, told her how well Earl looked. She wanted to quip: "Well, in this case, looks are deceiving," but she merely nodded.

Held at the New Christian Evangelical Tabernacle, Earl's funeral was long and, for Alice, exceptionally tedious. There were prayers, readings, and musical tributes by duets, trios and quartets. The coffin had been closed before it was brought into the church and that was a relief, except Alice had the lurking feeling that if she got up and opened the coffin, she would find it empty. Or Earl would open his eyes and grab her by the wrist and twist her arm backwards. Stony-faced, she remained in the front row, waiting patiently for it all to be over. As several old hymns were sung, Alice thought how good it would feel to get out of the clothes she was wearing, to go home and have a long hot bath. But there was still the graveside service and then the reception at the farm. Alice was glad to have her children and grandchildren, including her newest grandchild beside her. Throughout the service they sat quietly, except for Sonja's baby which fussed a little towards the end. Sonja pulled a bottle out of her bag and placed the nipple in the baby's mouth. The baby sucked contentedly for a little while, then began to hiccup. Lifting it up to her shoulder, Sonja started patting its back. At that point there was a momentary silence while the minister found his place in the text. Suddenly the baby let go a long gurgling fart. Somebody coughed and people shifted in their seats. Alice moaned. Near hysteria, she pushed her hands over her face and shook. Trevor and Sonja glanced at her. Those seated behind her mistook her laughter for weeping.

By 8: p.m., her children and grandchildren, their spouses, mates and friends, had all gone home to resume their lives. After the last of the neighbours had cleared out, after the dishes were washed and the remaining food put away, Alice sat down in the rocking chair. The dog, Skip, got up from where he was lying at the entrance, arched his back in a high upside down "U" then walked over and put his head on her knee. Alice put her hand on the dog's head, smoothed the soft fur over its ears and then leaned back. The dog slid to the floor, stretching out on its side.

She stayed in the rocking chair for over an hour. It was hard to believe that Earl was dead. Of course he had been away many nights but he always came back, and she always faced his return with excitement laced with dread. But not tonight. When her youngest daughter Lois had offered to stay over another night, Alice had refused, saying she might as well get used to being by herself.

She went upstairs, filled the bathtub with water, added bath oil, got out of her clothes and climbed into the steaming water. The old dog followed her upstairs and took up his post outside the door. Alice stayed in the tub until the water began to cool, then she climbed out and put on a fresh night-shirt. She unwound her dark hair, now well sewn with gray, brushed it and braided it loosely for the night. She slept soundly.

The following morning she got up, dressed, made scrambled eggs, toast and coffee, and after eating, sat down on the front porch. Around 8:30 am the telephone rang. At first she wasn't going to answer it, then changed her mind. It was her ex-hippie neighbour, Noreen, telling Alice that she was driving to Woodstock. "I could sure use some company," Noreen said brightly. "Want to go?"

"Well, I...no, I'd better... yes, I'd like that very much," Alice said. "What time will you be here?"

"Twenty minutes?"

"I'll be ready."

When Noreen arrived Alice, dressed in a skirt and blouse, was waiting at the door. They drove to Woodstock, commenting only on the weather and the errands Noreen hoped to accomplish, which included buying a pair of shoes. At the mall, they decided to separate and arranged to meet in one hour. Alice looked around Sobey's. There were a few good buys and bananas were on special. But there was so much food left over from the wake. She couldn't think of anything she needed, so she walked down to the Shopper's Drug Mart. Nothing she needed there, either. Then she found herself standing in the hall in front of the hairdresser's. Her eye caught a poster of the new short hair styles. She looked inside the shop. There were three chairs and they were all empty. The hairdresser smiled at her. In that split second Alice made up her mind. She walked in and asked the woman if she would have time to give her a hair cut.

"Sure do. It's a slow day. Sit right down here."

Alice sat down in the chair and the hairdresser smoothed a protective cape around her shoulders, tucking it carefully inside her collar. Glancing at Alice in the mirror she said:

"How do you want it."

"Short," Alice said.

"How short?"

"Like that," said Alice pointing to a pixie-faced teenager on the wall.

"Okay." The hairdresser unpinned Alice's heavy hair and let it fall. Then she lifted the scissors and asked again, "You're sure about this?"

"I'm sure."

"How long since you had your hair cut?"

"Thirty years."

"Man, this is a lot of hair." She started cutting, beginning on the left and working around to the right, then carefully placed each swath of hair over a chair back. After that she trimmed the remaining hair, short over Alice's ears and feathered down the back.

Alice kept her eyes shut until the hairdresser asked if she would like a little colour on it. Then she looked at herself in the mirror. The transformation was startling.

"Well, I only have a half-hour left," Alice said, glancing at the clock. "Perhaps another day?"

"Won't take but 20 minutes. We'll just put a rinse on, mask the gray a bit."

Alice had paid for her haircut and was just stepping out the door when Noreen walked past. Alice called out to her. Noreen stopped, turned and did a double take.

"Why, Alice. I hardly recognized you. It looks wonderful." Just then the hairdresser ran out with a package. "Oh, here, I've saved this for you. You may want to show it to your grandchildren." Alice looked in the box to see her long hank of hair wounded in a circle and tied with a ribbon.

"Thank you," Alice said, accepting the box.

"You're welcome," said the hairdresser. "Hope we see you again in a month or so."

"Well, now," said Noreen. "What do you say we take a run down to Global Textiles and see if they've got a new shipment in?"

"Sound's fine," said Alice. "I've never been there."

"Oh, it's a great place to shop. A thrift store. Though there are lots of new things, too. Stuff comes up from Boston, I've heard, Well, anyway, let's look around."

An hour later Alice and Noreen came out of the store carrying large shopping bags. Alice had bought three pairs of slacks, two turtleneck sweaters, a jacket and a pair of hiking boots. The clothes were wrinkled, but the slacks still had their tags and the hiking boots showed no signs of wear at all. Alice had spent less than $10. She could hardly contain her excitement. She had never worn slacks in her life.

"In celebration, I think we should stop at Colonel Sanders." said Noreen.

"Let's. I'm buying."

After her shopping spree Alice pressed her nearly new jacket, slacks and turtle-neck and, pulling a pair of Earl's white socks out of the drawer, she dressed and went for a walk up the hill. She kept moving her head around, surprised at the weightlessness.

As each day passed Alice got used to the idea of Earl being dead. She stopped shaking whenever a car drove into the yard. On Sunday she walked to church. There was a collected gasp as she sat took a seat in the middle pew where she'd always sat. People took one look at her short coloured hair and turned away. Only the young girls continued to steal glances at her during the service. Alice stayed until the last prayer, then got up and walked out of the church.

Alice Ferny grew up in Cedar Springs in the 1940s. The daughter of a farmer and a homemaker, she was the oldest in a family of five.

Along with the children of several other families Alice attended a one-room school, sometimes in her own neighbourhood or, if a teacher was not available, in the adjacent neighbourhood. Either way it was a three-mile walk.

A sensitive child, Alice had a miserable childhood. She cried a lot. Other children poked fun at her and called her stupid. Alice was 12 years old by the time an alert teacher realized that Alice was so near-sighted she couldn't see the blackboard. Until then Alice had gotten by on her memory and managed to pass into Grade 5, without ever really learning to read. At age 14 she left school to stay home and look after the younger children. Her mother was going through a bad patch. Her father had suffered a heart attack and was unable to work.

Alice preferred staying home. She was older than the other children and felt out of place in the school room. So she scrubbed and carried water and learned to cook. This was before the days of electricity, which meant there were lamps to clean and water to be carried from a pump in the front yard. She gathered eggs, milked cows, planted a garden, weeded and hoed, and took care of the others.

Meanwhile the younger children were doing better in school and when the Regional High School opened they all continued on to graduation. But not Alice.

When Alice was 15 she got noticed by Earl Grauhman, the son of an immigrant family. He was 21. Earl's schooling had been hit and miss. His parents, fresh from the old country, had worked for several farmers in different communities. The year Earl finished grade school, his father had managed to put a down payment on a farm of his own. There would be no further formal education for Earl. He was needed on the farm.

By then Earl had grown into a large, solid, stolid, hard and brutish man, with inborn anger and a sense that life would always cheat him somehow.

During the summers in the early 1950s, local farmers, after haying, allowed a field to become a baseball diamond. Farm boys and girls from around the community came out in the long summer evenings after the chores were finished, either to play baseball or to watch the games, or just to socialize. It was at these ball games that Earl met Alice. By then Alice, tall, pale-skinned, with thick dark hair, had a way of standing with her arms crossed over her breasts, as if by growing them she had done something shameful.

Earl borrowed his father's truck, and soon he was picking Alice up on the road and driving her around. That summer Earl's mother died of a ruptured appendix.

Alice had never had a boyfriend, and Earl found her ripe for the picking. They began having sex and they kept at it until Alice became pregnant.

A marriage was quickly arranged and Alice moved in with Earl, his father and two brothers and began taking care of the whole family. Then Alice had her first child, a son. Ten months later she had her second, a daughter, and 14 months after that she had a third, also a girl.

In those days there wasn't time for Alice to think about anything except keeping the children clean and fed, to keep bread baked, clothes washed and meals on the table. Fortunately, by then there was electrical power, and many of her tasks became easier. The most wonderful device Alice ever had was an electric wringer-washer, which put an end to the scrub board, nearly. She still churned all the butter, though, and washed the cream separator by hand.

Meanwhile Earl, fed up with farming and its ever-diminishing returns, joined the Army. After basic training he was shipped to Germany. Alice and her small family followed and soon she was settled in the married quarters of the army barracks. She made a few friends with other army wives, and cared for her small children, which by then included a baby girl. Earl continued in the service, often being posted to places such as Egypt where he would be gone for five or six months at a time. When he was home Earl was a good father. When the children were small he brought home treats for them. When the girls started singing and learning to play the piano, he proudly attended the concerts. He went to the games whenever Trevor played. The children looked on him with a mixture of love and awe. It didn't take them long to realize that Alice was afraid of him and that Earl despised her for it.

Alice was always tense when Earl was around, worrying that somebody might do something to offend him. He never struck the children, but there was a smirk in every snide remark towards Alice. He sniped about her cooking. He made fun of the way she stood, hunched over with her arms crossed over her chest. At night when the children were fast asleep, he would climb on Alice and have sex, never bothering to take the time to be gentle. Alice would have enjoyed love-making if she had had a chance to get in the mood, to warm up a little. Instead he pounced and then went at her like a battering ram, which left her sore and torn.

After four children, Alice wanted a tubal ligation. She knew there was no point in going to the doctor on the base because he would require

Earl's consent before operating. Instead, she had it done privately at a free clinic off base, by a female doctor who was using a new procedure which left no outward scarring. Also, since the army paid for such things as teeth and glasses, Alice got both. With the new glasses she could see well but she still couldn't read. This she kept to herself.

The Grauhmans came home in the 1970s. Earl got out of the service and bought a farm. But Earl wasn't cut out to be a farmer. The farm wasn't fit to grow potatoes, even if he could have afforded the machinery, which he couldn't. He bought cattle, and the calves died. He had riding horses, but nobody was interested in them. He tried working in the woods, but the bottom dropped out of the pulpwood market. Then he went to work driving truck, hauling potatoes down the Eastern Seaboard and bringing back oranges and peppers. Again he was away a lot of the time.

The family grew up. Rita went off to school. Sonja married. Trevor took a special course in welding stainless steel. Lois was in Grade 11.

When Lois was in her last year of high school, Alice decided it was time to learn to read.

She enrolled in a night school course and after a few nights with a good tutor, she was beginning to make headway. One of the teachers, a young man, drove right past her house. They arranged that he would pick her up and drop her off home after the course. Alice was delighted to find she could learn so quickly. She had long since stopped walking with her head down and her arms folded over her breast. Now she stood a little straighter. She was gaining confidence. Then Earl had engine trouble and the truck was off the road for a few days. He came home unexpectedly. He found the house empty. He strode up and down the road in front of the house, becoming more and more furious by the second. By the time Alice appeared at 9:30, he was livid. Standing in the shadow of a maple tree, Earl watched Alice say good night and get out of the car. He watched as the car drove off. Then he suddenly appeared in front of Alice. "Where were you?"

"At the high school."

"Who drove you home?"

"One of the new teachers."

"Well, how about I teach you a lesson or two." Earl slapped her, hard enough that she lost her balance and fell backwards. Her three-ring binder with all her exercises went flying. Earl then turned and strode into the house. Alice got up, gathered the contents of the binder and followed him in. She had planned to make a cup of tea, but instead she went straight upstairs to bed. But Earl wasn't through. "Who told you you could take night courses?"

"Nobody. I just wanted to. You were away so much, I just thought..."

"You thought. You thought. That's what you always say. Well, don't think, bitch. You're too stupid to think. What do you suppose the neighbours will say when they find out you're out running around at all hours, driving around with some young stud. Your place is here. In this house. And the next time I come home, you'd better be waiting for me."

Days drifted by. When Earl was home he and Alice attended church. She listened as the minister pulled out Bible texts which decreed that the man was head of the household, that the wife was there to do his bidding. And using the church as a stick, Earl kept the upper hand.

Alice found herself sitting, tears streaming down her face, week in, week out. Lois, busy with her last year of high school, felt impatience with her mother and stayed out of the house as much as possible. Rita treated her with contempt.

Alice tried to pray, to ask God to forgive her for her angry feelings about her husband. She asked for relief from the torment of his wrath. She asked the Lord to keep her from losing her mind. Winter turned to spring. Alice made an attempt to brighten the place up. After asking Earl if it was all right, she started working three afternoons a week, house-cleaning for an elderly couple. He agreed. The work was hard but the old couple appreciated it, and insisted on paying her. Alice accepted the money with gratitude. That fall she also picked potatoes. Anything to keep busy.

Then a group of young people from the United States bought the farm next door. These people had crossed the border during the Vietnam war and remained. They were the first hippies to come to the area and the old-timers shook their heads and waited for them to fail and go back to the United States. Instead they farmed using organic methods and became fairly successful in living their dreams. People talked about them, disapproved of them, but let them be.

Alice met one of the young women from the commune on the road and after a friendly exchange, she, Noreen, invited Alice over to visit. Earl had gone to Halifax for a week. Noreen, who operated a pottery shed and kiln, gave Alice tea in one of her own hand-made cups. Alice admired the cup, and talked about how brave Noreen was to move to a new country and start again. Noreen turned out to be a sympathetic listener. She drew Alice out about her home and family, her loneliness, her lack of purpose, and then suggested she take a correspondence course which she could work at when Earl was away.

Knowing Earl would be furious if he ever found out, Alice thought about it for several weeks. It was sneaky to do something behind her husband's back. But since God hadn't come up with any answers to her prayers, she decided to take a chance. She sent away for the course. When the books arrived she hid them. But she still had a more pressing problem. Her reading skills were so limited, the books were virtually useless.

While watching Alice one day, Noreen gently asked Alice if she had difficulty understanding the directions. Alice, in tears about being found out, finally admitted that she could not read.

"Well, that's no problem," Noreen said. "I'm home-schooling my children. You can join us and we'll all read together."

For nearly a year, while Earl was on the road, Alice would slip across to the next farm and sit at the kitchen table, drink coffee out of home-made mugs and learn to read. A sensible woman and a former school teacher, Noreen made every effort to stimulate Alice and to present reading material that was at her level. And one day Alice found she could stumble through a newspaper article, pronouncing every word and understanding most. The two women celebrated with a little home-made wine. The only time Alice had ever felt so gratified was when her children were born. It was time to tackle her correspondence course and go after a high school diploma.

Alice started by filling out a long, detailed set of questions designed to see where she was scholastically. Another set of books arrived and Alice began the course. She worked at it secretly for over a year before Earl found out. Usually the mail came in the morning and Alice picked it up before going to her housecleaning job. But this day the mail was late and Earl, coming home after being away for over two weeks, saw the flag up on the mailbox. He stopped, opened the box, pulled out a Sears Catalogue and some flyers and a brown envelope addressed to Alice. In the kitchen he placed the catalogue on the counter, then lifted the envelope and looked at it again. Opening the cutlery drawer he picked up a paring knife and slit the envelope. Inside he found a number of exam papers and the results of several tests test, plus a covering letter, which congratulated Alice on scoring 94 out of 100 percent on Grade 11 Math and English.

Enraged to discover Alice had mastered learning skills that would take her beyond him, Earl ripped the papers to shreds. Then he built a fire in the kitchen stove and burned them. Earl had taken many courses during his time in the army which brought him to a Grade 10 equivalent, but he knew he would never be an intellectual giant. He had been proud when his kids had done well in school. And now his stupid mouse of a wife had gone behind his back and had a better education than he did. Well, he'd see to that. In the army he took orders. At work he took orders. He took a lot of shit off his customers. The only one he could lord it over was Alice, and she wasn't about to get a chance to look down on him.

The more he thought about it, the more he felt betrayed. He searched the house, finally finding the text books and note paper. These he stuffed into the kitchen stove as well. On his search for the books, he found $120 Alice had earned house-cleaning and picking potatoes and he put that in his pocket.

After Earl left, Alice found her books missing. Also missing was the money she had stashed for her next course. Only Earl could have taken it. From then on she waited for the ax to fall. But he never mentioned the correspondence course and neither did she.

The years passed. Rita moved to Halifax. Trevor went to Ontario. Sonja married a missionary and moved to the Third World. Lois completed her Bachelor's degree and went to work in Saint John.

And then came the snowmobile accident. Last week Alice had been a wife, mother, grandmother, member of the New Christian Evangelical Tabernacle. Now she was a widow, barely tolerated by her children, ostracized from the church because of her hair, and propositioned by her late husband's so-called best friend.

There were two other major changes as well. Although the funeral expenses had eaten up most of the money she'd found in Earl's pockets, she still had $2500 which should tide her over nicely until she figured out her next move. More important, for the very first time in her life she had no obligations whatsoever. She was free.

But fate wasn't done with Alice yet. The following Monday she had a call from the bank. She learned that Earl had mortgaged the house and farm and that $68,000 was owing on it. On Tuesday the dealer came by and repossessed the snowmobile. He demanded the helmet back as well, but Alice hadn't seen it. While looking through Earl's wallet again, Alice looked more carefully at the two school pictures. The faces were so similar to those of Sonja and Trevor when they were small, that she hadn't noticed what the children in the picture were wearing. She carefully removed the photos from the plastic slots and turned them over. On the backs were printed: To Daddy with love, Naida, age 8, Grade three. Sammy, age 7, grade 2. Also on the backs of the photos was the photographer's stamp which included a telephone number. Alice dialed the number and was informed that it had been disconnected.

Alice then called the trucking company and learned that Art Elliot was just coming in the yard. She left word for him to call back. He didn't. She waited an hour and then called him at home. After greeting his wife, she asked if she could have a word with Arthur.

"Hullo."

"Arthur, what was the name of Earl's girlfriend."

"Uh, I don't rightly know." Alice could hear the uneasiness in his voice.

"Arthur, think about it. Otherwise I may take time off tomorrow to tell your wife of your late night visit...."

"No, he never mentioned it that I recall."

"You're lying, Art. Where did she live? Framingham?"

"Could be. I guess."

"Thanks for all your help." Alice placed the receiver back on the hook. Then she put on her boots and heavy coat and walked over to Noreen's.

"I'll be right in," Noreen called from the shed. "Put the kettle on."

As soon as Noreen, who had been working at the pottery wheel, had washed her hands, she came over to the table where Alice took out the two school pictures.

"So, who's this, then?"

"Apparently they are my husband's children."

"Earl's children? No." Noreen turned the photos over. "Hmm, Framingham, Mass. I know that area." She made tea. Then spoke, "obviously these children have a mother..."

"Yes."

"And you knew nothing about it? No, of course not. I'm sorry, Alice. That was clumsy of me. What are you going to do now?"

"Find her. Talk to her. Find out what in hell is going on."

"And then what?"

"I don't know."

"How do you propose to find her?"

"Well, Art Elliot knows, but he isn't saying. I called the number of the photographer but that phone has been disconnected."

"Have you tried finding a number for Earl in the Framingham area?"

"No. Gimme your phone book. What's the area code?"

"You'll have to ask the operator. Go ahead, use that phone. I have a special rate for calling my relatives in the U.S."

A few minutes later Alice had the number for Earl Grauhman in Framingham. She dialed the number. A child answered."

"Naida?" Alice asked.

"Yes."

"Is your mother there?"

"Yes." Alice heard the receiver drop on to a hard surface. Then she heard the child yell, "Mama, somebody wants you." A voice answered the child, "who is it?" Naida replied. "I don't know." Then Alice heard the receiver being picked up. "Hello?"

"Hello," Alice replied. "Is this Mrs. Grauhman? Mrs. Earl Grauhman?"

"This is Ardith Grauhman, yes. How may I help you?"

"My name is Alice Grauhman. I am calling from Cedar Springs, New Brunswick."

"Oh, you would be Earl's sister-in-law? His brother Bill's wife?"

"No. I am Earl's wife."

"Earl's wife. That can't be. I'm Earl's wife. We've been married ten years."

"When is the last time you saw him?"

"Well, it's been a month or more. My husband is a gypsy trucker. He travels all over Canada and the Eastern Seaboard. I talked to him, what, two weeks ago?"

"I don't think so."

"What are you talking about?"

"Earl died January 3 in a snowmobile accident."

"I don't know what you think you are playing at but..."

"I am not playing at anything. I have been married to Earl Grauhman for 28 years and I identified his body. I didn't know he had another wife for sure until just now. And that was only because of the photos of Naida and Sammy in his wallet." Alice listened to silence on the other end of the line which dragged on for the longest minute she'd ever experienced, then said: "Look, this is obviously as much of a shock to you as it has been to me. I've been cruel and I'm sorry." Then she set the phone back in its cradle.

"Don't go yet," Noreen said, watching Alice pulling her coat over her shoulders.

"Thanks, but I must."

So Alice was on her own. She had no husband and she would soon have no home. She hadn't even been left with enough dignity to prevent the advances of a pig like Art.

She squirmed around in the bed. Knowing it was unlikely she'd ever get back to sleep, she sighed, then swung her legs over the side of the bed, scuffed into her slippers and walked down stairs. In the shed was an inch of brandy in the bottom of a bottle that Earl had used to nurse a sick calf some years back. The calf had died anyway, Alice recalled, walking back into the kitchen. In the microwave she heated half a cup of milk and topped it up with the brandy and a teaspoon of sugar. She turned on the television and watched the news, and when her drink was finished she walked back upstairs to bed.

"I have to stop thinking about things," Alice said aloud. "I have to still my thoughts." Then with her eyes shut she stared at the lids of her eyes where a small white dot appeared. She watched the dot grow. Into her vision came a rush of pictures, some cartoons, some photographic stills, faces from her past, images of the children as babies. Some were collages of cartoons and film. All in total silence. The images rapidly changed to angles, planes, colours and then swirling junk; like a backed up toilet, all the shit that had ever gone down in her life came swirling up before something switched the power off.

Just before Alice awoke in the morning, she had another dream.

She was a child again, standing in the front yard. It was summer, very warm, and humid. At first it was so hot she felt as if she were breathing through vaseline. The heat paralyzed her in brain and body until she was virtually catatonic. Thunder rolled. The day darkened. She looked up as lightning flashed, blinding her momentarily. The first drops of rain spattered on the ground, raising the dust at her bare feet. Then skies opened and the rain poured down, washing her face, and she danced in the rain.

Again she looked up. The bruised and angry sky was suddenly shot with shafts of light, like that representing the Glory of God in an Biblical painting. She saw how the sun turned the rain into a golden waterfall as a rainbow arched over the east and a smaller rainbow echoed the first.

Now fully awake and feeling fine, Alice pondered her future. "What do I do with my life now?" she said aloud.

"Anything you can imagine," came a voice inside her head. The dog stood up, went to the window, looked out, came back to the bedside, and leaned his chin on the side of the bed.

I REMEMBER ANNA

At the restaurant this morning when I stopped in for coffee I fell into conversation with Grace, the waitress. I was her only customer. Until I walked in Grace had been reading the Fredericton paper.

"Good morning, Rose. Coffee?"

"Yes please, Grace. And maybe one of your wonderful date-nut muffins."

"Coming up. Says in the paper that the bones discovered over near Renous three years ago have finally been identified as belonging to Anna Walker, formerly of Brookside."

"No."

"That's what it says in today's paper. Did you know her?"

"Yes. Yes I did. But I haven't heard of her for years." Just then more customers came in and Grace, in her usual friendly, efficient way, set about making them welcome and taking their orders. I finished my coffee, dropped a dollar and a half beside the cash register and left the restaurant. I had planned to do some shopping, but instead I went for a walk along the river. Anna Walker is dead, has been dead for more than three years and I didn't even know. How is it we lose touch with those who have helped shape the person we have become?

I remember everything about Anna, her soft brown eyes, the lustre of her heavy dark hair. I remember her strength of purpose, her childlike curiosity, her infinite capacity for joy. I remember Anna's kitchen, fragrant with coffee and spices, flowers and rising bread, her table covered with a red and white checkered oilcloth, the white enamel kettle on the crackling wood stove. I remember the delicate chinaware tea cups, the blue and white milk jug. I remember canned vegetables standing in rows along her cupboard, the golden pink bottles of apple jelly and rose-hip.

I also clearly recall Anna's hands, strong, capable, warm. And her voice, low, mellow and melodious. When she laughed it was like little bells ringing, a happy sound like a hug set to music.

What brought Anna to Brookside that summer when I was 10 years old, I didn't learn until much later, but she taught me more in those few glorious summer months than anybody or any book has since. The first I knew, she had moved in one day, into the old gabled house at the end of the lane, not long after the last of the McAvitys died. She would have been around 50 at the time.

Just before my 10th birthday my father, Rev. David Bruce, came home one day with a bicycle. A couple in my father's flock had lost a son to leukemia. The boy had never really ridden the bike because of his illness, but the parents of the dead boy were getting rid of all the boy's things. So my father accepted the bicycle and passed it along to me. My mother, ever conscious of her role as the good Reverend's wife, did not wholeheartedly approve of my roaming around the countryside on a bicycle, but she grudgingly went along with my father's decision.

That bicycle, a maroon coloured CCM, was my ticket to freedom. It had reflectors, a headlight and a little tire-patching kit, buckled under the seat. But first I had to learn to ride it.

To start with, I couldn't keep it upright and get on at the same time. After a while I leaned the bike against the side of the shed and climbed on. Then I let go the shed wall and started pedalling. I wobbled out the driveway but I didn't know how to stop or turn so I went across the driveway and into the ditch where I was thrown into a heap. A quick check proved that no bones were broken, and a few more bruises meant nothing to me then. I leaned the bicycle against a tree and tried again. I pedalled forward and then backwards. Ah ha! To stop, all I had to do was pedal backwards. Then I found my balance.

One day, while I was riding my treasured bicycle past Anna's house, I saw her standing near the gate. I said, "Hello" and she said "Good morning." She asked me my name and I told her. Then she said, "You must come in and visit soon." For some reason I did not tell my parents about my meeting with Anna. In the first place I was a secretive child. And, secondly I had the sense, as children do, that it would not be well accepted at home.

A few days later I saw Anna digging around in her garden when I pedalled by and she called out, "Hello there, Rose. Would you care to stop for a raspberry cordial?" In my most courteous voice, I replied, "Why, thank you, that's very kind of you."

I climbed off the bicycle and leaned it against the porch out of sight from the main road.

When I went inside, I couldn't believe it was the same house. I had been there with my parents when the McAvitys lived in it. There had been dark green wainscotting on the lower part of the walls, grimy ancient paper reaching up to the smoke-blackened ceiling. I don't remember exactly what was on the windows or much else, except that the whole place smelled of kerosene, cats and gloom and that a bewhiskered old man sat in a creaking rocker by the stove, with a can of sand beside him, in which he regularly spat while poking angrily at the fire. The woman who looked after him I later learned was his daughter--you couldn't tell the difference in their ages.

They both had the same dolorous mien, a grim expression of having been cheated out of something.

Anna's kitchen was white, top to bottom, except for the red bows of the tie-backs on the starched white curtains, the red and white checked table cloth and the black stove. Even the stove glistened, especially the parts that were made of enamel or brass or chrome. She had painted the sills, the counters, the counters, even the rocker and the ladder-back kitchen chairs white, too. The polished wood floor was the colour of honey.

Sometimes I heard my parents talking in hushed whispers about Anna. But I couldn't follow much of what they were saying. The word 'fallen' came up. Unnatural. Ruined. But none of that made sense to me. I knew what ruined was--like my polka-dotted Sunday dress that I rolled down the hill in and snagged on a thorn, and the dilapidated school book I had accidentally dropped and knocked the covers off. But Anna wasn't snagged or torn. I didn't find her wild at all.

I didn't have any friends, what you'd call real friends my own age. We moved from place to place, so after a while I stopped trying to fit in. But Anna liked me, I could tell. What I liked most about Anna was that she knew things. She could tell a yarrow plant from caraway; she knew which mushrooms were good to eat and where the best berry patches were. She knew the names of all the different birds that flew into her yard. That Anna actually seemed to enjoy my company was a major plus. My father was not an approachable man. My mother was always bustling about doing good works, only now and then stopping to cast a despairing or disapproving glance in my direction. But Anna was never impatient. She seemed to have all the time in the world for me. I always loved getting her talking about the old days, what it was like when she was a girl. Why, she could talk about something that happened 40 years before I was born and it was just as real as yesterday.

Anna had definite ideas about what to do with trash--though she never seemed to have very much. It included flattening out tin cans, washing bottles, stacking newspapers, and all this was imparted in a serious but kindly tone.

Animals adopted Anna. Stray cats turned up one after another and made their home in her back shed. Sometimes one would find its way into the house and take up residence on the old rocker, occasionally reaching its front paws straight forward in long, luxurious stretches. I remember one day a stray dog walked into her yard. He was tan and grey and black and of a well-confused species. He had fleas and ear mites. His scraggly fur was matted with beggar ticks and burdocks.

Anna asked me if I wanted to help her give him a bath and I said, "sure." First she fed him. Then she rigged up the garden hose to the kitchen sink and carried it outside into the middle of the back yard and, together, we gave Dog a bath. He wasn't too keen at first as Anna lathered on a pungent mixture of herbs and something else to kill the fleas. After we'd given him a good scrub, I held him while she rinsed him off with the garden hose. Then she took some regular shampoo and we lathered him all over a second time and rinsed him off. You could tell by then that Dog had lost his fear and suspicion of us and that he liked the attention.

"What do you think we should call him?" she asked me, as Dog sort of spread his feet and lowered his body and then gave a wriggling, enormous shake. Anna and I jumped back, but not before getting showered.

"I don't know. I haven't thought about a name."

"But he needs a good name to go with his new shiny coat."

"What about 'Nimrod,'" I suggested, remembering the name I'd read on a mailbox during a country drive with my parents the previous Sunday.

"Nimrod," Anna repeated thoughtfully. "Nimrod, the hunter. Yes, I think Nimrod will do."

Nimrod rolled on the grassy lawn, then went over to the front porch where he lay down in the sun to dry. Anna made each of us a glass of iced coffee and we sat in the chair swing in the shade of an old maple, watching three kittens making mock battle at the foot of a lilac bush.

"What do you want to do when you grow up?" Anna asked me.

"I don't know. Maybe a teacher." (Our teacher at the one-room school I attended at the time was Edna Ewert. If we finished our school work early on Friday afternoons, she would read poetry to us. Although I didn't always understand the story in the poem, the rhythms of her reading would stay with me always. Through Edna words became a treasure to me, a privately enjoyed treasure as I mouthed them, scrambled them, wrote them down, and learned new ones. I made up serious poems and silly songs.)

"A teacher," said Anna, "And what would you teach?"

"Stuff."

"Just stuff? To teach you have to gain some special knowledge yourself. For instance, if you want to teach people about botany, you must first learn everything you can about plants and trees and flowers. If you want to teach archaeology, you must learn everything you can about the earth and the soil. If it is zoology, you must study animals, ordinary domestic animals like Nimrod to as well as more exotic animals like zebras and llamas. Although I wouldn't exactly call Nimrod ordinary."

"Maybe I should be a secretary," I said, thinking of a movie I'd seen with this beautifully dressed woman walking around an office in high-heeled shoes--to my seven-year old mind, the epitome of elegance.

"A secretary," Anna mused. "You would learn to type, to do accounts, to work for a man in an office, to become a servant to an office and the man who runs it. I wonder. No, I think you will want to do something more dramatic with your life. I think you will grow into a fine young woman. You are quick to learn. You are gifted with natural skills, talents and insights. You have curiosity and character. You have the capacity to go far." Just then a robin landed on the ground a few feet from Anna and looked at her expectantly.

"There," I said, laughing, "that robin wants to talk to you."

"Yes," Anna replied, but she wasn't laughing. She simply held out her hand to the robin and it landed in her palm, cocked its head right and left, then trilled a long note before flying back up into a branch. "I think it was William James who said, 'the whole drift of my education goes to persuade me that the world of our present consciousness is only one out of many worlds of consciousness that exist.'"

"You mean, like sometimes you know what animals are thinking?"

"Yes. But, if you stop, still your thoughts and listen carefully, you hear much more clearly."

"Real words?"

"No. Not necessarily. Think about your game of 'pretend.' Don't you sometimes almost hear answers from your pretend friend."

"You had a pretend friend?"

"Oh yes, many of us have them. Although when we grow up we push them into the background."

"I didn't know that."

"Ah, Rose, you have much to learn. But that's good. You have the capacity to learn."

"I think you are my only real friend," I told Anna.

"Yes. I am your friend, Rose. Always. Remember that. But, you will meet many people over your lifetime and in time, through experience, you will discover those who can become friends. Meanwhile, trust yourself, Rose. Trust your instincts. You have good instincts."

As it turned out Anna's positive prediction was off the mark most of the time. My life became a shambles of crab-like movements, successfully inching forward and sideways, only to drop back and break on the rock pile of experience. (Oh, Anna, why aren't you here now, when I need you?)

The year after I met Anna, our family left Brookside and moved to Cedar Springs. In my father's pastoral charge there were three churches and we travelled to three different places every Sunday.

I hated Cedar Springs at first. Nothing but trees, trees, trees. Cedar Springs still had gravel roads. The nearest neighbour was nearly a mile away and since they had only boys, my mother would not allow me to visit on my own. Most of the time I just rode my bike around the square. It was exactly seven miles. I could do it in twenty minutes if I wanted. But I used to stop and sit on a particular grassy knoll and gaze all around the county. I could even see Mount Katahdin in the State of Maine. I spent most of my time in the world of imagination, sometimes pretending to be grown up and living someplace else. In my fantasy I pretended to be living in the city, wearing high heels and looking elegant. I would wear my hair in a poodle cut and be very stylish.

The only company I had was my cousin Marie, who came up from Fredericton with her parents about once a month. Two years older than me, Marie was always the perfect lady when our parents were handy. When we were alone she alternately spent her time showing me how sophisticated she was or treating me with total disdain. One time I had the pleasure of grabbing her by the hair and throwing her to the ground, where I banged her head in the dirt. She retaliated by spitting in my face. That distracted me long enough for her to jump up and run into the house. My father came out with that despairing look on his face and ordered me to my room, where I spent the rest of their visit. When called down to supper I was still sulking, and refused. My stomach growled and gurgled until after everybody went to bed, and I slipped downstairs for bread with jelly and peanut butter.

One day I told my mother all about the process of menstruation and even though I wasn't exactly clear on the details, I had the general idea. "Where did you hear about this?" she asked.

"Marie told me," I said. "When you become a woman you bleed from your vagina, and if you don't bleed the blood all saves up and becomes a baby."

"Oh well," said my mother, "you don't have to worry about those things for a long time yet. Have you finished your homework?"

"Yes, mother," I said with a long-suffering sigh, cross that my attempt at grown-up conversation was being summarily dismissed.

"Then why don't you run along. I have things to do."

"Yes, mother."

I don't know why my parents named me Rose. I guess I should have asked my mother while I had a chance. When I got around to asking my father, he was no longer able to remember such irrelevant details.

Theresa Rose Bruce. I can still hear the kids in school chanting:
"Rose Bruce is a big fat moose.
"Her father is a Pole and her mother is a goose."

It was Chuck Riens (he later ran a bowling alley) who authored that nifty couplet. I took it for a while, but then I punched him in the nose and he went snivelling home to his mother. My revenge was short-lived.

His mother immediately called my mother. In episodes such as this, my mother never, ever took my side.

"Rose, Rose. What am I going to do with you?" my mother would say while wringing her hands and shaking her head from side to side. "You behave like a hoodlum. You shame us dreadfully. And your father, a minister, a man of the Lord. You struck that child. You must apologise at once."

"But he started it..."

"I won't hear any excuses. A minister's daughter does not fight in the school yard. You simply have to turn the other cheek."

Inwardly seething, I lagged along behind Mother until we reached the boy's parents home, where I grudgingly said "I'm sorry." Smirking and self-satisfied, he said, "It's okay." He'd won that round. But there would be others.

No, Rose was the most inappropriate name for me. The rose flower is sweet smelling, lovely, delicate, beautiful, open and inviting. I was lanky, awkward, loud, boisterous and sly. My hair, in mouse-brown braids, was always becoming undone. My knees bore permanent scabs from running or falling or climbing trees. As well as Rose Bruce, the big fat moose, there was the work of the Crestwell girls who came up with the yard chant of

"Rose, Rose, with the big fat nose.
Where did she steal it, do you suppose?"

And when I stopped to look in the mirror of my mother's dressing table, I saw that the other kids were right. I did have a big nose.

That summer I found some machinery stored at the back of a farm near our new place at Cedar Springs. Old stuff that had long since gone out of use, old rakes and hay-loaders, cutters and binders. There was a great contraption that ran a saw using horsepower, and there was a huge cylinder about three feet in diameter and 15 feet long that farmers used to roll the ground flat once they had seeded it. There was also an old threshing machine, all rusted except for some galvanized and canvas parts. I decided it would become my private space.

I took an old blanket and wadded it through the spokes and then climbed through myself. From there I could see out through the grass and get enough light to read by and, although the rusting iron frame of the threshing machine drew heat from the sun, there was usually a slight breeze coming through. I spent a whole summer in there, nearly. In the distance I could hear my mother calling, but only my empty stomach and darkness would drive me back to the house.

I missed Anna. I knew that she would have sympathized with my problem in the school yard. I also missed Nimrod who had turned into a second friend. Although he stayed loyal to Anna and slept most nights on her front porch, or in the front hallway when the weather was bad, he was always waiting for me when I pedalled my bike in the front gate. We played for hours. I had always wanted a cat or a dog of my own. But we never had one at home.

"Why, what would the neighbours think?" said my mother. "There is nothing worse than a barking, snapping dog around. Your father needs peace and quiet to prepare his sermons. And when people come to your father seeking counsel and guidance they don't need to be greeted by some barking, smelly dog jumping on them."

"But it would be my dog. I would take care of it."

"You have to go to school. Concentrate on your homework. As a minister's daughter it is your duty to set an example." (My mother was always big on duty.)

"What about a cat then?" I wheedled.

"Cats shed. And many people are allergic to cats," said my mother. "No, it just wouldn't do. Now run along and tidy up for dinner."

"Other kids have pets," I grumbled.

"Now, Rose. We've discussed this before," said my mother, looking at me directly for the first time. "Oh, Rose. Rose. Whatever do you do with your hair? It has all become undone." Reaching for the hair brush, she untangled the snarled strands, at the same time releasing some of her dissatisfaction with me by brushing hard and making my head sore.

"Ow. Ow," I whined. "You're hurting me."

"Oh why can't you behave like other little girls? Do you always have to run around like a tomboy?" My mother quickly restored my long hair to order in two thick braids. "Where are your hair ribbons?"

"I don't know."

"You've lost your hair ribbons again?" Mother slammed down the brush and holding onto the newly braided hair, she pulled me over to the sideboard. In the middle drawer she found a few inches of Christmas ribbon which she deftly tied to the braids after looping them together at the back of my head.

"You are such a disappointment. And your father has so many crosses to bear. Where oh where did we ever go wrong?"

I hated my hair. Most of the other girls in school had curly hair, which was worn in ringlets that bounced when they went through their prissy games of hopscotch or 'over and under' with the skipping rope. I had a skipping rope one time, but I lost it. The first time I saw the skipping rope with its two beautiful blue wooden handles, I was overjoyed. But no matter how much I practised, I never made it past three or four skips before I stumbled. I envied the other girls in the schoolyard, who skipped along like Alice in Wonderland, their curly hair flying as they moved like fairies.

Still, I had my bicycle, and my legs were long and strong. I could race any kid up hill or down. But that was only pretend. I rode my bike by myself. The other kids never raced with me. Then one day in April--I was eleven by then--I pedaled my bike over to Lasser's Pond, parked it beside a tree and stepped down to the water. I took my shoes and socks off and waded in. There were schools of fish nibbling around my bare legs as my toes disappeared in the soft muddy bottom, and there were lily pads all around me. The water lilies were like tiny yellow fairy cups. I reached for one particularly beautiful fairy cup and lost my balance, falling head-first into the pond. I flailed around and got back to the bank and when I looked down at my ruined dress, I saw that there were bloodsuckers attached to my legs and arms. I quickly pulled the leeches off. Then I lifted my dress and was looking to make sure none had gotten inside by clothes, when I became aware that somebody was watching me. When I whirled around, there stood the three boys from down the road.

"What're you looking for, Rose the Moose?"

"Mind your own business." I said defiantly, as trickles of fear prickled my back.

"So, who's going to make us?" said the middle one.

I didn't reply, but sat down and started to pull my stockings and shoes on.

"Why don't you show us what's under your panties?" said the oldest boy.

"Drop dead," I said.

"Now, that's no way for a preacher's daughter to act." Then turning to his younger brothers, he said, "Okay boys, I guess we've gotta look for ourselves." With that they pulled me over backwards. I kicked and bit and spit. But I was no match for them. Two of the boys held my arms and legs, while the youngest one pulled off my panties and threw them into the bushes.

Then the middle one opened his pants and pulled out his penis. I had never seen a penis before, but I had read enough to know what it was. I was scared and interested at the same time. He came over and kneeled by my face. "Want to touch it Rose?"

"No. Leave me alone," I said.

"Oh, come on Rose. Just touch it. It won't bite you."

I turned my face away and struggled until I got one hand free, then I slapped him as hard as I could.

"Oh, she wants to play rough," said the oldest boy. Then with the two others holding me, he dropped his pants and shoved his penis into my vagina. I screamed but one of the others placed his hand over my mouth. The hand tasted of pitch and salt. When he was through, he climbed off and the second brother took his turn. By then I had stopped fighting. It didn't hurt any more. I didn't lose consciousness, but I closed my mind to what was happening and waited it out.

When they'd had their fun they ran up the hill in a group, laughing and nudging each other. "What if she tells on us?" said the youngest boy.

"She won't say anything," said the oldest. "She wouldn't dare."

In that he was right. I would never have dared to tell my mother and father. Already I knew that I was a terrible burden to them. Telling them about this episode would bring nothing but more misery. I knew I was bad and worthless and had it coming. If I had been a nice girl with nice friends, I wouldn't have been caught down by the pond by the boys in the first place. I got up and brushed off the twigs and burrs. I picked up the hair-ribbons and found my underpants in the bushes and put them on. Then I got on my bicycle.

Mother was attending a church tea when I came home. She had left a note on the fridge, reminding me to do my homework. Father was in his study. I went straight to my room, stripped off my wet and stained clothing, and then climbed into the shower, where I let the water pour over me. My vagina was ripped and stinging and caked with mud and blood. I found a dead leech on the back of my thigh. I soaped my self gingerly but thoroughly, and patted myself dry. I put on clean underclothes and a clean dress and clean dry stockings. Then I burned the soiled underwear and ripped stockings in the wood stove in the kitchen.

When I started to braid my hair I looked in the mirror and changed my mind. I slipped into my mother's sewing room and, taking the sewing shears, I chopped all my hair off. The next time I looked in the mirror, all I saw was a big nose, two large wells of eyes and a nearly bald head. It was the same face and hair I was to see again 35 years later following several episodes of chemotherapy.

"Oh, Rose, Rose. Whatever have you done now?" said my mother wringing her hands. "Your lovely hair. Your crown of glory. You destroyed your hair. What a dreadful child you are! What did I ever do to deserve this?" Somewhere from the depths of his brown-walled study, my father must have heard the note of desperation in my mother's voice and he came in to the kitchen to investigate. He looked at me in horror, then told me to go to my room. Later that evening he and my mother opened my bedroom door and entered. I had pulled the bed clothes up to my chin and lay there like a stone.

"Because of your unseemly behaviour, you mother and I have made some decisions," my father announced. "You have behaved wilfully and unwisely. You have lost our trust. And for that you will be denied certain privileges. You will not ride your bicycle. You will not leave this house. You will not continue to shame us in this community. You will be confined to this room until I can think of a solution for your unacceptable conduct." With that he turned and left the room.

"Do you need to use the washroom?" my mother enquired, wringing her hands.

"No." I mumbled.

"Very well. I will be back in the morning." With that she turned and followed my father out of the room and closed the door. Then I heard a scraping sound and realized they had locked me in. How did I feel? What did it matter? Exhaustion took over. I slept.

I was still groggy when my mother unlocked the door in the morning to bring my breakfast and let me out to use the washroom. She waited outside the washroom door until I had finished, then locked me in my room again. The toilet paper I had stuffed in my underwear the night before showed traces of dried blood. I flushed it down the toilet.

I spent the next few weeks in my room. There were no books but I did have pencils and paper so I scribbled and sketched and slept and numbed out my mind as much as possible. One morning my mother unlocked the door and ordered me to get bathed and dressed, that she and father had decided it would be best all around if I went away to boarding school, that arrangements had been made and we would be leaving for Saint John within the hour.

The four years at boarding school passed quickly. Many of the other girls had been dumped there as a means of getting them out of their parents' hair. Like me, some had been "unmanageable" and the school was strict. Up at 5 a.m. for prayers. At 5:30 wash and dress and make the bed; at 6:30 breakfast; 7:30 chores. Since I tended to get caught swearing fairly regularly, I was usually assigned to clean the toilets, which was one step lower than working in the kitchen. At 8:30 there was a half hour of study time, and then classes until 11:30. There was a half hour break and then lunch at 12, followed by an hour of rest, reading or quiet. At 1:30 classes reopened and continued until 4:30, after which we all went outside and marched two by two for a three- or four-mile walk, returning in time to wash up for supper. Evenings were spent in the library or in study rooms and first bell was at 8:30 p.m. which told us it was time to wash up for bed. And lights out at 9 p.m.

We slept in dormitories, 40 girls to a room. Each girl's space was called a cell and it was large enough for a cot and a small bedside table. The cells were separated by curtains.

I think that was the hardest part, sharing a room with 40 others. Before I had always had my own room, no matter where we lived. But I survived and I look back on the boarding school experience as one of personal growth. After graduation I found a job in an office in Saint John and I stayed with it long enough to get enough money ahead for a few months' rent and a railway ticket to Vancouver. I thought of Anna from time to time. She, too, had attended a boarding school.

Of course, jobs were easy to come by then. I worked as a receptionist for a veterinary clinic during the day, and as a waitress at a jazz club in the evening. I made a few friends, went to parties and tried all the usual stuff going--grass, hash and alcohol. But I hated the feeling of being out of control. I liked working at the clinic, but I soon learned that if I was to make anything of myself, I would have to go back to school.

It took eight years of study and training before I had my degree and was able to open my own clinic. I loved working with animals. I was good at it. To nurse an animal back to health, to ease its pain is very satisfying.

Then I was diagnosed with uterine cancer and had to close my clinic. That was two years ago.

My move back to Cedar Springs is a new beginning for me. A beginning that opens with the breath of the past. Suddenly I am aware that it has begun to rain. I hug my body tightly as burning, streaming tears cleanse my spirit. I sob for the childhood that was destroyed. I weep for the lonely years I spent with only my animals for company. I mourn the loss of my clinic. I grieve for Anna.

At last the tears cease. And, there in the rain by the river I say goodbye to Anna, and thank the gods that be for bringing her into my life. Then Anna's face comes into my mind, warm, glowing, smiling, giving me strength to face whatever is to come.

FLY DOPE AND WHISKY

Fitzhenry White might have been 102, frail and feeble of body, but mentally he wasn't missing a link. Oh sure, he'd forget a name now and then, and once or twice he called his grandson Tommy instead of Teddy, but that was an easy mistake to make. Tommy was his own son, the one who couldn't wait to get overseas and fight in the war, and never came back. Almost like thinking of a stranger now, though. Teddy, or Dr. E. White as he was known to the community, was his pride and joy, a boy to be proud of. "But then," Fitz thought, "I shouldn't be calling him a boy. He is over 40 years old."

Fitz White's eyesight was good, but his hearing was a little dull. He had a hearing aid--in fact he had two--but often he took them out. He liked the silence and he felt at home with his own thoughts.

Every morning Fitz walked to the post office and picked up his mail. While there he overheard a couple of the younger men, Ron Goodall and Clayton Anderson, talking about it. Said the bones discovered up along the Renous highway three years ago had been identified as Anna Walker's, formerly of Brookside.

That afternoon Dean Booker stopped by for a visit. Fitz put his hearing aid in. They talked of the weather and changes in their lives. Then they talked about Anna Walker.

"They say Anna's bones have been found up there on the Renous," Dean said.

"Yes, I'd heard that," said Fitz. "Amazing what they can find out these days with all this new technology and everything."

Fitz pondered a bit and then continued: "Yes. I knew Anna Walker quite well. She belonged to the old judge--I forget his name just now..."

"Judge Thornton?"

"Judge Charles K. Thornton. His wife's name was Roslyn. She liked people to think she was a cut above the rest of us."

"You're saying C.K. Thornton fathered Anna?" said Dean.

"Yes, before he married Roslyn. The Thornton family thought he was too young to marry. Then again, maybe they figured Anna's folks were not of good enough stock."

"What happened to Anna's mother?"

"Well, that's a bit of a mystery. I daresay Doc Bartley could tell you, if he was still living."

"Oh yes, Doc Bartley. Died fairly young, didn't he?"

"Seventies, I think. He was pretty hard on himself. I used to play chess with him before he got to drinking so much."

"I knew he liked a snort now and then."

"Well, Doc Bartley always drank a little, but it got worse as the years wore on. Still he was a good doctor, practiced his own brand of medicine, lived by his own moral code, you might say. For instance when he discovered that one young girl in the community had been impregnated by her father, he gave the girl an abortion. And he threatened the father with a lot worse, I can tell you. And when Beulah Taggert went to him after her seventh child, he tied her tubes without Jim Taggert's consent. Hell, Taggert would have had a conniption. Obstruction of God's Will and all that.

"Anyway the Doc had known Anna Walker from the time she was a girl and he knew she belonged to the Judge Thornton, though he wasn't a judge at the time, just a horny young fellow like all the rest of us at that age. Her mother was a wild thing, had Anna when she was little more than a girl, and then took off for parts unknown. The grandmother raised her. The grandmother was straight out of the bogs of Ireland. Later on the judge must have had an attack of conscience, because he worked out something with the grandmother for the girl to attend boarding school in Boston. The school was run by a bunch of nuns. I doubt if Anna knew it was the judge right here in Cedar Springs who was footing the bill, but then she might have. God knows if Roslyn, the judge's wife, ever caught wind of it, she certainly would never have let on.

"Anna married a man from Boston and they moved to New Hampshire. His father had money, woollen mills, I think it was. I heard it wasn't a good match. The boy came from a decent family, but he was a brute. He began slapping her around no more than a month after they were married. Then she found herself with child and when she told him she was pregnant, he threw her downstairs. They were living somewhere in New Hampshire at the time.

"As I recall, Anna put up with things for about three years. When he was sober he could be a nice guy, but that type always fools you. When he was drinking he behaved like a raving lunatic. I suppose his family thought that marriage would settle him down a little. But the leopard doesn't change its spots. He was a bad one and he came to a bad end.

"The way I figure, it could have been an accident or it might not have been either. See, he kept horses, liked to bet them too, by the way, and even if he hadn't died he'd have run through everything sooner or later. But he used to keep a stash of liquor in the harness shed. Kept it on a shelf on the wall right next to the door. What he'd do is take a good swig or two from that bottle, then go in and have another drink. Now at that time the whisky was mostly bootlegged stuff. I forget if it was Prohibition--might have been. Anyway, the liquor bottle and the horse liniment bottle looked more or less alike in the dark. It seems that the hired man had mixed up some fly dope, made from water and some kind of powder. They used to have a fly-spray can, you pushed the plunger, like a bicycle tire pump, and it would spray a mist around the stables. Anyhow, he put the fly dope in an old whisky bottle.

"Now, the hired man swore he didn't leave the fly dope on that shelf near the whisky bottle. Nobody knew exactly how Anna's husband got hold of it--but he did. He'd come back from town where he was already rippin' drunk, and he took a good long pull at the bottle which turned out to be fly dope.

"Did Anna have anything to do with that? I've wondered. Certainly you couldn't blame her if she did. The family, his family had it put down as accidental death. Which it was in a way. He drank the fly dope by accident. The question is, where did he get it? Had someone replaced his ordinary whisky bottle with the one containing the fly dope? I guess we'll never know now.

"Of course, his family didn't make much of a stink. Face saving, mostly. Shortly after that Anna moved from New Hampshire. She must have had money, though you would never know it to look at her. In fact everything her husband had would have gone to her. I don't know, maybe he'd wasted it by then. But still, there were the race horses which she sold, and the farm. I imagine there'd be something left even after his gambling debts were paid.

"Then Anna moved to Maine and lived in a coastal village for about ten years before moving to Brookside. Bought that old McAvity house and moved in. I suppose the judge was following her movements. I don't know whether they ever met or not. Hard to say.

"Yes, sir, Anna was a strange one all right. But I rather liked her. She was self-assured, self-contained. Not flighty like some of the women around here. Anna seemed to be comfortable in her own skin, you know? Didn't need any of the fripperies other women do. Well, not as long as you don't count the big hats. But then, maybe because she was outdoors so much, she didn't want the sun on her face.

"I'm sorry the wife didn't take to her. I would have liked to make Anna welcome in the community."

"Still, Anna always seemed happy enough. She had a wonderful way with children. And a way with animals, too. Saw that movie the other night called The Horse Whisperer. Made me think of Anna."

"Well, that explains a lot of things. Like why Anna came back to Brookside."

"Maybe, maybe not. Hard to tell what Anna was thinking."

Dean Booker glanced at the clock. "Say, look at the time. I must be getting home. Janet will be wondering what ever happened to me."

"Come in again, Dean. It's kind a nice to reminisce a little."

"I'll do that. So long, now."

THE GIFT

"Zeke. Zeke." Hannah Hardlow woke her husband Zeke from a sound sleep.

"Whassamatter?"

"Oh Zeke. I had the awfullest dream."

"Ya, well, it's only a dream. Don't mean nothing. Go on back to sleep."

Hannah shifted her bulk into an upright position. "Oh, it was weird. I'll never get back to sleep now."

"Probably something you ate."

"No, no. It was ever so real. You know that bunch of bones they found up near the Renous. You remember it was all in the paper, and then yesterday it came out on TV that the bones were Anna Walker's? Well my brother Alfred used to talk about her. He met her when she came to Brookside. Said she was real strange, but kinda nice at the same time. Well, in my dream I saw those bones all rise up and there she stood. She was wearing this great big hat, and you couldn't see her face, but I knew it was her and she was saying, "Come on, Hannah, you can do it." And I said, "Do what," and she said, "You know, Hannah. You know what you have to do." And then the dream quit. Now what do you suppose all that means?"

Zeke turned over on his back, patted Hannah on her thigh and said: "Dreams don't mean nothing, Hannah. Probably something you ate."

"But I could have sworn she was right here in this room." Hannah flounced around on the bed. "Oh, I'll never get back to sleep now. I don't think I want to. The dream has left me crazy feeling." Swinging her legs over the side of the bed, she pushed her toes into her slippers and grabbed her robe. Then she lurched upright and headed towards the kitchen.

Zeke turned over again and closed his eyes. Anna Walker. Yes, he knew Anna Walker, though he'd never tell Hannah that. What happened was, Anna had left word for him over at the hardware store to come and see if he could do something about the septic system out at the McAvity place in Brookside. Before that he'd seen her on the street or out in the fields or sometimes near the covered bridge, but he'd never actually spoken to her.

The day he went out to look at her septic system, she had come out and walked around his truck a few times, looking at it this way and that.

Zeke wasn't paying attention to her so much as to that great big dog she had, the one she called Nimrod. Anyhow he got down to business, figured out how far the septic tank or cesspool was from the house, paced off 50 feet and began to dig. A few shovelfuls later he hit metal, so he knew he was on the right track. A few shovelfuls more and he had the lid off. Didn't seem to be full, but what he did notice was that the pipe that drained the sewage into the tank was right up against the baffle. That was the problem, well at least one problem. He got up, went back to his pickup and rummaged around, found a small handsaw and went back to the septic tank and cut a four inch length off the end of the pipe.

"Now, Miss, if you want to try flushing the toilet or pouring a bucket of water down the drain we'll see what happens." Anna walked back to the house but Nimrod stayed, sitting on his haunches watching every move Zeke made. Zeke stood where he was, brushing off a black fly or two while he was waiting. Suddenly a bit of sludge began to move and Zeke walked up to the window, saying "flush her again." He could hear the pump start. "Now turn on all the taps."

Zeke walked back to the septic tank, the water was pouring through clear and clean. "That's good. That's good," he called to Anna. "You can turn off the water."

In a few minutes Anna rounded the corner and walked over to where Zeke was working. "Nothing wrong with the sewer line," Zeke said. "And there's nothing wrong with the septic tank now. But that ain't the end of her." As he talked he paced off the top of the septic tank and stood on the ground above where the other end of the tank would be. His back was touching a 40-foot poplar tree, and behind him were several more, making a whole grove. "See, there should be weeping tile under here, and it's my guess that these trees have taken root right in the line so the water has no place to go."

"What do you recommend?"

"Well, I guess you could call someone with a back hoe. You probably need to invest in a few lengths of perforated pipe. See, what they usually do in a place like this, is: they dig a big trench, and then they half fill it with sand and rocks, then they lay the perforated pipe, and then they fill the trench up with sand and rocks. Then if you want you can throw a little soil and some grass seed on it, and you'll never have a problem again."

"Would you know anyone who could do that work?"

"Allison Boughan. He's a farmer, but he'd got a back hoe and he's got a gravel truck and likely he could find some rocks somewhere."

"I'll take your advice. Meanwhile, come inside out of the heat for a moment. There's raspberry cordial in the fridge." Anna walked back by the truck cab, glanced inside to see Zeke's violin case. Then, she said: "I don't suppose you'd feel like playing a couple of pieces. I've heard you play before. You have the gift."

"Ah, shucks. I ain't much good."

"That's not true, Zeke. When you play the angels sing."

"And sometimes the devils dance," said Zeke.

"Oh that, too. Zeke. Definitely."

When Zeke walked into Anna's kitchen, he could hardly believe his eyes. The kitchen was so warm and bright. The last time he'd been there all he remembered was dark and dampness and cat piss. Now, everything seemed to catch the light. Even the bottle of raspberry cordial which she set out on the counter.

"You can rinse your hands off there at the sink," she said. And handed him soap and a towel.

She filled two glasses with ice and poured the raspberry cordial over the top and set one down on either side of the table.

"So, where'd you learn to play, Zeke?" she asked.

"Ah, nowhere, really. I just taught myself. They used to have dances around the community, out there at Glassville and at the Silver Slipper. And when I was a young feller, I used to slip in to those dances and hunker down out of sight, just to watch the fiddlers. They had two or three real good ones and, boys, I wanted to do that. My fingers just itched to get hold of one. I was about 14 at the time and after I'd been going there to every dance for about six months, this one night the fiddler, big Sam McLaughlin--came from Cape Breton--looked at me and as he walked off the stage, he passed me his fiddle and bow. Said: 'Here, boy, I seen those fingers twitchin' for the cat gut.'

"Well, the rest of the band, the bass fiddle and the banjo and the piano player, they kept going right along. I stuck the fiddle under my chin, put my fingers on the strings and drew the bow. I must have made some awful squeaks and squawks but the rest of the band drowned me out. Then all of a sudden, I heard a note and another, and I got the timin' and then big Sam McLaughlin came back. He watched me for a minute or two, then he reached out and took the fiddle back. He said: 'Think you can learn the fiddle, eh?' Well, gosh, I didn't know what to say. I passed his fiddle and bow back. Then I sat back down and listened and watched right through to the end. Then on his way out, Sam said, "You'd better go on home, boy. But say, the next time you're in Cedar Springs, look me up. I got an old violin there and I could let you have it for $3."

"Well, boys, I thought about that violin for the next three weeks. I worked at everything I could find to earn a few nickels. Then that fall, I got lucky. I picked potatoes, first at Will Cranston's, then when he was through I went right over to Marlin Shaw's and I picked for about three days there, and then I went to the Goodalls. They were through picking, but I got a job racking potatoes, and before I was through I had enough money for that violin and then some.

"Well, Big Sam was good as his word. He'd gone out west to work in the logging woods meantime, but he left the fiddle with his landlady and she handed it over to me. I asked her for his address and she gave me that too, so I took the violin and went straight to the post office and I got Irene Parker to make me out a money order and I sent the money to him. Never saw Sam again. He went to work out there for BC Logging, ran a big crew up there around Port Hardy or somewhere. Then I heard he'd got crushed under a load of logs. Killed him."

"Yes," said Anna.

"Well anyway, I took that fiddle home and Pa was mad that I'd spent the money, but Ma just said, "keep it out of sight. He'll get over it." And he did. I'd walk down to the brook, right there where the falls is, and I'd sit there and saw away, and after a while I kind of got the hang of it. Boys that felt good. Still does." Zeke stopped for breath. "Lord, Lord," he said. "I don't know what's the matter with me, talking and talking and talking."

"I'd like to see your violin, Zeke."

"Well, I'll just go bring it in."

When Zeke returned Anna had placed two fresh glasses of raspberry cordial on the table. Zeke opened his violin case and gently lifted out the instrument, which he handed to Anna. Anna held it for a few minutes, shut her eyes as if she was listening for something, and then handed it back to him. Zeke gave his bow a rosin, then drew it across the strings. Zeke stood in Anna's kitchen window, looked out across the fields and played for half an hour. He played jigs and reels, a few old hymns, then ballad type tunes. As he played Anna, hat hiding her face, allowed the tears to flow. Zeke played trinkets of melody, some animal sounds, even played a groundhog snort, which brought Nimrod to his feet. Zeke moved on into songs of rejoicing, and Anna found herself laughing.

After a while he stopped. With a sheepish look on his face, Zeke said: "Sorry. I've overstayed my welcome."

"No. Zeke," said Anna. "That's not true. You have the gift, Zeke, and you have been kind enough to share it. The angels are smiling on you.

"Now, I haven't paid you for your work. What do I owe you?"

"Oh, whatever you think it's worth." Anna went into the back room and came out with $30. "Will that be enough?"

"Oh, that'll do. That'll do just fine."

Driving down the road that day Zeke had felt like a millionaire. He had a gift. She had said that he had "the gift." He reached over and lovingly patted the violin case. Yes.

"You awake, Zeke? called Hannah from the kitchen.
"Yes."
"I've made a pot of tea."
"Be right there," said Zeke. In the kitchen he looked at the clock, 4 a.m. What a hell of a time to be gettin' up. Oh well, he could always sleep later. Hannah placed a piece of hot buttered toast in front of him and poured the tea.

COVERED BRIDGE SECRET

Half carrying, half dragging the dead girl, he was almost across the old covered bridge when the carload of teenagers pulled into the pine grove and stopped. He planned to hide the body in the abandoned farmhouse a short walk south from the east end of the bridge but for now he crouched down and waited to see what they would do.

There was a soft wind that Halloween night of 1972, too warm for October, the kind of wind that promises rain before morning. In the car were five young people, June Schodak, Hazel Brimer, Allison Boughan, Carl Spencer and Ted White. They were supposed to be attending a Halloween dance at the high school.

While the others were giggling and whispering, Ted, the odd man out, sat drinking beer and playing with the car radio. Oldies by Johnny Cash, George Jones and Marty Robbins had been replaced by Dolly Parton singing *Joleen* and Tanya Tucker doing *Delta Dawn*. Ted had a crush on June. The beer and the fact that she was sitting with Carl made him depressed. He wanted to hurt something. "We ought to set that old bridge on fire," he growled.

"You're crazy," June said. "Why would you want to do that?"

"Nobody uses that old bridge anymore," Allison, son of a local farmer, pointed out. "You wouldn't run a truckload of potato barrels through there. Some of those planks are rotted clear through."

"You wouldn't dare," Carl challenged.

"What if someone catches you?" worried Hazel.

"You're all a bunch of squares," Carl sneered, as he got out, unlocked the car trunk, opened the spare can of gas, walked over to the bridge and splashed it on the dead grass beside the retaining posts. Allison tore a leaf out of a school book in the back window and handed it to Ted. With his lighter, Ted lit the paper and threw it at the bridge. There was a large whoosh sound when the gas caught.

In that first flash of light, Ted glanced up through the side of the bridge to see what looked like someone wearing denim crouching there. The next second flames licked up the walls and the whole area was covered with smoke. They jumped back in the car and drove the long way around back to town, where they parked in the school yard.

Excitement in the car was riding high. As the others planned what to say if questioned by the Royal Canadian Mounted Police, Ted was quiet, thinking. Was there someone on the bridge? Did they get out before it burned? Naw, maybe it was just the light, the fire shining on the old tar, maybe just shadows. But what if there was someone? There couldn't have been anyone out there. Some of the rest would have noticed. In the end Ted said nothing about what he thought he saw in the flames on the bridge that night.

Leaving the body, the young man ran through the smoke out the west end of the bridge, crossed the creek road and scrambled up a woods path to the railroad tracks.

By the time the fire trucks arrived the bridge was burned beyond saving. One of the few covered bridges remaining at the time, it was built around 1860 of local timber, and in its 112 years it had withstood a lot of wear and weathering. Horses, wagons, sleighs, livestock, tractors and gravel trucks had all crossed it one time or another. On the east side of the stream there had been several prosperous farms which had been operated for over a century. But one by one, in the early 1950s when the folks either died off, married and moved or left for Ontario to find work, the farms were abandoned. The buildings, except for part of one house, had collapsed into the earth. In the early 1970s, besides the beer drinkers, the only people who used the bridge were fiddleheaders in the spring, young boys who liked to climb the bridge trusses, or courting couples looking for a private place.

The bridge burning was just another halloween prank, folks said. There had been several false alarms that night and a lot of complaints about Halloween mischief throughout the town. The RCMP had their hands full checking each one out. Someone painted a farmer's barn with swastikas. Someone else opened a pasture fence and let a whole herd of purebred Holsteins out. The cattle walked almost to the town before they were rounded up. And it would be two more days before 12-year-old Gail Whitney, supposedly visiting her grandparents, was reported missing.

The morning after the fire only two smoldering heaps of ash remained at either end of the bridge. Pieces which fell into the water either sank or flowed downstream. Rain began around 5:00 a.m. and by daylight it was falling steadily. There were no tracks. No marks. No clues of any kind.

In a crowd of some three hundred teenagers, most of them in costume, no one took notice of the fact that five of them were absent from the dance for almost an hour the previous evening. No one saw a young man in blue denims who let himself in the back door of the empty house--his parents had already left for Florida--turn on the kitchen light and collapse into a chair. Even later, no one saw or heard the washer and dryer running as he washed the blood and mud and soot from his tattered clothing. And since he had seldom attended teen dances in the past, his absence was not noticed.

Further, no one in the village connected the young man to the girl's disappearance. No one even suspected he knew her. After all, he was a senior, and she was in Grade six. Although the police questioned everyone around, and although local service clubs raised enough money to offer a substantial reward for information, no trace of Gail Whitney was ever found.

But he had seen Gail Whitney all right. Attracted by her winsome face and her long silky fair hair, which resembled that of a blond model in one of the *Penthouse* magazines he had stashed in the basement, he was consumed by erotic fantasies. He had been out walking along the railroad tracks less than a mile north of the bridge when he first spotted her. Busy gathering the season's last few maple leaves and some fungi specimens for a nature project before going on to her grandparents' house a mile and a half further on, Gail didn't notice him at first. And when she did see him on the overpass, she didn't sense any danger. Although she had never spoken to him before, she had seen him around the school, so she continued walking and gathering leaves. About twenty minutes later when he suddenly appeared in the clearing in front of her, she was very afraid.

When he reached out and grabbed her she struggled but she was no match for him. There was no one near enough to hear her screams. The leaves she had gathered scattered in the wind.

Time passed. He stayed in school until Christmas, when he joined his parents in Florida for two weeks. But he didn't come back for the second term. Instead he moved to Toronto, hung out on Yonge Street, never speaking much to anyone. He found jobs but couldn't keep them. The only son of wealthy parents, he didn't really need the money. No one in the city cared to get close enough to find out anything about him. But during the 17 years he was there, in among the records of fires, murders and bombings, beatings, drownings, suicides, were pages and pages on unsolved cases concerning four more little blond girls who went missing.

All three of the boys who had been in the carload of teenagers the night the bridge burned finished high school and went away to college. Allison quit after a year and went back to farm with his father. Carl received a business degree from Dalhousie University and moved on to Halifax, where he married and settled down. Hazel also finished high school, worked at the local food plant for two years, then married a U.S. airman and moved to Texas. Ted enrolled at McGill to study medicine. In his third year he married June Schodak, by then a registered nurse. After Ted's internship at the Montreal General, he and June returned to the community and opened a general practice. Their marriage was a good one. They had two children, a girl and a boy. Their careers brought much satisfaction.

Ted sometimes thought of the night they burned the bridge, and finally told June of his fears about what he thought he had seen. June, ever the pragmatist, calmed him, saying that most youngsters did foolish things at one time or another--stupid, cruel, sometimes shameful things. It was all part of growing up. But what could be gained by stirring up old trouble? "You're a doctor now, and a darn good one," she told him. "Everybody respects you, and the community needs you. Let's just put it behind us."

June was right, Ted knew. There really was nothing to be done now. And most of the time he succeeded in putting the incident out of his mind, but on Halloween nights the memory of the fire would come creeping back.

On this Halloween night, Ted felt uneasy as he watched his kids getting ready to go to the Halloween party. Although eight-year-old Charles was his mother's favourite, twelve-year-old, blue-eyed, golden-haired Heidi was the apple of his eye. She was bright, good-natured, sometimes a little saucy, and he adored her. Not wanting to spoil their festivities, he hid his uneasiness. Over the years he had read dozens of textbooks, journals and papers on the workings of the human mind. These were not premonitions he was experiencing, he decided. Unresolved guilt was causing his anxiety.

Ted would come to wish he had heeded those feelings. June had driven the kids to the party. Charles, dressed as Garfield the cat, made a dash for the front seat while Heidi, as Bo Peep in an ankle-length frock, pinafore and poke bonnet, moved sedately to the back seat. Despite her mask, the long blond hair was unmistakable. After telling the children to wait inside the school until she came to pick them up at ten o'clock, June dropped them off at the edge of the school grounds.

Slamming the car door, Charles was half way to the school building when June looked back to see Heidi moving more slowly in that direction.

Instead of going straight home, June decided to make a call on an elderly woman, a patient of Ted's, who had recently been released from hospital. The woman lived alone and June wanted to make sure she had everything she needed.

Meanwhile Ted, having gone into the study to finish some paperwork, found he couldn't concentrate. He began pacing the floor. Charles's dog, a mutt called Darth, followed one step behind, stopping at each turn to look at him. After a few minutes Ted put on his jacket, found Darth's leash on the coat hook by the door and together they left for a walk around the square.

They met several cars on their way and Ted, pondering the

changing times, realized that he didn't know one make from another. In 1970 Ted or his buddies Carl and Allison could have named the make and model of every car in the neighborhood. Cars now, mostly compacts, all seemed to be the same size and the same colour. Just then a car passed him and as he looked towards it, he caught a glimpse of someone in the passenger seat with long blond hair. He didn't see the driver. He didn't notice the licence plate. Only the blond hair reminded him of his daughter. Turning the corner he and Darth picked up the pace as they walked towards home.

June and the kids were nearly due home when the telephone rang. "Dr. White," Ted answered. He heard breathing and then the line went dead.

Seconds later, the telephone rang again. It was June calling from the principal's office at the school. "Did Heidi go home on her own? I can't find her here, and Charles hasn't seen her. Is she there with you?"

"No. What do you mean, Charles hasn't seen her?"

"He said he hasn't seen her. He was hanging out with his friends..."

"Oh my God, what's happened?"

"Ted, hang on. I'll be right there. There has to be an explanation."

"Oh God, oh God, where is she? What should I do? Call the police? Hell, they're in Fredericton. No. We'll go look for her. June and I will call the other parents. We'll set up a systematic search. We'll..." Then he heard a car drive in the yard. It was June. She burst from the car with Charles lagging behind.

"Has she come back?"

"No." said Ted. "Charles, when did you last see her?"

"I don't know. She was hanging out with those dorky friends of hers.."

"Which ones?"

"I don't know. Bethany Lang for one."

"Lang. What's her father's name?"

"I don't know."

"Here it is," said June, scanning the phone book George Lang. "Let's call him."

No sooner had Ted started dialing than the door opened and Heidi walked in. "Where have you been all this time?"

"At Bethany's. We left early. Their dog's had puppies. And she's got some new CDs."

"But you were supposed to wait for June."

"Oh, chill out Dad. We were just messing around. The party was a bore. What's the big deal?"

"We didn't know where you were."

"So what? I'm not a baby."

Ted slapped her. The first time in his life he slapped one of his children. The slap shocked June and Charles. Heidi stared back at her father. On her face shock laced with pain hardened to fury before she turned and left the room. Ted was overcome with shame. June sent Charles to bed and went up to Heidi. With a cold cloth she bathed Heidi's face.

"What's the matter with him anyway?" said Heidi, still sniffling.

"Nothing to worry about. He loves you so very much. And he was afraid something bad had happened to you."

"Yeah, sure. What could happen around this boring old place?" Sittin on the side of Heidi's bed, June told her about Gail Whitney's disappearance. Heidi listened wide-eyed, then asked a lot of questions. June satisfied her curiosity but did not mention Ted and the bridge-burning episode.

"Now, will you promise me one thing?" June asked.

"Sure. What?"

"Before you decide to leave a party, call home so that we will know where you are."

"Yeah, Mom. Okay."

Ted remained in the den for another two hours. At first, relief at Heidi's safe return washed over him, then shame overwhelmed him. He had broken his own rule against using corporal punishment on his children. He wondered if time could mend the damage.

At last, Ted shut off the lights and went to bed. Emotionally exhausted, he soon drifted off to sleep only to be awakened half an hour later by his own moaning. He'd had a terrible nightmare, he told June. In it he saw Heidi driving away in a car with a stranger. He started running after them but no matter how fast he ran, the car stayed just ahead. Then the car started to cross the covered bridge and he could see Heidi waving and smiling at him. As the car disappeared into bridge he saw fire licking up the outside of the board walls. Before he could reached it, the bridge was engulfed in flames.

"It's only a dream," June said, holding him. "Only a dream. Heidi is in her bed asleep. Everything is fine."

Now wide awake, Ted stared at the ceiling for a while, then got out of bed and went to the bathroom. On his way back, he eased open Heidi's door and looked in, just to reassure himself. She was sleeping soundly. He closed her door quietly, then walked on to his own bedroom and climbed into bed beside his wife.

Up early, he was having coffee in the kitchen when Heidi came bouncing down stairs.

"Hi Dad."

"Good morning, sweetheart. I apologise for my behaviour last night. Can you forgive me?"

Heidi poured herself a glass of juice then came over and put her arms around him. "You're forgiven. I'm sorry I didn't call. I'll remember after this." Then she kissed him on the forehead, picked up her bookbag and set off to school. When Charles came into the kitchen a few minutes later he found his father sitting at the table, mopping tears of gratitude off his face with a paper towel.

"Hey Dad, what's the matter?"

"Nothing to worry about," Ted said, smiling fondly at his growing son. "I'm fine now."

Charles made toast and smeared it with peanut butter. "Dad, can I have a pair of roller blades?"

"You promise to wear a helmet?"

"Yup. And knee and elbow pads."

"I'll talk to your mother."

"Thanks Dad."

"Off you go to school now. Oh, Charles..."

"What?"

"I love you, son. I'm proud of you."

"I love you too, Dad."

THE JOURNEY

Down among the bulrushes tiny bugs flit across the brackish water, fireflies tip tiny pins of light into the depths playing across the sparkling baby trout. A moose has come to the water to drink. He dips his head down, then raising his giant rack of antlers, bugles softly into the dusk. Further on his call is answered.

A woman walks on the path, her feet silently rising and falling on the dusty earth. She doesn't seem to be in a hurry, yet she is moving purposefully forward. She is wearing a three--quarter length woollen coat of indeterminate colours and a bonnet, so it is not possible to see her hair, once raven black, now thinning and nearly white, wound into a bun at the base of her neck. Her dress is long and dun-coloured. She wears a heavy butcher's apron over the front. Her boots are sturdy and strong, scuffed at the toes. Over her shoulders she wears a grey shawl. One hand holds the shawl in place. In the other she carries a covered wicker basket. Along the water's edge she lingers, setting her basket on a nearby rock. She is tempted to take off her shoes and stockings, but contents herself with a short break. She has already walked nine miles over rough terrain but it is not far enough yet. She will walk until near exhaustion and then leave the path to rest in a small thicket.

It is early summer. Anna Walker is 71 years old. This is the second day of her last journey.

In the past few months Anna has experienced several disturbing episodes where her mind seemed to play tricks on her, even abruptly shutting down on her. One day she went out walking and looked down to see that she had put her shoes on the wrong feet. She'd mislaid her telephone book and forgot she'd lost it until one morning she looked in the fridge's freezer compartment and found it there.

Her recent dreams were awash in terror; her bed would be on fire and she would dash to the kitchen for water to put the fire out; nuns, purple-faced with rage, swooped in like demons and cursed at her. Her routines were suddenly disrupted by bizarre happenings. She would make her morning cereal, then pour tomato juice over it.

Although Anna had never given much credence to the medical profession, she had read extensively and knew that something was happening in her mind that she could not control. She made an appointment to see Dr. Ted White. Doctor White sent her to specialists and various tests were carried out. It was several weeks before she heard the results of the tests which, by then, she had come to accept herself. The disease of Alzheimers was stealing her mind bit by bit.

"How rapidly will this disease progress?" she asked Dr. White.

"Hard to say. Weeks, months, even years," he said. "Every one is different. Of course, keeping active and mentally alert as you can is said to help stave off the inevitable. Do you play bridge?"

"No. Math is not one of my talents."

"Chess?"

"No. I can't say I am good at strategy. I either know the correct answer or I don't. But I see where you are leading. Mental exercises may help."

"It's possible." Dr. White studied Anna for a few more minutes. He was a kind and good man, but troubled.

Anna stood up to go. "Well, you have other patients waiting. Thank you, Dr. White, for your time and interest. Then she looked closely at him and said: "Yes, Gail Whitney was on the bridge the night it burned. She was already dead by then. But her murderer is still among us."

"How do you know?"

"Some things I always know. But you, Dr. White, you will meet the murderer and you will know what to do." Then Anna picked up her basket and walked out of his office.

Dr. White sat back down at his chair. The nurse popped her head into the examining room, "Ready for the next one?"

"Give me a minute," he said.

Anna walked home from the doctor's office. It was a glorious summer day. The question was: what would she do now? When she opened the door to her kitchen she looked around for a second for her old dog Nimrod, then recalled that Nimrod had been dead for several years. She'd buried him at the back of the lot. She was about to set out cat food until it occurred to her that no cats had been near her place for weeks.

"I must be losing my mind," Anna thought. Then chuckled to herself. "That is exactly what is happening." She made herself a cup of tea and pondered her next move. The new Sentier NB Trail system had been set up on the old railway beds. She'd read somewhere that the last link had been connected. What she really wanted to do was hike that trail. And what better time to do it? She would go as far as it would take her. And so she closed up the old McAvity house. All the legalities had been taken care of more than ten years previously. Her will was in the lawyer's hands. She shut off the water and drained the pipes. She called NB Power to stop the electricity. From habit, she packed apples, biscuits, cheese, raisins and various foods that would see her through for a few days or weeks if need be.

She put on her large sun bonnet, threw her shawl across her shoulders, picked up her basket and walked out the front door, not stopping to lock it. Half way down the lane she turned and looked back. The house seemed to be saying goodbye to her.

Anna had always been a loner. Few people from Cedar springs ever came to the McAvity house where Anna had lived for more than 40 years. She hadn't had company for months. If people came around collecting, they found the house empty and moved on to the next. With the upcoming election an enumerator stopped by and found Anna's house empty. He went back twice after that. Then the people at the next farm told him: "You'll have a hard time catching her home. She's away a lot." Over the years Anna had come and gone sometimes for months at a time so the neighbours felt no obligation to check on her.

Back in Cedar Springs, Rose Bruce thought about Anna often and told herself she should go out and see the old woman but she put off the visit. Rose had been ill, battling cancer, using every ounce of stamina to fight the disease. Focussed on her own pain and fear, she let the chance of a reunion with Anna go by.

Anna Walker had her first out-of-body experience when she was attending a convent school in Boston. She was eleven.

"It seemed to start as daydreaming, as fantasizing," she told Rose Bruce years ago when they both lived in Brookside, where Rose's father Rev. David Bruce served for four years. "Put it down to culture shock," said Anna. "Put it down to my being confined. Up until then I'd lived with my grandmother on a small farm and I'd never been away from her. Put it down to loneliness. Put it down to feelings of being an outcast. Put it down to hormones. Put it down to growing pains. Whatever you like. One moment I was sitting at my desk with the books open in front of me looking at the back of the head of the girl at the next desk. Her neatly plaited hair was carefully divided into sections and tied with green bows. I felt like pulling one of the ribbons, but I didn't. Instead I held my chin in my hand and turned and gazed out the window. My thoughts turned to the tree outside and a raven I had seen flying around earlier. I remembered the "whap, whap" sound of its wings beating as it swooped down. I sat up to look, leaned back, pulled my long legs under the chair, and the next thing I knew I had quietly floated out the window. Let's be clear here: my body was still sitting upright at the desk. But my soul and spirit had fled.

"There was a feeling of weightlessness as I swept up past the rooftop, past the pine tree, past the crow balanced on a high branch. I was seeing the earth from a very different perspective. I was very happy. Peaceful, yet excited, a little like the feeling you have when the plane you are flying in has gained altitude and the warning lights go off, except there was no sound. Then, a split second later, I became aware that I was still at my desk and a purple-cheeked nun was breathing foul air into my face:

"I asked you, Miss Daydreamer, to name the various ducts in the human body" the nun demanded.

"Ducts?" I wondered blankly. "Ah, em. Well, there are tear ducts and bile ducts,.....er....aqueducts and...." The other girls began to giggle.

"That will be enough. Perhaps you would care to glance at the lesson we are working on today." I looked down at the notebook where I had neatly written my answers to any question the nuns might ask. My face was as red as the nun's. I knew the lesson, could have sung it, piped it on a tin whistle, drawn it or spouted it while turning cartwheels. But my mind was blank. After that concentration on school work was difficult to maintain.

"But I knew I had found the key to freedom and it would stay with me for many years to come. I learned how to slow my breathing, to still my thoughts, and float away to a sandy beach with the setting sun glowing pink across the water. Well, floating isn't exactly the right word. It was levitation with movement."

"Weren't you scared? Rose asked.

"No." said Anna. "Surprised. Delighted. My grandma had what they called 'second sight' in the old days. Perhaps I inherited some of her genes. Maybe you'd say she was clairvoyant now."

"You mean she could see into the future?"

"Well, now. I'm not really sure. What she seemed to do was read your thoughts. On the other hand, perhaps I was an easy study. I lived with her from the time I was two."

Rose was still pondering: "Second sight. Clairvoyant. Wow."

"But these are only labels," Anna said. "It wasn't a talent you could depend on like, say, learning to play the piano or type a letter, that you would always achieve the same melody or write the same sentence. It was a frivolous and whimsical talent. Sometimes there. Sometimes not. And, of course, a lot of it was sheer unfettered imagination. There was no set pace, time seemed to be irrelevant. Photos or phrases could trigger my mental travel. Even advertising layouts were enough to spring me from my confinement. I moved through the mountains in liquor ads. I wore glorious dresses in mansions. I rode horses. I was a cavalry officer. Sometimes I simply floated around, but most often I went to my grandmother's kitchen where I'd sit at her table and bask in the warmth of that room, studying the fresh vegetables by the sink, the shiny row of canisters on the shelf, the singing kettle on the stove, the breeze undulating the curtains. When Gran was in the room she didn't actually talk to me but she'd often smile in my direction.

"Sometimes I'd catch Gran in her garden, hoeing, or down on her knees, weeding. One day, while kneeling, she sat back on her heels, took her gardening glove off her right hand, and lightly mopped her forehead. Then she said aloud: "I know you're homesick, Anna, but this will pass. You'll be right fine." Just as she said that, I felt a snap, like I'd been pulled back into my classroom by a rubber band and for a few seconds my heart stopped.

"My grandmother died when I was 15, a year before I finished convent school. I was not allowed home to attend her funeral, but she came to visit me in my dreams to say goodbye. I, in turn, sent my spirit to the old house where her lifeless body lay. At first I saw an emaciated body in a dress too large, with tiny waxen fingers folded. Those didn't look like Gran's rough capable hands. Then as I looked away from the coffin I saw Gran as she must have been when she was a young woman, straight and strong, hair nearly waist-length. She had on a white gown and there was a wonderful warm glow all around her and then she smiled at me. She smiled at me, and disappeared."

Rose noticed tears flowing down Anna's face as she told the story. Rose had never seen an adult cry. She didn't know quite how to handle it. After a while Anna took up her story again.

"When school ended that June and I was ready to go out and face the world, I had a moment of sheer panic. It happened when I was in a shoe store looking for the proper footwear for a young working woman, something more fashionable than the brown oxfords I'd worn for so long. There were a lot of people around. The clerk was harried. There were so many, many pairs of shoes to choose from, I felt at first confused, then overwhelmed. And then I suddenly realized that my childhood was over, that my schoolmates had all gone home to their families in and around Boston, and that I would be left alone again to fend for myself. Then I heard Gran's voice. "You are doing fine, Anna. Everything will be all right." The voice was so real, I stood up and looked around. But there was only the clerk, with armloads of shoe boxes, moving the metal foot measuring device over my way. And somehow I knew I would be okay because I had my Gran to guide me. Or maybe she was an angel, an angel who smoked a corncob."

"A corncob pipe," said Rose, "that's funny."

"Oh I imagine a lot of the fine ladies of Cedar Springs thought Gran was rather peculiar. But Gran didn't mind...." Anna stood up, while Rose raked the weeds into a pile, and they both moved on to the next row.

"I continued the breathing exercises and the thought concentration that resulted in my spirit floating through the air, moving along over the rooftops, looking inside restaurants to see who was sitting there and what they were doing or talking about," Anna said.

"I found a job doing housework for a Boston society couple. I worked in the kitchen where I learned to cook from some of the finest chefs is New England. I stayed there six years, saving every penny. My only outings were my daily walks to early Mass and my weekly walks through the parks in Boston.

"And then I met someone and my life took a different turn. But that's enough for now, Rose. You'd better run along. Your mother will be looking for you. You are a dear person, Rose. Thank you so much for your company."

Rose came back again the following day and Anna took up her story again. "I served notice to my employers, who seemed sad to see me go. I had been a quick study, I knew how to serve a meal, to slip in among the guests and provide refreshments, to move about the parlour without being seen. In fact I prided myself on being invisible. That way, as long as I performed my duties to the best of my abilities, I was free to dream. But I had fallen in love. Foolishly."

"What's foolish about falling in love?" said Rose.

"Oh, I don't know that it's foolish exactly. I was young and lonely, a silly goose really, and so naive I couldn't tell romantic love from infatuation. I guess I loved the idea of love, without really knowing the man first."

"Did you get married?"

"Yes, but Rose dear, I don't want to talk about that just now. Not on a day so fine. Let's talk about something else."

"So tell me about your Gran."

"Oh, I loved her more than anything in the world. She was short, always wore a bandanna tied under her chin. And as I said before, she smoked a corncob pipe. Every evening after we'd finished the chores, she'd fill the pipe and we'd sit, usually not saying anything. We didn't need spoken language. Why, just sitting near her was like being wrapped in warm strong arms, and you knew you were safe from everything.

"The day came when I returned to Brookside. I went to the old house where Gran used to live, but another family was living there. Gone was the garden and the grassy lawn was tangled over with weeds and trash and junk car parts. The house was badly in need of paint. The living room window had been smashed and was covered with plastic. But as I stood there feeling sad Gran's voice said: 'My journey has ended. Yours has hardly begun. You'll find your own place.' And she was right. I found this." Anna swung her arm to include the house, the garden, the duck pond, Nimrod, and Rose and the farm land beyond.

Another morning while Anna was gardening, Rose came along on her bicycle and sat down to pet Nimrod.

"I've been reading Irish legends," Rose announced. "What is a familiar?"

"A familiar," said Anna, "is that little person that sits on your shoulder and whispers in your ear. Sometimes my familiar talks in my Gran's voice.

"When I arrived back at Brookside days came when I felt restless. I was settled down. But down is not where I wanted to be. Up was what I wanted to feel. Joy, sunshine, progress, star swinging up. Up was where I wanted to be. I wanted to feel alive, I wanted to take wing, to fly up, to soar through the air. To reach up to the sun. But, by that time I was old enough to know that too much sunshine burns, consumes, and leaves only ashes. Then I heard Gran's voice: 'True, and from the ashes rises Phoenix.'

"Another time, in the Spring, I was feeling slightly melancholy. Gran had been dead over 10 years by then.

'Perhaps it's Spring,' came her voice. 'As a girl I was always restive in the Spring.' I liked to think of Gran as a young girl." Anna paused, lost in thought.

"What was Spring like when you were a little girl?" Rose asked.

"That was the time of year when spring cleaning began," Anna said. "So there's probably a genetic disquietude inherited from countless generations of female ancestors who have been conditioned to commence spring cleaning, an annual ritual of exorcising one's home of its winter humours. For centuries each March and April, goodwives in our part of the country have launched an all-out attack on the winter's accumulation of dirt, dust, grease and wood smoke, while dogs hide under the front porch and cats make themselves scarce.

"When I was a child, spring cleaning was an event. It began as soon as it was warm enough to let the fires out. Right after breakfast on the appointed day, the stove pipes were taken down, cleaned, put back up and freshened with aluminum paint.

"Wood ashes were soaked and poured over old fat or bacon grease, and stirred in a jar, before being poured into frames to harden for soap.

"Rugs and carpets came next. These were pulled up, taken outside and beaten with great paddles. Feather mattresses were aired and plumped. In some homes, straw mattresses were emptied and filled with fresh straw.

"As a small child, what I remember most about spring cleaning was carrying water. I carried water by the pailful and boiled it by the tubfull. Besides the tank of hot water on the side of the kitchen stove, large covered boilers full of water steamed on the stove for weeks. Curtains were taken down, washed, dipped in starch or sugar and water, and then stretched on frames to dry.

"Kerosene was the great cleaner of the day. Kerosene removed spots. Kerosene and vinegar cleaned the wooden furniture. (It was also used to rid children's hair of lice, and an elixir of kerosene and molasses was spooned into squirming 'peak-ed' youngsters, to rid their digestive system of worms.)

"Yeech," said Rose.

"Oh, but it worked, we were healthy. Then I recall that a mixture of flour and kerosene the texture of silly putty was worked into globs that cleaned the smoke and grease off ceilings and wall-paper.

"After a thorough cleansing, floors, stairs, banisters and newel posts were varnished. Drawers were upended, wiped out and lined with fresh paper.

"Women made their own wallpaper paste. Gran riced raw potatoes and added them to boiling water, which made a fine paste. Some people used flour and water and slathered this gummy substance on the wall-paper before patting it into place.

"Windows were covered with scratchy white Bon Ami, and wiped clear with old newspapers, or else vinegar and water on a soft cloth. Storm windows were removed and put away for another year. Screens were tacked into place.

"There was no such thing as bleach. In those days, everything in the laundry was boiled and washed, rinsed in bluing, and hung outside on the clothesline in the sun. Or starched. The starch had to be made with boiling water, and at the right consistency, or it would stick and burn. Then the laundry was brought in and ironed, and folded over clotheslines strung across the kitchen just below the ceiling. But first all the starched items had to be dampened down. We used a bottle of water with a screw cap, in which we had punched nail holes to sprinkle the laundry.

"Sheets, table-cloths, dresser scarves, antimacassars, doilies, runners, shirts, slips, house-dresses, aprons, everything, it seemed, had to be starched and ironed...."

Rose thought about dressers wearing scarves, the kind you wear around your neck. Then she asked: "what are antimacassars?"

Anna explained that these were usually white linen napkin-shaped cloths that were tacked to the back and arms of chairs to keep them from being soiled. "Men wore pomade in their hair, an oily substance, and when they leaned back the pomade was transferred to the plush on the chairs and quickly gathered dust and grime. So the women of the day protected their furniture with antimacassars.

"Before the days of electricity there were flatirons with detachable handles that you heated on the stove. When one cooled, you exchanged it for a hotter one. Later there were gas irons and Coleman irons. And then came electric and steam.

"We put whitewash on the shed walls, and lime in the outhouses, that the men previously emptied with shovels.

"We mixed Muresco, which we painted on the ceilings. This was a white powder stirred into water. Some people coloured the Muresco with dyes before covering the walls and ceilings of their homes.

"While all this was going on, fires were kept, stoves were blackened, lamps were filled (again with kerosene) and polished. Cream separator disks were scoured and rinsed, bread was baked, furniture was dusted, meals were prepared, dishes were washed, eggs were gathered and butter was churned.

"Then the sheep were sheared, the wool gathered and washed. I carried pails and pails and pails of water from the spring, filling tub after tub. The wool (which smelled like the Scotch whisky to me; Gran used to have a cup of it now and then) was given several rinses before being spread out to dry on the new grass. As soon as it was dry, we picked out every twig and every burdock. After that the great fluffy mounds of clean wool were sent to the mill for blankets or yarn to be knit into socks and gloves and mittens and scarves and hats, even underwear. You can safely bet there wasn't much time left for boredom....

Anna paused from her weeding, then stood up to get the kinks out of her back. "No, Rose," Anna said: "Don't ever believe people who talk about those good old days. It was hard work from dawn to dusk. Hard work and no pay, and especially difficult for women. I had no idea how poor we were.

"Today we have non-iron sheets and shirts, granulated soap and bleach, spray cleaners, automatic washers and dryers, vacuums, scrubbable prepasted wallpaper, double glazed windows, electric heat. A whisk here, a squirt and a wipe there, a roller of paint, and that's it. Somehow these days spring cleaning isn't quite the same. And thank goodness!"

"Didn't you ever have time to play?" asked Rose

"Yes," said Anna. "Oh yes. It wasn't all work, growing up on the farm. Sure, there were specific chores I was expected to carry out...filling the woodbox, fetching the water, gathering the eggs, carrying warm mash or kitchen scraps to feed the hens and hogs, and so on, but besides those duties, I found plenty to occupy the days.

"Much of our entertainment we created ourselves. As a child I recall gathering pussy willows and making furry Easter bunnies. You stirred flour into a couple of teaspoons of water in a cup to make a paste, and then stuck the fat silvery catkins onto a sheet of cardboard.

"Gran showed me how to whittle off a small branch from an alder bush the thickness of your little finger, and cut a notch about two inches from one end. Then with the handle of the jackknife, gently tap the bark round and round until it loosened. The loose bark was worked carefully off and you shaved a small chip of wood off one side. When the bark was pushed into its original position and dried, it made a lovely whistle.

"The arrival of the downy yellow chicks each spring was a special spring event. We kept them in a box near the stove in the kitchen. They drank from water in a sealer jar, placed upside down in a saucer. Peep-peep, peep-peep, they would sing as they settled into your hand. Peep-peep.

"Somewhere a barn cat would have a litter of kittens stashed, but I'd find them sooner or later. These kittens only gained entrance to Gran's house illegally under someone's coat or sweater, bringing with them their own retinue of fleas."

"Your coat," Rose said.

Anna smiled: "Then came the polliwogs in the brook. Jellied masses of frogs eggs with hundreds of black dots that would turn into tadpoles. As the tadpoles metamorphosed into frogs, spring changed to summer and then came weeding and hoeing and summer company, and shelling peas......until that lovely rainy day came along. Then right after the milking was finished, Gran and I shovelled earth and gathered a can of angleworms, cut a pole from an alder bush and struck off trout fishing.

"We played horseshoes--with real horseshoes. We rode, too, but we considered that work, since we usually ran errands or went out after the cows on horseback."

Rose loved Anna's stories and pummelled her with questions. No matter what Anna was doing, weeding, or sorting or drying or hoeing or any number of the summer tasks she had set herself, she would take time to talk to Rose.

"Times have changed so much since I was a girl," Anna said, kneeling down and taking up her spade again.

"What do children look forward to in the Spring these days? Do they ever get to know the tang of the sorrel plant, the sharp sweet bite of the wintergreen, the refreshing taste of cool clear sweet sap. Are they excited by the first foray along the riverbank for fiddleheads, or deeper into the woods for the dog-toothed violets and purple trillium? Do they know the delight of catching fireflies to glow in their cupped hands? Are they ever soothed to sleep of a summer evening by the rhythmic lullaby of the bullfrogs? Is there a future?"

Then Anna answered her own question. "Oh yes, Rose. There is a future. There is a fine future for you. But you must chart your own journey."

On another day when Anna was talking to Rose Bruce, Rose asked her more about astral travel. Anna said: "During my experience of astral travel, I didn't seem to be bothered by the atmosphere. Whether it was snowing or raining or super hot, I never felt anything but freedom. And speed! Speed was something else. A little distorted, like what happens to marijuana smokers on the third roach."

Rose looked at Anna: "You tried marijuana?"

"All of us have our own journeys, Anna. I've tried many things, kept some, discarded others. Like thoughts, ideas, truths. As will you.

"Anyway, as I was saying, I could move from Boston to Brookside as quickly or as slowly as I liked. Floating along I would see a sign for Belleville, say, and I might drop down and move along the residential streets, just to look at the flowers. Once, I noticed a man standing urinating next to the side of a house. It was embarrassing. Suddenly I found myself back in my own living room.

"And all the time I was in the city, whenever life became unbearable, through boredom or physical pain or shattered romance, I continued to take my astral journeys. While curled up in a knot of grief over a lover's casual goodbye, I started floating. Pain was immediately replaced by euphoria, as I climbed out of my room, out of my despair and into another sphere."

"Did you have many lovers?" Rose asked.

"Oh, Rose. Not many. But I've known love. And you will too. But I want to tell you about what it is like to be an astral traveller.

"Oddly enough, nighttime was never a problem. The darkness was not in the least frightening and I could see as well in the dark as the daylight. Bats seemed to know when I was in the vicinity and shrieked warnings to each other.

"I often listened in to other people's conversations. In a small pub once, maybe it was the Clarendon, I squeezed into a seat where businessmen were drinking beer and philosophizing. It was warm and cosy. The tobacco smoke was thick. For a short time I listened to the conversation, but it was the same old shlock from my grade school days, gussied up in modern slang. Look before you leap, they say. Stay safe, they say. Cover all bases, they say. Don't take chances. Give yourself a safety net. Hedge your bets, they say. Don't burn your bridges. I wanted to shriek at them: But how can you reach the mountain top with one foot on the ground? I wanted to tell them: Sometimes you have to take two steps into the dark. Reach into the unknown and take a good look at what you find in your hand. Smell it. Feel it. Taste it. Sometimes you have to let go the rope. In order to progress, you have to try new things. You cannot experience life and remain in the womb at the same time.

"Then an older woman at another table, as if hearing my thoughts, took up the conversation. 'In my lifetime, especially in my early years, I took so many chances and ran scared so often, terrified seemed a normal state of feeling. I ran away from home, I ran from responsibility. I refused to collect material things. I talked to strangers, slept by the roadside, swam uncharted streams, followed dreams. I tried the panaceas of the 1960s, heard the gurus of the 1970s, and wondered, what's next? I attracted a lot of pain.'

"But what did you learn from this?" I wondered.

"Many, many things," she cackled. "But then rheumatism and old age caught up to me. I yearned for safety, surety, security and sanctuary." The crone raised a glass: Looking directly at Anna, "To your journey," she said.

"Yes, the journey."

"Did you ever live anywhere else?" Rose asked.

"Yes. I lived in New England for a time, and in Maine. And I have travelled all over the world, by ship, by plane, train and on foot.

"Where did you like living best?"

"Right here, Rose. Right now. This is as good as it gets," Anna said, lifting her face to the sky.

The days have been warm and sunny, the nights mild. Anna has been walking for nearly a week, resting now and then, curled up at the foot of a tree. One night it rained, she strung a nylon sheet between two trees, crawled under it and kept dry.

One morning she awoke and had no idea where she was, who she was, or what she was doing there. A large raven squawked and swooped down to land nearby. Anna looked at the raven as it hopped towards her, then stopped to peck in her basket. Anna shooed the raven away. She stood up, walked behind a tree and urinated. Alas, she had forgotten to pull down her underpants. As she walked that day she wasn't aware that her clothes were soiled. She stopped to sit on a bench late in the afternoon. Two cyclists glanced at her as they pedalled by, heads down, rear ends in the air. They could smell human faeces as they passed. They were on their way around the province before summer school started. Neither would remember seeing an old lady who smelled of shit, sprawled on a park bench.

Anna walked on. She left the trails and moved on up to walk parallel to the highway. Afraid of the big logging trucks and transports, disturbed and confused by the noise, she walked near but not on the highway. Lying down to sleep, getting up and walking on, one day she looked around for her basket to find something to eat and realized she must have left it somewhere. A little hungry, she came to a field and spotted wild strawberries. She picked several handfuls, ate them, and moved on.

Then early one evening Anna became very, very tired. She wandered through the trees until she found a tree she liked and settled down in front of it, tucking her legs up under her skirts, and pulling her shawl down over her head she went to sleep.

Then she became aware of light, magnificent, warm, glowing light, like a million aurora borealises rolled into one. A glorious scent filled the air, as if a billion blossoms caressed her. And from the light came her

Gran's voice. And a hand reached out to her. "Come Anna," said the voice, "Your earthly journey is over, Anna. A new journey begins." And for a few seconds all the forest noises stilled. No moose bugled. No bird sang. No squirrel chittered. No porcupine or bear grunted. No fox yipped. Then somewhere nearby, a coyote lifted his nose into the sky and howled a long and reedy note. From further in the forest other coyotes took up the chorus as Anna's soul and spirit quit this earth. And the essence of Anna was gone.

Anna would have been happy to know that her last gift to the animals she so loved, had been nourishing food, untainted by formaldehyde and embalming fluids.

In less than 24 hours coyotes, maybe the same, maybe another pack, scented decay and followed their noses to the spot under the tree. They circled the body and pulled away the shawl. Ravens flew down to peck at the blackened face. Coyotes ripped away the woven materials to get at the flesh. Smaller animals showed up in turn for their share of the feast, smaller and still smaller until by the following spring insects had cleaned the bones.

CULVER'S LAST RIDE

On the grim February day Culver was buried, the steep banks of snow on both sides of the driveway leading to Cedar Springs Cemetery offered welcome protection from the driving wind. Everyone remarked how fortunate that the snow held off until it was all over.

The graveside service, like the Church of England ritual which preceded it, was mercifully short. Returning to the comfort of their Buicks, Chryslers and Lincolns, the mourners' tears soon dried with a wash of warm air from the heaters as they headed to the Elk's Hall for the reception.

The funeral director and the minister watched as the last of the mourners, Fitzhenry White, left the cemetery pushing a walker, while being steadied by his 80 year old daughter.

"How old would he be?" said the minister, "did someone tell me he's 102?"

"Yes, I think so," the funeral director replied. "Hardly worth going home, is it?"

Meanwhile the director's assistant lifted the green carpet grave dressing covering the raw earth, deftly folded it and placed it in the supply van. He then dismantled the casket-lowering device and loaded it last.

Both the minister and the funeral director were acquainted with Culver. Everybody knew Culver. Too well, in the case of the funeral director, who for many years had held the suspicion that Culver had slept with his wife. It gave him a certain sense of satisfaction to put Culver somewhere safe where he could no longer get his hands on other men's wives at least in this life. Even so, he handled Culver's send-off with great dignity and attention to detail. After all, Culver had a large following, not to mention a large family connection, and Catelle's Funeral Home of which he was now sole owner could certainly use the trade, especially with the new Co-op Funeral Association taking a great whack of his business.

Saying their goodbyes, the minister, the funeral director and his assistant drove off. As if on cue, a yellow backloader clattered in to the cemetery and squealed to a stop beside Culver's grave. With a few expert sweeps the grave was filled and the excess soil scooped up and levelled over another grave that had sunk under the weight of the winter snows. Within a few short months, grasses would knit roots across the grave, erasing any earthly trace of the man who had affected so many lives during his 64 years. By that time an orange-coloured, rather phallic 15' granite obelisk would have been erected on a large base at the head of the grave, a fitting symbol for a man known for his conquests, sexual and otherwise.

The reception started out as a glossy affair with fresh-cut flowers on every table, platters of miniature chicken sandwiches, trimmed pimento triangles, rolled asparagus with cream cheese fingers, geometrically arranged vegetable trays, tiny cakes and squares, and imported coffees, all tastefully served on delicate Wedgwood plates, with linen napkins, crystal goblets and china cups. But with the generous and rapidly repeated servings of liquor, the late afternoon soon turned into the kind of merry melee that Culver enjoyed most, where even the most respectable and uptight community leaders, albeit with slightly tilted aplomb, might let down their hair. It would be the talk of the village for weeks.

Culver's funeral was one of the biggest in the county. Family and friends, almost everyone in the village attended, as well as dealers, company reps and various members of the Legislature. Culver would have chuckled over the pomp and pageantry and found a way to pinch the pretentious, given a chance.

Neither Rachael Lawson nor Theresa Grant attended the funeral. Theresa had made an appearance at the wake the previous evening. Rachael had planned to attend. In fact she was already on her way, wearing her fur coat over her basic black, when she changed her mind.

Because of faulty wiring, the radio in Rachael's car went off and on sporadically. It had been silent when Rachael started out. Then suddenly it came to life, at the beginning of an old Hank Williams' tune. *"Have you ever heard a whippoorwill? He sounds too blue to fly. The moon just went behind a cloud. I'm so lonesome I could die."* Hank Williams...Culver's favourite singer. Talk about coincidence.

Rachael disliked Country and Western music. In the 1950s, she and Culver had had many a boozy argument over whether Hank Williams was a singer or poet or just a damn droning noisy irresponsible drunk.

With the size of the funeral and the number of people expected, there would be standing room only, and probably that outside, she told herself. Instead she drove through the centre of the village and stopped in Theresa's driveway. Culver was dead. Today her place was with Theresa, her lifelong friend, who also happened to have been the "Other Woman" in Culver's life for the last 15 years. God, thought Rachael, has it been that long? She and Theresa had a lot in common, including being, at different times, Culver's lovers. Rachael had never discussed her early fling with him with Theresa. Besides the relationship, such as it was, had ended at least 30 years before. Where had the time gone?

By the time Rachael returned to the Maritimes in the early 1980s, all that was left of the early passion melted into a quiet friendship. If she happened to meet Culver in the Village she smiled and waved. At the Elks club she always saved him a dance. But that was as far as it went. Or would ever go.

Now in the afternoons, Rachael and Theresa played Mexican Rummy or similar card games once or twice a week, smoked, sipped coffee and talked about anything and everything, although rarely about the past, of which they had shared so much. They sat at a circular oak table where they could see out the window facing the road. Today, Theresa plugged in the electric kettle, spooned instant coffee into their mugs and after a few minutes, filled the mugs with boiling water.

"What time did the funeral start?" Rachael asked.

"Two o'clock."

"What is it now? Five after?"

"About that," Rachael replied.

Both sat watching the road, each with her own thoughts. Theresa stubbed out her cigarette and sat silently, absent mindedly rubbing a stain on the terry-cloth table cover. Rachael studied her friend, and realized that she was at last beginning to show her years with the deep wrinkles and soft down on her cheeks, the flesh hanging loose under her chin. Theresa was only five years older than Rachael.

Rachael, fully aware and accepting of her own aging process, had come to terms with it years ago. What the hell, was Rachael's attitude. "It was fun while it lasted, and certainly I had my share of the good things in life, including the pretty boys. But I will miss Culver," she thought. Just knowing he was in the neighbourhood had given her a warm feeling. A certain security. His friendship was important to her. The secrets they shared, precious. If she had ever needed help, she knew she could have gone to him immediately. But....no more. For some reason the lines of "*Kawlaiga, the Wooden Indian,*" passed through her mind, followed by strains of lyrics from other old Hank Williams tunes. Culver's idol, she thought.

Culver hadn't always been comfortable with women. He was a scrawny youth with a long face, reddish brown hair and spots. Few girls noticed him in high school, which was probably just as well, because Culver was painfully shy. He was also afraid of rejection.

What he did have was a bull-terrier's way of sticking with it, of seeing something through. And, as many women discovered, he had a sense of the ridiculous that always took one by surprise. When he was 14 he skipped school in the fall to drive a potato truck, promising his father he would catch up on his studies by Christmas. He did. In the spring, he worked on the potato planter. And in summer he hauled pulp. When he was 18 he bought a used truck for $150 and started hauling potatoes. A year later, he bought a backhoe and payloader, and soon had a good-sized heavy construction business going.

Meanwhile he started dating Jean Vale from Portland, Maine, and within six months they were married. Jean was 19. He was 23. The first two years of their marriage were reasonably happy. Their oldest daughter Alice was born within the year. Thirteen months later along came Tom.

"When Jean was pregnant, she was easy to get along with," Culver told Rachael. "She didn't want sex, and I didn't bother her. And when she wasn't pregnant she was always busy with the kids. But she was a great mother. I'll say that for her."

Despite her mothering instincts, Jean had a darker side. Although she had been impressed by Culver's business acumen, and smart enough to see him as a meal-ticket, she gained her personal power by withholding complete approval of anything Culver did. She didn't exactly put him down. She showed no interest in his business and soon he stopped trying to discuss it with her.

Culver meanwhile, hormones hopping, started having one-night stands with women in other cities. It didn't take long for him to contract a nasty dose of gonorrhoea. Alas, his twice yearly sexual encounter with Jean took place the following week before the symptoms appeared.

"She was not amused," he told Rachael later. "She was furious and I couldn't blame her. I could have kicked myself all over the county. Anyway I hied us both up to old Doc Bartley and had it looked after in no time. But that gave Jean a good and permanent reason, at least in her eyes, for cutting out sex almost entirely."

"Yeah, sure," Rachael said.

Although Jean always appeared with Culver in public, stylishly dressed, always playing the role of doting wife, she could be scathing in private. Anyone seeing them at Lodge or at the Legion dances would take them for the perfect couple. Then Culver started playing closer to home. One night, when Jean stayed in to nurse a cold, he found himself in the genial company of the funeral director's wife. They left the Legion boozily singing *Kawlaija was a Wooden Indian.* Culver realized he was too drunk to drive. So, avoiding the parking lot, they cut through the trees at the back of the legion arm and arm and headed up to the top of the knoll, stopping along the way to kiss. "I tell you, I pole-vaulted the last 50 feet," Culver told Rachael later, "but she beat me to the ground. By the second round, I was beginning to sober up. And it occurred to me that she was at least 15 years younger than I was. But by God, she knew how to make a man feel like a million. I guess, though, when she got home, her old man was there in the door waiting for her. I don't think he believed the story that she fell down and got her clothes all mussed and grass-stained. But on thinking back, I doubt if I was the first extracurricular activity she had had."

In time, though Culver got no handsomer, he did get a reputation as a lady's man. He liked married women because they weren't much of a threat. He stayed away from single girls except for Irene Parker, but that was much later on. Meanwhile his business did well. If he wasn't really well off, he at least gave the appearance of success. He built a new garage to house his heavy equipment, had about six acres of yard paved and did a lot of travelling, lobbying various government officials.

Often when he was in Toronto, he'd stop at Rachael's. Later when she became involved in a more serious relationship, he still called her and they'd go out to lunch and catch up on the news. She was one damn fine-looking woman, and he always got a kick out of the envious glances he got from other diners when Rachael walked into the room.

One of Culver's many talents was the ability to listen. Although it didn't draw women to him, it kept them captivated afterwards. His power in the community was a turn-on for most. And he highly enjoyed picking off the "good" girls, the sweet young wives of the pious fundamentalists and the energetic busty matrons in whom he kindled more than a passing interest.

One day he discovered to his own amazement that he truly loved women. He liked their company. He liked their smell, their way of thinking. He liked their voices, and he sure liked the sex. That's women. All women. Well, most anyway. But when he pulled Theresa from the water the night of her accident, all that changed. From then on, she was the only one he wanted. He felt he had found and saved a treasure, a soulmate, and for all his misadventures, through his love for her, he felt redeemed.

From then on he spent as much time as he could with Theresa. He began taking her on trips. He doted on Theresa's Ellen the way he did on his own kids.

Although he didn't discuss one with another, it was safe to say that neighbourhood gossip had got back to Jean that he was spending a lot of time with Theresa. Jean, certain of her role as wife, chose to ignore it. After all, she had what she wanted. She had her children, her lodge, her position in the community and her connection with the church. She had begun going to church about the same time as Culver gave her the clap, and she had continued to go. It was another way of silently berating Culver for his adulterous ways. Most important, she would no longer have to go through the messy ordeal of sex with Culver. Or anyone else, for that matter. For her sex had always been a means to an end, the children. That's all.

There was no joy in the sex experience for Jean. One time when she got tiddly with a couple of women friends after a Tupperware party, the talk got around to sex, with the other women cracking jokes about their husbands' ineptness in bed. One related that she didn't care much for it, since her husband always managed to get his elbows between her ribs at the worst possible time. Another said she was thrown off, especially when the kids were around because her husband was such a "noisy comer." Then the last one said the only thing quicker than making love with her husband was preparing "instant breakfast." Waving her glass for more sherry, Jean said her problem was just the opposite. "My husband thinks he's in a marathon. Sawing away. I usually try to think of matching wallpaper and drapes."

"Big wake?" Rachael asked.

"Oh yes," said Theresa. "Culver would have been delighted. Jean stood next to the coffin, managing to look both grim and smug at the same time. As I expected, she looked straight through me and reached for the person behind me. I didn't put out my hand either, just kept walking towards the casket. Alice and Tom and their families were there in the receiving line. Alice got home from the west last night. Tom went down the airport to pick her up. I guess they had a hell of a trip back. Lots of black ice. That's a miserable stretch of road down along the flats, especially if it's sleeting. Anyway they made it. More coffee?"

"Not just now, thanks."

Theresa lit another cigarette and inhaled deeply. *Did you ever hear a whippoorwill? He's just too blue to cry.* Although her grief was all-enveloping, she didn't feel like crying. She wanted to hug herself and moan. Or start keening as she had in the night.

Culver's death was so damn sudden. So unexpected. And, Christ, he was only 64, a year older than she was. She and Culver had known each other since high school. They hadn't dated. Both had married at 20, the standard age for marriage in the county. Culver had married Jean Vale of Portland. Theresa had gone to teacher's college and taught until she found herself pregnant by Larry Grant. Their first child, Melany, was born seven months after their hasty marriage. A son, Lawrence, followed 12 months later. Six years passed before their last child, Ellen, arrived, and six years after that Larry was killed working in the woods.

At the time Larry died Theresa felt more anger than grief. Larry had been a hard man, given to anger and sudden rages. He was hard on himself and when he drank he would throw up the fact that he and Theresa "had to get married." He couldn't accept the fact that he had as good a wife as any in the county. She was not only faithful, but she was also aa good home-maker, an excellent mother and cook. He could not see that instead of marrying beneath himself, he had in fact married well. Secretly he felt that she was more intelligent and better educated than he was. That also made him angry.

Just before the accident, Larry had announced that he planned to leave Theresa, and that she could go to hell as far as expecting support for either her or her children. And how was he to be sure they were even his? After all, Ellen had bright red hair, and there sure as hell was no red hair in his family? True to form, Theresa thought.

The next ten years were hard ones for Theresa. She didn't have a proper teaching license so she worked at other jobs. She did papering and painting for friends. She worked on the potato harvester. She took in children. She scrimped and saved until Melany and Jim were through school. They were good children, well behaved and enterprising. Jim had a part-time job at a garage, where he turned himself into a first-class mechanic. Melany became a stewardess. And then it was only Theresa and Ellen sharing the lonely old house. Theresa's only social life was through the Liberal Association, where she served as secretary. Then an accident changed Theresa's life forever.

On a back stretch of highway between Perth and Plaster Rock where Theresa had attended a political meeting, she was nearly killed. The torrential rains had washed a bridge out and she drove straight into the water. As fortune had it, Culver, who had attended the same political rally, came along and managed to drag her out of the car before she drowned. Theresa had a dislocated shoulder. Her face was badly cut and she was unconscious, but he carried her to his car and drove her to the Tobique Valley Hospital where she remained for over a week. It would be three days before she regained consciousness. Then she awoke to see 15-year old Ellen, smiling and sobbing at the same time. Even with a red nose and streaming eyes, to Theresa Ellen was a beautiful sight.

"Ellen, oh Ellen." was all Theresa could manage before she slept again. When she awoke near suppertime Ellen was still seated beside her. "How long have you been here?"

"A couple of hours," Ellen said. "How are you feeling?"

"Groggy and sore. They must be giving me something."

"Yeah, the nurse gave you a needle a while back. You've been snoring."

"Snoring? I have never snored in my life," Theresa said.

"Like a buzz saw," said Ellen laughing.

"How did you get here?"

"Well, Mr. Culver drove me. And I've been staying with school friends just down the road. Mr. Culver brought me here the night of the accident, and then hung around and got me settled in with my friends. I guess he knows their parents or something. Anyway, they've been real nice."

"Mr. Culver?"

"Yeah, Mr. Culver. Do you remember the accident?"

"Not really. I just remember the driving rain. The windshield wipers could hardly move it. Then nothing...."

"There was a bridge washed out. You went right into the water. He was coming along behind and stopped just in time. A few seconds more and you'd have drowned." Ellen began crying.

"Oh my God. There, there, baby, there, there. I'm all right. We're together. We'll be all right."

"Oh Mama, I couldn't lose you. I couldn't manage without you. I'm so glad you are going to be okay."

"Yes. Well, why don't you run along to your friends. It must be nearly suppertime. Tell them how grateful I am that they are looking after you. I'll meet them as soon as I get out. Bye, bye, dear."

After Ellen left, Theresa realized she had to use the toilet. She turned back the covers and swung her legs over the side of the bed. The room swam before her and grabbing the edge of the bed, she rolled back into it. A nurse stepped through the door and asked her if she needed help.

After she had used the toilet, Theresa stood up and looked in the mirror. Her forehead was covered in a crusty blood-stained bandage. Her eye was black and there was a mean bruise on her cheek. "Why, I look as if I had had an encounter with Larry," she thought ruefully. "What this old face has been through."

By the time she got back into bed she was totally exhausted, and slept soundly. Late in the evening, when Culver, driving a load of lumber in to Plaster Rock, stopped at the hospital and poked his head into the room, she was sound asleep. But her colour was good, her breathing fine, and he found himself truly relieved at her progress.

Culver was again there to meet her when Theresa left the hospital. Feeling weepy and fragile and a little afraid, she huddled near the door in the front seat of his car. Culver cut his usual speed of 120 kms down to the 80 limit. "You're going to be fine, Theresa," he said. "Just fine."

"Yeah, I know. It's just....it's just, well....Ellen is nearly grown now. She is a level-headed young woman, much smarter than I was at her age. But in another year she will be in university, and then I'll be...I'll be..."

"Alone? is that what you're worrying about?"

"Maybe."

"But we are all lonely at times. Maybe those of us who are married are even more so."

"Now, Culver," said Theresa brightening, "everybody knows Jean adores you."

"Don't believe all you hear. Don't even believe what you see."

Theresa remained silent until they were almost home. Culver pulled the car up close to the steps and went around and opened the door for her. Theresa climbed out and stood trembling, wondering if she would make it inside. As she moved forward, her world began to whirl and her knees buckled. Culver swept her up in his arms and carried her to the landing. He had to set her down for a few seconds while he retrieved the door key she had dropped, but he soon had the door open and carried Theresa inside, where he set her down on the living room couch. He looked around for something to cover her, and found a blanket on the chest in her bedroom. When he came back to the couch where she was lying, he was startled to see tears pouring down her cheeks. Her distress was palpable. Again he pulled her into his arms and comforted her like a sobbing child. "There, there," he said. "There, there. It's going to be all right. What you need is a cup of tea. I'll make it."

Theresa remained on the couch while Culver rummaged in the cupboards. He came back after a while with a steaming cup of tea on a tray which he set down in front of her. "I saw a bottle of Canadian Club under the counter when I was looking for the teapot" he said. "Mind if I have a drink?"

"By all means, help yourself," said Theresa. "Small payment for all you have done for us. I don't know how I can ever thank you."

"No need. No need at all." Culver downed the whisky in two gulps. "I should be getting down to the office. Are you going to be okay now?"

"Yes, I think so. Ellen will be home any minute. I think I'll just stay right here."

Culver leaned down, kissed her lightly on the forehead saying, "Take care, now. I'll be back to see how you are doing a little later."

"Thanks again for everything."

And that is how the relationship between Theresa and Culver began. Within a month they were lovers and remained so until three days ago.

"What time is it?" said Rachael.

"Two-forty. I should think they'll be along any time now."

No sooner had Theresa spoken these words than two police cruisers slowly and ceremoniously passed, followed by the long gray hearse. Tears began to fall as Theresa stared mutely at the procession. Rachael, too, felt a deep sadness as she shared her friend's grief.

The funeral procession faded from sight.

"Good bye, Culver," said Theresa.

"Yes," said Rachael, "Goodbye, old friend. You were one of a kind."

Did you ever hear a whippoorwill? He sounds too blue to fly. The moon just went behind a cloud. I'm so lonesome I could die.

MOTHERS DAY

Hurrying west on Wellesley, Ruth Gilman saw her bus pulling away just as she reached Parliament Street. No taxis were to be had this time of day, so it would be fastest to walk now.

Back in the city to take part in a well-publicized television special, Ruth realized it had been three years since she'd left Toronto for the peace and renewal of life in a small New Brunswick village, Cedar Springs. She had almost forgotten the manic Toronto of rush hour. Crossing over at the lights, she picked up speed, dodging bikers, pedestrians, wine bottles, gobs of spittle, spilled ice cream, dog excrement and soft tar, reaching the hospital about 20 minutes later.

As she made her way along, she wasn't really aware of the morning's chill, and the gusts of raw air moving up from Lake Ontario to tangle with gutter halitosis, gas and diesel fumes. When she had booked into the hotel the night before, there had been a message waiting for her from someone by the name of McVickers, a patient at the Princess Margaret Hospital. When she'd settled into her room, she returned the call.

"You don't know me," Ellen McVickers said. "But it's most important I see you as soon as possible. It's about the child you had 32 years ago."

Ruth's heart lurched. "There must be a mistake. Is this some kind of a joke?"

"No. But you must hear what I have to tell you. You must believe me."

"I lost a baby 32 years ago," Ruth replied coldly. "It was born dead. Who are you? And why are you doing this?"

"Your daughter didn't die. She's alive. I raised her. Please listen to me. For the past two months, I've been in the Princess Margaret Hospital. The cancer has metasticized and my time is limited. I saw in the Star where you would be arriving today, and I called five hotels before I found you.

"You see, everything has been preying on my mind. I must talk to you. For your sake as well as mine. I'm in Room 317. Could you come tomorrow?"

"Yes," said Ruth, "I can be there." With questions whirling through her brain like swirls of snow buntings, Ruth canceled her next day's appointments, then spent a fretful night.

Dressed in a pale green linen suit, a cream silk blouse, a star-burst pin on her left lapel, carrying a briefcase and a soft leather shoulder bag, Ruth presented the image of someone in charge of her life, someone who had achieved the success she had dreamed of those many years ago, when she had walked this same street, lost, empty, and alone. Yet, even now while living a more exciting and productive life than she could ever have hoped for, the pain and bitterness which had burned so deeply into her psyche could never be fully erased. Over the years she had learned how to channel that bitterness and rage into energy, which ultimately pushed her to the top in television communications, a profession nearly closed to women. At the beginning of Ruth's working career, equal opportunity for women was still decades in the future.

Entering the hospital through the main doors, she met only a cleaner as she moved towards the elevator which took her to the third floor. Ground floor, first floor, main floor, mezzanine. She pressed number three.

Stepping off the elevator she turned left and walked along to Room 317. The door was closed. Ruth paused. It was still not too late to turn around and go back down the elevator, walk to the Wellesley subway station and catch up on her appointments. Maybe, since the door was closed, the woman was already dead, taking her answers with her. Ruth's heart seemed to be pressing against her lungs, allowing only tiny shallow breaths. If she was still alive, could Ruth bear to hear what she had to say?

After all the despair she had borne over the last 30 years, the heartache, the agony of looking in other baby carriages, of watching other new parents proudly describing the antics of their children, of passing a school yard and hearing the shrill, merry voices, Ruth had become accustomed to the feeling that some special part of her had been cut out and that something vital had been taken from her. She'd learned to quell the longing, to suppress the pain of attending graduations to watch other people's children, in robes and rakishly tilted mortarboards, walk down the aisles. Listening, and dying a little, as her sisters and brothers described their grandchildren.

Ruth had come to accept the emptiness, and sometimes even stopped blaming herself for the loss of her baby, tossing aside magazines which printed statistics saying that smoking was bad for the foetus, drinking was bad for the foetus, caffeine was bad, etc. etc., although she had smoked and drunk coffee and alcohol. But there was another aspect of her loss which she guiltily acknowledged from time to time. It was the relief she felt that responsibility for another human being had been taken from her. On low days, she wondered if she would have had the courage, the emotional stability to raise a child on her own, to face the rancor of her parents. And where would she have found the money?

Times were different in 1957 when Ruth found herself alone, pregnant and nearly broke. To gain shelter for herself and her unborn child,

Ruth took a job offered in the Toronto Telegram Classified Ads section "Unwed mothers welcome to apply," keeping house for a young professional couple with three children. She stayed with a couple in Rexdale, a northwestern suburb of Toronto, and looked after them and their family until she went into labour half way through her ninth month. A doctor was called and she was given an injection. It was five days later when Ruth became fully awake. The woman for whom she worked seemed agitated. Leaving Ruth's room, she quickly returned with the doctor who explained that Ruth's baby had been born dead. When Ruth asked to see it, she was told that due to complications she had been unconscious for several days after the birth and that they had had to dispose of the baby's remains. The doctor prescribed Stilbesterol to dry the milk in her leaking breasts.

Numbed by grief, physical weakness and shattered hopes, it didn't occur to Ruth to question the doctor further. At that time, she would never have dared challenge his authority. She accepted the statement as fact and a few days later she moved away from Rexdale and never saw the couple or the doctor again.

Easing open the door to Room 317, Ruth found a small emaciated woman who motioned her to a chair near the bed.

"Mrs. McVickers? Am I too early?" Ruth asked.

"No. It'is a good time right now. Later in the day, the medication makes me very confused."

Reaching a pale clawlike hand towards Ruth, Ellen McVichers said, "I don't know where to start."

Ruth allowed the woman to take her hand and waited.

"You see Arthur--that's my late husband--and I couldn't have any children," she began. "We wanted a family so much. We had a good marriage and a lovely home in Rosedale quite near the ravine. We had been married ten years when we decided to adopt. But Arthur was Jewish and I'm Catholic and for that reason we were never accepted as adoptive parents. Then one day, Arthur came home from the office--he was a partner in the law firm, Smedly, West and McVickers--anyway he came home and told me that he had had a call from a contact of his who told him a new baby would be available within the next day or two, and that if we could come up with $5,000, the baby could be ours.

"Are you saying you bought a baby?" Ruth asked.

"Oh, no. Arthur told me the money was to go to help the baby's birth mother pay her hospital bills and continue her education.

"Well you can't imagine how I felt when the very next day, this infant, only a few hours old, was placed in my arms. My husband took care of the business end of things and I had this wonderful perfect exquisite little girl of my own.

"I was so thrilled with her, I wouldn't even leave the house to go shopping. I sent the maid out to buy the things we needed. I had an interior decorator come in and create a room for my Linda--I named her Linda Louise, after our mothers. We had her room done in yellow and white. It was a big and airy room, with windows on two sides. The wallpaper had teddy bears with drums in the pattern. We bought her stuffed toys.

"From the time she came to us, Linda filled our lives with sunshine. She was so quick and smart. She was walking at eight months, and talked in whole sentences by the time she was two. I kept a baby book, and later on a diary, which she still has today. Of course, she had the usual childhood diseases--measles, mumps, chicken pox--and I worried myself sick. But we had the best pediatrician in the city and she quickly recovered. She ran through the days as light as laughing air.

"We bought her a puppy, a beagle. She named him Popeye. From then on, wherever you found Linda, asleep in bed, in front of the TV set watching "Howdy Doody Time," or riding her tricycle in the garden, Popeye was always there by her side.

"A few days after Linda's eighth birthday, Arthur suffered a sudden heart attack while at work. They rushed him to the hospital, and tried every measure available at the time, but he never regained consciousness. A few days after the funeral, I had a call from one of his partners, asking if I wanted to go in and clean out his desk, or if I wanted them to handle it. I said I would go.

"Arthur's secretary was away that day, and another young woman showed me into his office. She was very helpful. She found some cardboard boxes, and the keys to his desk. It felt strange to be sitting at Arthur's desk where he spent so much of his working life. I looked through the drawers, and skimmed the files, which all had to do with cases he was working on. I set those aside for his secretary to look after. Then, over on the credenza, I saw the new briefcase I had bought for him at Christmas time. I tried to open it but it was locked. I had noticed several keys in his desk, so I tried one of them and sure enough it worked. At the same time, I tried another key in the drawer in the credenza, and it worked too. There I found Arthur's personal files. I slipped them into the briefcase. Then I placed his books and other knickknacks, pen set, clock, radio, etc, in the boxes and arranged to have them dropped off at the house.

"Well, there was so much to attend to after Arthur died that several months went by before I got around to looking through his personal files."

Ellen McVickers rested a moment, and then reached for a glass of water. Ruth held the glass for her and steadied the straw between her lips.

For Ruth, the confusion of emotions concerning what she might be about to hear had short-circuited all rational thought. She waited.

"In among Arthur's papers were some clippings. At first they meant nothing to me and I nearly threw them out, but an article caught my eye about a doctor charged with stealing babies. The dates on the clippings were about six months after Linda came to us. I don't know how Arthur managed it but there was a copy of Linda's birth certificate, listing us as her birth parents. Well, when I saw that, I knew immediately something was wrong. I sat down and carefully went through each piece of paper. Your name was also there among his notes. Then I put everything away in the safe at home to give myself time to think about it.

"Looking back, I can see now I was disorientated by the grief of losing Arthur, and I couldn't handle anything else. The idea of having to give Linda up was unthinkable.

"You see Linda was only eight years old. Arthur was gone. She was my life. She was my strength. Linda meant everything to me. You should have seen her, she was so beautiful. She was taking piano lessons and when she was barely six, she could play "Boogie Woogie" just like a professional.

"Arthur's death was hard on her, too. He had always doted on her. He took her to Yorklea Stables every Saturday morning for riding lessons, and he bought her a fine chestnut gelding. Linda looked splendid in her riding clothes, so sure in the saddle. It seemed that whatever she set out to do, she became committed and gave it her very best. I don't know how we got through that dreadful time after we lost Arthur, but we stayed busy and soon she was her happy, sunny self again.

"So I thought it all over and decided to say nothing. At first I rationalized that Linda was too young to be told so soon after Arthur's death that she was adopted.

"But I knew I couldn't give her up. I couldn't take a chance on losing her. As time went on I put the whole thing out of my mind and concentrated on giving Linda the best possible upbringing I was capable of."

A sheen of perspiration covered Ellen McVickers' gray wasted face. Just then a nurse bustled in with a hypodermic. Ruth stepped outside. When she came back in Mrs. McVickers seemed to be sleeping.

Ruth waited. A girl. Linda. Funny, though she'd never seen it, she'd known her baby had been a girl. From time to time she had dreamed of a smiling little girl with pigtails running towards her open arms and then fading away again. Her thoughts went back to her own beginning.

Born near Sussex, New Brunswick, Ruth had quit high school to get married. Her father, distant, domineering, religious to the point of fanaticism, had strict codes of behaviour for his daughters. Any kind of emotional warmth was seen as weakness. Her mother went along with her father's wishes. When Ruth met Allison Gilman, fresh from the Korean war and newly discharged from the army, she thought she had found a way out. They never really dated. Instead they ran into each other at the diner. He borrowed his brother's pickup and they drove around. Then one day he told Ruth he wanted to go to Ontario, and he wanted her to go with him. She spoke to her father. After a sermon about her waywardness, he agreed to sign the necessary legal documents, since Ruth, having just turned sixteen, was considered under age.

The Gilmans moved to Bowmanville, found a two-room apartment, and within days of their arrival Allison was hired by General Motors. Married to Allison, Ruth soon discovered that she had traded life with her cold, domineering father for life with a hard-drinking, abusive husband. She stayed with him for eight months. Soon Allison's weekend drinking spilled over into week days. Working shiftwork, he came and went on no set schedule. Ruth tried to have something cooked and ready when he got home, but she never knew when that would be. If the meals she prepared didn't suit him, he flung them against the wall. She began spending time in the library, until one day she didn't make it home before he arrived. He broke her nose.

Sex hadn't been that great between them, and each time Allison reached for her when he was drunk Ruth found it harder and harder to submit. If she begged off because she was tired, he demanded sex before she could sleep. One night his thrusting and grunting repelled her so she became nauseated. Soon she was choking on her own vomit, but he still didn't stop.

The next morning, while he lay sleeping off a night's drinking, Ruth removed $30 from his billfold, packed a small suitcase, and slipped away to the bus station, where she caught a bus to Toronto.

Ruth found a small room in Parkdale. Then she landed a job at the Pickin' Chicken restaurant on Lakeshore Boulevard in Mimico. She worked as a car-hop from four in the afternoon to 11:30 in the evenings. She discovered the Parkdale Public Library, and each day, shortly after it opened, she went in, found something to read and sat down. She often stayed at the library until it was time to go to work.

When she had been in Toronto a few months, a fellow by the name of Jerry Stewart began arriving at the restaurant about half an hour before closing time. Soon he was driving her home from work. To Ruth, this handsome, laughing, charming man was everything Allison was not. Jerry sold cars at a dealership on Bay Street and by the way he threw money around, he seemed to be successful at it. He took her for a weekend to Wasaga Beach. He took her to the race track. They went walking in Sunnyside. It wasn't long before they began going to a nearby motel and Ruth soon became pregnant. When she told Jerry she was having a baby, everything changed. "How do I know it's mine?" he asked.

"Because I have never been with anyone besides you," she cried.

"Well, it doesn't make any difference one way or another," he said. "I've already got a wife and five kids in Don Mills. Maybe you ought to go back to your husband."

And so ended the affair between Ruth Gilman and Jerry Stewart. Ruth stayed at the restaurant until her pregnancy became visible and she was fired. She then answered the ad with the couple in Rexdale.

Walking across the bridge over the Humber River on her way out of Rexdale, Ruth looked down at the swiftly flowing muddy water and considered letting the water take her. Then from under her despair came a will to survive, and in a few minutes she continued over the bridge.

After she lost the baby, Ruth went back to Parkdale and found another rooming house at Jameson and King. For the next few days as she settled in she considered her options. She could go back to restaurant work, or she could try for something in a factory which would be better money and maybe take a night course in shorthand-typing. In the meantime, on Saturday morning while doing her laundry in the basement, she met Lois who also lived at the rooming house. Lois invited her to a party to take place in the common room on Saturday night. Ruth worried what she should wear but Lois assured her that wasn't important. These were actors and beatniks and musicians and friends. It wasn't a dress-up party, just group of people she might enjoy meeting. The plan was that everyone contribute $2 towards the beer and food, and come along any time after eight.

Ruth entered the common room about 8:30 in the evening. Jazz was playing on the hi-fi, progressive jazz she would later learn, big band stuff with Stan Kenton. Two handsome young men stood near the door. "I'm Jack," said the first. "I'm Ed," said the second. "Could I get you a drink?" She talked to Jack until Ed returned with a bottle of beer for her. "Let me introduce you around," Jack said. Although Ruth repeated the names, John, Ralph, Vibka, Reuta, Polly, Janet, Virginia, Joan, Wesley, Malcolm, Jane, Jane's husband Allen, Miles, Alex and Jimmy, it would be weeks before she could remember them all. As the evening progressed, Ruth learned that some were actors who had day jobs. Some were unemployed. Janet was a folk singer. John Egan was a cameraman with a film company, and played sax in a nearby club. Ralph Hicklin was a drama critic newly started with the Toronto Telegram. Virginia was a teacher, divorced, with a small son. Polly was a reader for a book company. Vibka played the piano and worked in the blueprint room of a steel company. Joan, an executive secretary, was also an actress appearing in a play at the Little York Theater, with Jimmy Rutherford. Jack and Ed also had something to do with the play, costumes, stage props. She would later learn that Jack and Ed were a homosexual couple, destined to live together for over 30 years until Jack was killed by a passing motorist as he stepped out of a taxi.

With these people, for the first time in her life, Ruth felt at ease. Polly made room for her on the chesterfield and began discussing manuscripts. Having spent so much time in libraries, Ruth was familiar with most of the current authors and their works. Starved for conversation, she was the best kind of listener. What these people had in common were dreams, dreams of something better, and the way they talked of these dreams to Ruth made it sound like anything was possible.

After the party the others at the rooming house seemed to accept Ruth as one of them. She found a job as a waitress. On her nights off, she went with one or more to the Little York Theatre. She went with them to poetry readings. She accompanied them to the Village Corner, one of the first coffee houses to open in Toronto. They took her to the museum, to the art gallery and to Toronto Island.

Ruth began keeping a journal and she wrote in it constantly. She poured out her feelings, her fears and her hopes. The rooming house, with its daily smorgasbord of tragedy and low comedy, positively vibrated with creativity. When not having nervous breakdowns or running from the police, the bill collectors, ex-lovers and their own demons, everyone was doing something imaginative. She came to love all these creative, energetic, accepting, wonderfully flawed and quirky people.

With her new friends life took on a special glow. She wrote sitting in a bay window, watching the sunrise over Lake Ontario and hearing the first streetcar of the morning rattling along King Street. She tried her hand at poetry.

One time after she had been at the rooming house about six months, Ralph, the drama critic, while cruising the bookshelves for something to read, opened a magazine which Ruth had been using to write on, and one of her poems fell out. He picked it up and put it in his pocket.

That night there was another party and, about halfway through, when the topic of writing came up, Ralph pulled out the poem and read it to the crowd. "I don't know where this came from," Ralph said. "But I want you to hear it." Ralph, who had done public readings of his own work, read slowly and with feeling. Listening to him was such a delight that for a second or two Ruth didn't recognize her own work. And then she did, and her heart stopped.

"Very good." said someone when Ralph had finished.

"Excellent. Profound, very moving," said another. "Was this submitted to the Telegram?"

"No," Ralph said. "I found it right here on the bookshelf among some magazines. Does anyone know who wrote it?"

All shook their heads. Ruth, still too stunned and embarrassed, said nothing. Instead, she left the party shortly afterward and walked down to the lake. The knowledge of what had taken place was almost too much to take in at once. She had written a poem. It had been read in public. They had thought the poem was good. The way Ralph had read it, it even sounded good. Suddenly she understood that she had created something worthwhile. For the very first time she realized she could be more than an uneducated loser from the Maritimes, on the run from a brutal husband. And finally, the pain of losing her baby began to lift. That was the push she needed, the real start of her career in newspapers, radio, and television journalism.

Ruth, who had been sitting motionless throughout her reverie, realized Ellen McVickers was awake and once again studying her.

"Did you ever tell Linda about her beginnings?" Ruth asked.

"No," said Mrs. McVickers. "No, I didn't. But I did discover what had happened to you. The first time I saw you on the television, I did some checking, enough to satisfy me that you were Linda's birth mother. I was really impressed with you. You had such assurance. You had such poise.

"See, I had never worked out. I had lived at home until Arthur and I were married. I had never wanted a career, I wanted to be a wife and mother, to keep a nice home for my husband and children. I didn't think I was any good for anything else.

"But when I saw you, I thought to myself, there's somebody who knows where she's going. You were moving up in your career. You appeared to have such strength, such control. You had everything I didn't have. So I told myself, she already has everything. She is somebody. She doesn't need Linda. Linda was all I had to live for. I couldn't take any chances in losing her.

"It seemed like no time until Linda was going to high school. It was a private school, one of the best in the city. She sailed through with top marks in every subject. We spent our summers at Georgian Bay. Friends of ours had a sailboat. She swam and sailed and water-skied. For her sixteenth birthday, I bought her a little red Firebird. She loved that car. At eighteen she enrolled at University of Toronto. The next summer we decided to go to Europe, Spain, Portugal and Italy. Another year we went to Switzerland. She loved to travel. I was frightened to death half the time, being that far from home, but she loved to organize and plan our days. We went everywhere: castles, museums, ruins, restaurants. In the winters we took a cruise, the Bahamas one year, the Marianas another.

"The year she received her law degree and was called to the bar there were only three women in a class of 125 men. Oh, she was smart. I can't tell you how proud I was to see her there at the front of the hall. She had turned out so well, better than my fondest dreams. Charming like her father, educated, capable, all those things I never was. How I wish Arthur had been alive to see how well our girl turned out.

"Even before she left university she had a job lined up. She worked for three years in a large law firm, and then opened her own law practice."

Ellen McVickers lay back on the pillows, seemingly exhausted from the effort of talking.

"Where is Linda now?" Ruth asked.

"Oh, she and her husband will be here later this evening. She pops in every day on her way home. Did I tell you she was married? Such a lovely wedding, seven bridesmaids. They were married at the Holy Trinity Church. We had the reception on the back lawn in Rosedale. Just a perfect June day. Linda was so beautiful. Her husband Greg--he is a lawyer, too--looked so dashing in his tuxedo. What a handsome couple they made. They went to New Zealand on their honeymoon. They met soon after she went into practice. Now they have their own law firm, Johnson and McVickers. Linda kept her own name, even after her babies were born."

"Grandchildren?' said Ruth wonderingly.

"Montgomery--they call him Monty--is three, and Elizabeth is about 18 months old. Perfectly darling children. They have their own nanny who lives right on the premises. Linda and Greg bought this big old house in Mississauga. Lovely. Of course, Linda is very busy at the office, and they have lots of help, a housekeeper, and someone who looks after the grounds."

At two in the afternoon a nurse came into room with a hypodermic and soon Mrs. McVickers slept. Ruth moved around the room, then out into the hall. She had had nothing to eat all day, but decided she was not hungry. Instead she got a cup of coffee from a dispenser near the lunch counter and returned to Mrs. McVickers' room.

Ruth recalled those early years, the struggle to make ends meet while she learned how to write. She had driven a coffee wagon, she had modeled coats. Then through her old friend John Egan she got a job as story editor at CBC Radio. She was good at it. She had lots of ideas and she created interesting programs.

In 1965 she moved from radio to television and began appearing regularly doing book reviews. She later left CBC and went to work on a rival television network. Within a year she had her own show. By then she was earning good money. She had a luxury apartment. She had books and paintings. She had traveled, albeit usually on working trips, which left little time for sightseeing. At age 50 she decided enough was enough. She wanted out of television. She wanted out of the city. It was time to devote all her energy to writing. And so she had found the snug little cottage near Cedar Springs. Life was very good indeed. She had almost refused to take part in the television special, but then decided it would be an opportunity to renew acquaintances and lunch with old friends.

It had not been an easy life, but taken all in all it had been a good life, Ruth thought. She had held her age well. There had always been men in her life. But never again would Ruth lose control of a relationship. Because of this very control relationships which had a warm, passionate beginning, tended to cool over the years. In time old lovers became friends.

And now to learn that she actually had a daughter, that she had grandchildren, it was almost unbelievable. She thought about Linda's children and their nanny. How very different Linda's experience had been from hers. The center of a loving family, doted on, supported, championed at every turn. Backed by wealth and social status, Linda could never know what it was like to be alone, broke, scared, pregnant and then losing her baby, with all the emptiness that followed. Ruth remembered the one and only time she had discussed it with her family. She chose to speak to one of her married sisters. It was a mistake. "How did you get rid of it?" her sister asked.

"Get rid of it? I didn't get rid of it. I lost it."

"Well," said the sister, "it's probably just as well. How would you have looked after it? What would you have told Mom and Dad?"

How and what indeed. Ruth didn't know, and in a way felt relief that she would never have to find out.

Late in the afternoon, when another dose of medication eased Mrs. McVickers into sleep, Ruth walked down to the cafeteria and had a sandwich and tea. Although she was only gone for a few minutes, when she arrived back at Room 317, she saw a change in Mrs. McVickers. Her face and hands had a waxy hue. Her breathing had slowed to a shallow whisper. Ruth rang for the nurse. Immediately the nurse bustled into the room, brushing the crumbs from her supper off her white pants. As she checked for the pulse, Mrs. McVickers sighed softly one last time. It was six o'clock.

"Her daughter usually arrives about now," the nurse said. "I'll just call her office and let her know what has happened. If you would like to stay until she arrives, I am sure that will be fine."

Ruth sat down again. As she looked at the still form, she searched her mind for answers. "You had no right to keep my baby from me. You had no right. I almost wish you hadn't told me," she thought.

But the fact was, although she had lost her baby and suffered from that loss for over 30 years, for Linda's sake maybe it was for the best. Linda had had everything money could give her. Ruth had no money in those early years. God knows how she would have managed with working and looking after Linda at the same time. It was all she could do to support herself.

And still she felt robbed. Robbed of some very vital part of herself, robbed of motherhood, robbed of the experience of watching Linda grow up, robbed of the mother-daughter relationship. Thirty years of feeling that she was less than a woman, that everyone else had children but she. That she was inadequate. She recalled with bitterness how hurt she was when her father, while proudly presenting his grandchildren to visitor, explained that these were his other daughter's children. Then he added: " Ruth never had children. She was barren and fallow."

Suddenly Ruth pulled herself together. Wallowing in old pain, dredging up old hurts, picking scabs off old wounds could serve no purpose. Then she heard the elevator doors open and footsteps in the corridor coming towards the room. Ruth stood up to leave as Linda entered the room. Nodding, she moved to Ellen McVickers' bedside. Ruth studied her. Tall, lithe, plain-featured, Linda's dark blue eyes were like Jerry Stewart's. Ruth couldn't see her own features at all.

"I'm sorry," Linda said, "But I don't know you. How did you happen to be visiting my mother."

"She called me and asked me to come. There was something she wanted to discuss."

"I don't understand what that would be. Since she became ill, my husband and I have been handling all her affairs. What exactly was the nature of this business she called you to discuss."

"She never really had a chance to tell me everything," Ruth stalled. "I am not sure exactly what she wanted."

"Well," said Linda. "Whatever it was it is too late now. If there is anything else you can call my office. I want to be alone with my mother."

"Yes, of course," Ruth said. "I am very sorry."

CELL PHONE

Punching, biting, spitting and scratching, Gloria Coty and Hazel Foster flew at each other like she-bears with new cubs. Gloria, the larger of the two, was a mixture of muscle and lard. Hazel, on the other hand, was quick and wiry, but her long hair was her downfall. Gloria grabbed Hazel's hair as it swung past her face and hung on. She stood like an ox, with Hazel's pony-tail in one hand and her ragged T-shirt in the other, and swung round and round. Hazel's feet left the ground and for a moment she was airborne, just before she landed head-first in a lilac bush.

"Stupid, crazy bitch." said Hazel.

"Lying, thieving sneak." Gloria retorted. "Little whore."

"Fat cow. You just wait. I'll get even. See if I don't." Hazel picked herself up and stomped away.

"Aw go screw yourself."

"Why should I with you around."

The row started after Gloria heard her daughter scream. She ran outside to see Hazel's boys tossing her daughter's new kitten back and forth over her head. As the little girl ran to catch the kitten, one of the boys tripped her and she sprawled on the ground, striking her chin on a rock. The kitten, frightened and disoriented, scurried away under the porch. But Gloria caught the larger boy, a lout of about 14 and clipped him on the side of the head. Hazel, sitting at her kitchen table reading a Harlequin Romance and sipping a Moosehead, hadn't paid any attention to the yelling, until her son came into the house snivelling.

"What's the matter with you?"

"She hit me."

"Who hit you?"

"Old Gloria?"

"Why did she hit you?"

"I don't know. I wasn't doin' nothin."

"Well, we'll just see about this." Hazel stubbed her cigarette out in the ashtray and walked across the road to Gloria's.

"Just what in hell do you mean by hitting my son?" said Hazel as Gloria opened the door.

"Why'n'cha ask the little bastard?"

"I'm astin' you. Did you hit my son?"

Gloria stepped outside. "I certainly did. He tripped my Jaime and knocked her flyin'. Him and that other brat of yours were tormenting her kitten. And I'll swat him again if I catch him doin' it again."

"Oh, you will, eh?" Hazel doubled her fist and punched Gloria square in the face.

Gloria shook her head and came after Hazel. The women fought until Hazel landed in the lilacs. Gloria had clearly won that round. Hazel wasn't about to forget it.

Back inside her kitchen, Hazel lit a cigarette and finished her beer. Her head ached and she was filthy from the scrap. And she was madder than hell. She tossed the bottle into the box of empties. Then she pulled the phone book out from under a stack of pot-holders, sat down at the table, pushed the Romance novel aside, riffled the blue pages until she came to the "W"s. Under "Welfare" she read: See, Human Resources Development. Then she looked under the "Hs" and found Health Services, Family and Community Social Services. She got up went to the fridge, twisted the cap off another Moosehead, took a swallow, lit another cigarette, and then dialed the number. When she got through she said: "I'm calling to report Gloria Coty. She's been workin' and collecting welfare both and that ain't right."

The following day an investigator showed up at Gloria Coty's and there was no one there. She called back at 3:30 and one of Gloria's girls answered the phone. "Naw, she ain't here. She's workin'." Asked where her mother was working, the girl simply answered, "the plant."

The investigator then visited the personnel office of "the plant" and discovered that Gloria had been working off an on all summer. At the same time she was collecting social assistance for herself and her children. If the investigator had been thorough, she would have learned that Gloria had three turkeys stashed in the fridge from Christmas boxes, and a good assortment of canned foods from the local food bank.

Gloria saw herself as a survivor. Whatever she was able to grab from the government or charities, she took. She felt she had it coming to her. Both of the men she'd lived with had been no damn good. All she'd wound up with was more mouths to feed and more diapers to wash. Okay, so she was milking the system. Why should everybody else have all the good things? She couldn't depend on work at the plant. It was even less than seasonal, and she always got called at the last moment when somebody else didn't show up. If she gave up her welfare, it would take her months to get back on and she didn't have enough food stashed to see the girls through. Nosiree. She was looking after herself and by God, she was going to see that her girls had everything she could get.

And she kept saying she was through having kids. She'd tried the pill and it made her bloated. She kept planning to get her tubes tied, but just hadn't got around to it. Trouble was she got lonely and she deserved a little lovin' just like anybody else. So if a fellow showed up with a case of beer why shouldn't she have a little fun? In fact, before the fight, she and Hazel had often partied together with a bunch of guys.

Gloria had never been svelte and lately she had let herself go, so it wasn't as if she had men coming out of the woodwork, but usually there were one or two who came around after the dance or when the Legion closed. She had long since accepted that she'd never walk down the aisle dressed in white. What man would want to take on three kids? The two older girls--15-year-old Cayle and 13-year-old Gemma--were real good kids. They looked after Jaime when she worked at the plant. Nosiree, men were only good for one thing and she knew what that was.

Despite always grinding for money, Gloria managed to keep her family fed. In her own way, she loved her kids and was doing the best she knew how. She'd only been 14 when Cayle was born, a year younger than Cayle is now, and her mothering skills left a lot to be desired. Her house, provided by the government, wasn't the cleanest, nor the tidiest. She could cook a turkey, boil potatoes and make a cup of instant coffee. She had canned milk when she could get it. She could have used the money she made more wisely, but she had never been taught how to budget. On top of that Gloria was a sucker for every TV ad that came on. If the kids wanted something and she had money the day her welfare cheque came in, she bought it. Gloria didn't read Harlequin romances like Hazel, but she had a 25-inch TV and a satellite dish.

The social worker showed up again Saturday morning. Gloria's hangover from Friday night drinking at the Legion felt like fifty fiendish cloggers running amok in her head. Still, it didn't take long for her to grasp that she was in trouble, that somebody had ratted on her and she was going to have to go to court. Well, it wouldn't be a first. She could handle it.

When the social worker left, Gloria made a cup of instant Nescafe, rolled a cigarette--the tailor-mades were all gone--and thought about the situation. Then she yelled:

"Cayle. Gemma. Get yer arses in here."

The girls came into the kitchen. Cayle, moon-faced, already starting to gain weight from a diet of chips and sugar corn pops, had been watching The Simpsons with Jaime.

Gemma, slender, dark-haired like her father, had been in the bathroom, studying her reflection in the mirror.

"Wassamatter, Ma?" Cayle asked.

"Has there been anybody in here, snooping around?"

"No, Ma."

"You haven't let anybody in while I've been gone?"

"I said no, Ma."

"Okay, don't start sulkin'. I jest ast you a question. I want to know how in hell Social Services found out I was workin'. Cripes! I'm only trying to get enough money to raise my kids. Your no-good fathers have been no help. What am I going to do now?"

"I don't know, Ma."

Throughout this exchange Gemma said nothing. She remembered the phone call that Jaime took, when she said on the phone that Ma was working. Gemma had warned Jaime at the time. It wasn't safe to let people know there was no adult in the house. It wasn't even safe in the house, sometimes, when some of Ma's boyfriends slept over.

For once the wheels of justice passed quickly. A young lawyer, Sarah Whitmore, was passed Gloria's case through Legal Aid. Having been run off her feet at the office with cases piling up, and knowing her client probably had no means of transportation, Sarah decided to drive to the Cotys and interview Gloria there. Coming straight from court, Sarah was dressed in a charcoal gaberdine pantsuit with a cranberry silk blouse. At a height of nearly six feet, Sarah always made a strong first impression. People immediately saw her as a capable, in-charge kind of person. In time a select few would learn there was a warm, jelly side to her nature, but that would only show much later.

Gemma watched Sarah drive up, but it was Gloria herself who opened the door. Sarah explained that she was a court-appointed lawyer and she was here to see what could be done to represent Gloria.

The two women sat down at the kitchen table and, after Gloria had told Cayle to shut off the TV and take Jaime outside, they discussed the case.

Sarah asked Gloria if she had ever been in trouble with the law before and Gloria said no, but not before a narrowing of her eyes gave away the fact that she was lying. Sarah did not pursue that line of questioning, she merely explained that Gloria would have to appear in court, and that she would likely be fined.

"So, let 'em fine me," Gloria said. "I ain't got no money anyways. All I was doin' was tryin' to buy some stuff for my kids. It ain't easy, you know, raisin' three kids all alone. Every time you try and get ahead, and the government jumps on you."

Sarah did not argue. As she was taking her leave she spotted Gemma standing just inside the living room door. An elfin child on the cusp of puberty, she had a winsome little face. Sarah smiled at her. Gemma reminded her of somebody. That evening in the shower, she remembered who it was; herself at that age, at a time when the whole world was opening up to her. Sarah wondered what life held in store for Gemma.

Meanwhile, Gemma stood in front of the bathroom mirror holding her head high, standing as tall as possible, reaching for an imaginary briefcase. She had memorized every detail of Sarah's appearance and vowed that she would some day be just like her.

The following week Gloria appeared in court with Sarah at her side. It was late afternoon. All stood as Judge Sappier walked in. He had just got off the phone after talking to his wife. By the querulousness in her voice, he knew she had been drinking. He was fed up. He took a look at Gloria, bloated and bovine, and shook his head. One sorry loser after another. He felt like hurting somebody and there stood Gloria. Judge Sappier scowled at her, then he outlined the evidence and fined Gloria $1,000 or a month in jail. Sarah was appalled. Before either she or Gloria had a chance to recover, Judge Sappier had left the room.

"Well, what happens now?" Gloria said. "I still ain't got no money."

In the end Sarah was able to arrange that Gloria do her time on weekends, when Cayle and Gemma were home from school to look after Jaime.

On Friday afternoon a young RCMP officer showed up at the Coty residence and took Gloria to jail for the weekend. On Sunday afternoon another RCMP officer picked her up and took her home.

Gloria had not had a nice time in jail. But she had learned a few new tricks. If everybody was out to get her, like that stupid Social Services woman and that mean judge, and all the useless men that had rooted and pawed around her bed, then it was time to get her own back, and she knew how.

The next Friday afternoon, the same young officer turned up at her door. Gloria opened it a crack and said: "I ain't goin'."

"Pardon me?"

"I ain't goin' with you. Last time you tried to rape me."

The officer's face was a study. The idea of even touching this fat, slovenly woman was repulsive to him. What was he to do? He didn't want to manhandle her right there with five children watching. Without a further word he turned and walked back to the cruiser. He called the detachment office and asked for a female officer. The only female at the detachment was out on the road. He then pulled out of the driveway and went to a pay phone. From there he called his supervisor in Woodstock and outlined the situation. Eight months previously an officer in the Cedar Springs area had been falsely accused of sexually molesting a female in a police vehicle. That case was still not settled. The supervisor didn't need another. As always, when there was even a whiff of investigation about an officer assaulting a female, the smell just wouldn't go away. It could ruin this young man's whole career. "Okay," the supervisor said. "I can't find anybody to go with you. What you do is tell the Coty woman she is under house arrest, until we figure something out."

The officer went back to Gloria Coty's house and explained that she was under house arrest, that she was not to leave the house under any circumstances, that she was to be available to answer the phone at any time day or night. Gloria agreed. Then with all the dignity he could muster, he strode back down the driveway to the cruiser and drove away.

Gloria laughed to herself as she watched him leave. Then she turned around just in time to see Hazel at the window watching the cruiser pull away. Hazel poked her head out and said: "What was that all about?"

"Now, wouldn't you jes' like to know!"

Meanwhile Gemma, after listening to the exchange between her mother and the RCMP officer, went back to her homework. Inside the top drawer of the chest on her side of the small bedroom was a stack of exam papers, and every single one sported a fine big A. When Gemma's teacher sat her down and told her she was a model student and that she had the ability to go far, Gemma believed her. She just didn't know what she wanted to do. But after seeing her mother's lawyer, Sarah Whitmore, Gemma knew.

In Grade 10, Gemma and other high-achieving students were offered an option to work and study in an apprenticeship program. Gemma did not hesitate when the opportunity came for her to work at Sarah's firm. She carried out the scut jobs assigned to her, learned how to do research with the computer and through law books. Sarah took a special interest in Gemma and spent as much time with her as possible. For this mentoring Gemma would always be grateful.

Thanks to her mother's continuing poverty, Gemma knew her way around a second-hand clothing store. In a fashion time of grunge, Gemma learned to choose outfits of quality, items that could be starched and pressed to look like new. Unlike her mother and older sister, Gemma always appeared well turned out. Two years later at graduation, when she was called back time after time to be presented with a variety of scholarships and have her hand shaken by the principal, Gemma was the only graduate who didn't have a parent in the audience. Gloria had been going to attend, but the day was hot and the room so crowded and she had nobody to stay with Jaime. However, Sarah Whitmore was there, at Gemma's invitation, and when it came time to take pictures, Sarah posed with Gemma and a schoolmate, then took Gemma out to dinner. A few years later when she graduated from law school in Toronto, Gemma sent Sarah a newspaper clipping and a note of thanks. But Gemma would never come back to Cedar Springs.

THE LAWSON HOUSE

Beyond the structure, size, floor plans and decor, every house in Cedar Springs has a character of its own, something that distinguishes it from all others. I'm not in the market for a house, even if I could afford the prices they're asking these days, but I like to drive around the country and look at all the new places going up. I also like to think about the houses that I remember as a child, the parties, games, dinners, showers, sings and wakes held in them. Over the years I've seen so many homes that were once sturdy and strong and teeming with life, collapsed back into the earth, or levelled by fire or bulldozer. Perhaps all that's left to mark the site is the rusty remains of a hand pump, a few apple trees or lilac bushes. It's sad how fast houses fall to ruin when they've been abandoned.

Driving along the river last week I counted six "For Sale" signs. I could swear these same houses had "For Sale" signs on them last Spring or maybe the Spring before. Then other day in Tim Hortons I ran into Sheila Meizner, who's just opened her own real estate agency. I went to school with Sheila--her name was Belyea then. Sheila sold real estate in Toronto for years before moving back to Cedar Springs. Anyway I mentioned the fact that these same houses always seem to be changing hands and she said, "well, there are such things as orphan houses. For instance, a new subdivision opens and all the houses are snapped up right away, except for one. That house takes longer to sell. The buyers move in and six months later the husband gets transferred. The house goes on the market. New owners move in and then they separate almost as soon as the ink on the deed dries. Then the house is vacant for a while. The third or fourth owners live there a year or two and, after some family disaster, they move away and the house becomes vacant again. Meanwhile most of the other houses in the subdivision are still owned and occupied by the original buyers. But the orphan house takes on an aura of despair and it becomes very hard to sell. Sometimes these houses are actually torn down and replaced."

On the way back from town I thought about the orphan houses and the strong positive or negative feelings I experience when I enter a house for the first time. Maybe it has something to do with polarities, with electromagnetic fields, with the quality of light, with the land the house is built on or the chemicals under the earth. Some houses I feel comfortable in and others seem so malevolent I can't get out fast enough. Do houses have souls, personalities, spirits? Do houses have memories? Do they draw the ghosts of the people who have lived in them?

The Lawson house definitely has its own character and, for me a special charm. I've been in it many times over the years. I have known everyone that has lived in that house and I've always felt welcome there. When I drove by today, I noticed a stack of asphalt shingles in the yard. The new owners must be getting a new roof.

When POW Mark Lawson returned home in 1946 he was 22 years old. Lying his age to get into the army when the war began, he'd trained with the Carleton & York Regiment, volunteered with the Royal Rifles and was shipped to Hong Kong, where at 3 p.m. on Christmas Day 1941 he was taken prisoner.

Mark spent the next four years in a prison camp, the first two moving a mountain, literally, one sack of earth at a time. Later he worked building ships in Yokohama. Like all of the Hong Kong prisoners of war Mark suffered unspeakable abuse and near-starvation from his captors. He also had malaria, dysentery, beri-beri and the continual discomfort of fleas and lice. When he arrived back in Canada he weighed less than 90 pounds. He hadn't had a letter from home in five years. Nobody met him at the train.

Mark hitched a ride from the train station to the outskirts of Cedar Springs, only to find the home place empty. From the neighbours he learned his mother had died two years after he went overseas, and that his father had married again and moved with his new wife to Ontario. As far as the neighbours knew, his father still owned the farm.

Mark spent his first night home sleeping on the couch in the kitchen, wrapped in blankets, getting up from time to time to stoke the fire. Between the dampness and the early October frost, it was all he could do to stay warm. The following day he talked to his father in Oshawa. His father invited him to come to the city but Mark said he felt he'd done enough travelling for the time being.

"Well, what will you do then?"

"Look for work around here."

"Thinking of farming?"

"Maybe, later on. Over the last few years, I've become a fair carpenter. I was thinking of setting up my own shop."

"The farm is yours, Mark. I've kept the taxes paid. I've got a good job here at General Motors; pays decent money, money you can count on, not just shove back into the farm. The wife likes it here. We already bought a house. And after losing your mother there are too many bad memories for me in Cedar Springs."

"Sounds as if you're pretty well set."

"Yes. Look, I'll send you the deed and a copy of your mother's will.

I'm sure glad you're back, son. I hadn't given up, I saved the farm for you. But after all that time...none of your mother's letters were ever answered."

"It's a long story, Dad. I never received any mail. But there's no sense going over the past."

"No. Well, see what you can do. Maybe you could get up and visit us at Christmas?"

"Thanks, Dad. I might just do that."

In daylight Mark had a good look around. The old farm house had fallen to ruin. It was much worse than he had thought. In the end he decided to use some of his pay and his hard-gained skills as a craftsman to build a house of his own. It took him over a year to finish it; each board was sawed and fitted and nailed by hand. Two bedrooms, a bathroom, living room, kitchen and a front hall. All the interior woodwork gleamed, the closets, the kitchen cupboards, the shelves all felt silky to the touch. By then he had got his strength back.

When the house was finished Mark built a small shed which he planned to used as a shop.

The white bungalow still stands well back from the road. Mark told a friend in later years that he had an aversion to any building with more than one storey, and for good reason:

"It happened New Year's night in 1944," Mark recalled. "We'd built a little bonfire. We didn't have a stove or anything. The camp was built with just open sand in the middle, you know. That night we had a big snowstorm--maybe four or five inches of snow. The roof was all tile--all the roofs in that part of the country were constructed with tile. The building was flimsy and not too sound, and with the weight of the snow on the tiles, about two o-clock in the morning it caved in.

"It went right sideways. I was over on the southeast side. It went down over me, but it was two stories high, with rooms upstairs and down. There might have been 150 men in it. And when she went, people cried and hollered. There were eight people killed and a lot more were hurt.

"The dead were taken out and buried. Those that got hurt either got well or died. There were a lot of broken bones, legs and arms. We had two orderlies in the sick room, but they couldn't do much without any medicine."

"After that they let us build steel huts..."

When the house was finished Mark looked around for something to do. He didn't feel like taking on the responsibility of farming, but a new business had started in a nearby village which produced farm machinery and did metal work. He applied and got a job. The pay wasn't great, but it was steady work. In a short time he became adept at planning and costing out a project, a skill not lost on the boss. In the early 1950s they made him Vice-President.

At the Saturday night Legion dance he met Mary Downy, a young widow whose husband had been shot down over Holland. She was two years older than Mark and already had an eight-year-old son, John. After a short courtship they married and moved into Mark's new house.

For the next 22 years Mark and Mary lived quietly and happily together. Mary bore him a son, Luke. Mark's nightmares frightened her, but she got used to them in time. Despite the nine-year age difference, John and Luke were friends as well as brothers. An easygoing, undemanding woman, Mary doted on Mark and the boys, taking pleasure in nurturing them well. John wanted to stay on the land. He attended the agricultural college, started an apple orchard and began raising vegetable crops. Luke was not interested in farming. Instead he attended UNB, got his Master's in Business Administration and moved to Toronto.

Then Mark suffered kidney failure. Despite the new renal dialysis equipment they brought into the house, he died within six months.

After the funeral, Mary looked around her and decided she had to do something useful. Her children had flown the nest and at 48 she was alone. She took a Registered Nursing Assistant's course and was immediately accepted at the Woodstock hospital. It didn't take long--only one winter skid off the icy road late at night--to convince her she wanted to live in town. Mary found a bright, cosy apartment facing the river and a five-minute walk to the hospital. After talking it over with John and Luke, she put the house and 15 acres up for sale.

Soon Mary was leading a busy, rewarding life. She enjoyed nursing, was good at it and very well liked by patients and staff. She joined the United Church choir. When the house was sold a few months later to Nedra Hanning, Mary drove from town and spent several hours recalling the happiness and grief she had known in the small bungalow her husband had built. She remembered the rough-and-tumble boyhood years of her two fine sons, the worrisome time of their teen years, the final phase of Mark's illness. Although she had seen Mark's casket lowered into the earth, she felt his presence around the house and grounds more than anywhere. She walked through his shop and felt a sharp stab of grief. She stopped to cut an armload of rhubarb. Then she drove back to town.

The remaining land went to John and Luke. Within a few years John raised enough money to buy Luke's share and later John and his new wife had a large and stately home erected on the northeast corner of the property overlooking the apple orchards. Only in winter when the leaves were gone could they catch a glimpse of the house their father had built.

Nedra Hanning loved the Lawson house. She liked the roomy kitchen, the fine cabinet work, the counter space and the built-in closets and cupboards. For 24 years she lived there with her dog and cat and a wealth of friends who stopped in. In summer and fall she often had friends from Alberta, Ontario, Quebec or the States staying with her.

Nedra had one sister, Joan Prentiss, but they had never been close. Born a year apart, Nedra and Joan had little more in common than genes and gender. They did not look, think, or act alike. Joan set goals and met them, made plans and carried them out. Nedra was a dreamer and a dabbler.

No sooner had they grown out of the frilly pinafores their mother dressed them in as children, than they went their separate ways. In high school Joan wore tailored shirts and blouses. Nedra favoured worn jeans and sloppy sweatshirts. As adults they rarely visited. In fact Nedra had been dead for two weeks before the news reached Joan during her annual winter getaway in the Bahamas.

Joan Hanning Prentiss was a model of consistency and efficiency. Joan had been an obedient child, diligent through high school, graduating with a B+. She went on to train as a nurse in Montreal. She finished her training, nursed for a year, then married a chartered accountant. They began marriage with a starter house and sold and bought up to an eight-room house with a pool and two-car garage. They had two children, whom they raised and put through university. They joined the United Baptist Church and the Masonic Lodge where Joan worked her way through the offices in the Eastern Star while her husband became the Grand Pooh Bah. When her daughters were grown, Joan spent two afternoons a week with a bridge club, and Friday mornings volunteering at the Cedar Springs nursing home.

Joan's house sparkled. She kept physically in shape and read glossy magazines about toning up her love life and her marriage. Each morning she showered and prepared her face with a series of creams and emollients, dusts, erasers, blushes and highlighters, before venturing out to meet the day. At night she brushed her hair 50 strokes, and carefully removed layer after layer of makeup with a series of cleansers and replaced those with a night cream.

Nedra, on the other hand, never got it right. After quitting high school in Grade 10, Nedra moved from factory jobs to waitress work to the most menial of office tasks. She did manage to learn enough typing and shorthand to handle clerk-typist jobs or serve as a member of the secretarial pool. She had never got far enough in the touch-typing manual to handle figures; her awkward left-handed shorthand was fortunately backed up by a fair capacity to listen and to memorize. So she earned a living. She married young and unwisely and 12 years later was divorced. She married again and was subsequently divorced. She had no children. "My first husband wanted a mother," she confided in a friend. "Then my second needed a nurse."

When she was 36 she received a fairly large inheritance from her grandmother. With part of that money Nedra was able to purchase the Lawson house. She had love affairs.

Between affairs Nedra embarked on self-improvement projects. One year she purchased a correspondence course to upgrade her education to Grade 12 equivalency. She chose four subjects to start. In English and history she whizzed along. In math she stumbled through three lessons. The diagrams threw her. Science and Physics, which started with various pulleys going in different directions, made no sense to her at all. She quit the correspondence course.

Meanwhile Nedra's house became a drop-in centre. People of all ages from children to octogenarians came to talk, to air their thoughts and miseries. She served cocoa to teenagers who groaned their angst or sighed their despair. She poured tea or coffee while farmers worried about blight and contracts. She listened to young wives wondering how they would manage another child or a straying husband or a demanding parent. She heard about divorces, abortions, incest, illnesses, disappointments and even some successes. She had a wry sense of humour. She could make one see the funny side of almost any misery. People who spent time with her always went away feeling better about whatever situation they were in.

Just by being Nedra with her ever-ready cups of tea or coffee and her sympathetic ear, she probably did more good than all the psychiatrists and therapists, guidance or grief counsellors put together. Nedra showed people how to lose and carry on, how to put pain behind them. What's more, Nedra kept her mouth shut. Oddly enough, despite all the people she had comforted over her lifetime, despite all who had sat at the kitchen table of the Lawson house, she was alone when she died.

It was hard to establish what Nedra was doing in the weeks before she died. As was her habit, she seemed to have had a dozen projects on the go. In the spare bedroom, a very large room, a treadmill was pushed against the wall, the gathered dust evidence that it hadn't been used in some time. In the centre of the room, a half-finished quilt sagged in a frame; its middle, which contained tangled spools of thread, was soiled and crawling with cat hair. Near the north window an easel stood, with a stretched canvas on which had been sketched a few meaningless lines. On the nearby stand tubes of oil paint and brushes dried.

At a desk in the hall was a home computer plugged into a surge protector, its light flickering hopefully. Nedra had turned it on, started a letter, stopped, shut it off and then had gone on to something else.

In the shed was an abandoned pottery wheel and kiln. Several cracked, lopsided bowls were stacked on the shelf along side trays of dahlia and gladioli bulbs, as well as drying onions. There were ice skates, unused for 20 years, roller blades tried once, used snowshoes with a broken harness. There was a wetsuit and deep-sea diving gear.

In the kitchen, several of the drawers had been upended on the counter, where the contents were partly sorted. Hard to say how long the stuff had lain there. A sheet of paper had slid over next to the toaster. On it was written:

"This grand show is eternal. It is always sunrise somewhere: the dew is never all dried at once, a shower is forever falling, vapour is ever rising. Eternal sunrise, eternal sunset, eternal dawn and gloaming, on sea and continents and islands, each in its turn as the round earth rolls," (a quotation by naturalist, explorer and writer John Muir (1838-1914).

Always wildly enthusiastic at the beginning of any new venture, Nedra undertook music appreciation, understanding psychology, the study of paintings by the old masters, poets of the 16th century, Shakespeare's plays, Canadian short story writing-- you name it. Trouble was, after a few weeks, days or hours, she lost interest. It was a pattern set early in life. One late September morning she awoke and she was 50 years old.

Fifty. As she walked the dog along the road, where she had walked every day for the past 14 years, it struck her that she really hadn't accomplished much of anything. Despair overwhelmed her. She returned from the walk and sat in her kitchen, drinking coffee and staring into space. The phone rang. It was the receptionist from the doctor's office reminding her of her appointment to get the results of some tests she'd had a few weeks previously. She'd forgotten about them.

In the doctor's office, she had hardly had time to sit down when he came straight to the point. "Nedra. There is no easy way to tell you this," he said. "You have pancreatic cancer."

"I see. That's inoperable. Right?"

"Yes, it's inoperable."

"And means a rapid death."

"That's usually true."

"How long would you say I've got?"

"A few weeks. A month."

"And there's a lot of pain."

"Well, now there we can help. We have a variety of new painkillers, and I think we can keep you comfortable. Also, there's a hospice right near here. I can arrange to have a bed for you there."

"I'll have to think about it."

"Well, let me know when you've decided."

"Thank you, doctor. I will."

Nedra left the doctor's office. The late afternoon sun was slanting through the trees. The street, lined with maple trees--crimson, orange, green and brown, was quiet. She looked up into a cloudless blue sky and inhaled deeply of the fall air. She could smell wood smoke. She drove home.

For the next few hours Nedra wandered from room to room with the dog and cat following. Every time she sat down, the cat jumped into her lap and the dog stretched out across her feet. Nedra thought about calling Joan, but procrastinated. She thought about updating her will but she had hardly enough money in the bank to bury her. The house would go to Joan. What difference did it make? Joan would sell it and her precious accountant would turn the money into a new fortune. The one thing she did have to do was find her pets a new home. She called the Cedar Springs animal shelter and explained the situation. They were sympathetic and promised to take them if she failed to place them elsewhere. Nedra put ads in the local papers and on the radio station. She walked around her property and noticed that some of the spruce, fir, cedar and pine trees she had planted 25 years earlier had seeded the field beyond. then she sat down at her computer and wrote:

THE TREES - MY LEGACY

Third Thursday in May. Arbour Day.
Arbour Day, tree planting day. So
Plant a tree.
Plant a great tree.
Plant just one or two or three.
Plant a tree,
Just a small tree.
Any tree will be a tall tree
All that's needed is a seedling
And a shovel or a spade.
Plant a tree.
Plant a new tree
Plant a pine or beech or yew tree
Plant a cedar, oak or spruce tree.
Plant an aspen, ash or bass tree
Plant a willow for the shade.
Plant a tree
Plant a crab tree.
Plant a hickory or a walnut.
Plant a butternut or chestnut
Plant a hazelnut or beechnut
Plant a cheery cherry tree.
Plant a tree.

Plant a tree.
Plant a tree now.
Plant a tree and watch it grow.
See it changing with the seasons.
There are hundreds of good reasons
Why we all should plant a tree.
Plant a tree.
Watch the birds come
And with straw and twigs and mosses
Building nests among the branches
Safely cradling and sheltering
Their new babies in the shade.
Plant a tree.

Two weeks went by. Nedra was back and forth to the doctor's office, getting pain medication. The third week she became so ill the doctor suggested she be hospitalized. Then when she hesitated he ordered a nurse from the Victoria Order of Nursing to stop by her house to give her needles. Although those helped, the pain-free periods became shorter and shorter. She did get several calls about the pets, and luckily a young man who had just moved to the area wanted both of them. He came by and picked up the animals and all their paraphernalia. Nedra was reassured to see that they went willingly.

The VON asked her if she had made funeral arrangements. Nedra, who happened to be looking in the mirror at the time, newly amazed at the rapid changes in her looks, said, "Yes. A while back. But since then I've decided there's no need for one. None of my relatives are left in Cedar Springs except my sister and her family and they're likely to be away. My sister fills in her daytimer at least a year ahead. She'd view my funeral as a dreadful inconvenience.

"Go on with you."

"Well that may be stretching it a bit. But I really don't see the point in a funeral. As a matter of fact I ran into the Cedar Springs funeral director just before I was diagnosed. We went to school together, you know. He was going for coffee at Tim Hortons and I joined him. Naturally we got into a discussion of the burying business. I told him, no funeral. Just a shake-and-bake. Keep the ashes, and when the driveway gets icy use them for traction."

The following night Nedra's pain was excruciating. She searched around for the pain-killers and couldn't find them. Then the pain grew so bad she lost consciousness. "Help me," she moaned, "Oh, sweet Jesus, help me. I can't stand it any more."

Suddenly she was pain-free. The darkened bedroom was diffused with light. For a moment or two she seemed to be hovering just below the ceiling. She looked down and saw the still body, hers, half off the bed. Then she turned and was drawn into the light.

When the VON arrived in the morning she knocked on Nedra's door and, getting no answer, opened it and walked in. Finding the body, she made appropriate calls which resulted in the corpse being removed by the undertaker less than an hour later and sent to Saint John for cremation. An attempt to contact Nedra's sister Joan, whom Nedra had listed as next of kin, was made through Joan's daughter but as far as she knew Joan and her husband had already left for the Bahamas. There they had joined friends on a yacht and had told no one where they were going.

Several weeks later when Joan heard the news of her sister's death she was at first astonished, and then furious. "Typical, just typical," she raged. "Couldn't even manage to let me know she was ill."

"Well, what could you have done?" Joan's husband asked reasonably.

"I don't know. But this is such a shock. Such a shock."

"But you weren't that close."

"We were sisters, for heaven's sake."

"I mean you didn't visit much."

"You wouldn't understand. Anyway it's over and done with now."

"What about a memorial service?"

"Where? In our church? I'd be mortified."

"What about her house? Would she have had a will?"

"Knowing Nedra, I doubt it." Sighing, Joan sat down to make some phone calls, the first to Nedra's doctor and the second to her own lawyer. She learned that Nedra had named her as her beneficiary. The third call was to a real estate agent to put Nedra's house--the Lawson house--on the market. Best price. As is.

In time the little white bungalow would be purchased by Lilian Oakes, a deaf-mute artist, who would come to love it even more than Mark and Mary Lawson and Nedra Hanning had.

A LIFE FOR LILIAN

The emaciated form in the Princess Margaret Hospital bed uncurled slightly from the foetal position. Natalie struggled out from under the fog of the painkiller she had been given half an hour earlier.

"Natalie, it's me, Brenda. Wake up. I need to talk to you."

"Brenda? The children?"

"They're fine. They miss you. But they're fine. Look, Natalie. I want to show you this," and Brenda held up an 8x10 sheet of paper. "Here, Natalie, look at this. Who does it remind you of?"

Natalie focussed on the picture and attempted a smile. "Zoe? Zachry?"

"No. It isn't Zoe or Zachry. Look again."

"Me?"

"Well, that's what I'd like to know."

"Where did you get it?"

"Off the computer. My boys' father bought the children a computer for Christmas. First time he's turned over anything to their keep."

"The computer."

"Yes. Paul was playing around and found a place on the computer where people are looking for their adopted children, and adopted children look for their birth parents."

"Birth parents?"

"Yes. Remember, you told me one time you were adopted."

"Three years ago. That's when I learned. Before I got kicked out. That's when they told me."

"Do you know where you were born?"

"No."

"Okay, so what is your birth date?"

"February 6, 1974."

"So, what do you think." But Natalie had shut her eyes.

"Natalie?" The painkiller had kicked in. Natalie was no longer conscious. Brenda placed the picture in Natalie's hand and left.

All the way back on the streetcar, Brenda thought about what would have to be done. Since her friend Natalie had been diagnosed with HIV, Brenda knew worse was to come. Natalie was dying. A drug user and promiscuous since her teens, she was dying of AIDS. It had been bound to happen sooner or later. Still Natalie had managed to stay clean while she carried the twins, and that was something. And you had to hand it to her, Natalie had given the children good care until she became unable to carry on. As well as her own children Brenda had been looking after Zoe and

Zach for nearly three months. Five kids and on welfare, and that asshole she'd married, all he'd come up with was a computer for the kids for Christmas. Oh, well. What's the use in getting all exercised about it. That was the way he was.

But when Natalie died, someone was going to have to take her children. Brenda thought about trying to get in touch with Natalie's adoptive parents, but figured that was pretty well a lost cause. They'd never come near. Probably didn't even know Natalie had children.

Brenda sighed. Her legs were sore, but she had only two more streetcar stops and she would be back at the apartments on Sackville Street. It was a hell of a place to raise kids, but what could she do?

At the house she called out to her teenage son, "Paul?"

"Yeah, Mom, whassup?"

"Where are the children?"

"Twins are sleeping. Jenny's at her girlfriend's. The boys are outside."

"What are you doing?" Brenda walked towards her son. He quickly started tapping the computer mouse. Too late, he was in a program called Java, and there in living colour on the screen was a nude oriental woman having sex with two men.

"Right. Now, Paul, I told you I didn't want you looking at that disgusting muck. What if one of the younger ones came in?"

"Sorry, Ma. I won't do it again."

"Yeah, sure. Well, now you can just redeem yourself. You find that place where you got the picture that looks like Natalie and the twins. I want to see that again. I'm going to get a cup of coffee and check on the others."

"Okay Ma, give me a minute." Paul punched a few more buttons and the erotic picture disappeared. Then he started checking for the picture his mother wanted. After a few minutes, he called:

"Got it, Ma."

"Be right there." By then the twins were awake and running around. Both had to be changed. Brenda got them settled in the living room with some arrowroot cookies in front of the TV.

"Here's the picture. There are a couple."

"Print them off for me, will you?"

"Sure."

"Does it give a name or an address?"

"E-mail. Lilian Oakes. They're actually paintings. This Lilian Oakes is an artist. So they may not be real people."

"Send her a message. Ask her if she knows a Natalie Golder, born February 6, 1974."

"You think this person is related to Nat?"

"I don't know. So let's find out. Put that nice computer your father bought to some proper use."

Paul carefully phrased his question and sent the message.

Nearly everybody in Cedar Springs found their way to the new Helen Grafton Memorial Gallery during the month Lilian Oakes' art was on display. The first night there was the usual core of gallery supporters and culture vultures that attend every new showing. After that news spread by word of mouth, by phone, by fax and by e-mail. Everybody in Cedar Springs showed up to gaze at the paintings, in which they were nearly all represented. Most viewers got a kick out of seeing themselves immortalized in paint or charcoal. Others were furious, having been caught in attitudes that were less than flattering and in company with whom they would have preferred not to be seen.

There was no doubt, however, that the art showing was a huge success. With collectors coming from as far as New York and Toronto, $100,000 worth of art was sold.

Over the month, the deaf-mute artist Lilian Oakes stayed at the gallery every minute the doors were open. She kept busy with her sketch pad, allowing people to watch her work. She was pointed out, stared at, smiled at, and sometimes ignored. She, in turn, studied each face that came through the door. The one face she hoped to see did not appear.

Up until a few months previously Lilian had lived in the house she was born in. She had looked after her parents for more than 20 years. Her father, who had suffered a stroke, was bedridden for over six years. Her mother, a diabetic, developed Alzheimer's and the last two years of her mother's life were unremitting hell. She became blind and violent. In the end she died of kidney failure. Through it all Lilian had shouldered the burden.

Lilian's brother was against Lilian getting her own place. First, he'd suffered financial losses and couldn't pay the mortgage on his new house, so he had plans to move back to the home place as soon as his mother was gone. The second reason was Lilian's disabilities. Like so many others, when it was discovered that Lilian couldn't hear or speak, he assumed she was retarded. She'd never make it by herself, or so he told himself. Lilian was a good worker and a good cook. With five children he and his wife could use all the help they could get.

When talking about Lilian living with them he'd told his wife, "It isn't that she is really weird or anything. But she's never gone to school. Ma was against sending her away at the time. Then when she was 17 Lilian got knocked up. She'd never say who the father was."

"What happened to the baby?"

"Put up for adoption. After that Ma and Pa kept a pretty tight rein on her."

Despite Lilian's handicaps, and her brother's misgivings, Lilian had learned to compensate. She had never watched a lot of television, except Sesame Street, which she liked because of the children. It was through television's Sesame Street she learned to read and write, but she kept this to herself. Over the years Lilian had become a woman of secrets. She had so little control over her life that her secrets were her only source of power. She refused to say who had fathered her baby.

Lilian had another secret talent. She could draw. When her baby was taken Lilian grieved and grieved; a little girl so perfect in every way. But Lilian's wishes did not come into it. Ma said she was unfit. Ma knew best. Or so Lilian was led to believe at the time. The adoption was carried out in secret. Lilian never knew where the baby went, and her dreams from then on were coloured by her loss. After her baby was taken she spent many late night hours, when her parents were in bed, drawing the tiny perfect face. Later she worked on birds and flowers. Her drawings were made on brown paper, wrapping paper, tissue, and note pads. She had found a child's set of paints on the road. Most of the paint pools were nearly empty, but the brush was there. All this she kept out of sight in her room. She also drew and painted on the nights when her mother went to play Bingo.

When her father became ill, the outside work fell to Lilian. And she did it as a matter of course along with the housework. She sketched her father in all the stages of his illness.

Without a complaint she looked after both her parents. As her mother's condition gradually worsened, Lilian thought about her own future. Two months before her mother died, Lilian sat down and wrote to a lawyer, Sarah Whitmore, explaining that she was deaf and mute. An appointment was made by letter and then she met her lawyer face to face. In the letter Lilian had included the fact that she had no money.

Sarah, though far from being a sucker for a sob story, was touched by this woman's courage. She took a yellow-lined pad and began writing. Lilian studied her face while she wrote. Sarah would look into the situation and find out what options Lilian had. She asked that Lilian come by in two weeks.

On the second visit Sarah informed Lilian that her brother had been given power of attorney and that he had been made executor of her mother's will. Also, she told Lilian that because of her handicap, Lilian's mother had been receiving money every month from the government for her care. Lilian had never seen a penny of this money. She had thought that her brother had been giving her $20 a month out of his own pocket.

"Family quarrels are always difficult to resolve," Sarah said. "You could sue. But first we should establish legally that your handicaps don't make you unfit to handle your own affairs. I can certainly help you with that."

By the time their mother died, Lilian and her brother were barely civil to each other. Less than a week after the funeral, he and his family walked in and took over the home place. Again Lilian turned to her lawyer.

"Do you want to remain in the house?" Sarah asked.

"No," Lilian wrote, "but where would I go?"

"I could help you find a few rooms or a small apartment while we see what can be done about getting your share of the inheritance."

"Thank you. Yes," Lilian wrote.

A few days later Sarah noted that the Hanning (formerly Lawson) house, which had been on the market for several months, was still being listed, but the price had dropped. So the house wasn't selling. She called the real estate agent and asked if he would be interested in a rental. Yes. It was better, considering the cold weather coming on, to have the house occupied.

It had been a fairly simple procedure to have Lilian pronounced fit to handle her own affairs. Sarah got a statement from the family doctor; she had Sarah tested by a psychologist. Sarah wasn't surprised to learn that despite Lilian's handicap, she was very bright. Lilian's government cheque was immediately transferred to Lilian's newly set-up bank account. Although Sarah hadn't made much headway in getting Lilian her share of the inheritance, she was optimistic. Meanwhile she could afford to pay rent. She took Lilian to see the Hanning house.

The house, a bungalow, had been built by Mark Lawson immediately after World War II. He and his wife lived there for over 20 years while they raised their family. When Mark died his wife sold it to Nedra Hanning. Nedra later died of pancreatic cancer and the house was inherited by Nedra's sister Joan Hanning Prentiss who, already having her own elegant home in town, put it up for sale.

When Lilian and Sarah walked into the house, it was just as Nedra Hanning had left it. Lilian's reaction was one of awe and delight. Yes, the house was grungy, and yes, repairs were needed. But it would be Lilian's own place. Nobody could rule her any more.

They went back to Sarah's office where Sarah made a few phone calls. Then they drove to Lilian's family home, where Lilian quickly packed. The brother was at work. His wife walked around after them nursing her baby, whining that Lilian shouldn't make this sudden silly move and warning her that her brother would be furious. Lilian ignored her. With Sarah's help she carried her two boxes of belongings, one containing clothes and the other containing drawings, down to the car and they drove the 26 miles to her new home.

When they pulled in the drive, Sarah turned to her and said, "You'll be all right?" Lilian smiled and nodded, then impulsively she leaned over and kissed Sarah on the cheek.

Inside the house Lilian shut the door, locked it and then stopped to admire. "My place," she thought. Then the house seemed to speak to her. A voice came into her head, saying: "Yes. It's your turn now. Life is full of possibilities." Lilian felt blessed.

Lilian took several more tours of the house and returned to the kitchen. Seeing an upturned kitchen drawer, she replaced the papers and other junk and returned the drawer to its proper place. She would go through it more carefully later. Then she got busy and cleaned up the kitchen, starting with emptying and defrosting the fridge.

When the kitchen was shining, Lilian made a pot of tea. Then went to her box of drawing materials, took out her sketch pad and charcoal, sat down at the kitchen table and drew a face. Then she sketched another and another. Each time she finished, the word "Yes," came into her mind.

The afternoon slipped away, the tea pot was empty, the washer had stopped. Lilian moved the clean laundry into the dryer and filled the washer again. She went into the bedroom. It was a shambles, too much to finish in one day. She went back to the living room, stripped off the soiled cover of the futon and found a reasonably clean mattress underneath. Then she opened a linen closet, pulled out two sheets and a blanket and made up a bed on the futon.

In the kitchen cupboard she discovered a tin of ravioli, which she opened, heated and ate for supper. She rinsed out the dishes, folded the clean laundry, and stretched out on the futon. "My house," she thought, "my very own place." And again the house seemed to answer, "yes."

When she awoke it was morning. Outside snow was falling.

During the next few days Lilian created some order in her new home. She cleaned and rearranged the bedroom. She framed several of her better drawings in picture frames she found in the shed, and hung her own art. In the workroom, she stood for 10 and 20 minutes at a time in front of Nedra's sketch on the easel at the north window, studying it from every angle. She looked at the half-finished quilt in its frame, but couldn't make up her mind what to do with it. She fixed those things in need of fixing, including the clothes in the laundry basket and the snowshoe harness in the shed.

One Saturday morning Lilian glanced out the kitchen window to see Sarah Whitmore waving at her. Lillian's face lit up with delight. She opened the door and motioned Sarah in, then grabbed her pad. "My first company. Welcome." Sarah smiled in return. Over coffee, through a series of gestures and the note pad, they conversed. Then Lilian took Sarah for a tour of the house. In the bedroom, Sarah stopped. "Where did you get the prints?" she scribbled.

"Not prints, paintings, mine," Lilian wrote.

"This is your work? It's wonderful."

Lilian lifted her hands palms up, as if she thought the art was ordinary. But she was secretly very pleased that Sarah liked the watercolours. In the work room, where she had stashed her box of drawings, Lilian pulled out a folder of paintings, beginning with those she had created with the child's paint box and ending with those she'd made with Nedra's salvaged paints. Sarah studied each one. "You really have talent!" she told Lilian. "I'm not just making nice. I'm serious. I took an art course one year at the university."

Lilian then sifted through the drawings and drew out three. One of a little girl in profile, seated at a piano, another of daisies and paintbrushes in a field, and another of a flop-eared dog sitting with its nose touching that of a horse on the other side of a fence. Then on her note pad she wrote: "Choose one. For you. A present."

"Oh, I couldn't," Sarah said. "These are worth money. They really are."

"I would like you to have one. I can make more."

"Well, if you're sure. Thank you. Thank you so very much." She chose the horse and dog.

Lilian spent the rest of the winter delighting in her new home. She didn't go out much, except to shop for food. Otherwise she found enough around the house to keep her busy. She had filled several cartons with clean, mended clothes to go to the Salvation Army. She had also found a tutorial for the computer and began learning to operate it. Sarah came by several times. When she found that Lilian was trying to learn the computer, she brought her a book on touch-typing.

The days sped by. Lilian was never lonely. She enjoyed her newfound friendship with Sarah. And she did carry on imaginary conversations with the former owner of the home whose presence she felt quite often. It was a benign presence, friendly and comforting.

Then one night Lilian had her dream again. It was a familiar dream....she hears a baby crying. Lilian tries and tries to reach it, but she can't move. She sees a small girl at a window, still crying. Again she tries to reach out to her but can't. The girl turns into a young woman. She is taking pills and more pills. Lilian knows the pills will kill her and tries to stop her.

Lilian awoke. The dream left her sad, so sad.

Sarah enjoyed her visits with Lilian, who seemed to be blossoming daily. Sometimes, despite her growing practice and her success in the courtroom, Sarah felt that she was missing out on things. In her busy life there was no time for family. She didn't have a regular boyfriend. Men found her overbearing, scary. As her late great granny might have said: "No man wants a woman who is smarter than he is." The other thing she liked about visiting with Lilian was the peace that reigned. Also Lilian always seemed overjoyed to see her. As time went on, Sarah realized that as long as Lilian was watching her, she could dispense with the note pad. Lilian understood everything she said. She could also sense a mood. One Saturday morning in winter Sarah came by. Over coffee they looked out at the falling snow. "We should go snowshoeing."

"There are snowshoes in the shed." Lilian said.

"Great," said Sarah "I have some in the trunk of the car."

The two women bundled up, strapped on snowshoes and set out across the field. They circled the property and then took a woods road for about a mile. Sarah, who was leading, stopped and turned to see how Lilian was making out. Lilian had stopped about 200 feet back at the edge of the clearing. Sarah started to call out but realizing Lilian couldn't hear, she turned and started back towards her. Just then a bull moose was walking into the clearing. He lifted his head into the sunshine, turned towards Lilian, gazed at her for a few seconds, then nodded his head and disappeared into the bushes. It was as if some communication had passed between Lilian and the animal. And the other really strange thing was that Sarah had not heard the moose approach, nor did it make any noise as it slipped back into the woods.

As Sarah approached her, Lilian's face broke into a wondrous smile. "Wow!" Sarah said. "Wasn't he huge?"

Lilian nodded.

Back at the house, they got out of their snowsuits and boots and Lilian made them hot chocolate. As Sarah sipped, Lilian pulled out a sketch pad and rapidly drew the moose, raising its head towards the sunlight. Then she drew herself in profile and lastly she drew Sarah, her toque falling off the side of her hair, her mouth a wide O of astonishment. Then she ripped off the sketch and handed it to Sarah.

Sarah loved the drawings but she felt guilty taking Lilian's gifts.

"Lilian, would you like to sell some of your paintings?"

"Do you think people would buy them?" Lilian wrote.

"I'm sure of it."

"Why sure?"

"There is such a quality of mystery about them. They are alive. The paintings really speak to you. I know that's trite, but I get a real sense of communication with them. On top of that, with most of your pictures I feel better having looked at them. Most of them. Not all."

"Which ones don't you like?"

"It isn't a matter of liking. The work is very, very good. Some of the pictures make me feel sad. Desperate, even."

"Explain."

Sarah got up and walked into the workroom where she opened Lilian's portfolio. She riffled through until she came to one of a man standing in front of a collapsed building, a look of horror on his face. She found one of an old man in bed, obviously dying, another of a woman, gazing backward at four shadowy figures of men. Then she pulled out the pictures of the newborn, the child being removed from its mother. Although the mother's face was in profile, her pain was evident. With the little girl at the piano, again the mother's face was in shadow. Turning to Lilian, she saw that tears were pouring down Lilian's face.

"Oh my dear, I'm so sorry." Sarah said, pulling her friend into her arms. "I'm so sorry. I didn't mean to hurt your feelings."

Lilian stopped weeping, made a deprecating wave of her hand as if to say forget it, it's all in the past.

"I'd better go now," Sarah said. "I've got an appointment this afternoon."

Lilian nodded. On the way out through the hall, Sarah noticed the computer. "How are you making out?"

Lilian nodded in the affirmative.

"Are you on the Internet?"

"Not."

"Why not? You'd really get a kick out of the net."

"Doesn't work."

Sarah put down her boots and walked over to the computer, punched a few keys and up popped the message "connection to other computer cannot be made." She punched a few more keys, then looked at the back of the computer, to ensure that it was plugged into the phone jack. Lilian watched her carefully. Finally Sarah picked up the telephone receiver. There was no dial tone. Of course there was no dial phone. Lilian was deaf. Why would she have a phone?

Sarah then explained that the phone line had to be hooked up so the Internet would work. "Want me to look after it?"

"No thank you. You're busy. I can do it."

"Well, if you're sure."

That afternoon Lilian sat down and wrote to NB Tel. Two days later a lineman reconnected the telephone line which had been disconnected when the house had changed hands. The next time Sarah came to visit, Lilian took great delight in showing her how proficient she was with the Internet, and all the new sites she had discovered.

"Wonderful," said Sarah, amazed at Lilian's progress. "Wonderful."

After Sarah left Lillian got up, put her coat on and went outside to walk along the well-trodden path around the property. Another thought crossed her mind, "Are you haunting me, Nedra Hanning?" And clearly the answer formed in her head, "No, just keeping you company." Lillian smiled. "Here I am, deaf as a post, listening to dead people talk."

"Yes," came the voice.

In the early spring Lilian wrote off to Vesey's seeds for seedlings. She would plant a new tree next to the road.

One morning she opened the back door to find a dog curled up on the mat. The dog quickly slipped past her into the kitchen where it nosed around the fridge and stove looking for food. At first Lilian was a little frightened. She was not familiar with dogs, never having had a pet. The dog sat, wagging its tail against the floor and looking up at her expectantly. Lilian caught the message. She found the stainless steel pet food dishes she'd cleaned and put away. She also found the half-bag of kibble in the broom closet. She filled one dish with kibble, and one with water, then stood back to watch the dog eat. When the dog had finished the kibble, it turned to the water dish where it lapped and slurped, spraying water about a foot around. Finally it stopped, raised its head, then settled slightly and gave a great wriggle before walking into the hall. It sniffed the floor, as if tracking something. Lilian followed it. At the master bedroom it stopped, then walked back to the hall, found a spot, circled it three times and flopped down onto the rug.

Lilian had breakfast and went about her morning chores. The dog remained on the rug. At noon she opened the back door. The dog raised up and looked at her, then at the door. Audibly sighing, the dog walked outside and down the driveway.

The next day the dog was back. The third time, Lilian got up the courage to pat its head. She delighted in the feel of the soft fur. As the dog ate, she sketched it. As it circled to lie down, she sketched it and she sketched it in repose. She wondered whom the dog belonged to. It was not wearing a collar with identifying tags.

Then while Lilian was out walking she saw a poster tacked to a telephone pole advertising a lost cat. The sign gave her an idea.

Lilian went home, made several sketches of the dog and above them wrote: "Found dog. Owner please call at 23 Cedar Springs Road." She tacked some on telephone poles, and she placed two on store bulletin boards. But she did not receive any reply. The notices with the sketches disappeared.

The dog food ran out. On her next shopping expedition she bought more. She also bought the dog a collar. When she got home the dog was waiting on the back step.

"Well, dog, I guess you've been adopted," Lilian thought. The dog, busy chomping kibble turned, looked up at her, wagged its tail, and went on eating. That night Lilian gave the dog a bath in the shower. She stripped off and got the dog into the shower and shut the door. Holding his collar, she sprayed him with warm water and shampooed him. Carefully rinsing away the shampoo, she added conditioner and sprayed him again. When he was finally clean, she wrapped him in a big brown beach towel, but not before he settled down into a crouch and then shook, spraying the bathroom with water from top to bottom. After the dog was bathed Lilian herself showered and put on fresh jeans and T-shirt. She found a brush and brushed the dog carefully, dislodging nearly a shopping bag full of loose hair and fur.

Once clean, the dog was handsome. His coat was a brindle colour with red and black highlights and his tail was a fine bush. He had a lovely little expressive face. Sarah made more sketches of the big wriggle, and of the different facial expressions. Lilian now had a roommate, one she had to remember to step over on her way to the bathroom in the morning. She loved the feel of the warm silky fur on her feet as she welcomed the day.

A few days before the three-month lease was up, Sarah came by with bad news. There would be no inheritance. Her brother had spent the money, and he had mortgaged the house, which had been in his name, to buy a car.

"But I must stay here," Lilian wrote on her pad. "This is my home now. I love this house."

"Well, the real estate agent says there have been enquiries and he wants to begin showing the house."

Lilian's face registered despair.

"What about selling your paintings?"

"How?" Lilian wrote.

"Let me talk to a dealer I know. She's also a gallery owner in Fredericton. In fact, loan me three or four and I'll get her to look at them."

As always, Sarah was as good as her word. The gallery owner liked the paintings, and arranged a showing. Lilian had two weeks to get ready. The showing was advertised. Critics were positive. The paintings were sold. But Lilian would never see a cent of the money. The gallery owner had been behind on her rent, she also owed money to printing houses and a marketing company. She'd been juggling accounts and lost. The bank sealed her accounts. And the gallery went under.

Feeling responsible for Lilian's losses, Sarah offered to co-sign a loan, but Lilian refused. They would have to think of another way. Meanwhile, the real estate agent started showing up with potential buyers.

Lilian grew frantic. Then one day Joan Hanning Prentice knocked on the door. She introduced herself as the owner of the house, having inherited it from her sister Nedra. She then said that she had heard about Lilian's art show, and she'd heard so many good things about it. Did she have any other works in progress?

Lilian showed the woman her paintings. Looking at the miniatures, Joan Hanning Prentiss said, "Oh, these are sweet. They would make delightful greeting cards." Lilian smiled. They went on to later work. Then Joan caught sight of the sketches Lilian had made the day she moved into the house. "Why that's my sister Nedra," she said in surprise. "You've caught her perfectly." Lilian looked from Joan to the painting. She saw a similarity. On her pad, she wrote: "This portrait reminds you of someone?"

"My sister Nedra. Did you do them from photos?"

"No," wrote Lilian.

"But you must have known her a long time." Holding up one of the paintings, "this was when we were about 16. There she is 26." Pointing to a third painting, "That was just after her second divorce. I remember the outfit." And, looking at the last one, "Oh, God. That must have been done just before she died."

Lilian studied the woman, seeing the range of emotions that flickered across her face, but said nothing. Throughout the conversation Joan kept turning her face away so Lilian missed a lot of what she was saying. In the end Joan bought two pastoral paintings and paid by cheque. Lilian thanked her and saw her to the door.

The cheque was for $200. It wasn't a down payment on the house, but it did give Lilian an idea. The following day she took a bus to Fredericton and went to several printers. In the end she chose one and made arrangements to have a small printing of cards and envelopes. Then she designed a sign, and went to the local farm market. Just before Christmas, the cards sold within two hours. She could pay the printer and still have $1,000 over.

When she got home there was a message from the real estate agent. The house had a potential buyer. She would have to be out within 30 days.

"Thirty days," Lilian despaired. Sarah dropped by the following morning. She had never seen her friend so down.

Lilian handed her the note from the real estate agent. Sarah studied it. "This says potential buyer. That doesn't mean it's etched in stone. Thirty days. Anything can happen in 30 days."

That afternoon Lilian paced the floor with the dog right behind her. Every time she stopped and turned, the dog stopped and turned. Once she took a step backwards and nearly tripped over it. She took her sketch pad and drew a series of cartoons, of herself walking, the dog following, the dog's expressive little face, its eyebrows raised like dancing commas. Then she threw down her sketch pad and went for a walk.

All around the property she trudged, the dog darting back and forth, yipping, sniffing. She looked at the pine trees which she had come to love, she looked back at the little bungalow in which she had invested so much labour. She looked at the dog which depended on her. "There must be a way," she thought. "There has to be a way for me to keep this house."

Two days before Christmas Lilian went to the store for groceries. A woman with a small child followed her through the check-out. The child was fussy and had a runny nose. As Lilian bent down to retrieve her canned goods the child leaned over her basket and sneezed in Lilian's face. Lilian came down with the flu. Every bone ached. She was hot, she was cold. Even her eyebrows hurt. For the next week she got up and down only to tend the dog and cat and go to the bathroom. Sarah had gone home to Saint John to spend the holidays with her folks. Lilian's temperature rose and fell. She didn't really sleep as much as doze and dream. In her dreams she was outside, standing looking at the house. She was nowhere. She could see hundreds of people walking, running, children skipping back and forth silently. And behind it the house, but she couldn't get in. Then she was holding a baby, just for a second, then someone or something pulled the baby from her arms. She awoke moaning.

By the time she was back on her feet several days had passed. New Year's day she had a visit from Sarah, who'd returned that morning from spending Christmas with her father. Sarah said she wished Lilian had been able to get in touch with her. She could have come back early and looked after her. Then Sarah said, "Come here," walked over to the computer and turned it on.

Lilian signalled a question mark.

"e-mail, my dear friend, e-mail. Why didn't I think of it before. Here, I'll show you how to set it up."

Lilian made them cocoa and they celebrated the coming of the New Year. At midnight Lilian got up and opened the door, looked out, then closed it again.

"What was that for?" Sarah said.

"To let the New Year in," Lilian wrote.

When she was leaving Sarah said, "check your e-mail in the morning."

That night, despite her continuing worry over losing the house, Lilian slept soundly. The following morning she arose early, ran with the dog around the lot and then returned for breakfast. Then she switched on the computer. Pressed "read mail," and waited. A few seconds later, she read on the screen "You have one new message." Lilian opened the message.

"Good morning, Lilian," it said. "Here's wishing you the very best year 2001 possible. I am so glad I know you, my dear friend. With love, Sarah."

Lilian read the note several times. Then she replied. "Dear Sarah, you have enriched my life in countless ways. I am truly grateful for your friendship."

Then it was January 20, and Lilian had less than a week to get out of the house. For some reason she put off packing, justifying her procrastination by saying to herself that she could take care of it in an hour.

She did look in the local papers to see what was available in the way of accommodation and continued to worry about how to look after the dog if she lost the place. In the end she broke down and went to visit her brother. She asked him and his wife if they were willing to look after her dog until she got settled in a new place. They weren't. They already had a dog. Further, how could she be so stupid as to take in a dog that she couldn't look after?

On her way back to the house Lilian chastised herself. "Well, I asked for that," she thought. Then since she was going by, she visited the real estate agent, first to ask if they might know of a place she could rent that would accept a dog. The agent was out, but the secretary was there: "Oh, I tried to contact you, but I couldn't get you on the phone." Lilian studied her.

"We thought we had a buyer, but they changed their minds. He's with the military and they have been transferred."

Lilian's heart began to beat faster. She pulled out her note pad and wrote, "Then may I keep the house a little longer?"

"Well, I'll have to ask about that. But I can tell you we aren't advertising the house right now. I mean, nobody moves this time of year. Not until spring."

Lilian wrote: "The reason you can't get me on the phone is because I can't hear. But I do have e-mail."

"Right, well, when the boss comes in I'll explain the situation. Gimme your e-mail address." Lilian pulled a small card out of her pocket which contained her e-mail number and a drawing of a perky little pup in one corner.

"Oh, this is so sweet," the secretary exclaimed. "Where did you get these made?"

Lilian smiled. "It's an original," she wrote. "One of a kind." Then she took a small pad from the top of the desk and quickly sketched the secretary, and passed the pad to her.

"Oh, this is marvellous. Marvellous. Thank you." Lilian smiled and left.

On the way home her mind was buzzing. For the first time in days she felt a glimmer of hope. At home, she hung up her coat, took off her boots and scarf and put the tea-kettle on to boil. Then she went in to the computer and checked the e-mail. No message. She went into a WORD program and began brainstorming a list. Paintings, greeting cards, calling cards. She got up and made tea. Then she went back to the net and typed in "Printers." This brought up all the different kinds of printers for home computers. She tried "printing companies." Then she found what she was looking for, a list of items she could create. Napkins, invitations, place mats, posters, menus, cups. Then the dog jumped in her face, almost knocking her off the chair. Someone was at the door.

Lilian got up and looked out the window. The mail lady with a parcel. Lilian quickly opened the door and, mouthing the word "thank you," she signed the book the mail lady held out to her. Back in the kitchen she opened the parcel. It contained her order from Vesey's Seeds.

Possibilities.

Leroy Martin returned from Toronto to Cedar Springs after a 25-year absence to visit his ailing mother. During the time he'd been away he had married, fathered four children, started a construction business, become an alcoholic, lost that business and built it up again from scratch.

Forty-seven years old, he had been sober nearly six months when he came home to a note on the table saying that his long-suffering wife was gone. She wanted nothing more to do with him. "Have a nice life," she'd written. She had left no forwarding address. Two of his children were married, one was in university and the youngest had disappeared into a Yonge Street life of Ecstasy, Raves, rock and rap. Leroy had no idea what he lived on. He'd left home at 17 and been gone for three years. Leroy had stopped worrying about him. He, Leroy had left home at 15, and made it on his own. More or less.

Leroy's first thought was to go to the liquor store. He went so far as to get his coat on and drive down the street, then changed his mind. Instead he went to an AA meeting.

In all fairness, he couldn't blame his wife. She had put up with his shenanigans for 23 years. She'd been steady all during the time they were raising his children. He'd had one-night stands that had led to affairs, and on a couple of occasions he had slapped her around. The memory of his behaviour shamed him deeply.

There was something else that haunted him. It had happened when he was 19 years old. Driving a dump truck, he picked a girl up on the outskirts of Cedar Springs and dropped her off near the high school. He picked her up every day for a week. She smiled at him, nodded, shrugged her shoulders, or shook her head. But she never said a word. Then one Friday he took her to the abandoned gravel pit overlooking the river and had sex with her. She had seemed willing enough but he had been fast and rough. She'd cried a little and he couldn't get her out of the truck fast enough. The memory of the experience left him feeling squeamish. Although she was 16, she looked more like 14. Jail bait. The following Saturday night Leroy picked up his pay and went to the Legion dance. Three of his buddies were going to Toronto, leaving in the morning. Leroy went with them.

In Cedar Springs, while his mother recovered from a hip replacement, Leroy spent his time making repairs on her house. The eavestrough needed replacing. And while he was at it, he stripped off the old siding, wrapped the house in insulation and put on new vinyl. The last day before he intended to leave for Toronto he was in the hardware store when he bumped into Lilian. Literally. Lilian had been choosing tubes of paint from a shelf, turned around and, wham, they collided. The tubes of paint went flying. He recognized her immediately as the girl he'd taken in the gravel pit. She'd changed very little.

Leroy, however, had aged. His hair was white, his features had coarsened. He followed Lilian to the counter and waited while she paid for her paint. Then as she was leaving he called after her to wait but she continued walking. The clerk knew Lilian, who had been coming to the store for some weeks. He turned to Leroy: "She can't hear you. She's a deaf mute. But she can read your lips. Read your mind, too, I think sometimes."

Leroy paid for his purchases but by the time he got out of the store, Lilian was nowhere in sight. He drove on home. During supper he asked his mother if she knew of a deaf-mute woman that lived in town. She couldn't recall anyone like that.

That night Leroy awoke with the night sweats. It had happened to him often since he'd become sober. During his wakeful state he knew he had to get in touch with the girl--woman, and ask her forgiveness. God, what a stupid, callow bastard he had been.

The following day he returned to the hardware store but that was the clerk's day off. He asked the owner if he knew of a customer who was deaf-mute. The owner said he was new to the area and couldn't recall any. Leroy thanked him and left. There had to be a way to contact her, but how? He didn't know who to ask any more. Most of the people he had gone to school with were gone. The man for whom he'd driven the gravel truck had been dead for years. He made several trips around town during the time he had left, but he did not run into her again. He returned to Ontario.

Back in the city, he found himself at loose ends. The business practically ran itself. He attended AA meetings, but he couldn't seem to settle into anything. By then he'd heard through his children that his wife had settled in British Columbia. He called her but she was adamant that she would not return. Not then. Not ever. He could file for divorce or go jump in Lake Ontario for all she cared. She'd served her time. Funny, Leroy thought, she hung in all the years I was drinking. It was me sober that she couldn't stand.

Within a month he sold the house and his business and realized a decent profit from both. He sent a cheque for half to his wife in British Columbia. Then he turned his five-year-old pickup in on a new four-wheel drive, packed his carpentry tools and several saws and headed east. At least he could be handy if his mother needed him.

By the time he got past Bowmanville, the traffic thinned out. Leroy's thoughts flitted back and forth. "Forty-seven years old, and what have I got to show for it. Oh sure, there had been some big projects, and I built the business back up. But now, what? I don't know. If I list the negative things: I've abused people. I was a lousy husband, and an indifferent father. I've screwed up often. I've smashed up a dozen vehicles and I have a license hanging on by two points. But, hey, at least I haven't killed anyone--at least I don't think so. There are still the blackouts where anything could have happened." Shame and fear coursed through his body. Then he made a conscious effort to control his thoughts: "Hey, Leroy, take it easy, one day at a time, remember?"

By the time he got to Riviere-du-Loup, Leroy had made up his mind he would find the deaf-mute girl and make some kind of reparation. The thing was, how to find her. It turned out to be an easier task than he expected.

At home Leroy settled in with his mother, temporarily. Her querulous voice almost drove him crazy. Even his long-suffering wife's nagging hadn't grated on his nerves so much. What he needed was a project. He set up a work bench at the back of the garage, and began working on a Morris chair, with a design he found in a "Popular Mechanics" magazine. It kept him out of the house.

About once a day he would jump in the truck and go for a drive. He even drove 30 miles out of town to the abandoned gravel pit where he had taken the girl so long ago, and he drove along the road where he picked her up. Despite his poor memory and boozed-out brain cells, he could remember her clearly.

Another day, while cruising around looking at houses for sale, he got the idea that he might buy a place, fix it up and resell it. Or, he might buy some land and build a house and sell it. He stopped by the real estate agent's office. He looked through the catalogue and came upon the Nedra Hanning house. "What about this one?"

"Well, it's for sale, at a very good price. But it's rented until April 1."

"April Fool's day. Hmm. Any chance of having a look inside?"

"I suppose so. We took it off the market for the winter, but maybe if you like we could go out and ask the woman if she'd let us look around. Want to go in my car?"

"No. I'll follow you."

Leroy followed the real estate agent's Camry to the outskirts of town. They pulled in the driveway and got out of their vehicles.

"By the way Mr. Martin, I should warn you. The lady who rents the house is deaf-mute. But she reads lips, so she has to see you to understand what you are saying."

Lilian opened the door and looked out to see the two men standing there. She recognized the agent and allowed them in. "This is Leroy

Martin," said the agent, "he's interested in buying the house. You don't mind if he has a look around?"

Lilian hesitated, then made a palms up gesture, saying "go ahead." Lilian had been painting at her easel, but while they walked through the house she stayed in the kitchen, thinking... "that's Leroy. After all these years."

Meanwhile, with the dog sniffing at his heels Leroy took a careful look around the house. When he got to the workroom and saw the paintings, he stopped.

"She's good, isn't she?" said the agent.

"Very good. I don't know much about art, but I like these a lot. Does her work sell?"

"I wouldn't know. I do know that she wanted to buy this place, but she couldn't come up with the money."

"How long has she been here?"

"Just since last fall." On their way through the kitchen Leroy spoke to Lilian.

"Thank you. I hope we haven't inconvenienced you too much."

Lilian shook her head, all the while studying every feature of his face.

Back at their vehicles, Leroy told the agent. "I'm interested in this place. What is the down payment again?"

"Ten thousand."

"I've got to do some banking. I'll be in touch tomorrow."

"No hurry. Not too many takers this time of year."

Leroy got in his truck and drove to Tim Hortons. He had coffee and a doughnut, and thought about Lilian and the house. He really needed a drink. Uh oh. Bad idea. He finished his coffee, went to the bank, and then, instead of going home, he drove back to Lilian. He got out of the pickup and raised his hand to knock, then remembering she was deaf, put it down again. The door opened and she stood before him. They studied each other for several seconds, then she beckoned him to come in. He followed her into the kitchen. She lifted the pot of coffee and looked at him.

"No thank you. I just came from Tim Hortons. I really just want to talk to you."

She signalled him to sit down, then sat down at the table across from him.

"I don't know where to start," he said as he watched her eyes darting back and forth exploring his face. "You may not remember me...."

Lilian raised her hand palm towards him, then pulled out a small pad. Then she quickly drew a dump truck with him leaning out the window of the driver's side.

"You remembered."

She nodded.

"I have always felt ashamed of myself for what happened in the gravel pit." Lilian waited. "You know, three of us left the following day. Went to Toronto."

Lilian watched him.

"I want to say I'm sorry for what happened. I have to add that I was young, stupid and you couldn't have been more than 12 or 13. I got scared. I'm ashamed. Many, many times over the years I've thought of the incident and felt rotten about it. Then I tried to put it out of my mind. But it would keep coming back."

Lilian wrote on her pad and pushed it toward him. "Tell me about your life."

"How long have you got?"

"As long as it takes," she wrote. "You went to Toronto...."

Leroy talked about arriving in the city, landing his first job, getting married. He talked about his drinking, his business, his children, his slide into alcoholism, his long road back. Throughout his recitation Lilian's eyes never left his face. Then she wrote:

"What will you do now?"

"Well, I'm thinking I might buy a house, fix it up and resell it. I need to have a project."

"This one?" Lilian wrote.

"It's a possibility. What are your plans?"

"Survival."

"No, I mean, what will you do when the house sells?"

"I don't know. I hoped I'd be able to buy it, but..."

"Look, Lilian. I know this isn't my place to butt in, and this in no way makes amends for what I did to you. But let me make the down payment. I can find another property. Or maybe a building lot or start from scratch."

Lilian studied him for several minutes. Then she nodded and wrote: "A loan. When I arrange another art show, I can start paying you back."

"A deal."

Lilian put her hand out, and he took it. Then she lightly kissed him on the cheek. Back in the pickup Leroy turned on the radio to hear a song by John Denver: *Gee, it's good to be back home again.* Leroy, an enormous weight lifted off his shoulders, sang along.

After Leroy left, Lilian did a series of drawings, starting with the young boy, the man, and the man today. Then she put them away beside earlier drawings of a newborn, of the child being taken from its mother's arms. She had a lot to think about. Would he keep his word? Yes, she felt he would. Was she right to take the offer of the loan? Yes. For both their sakes.

That evening Leroy found an AA meeting. In the morning, he was waiting at the real estate office when it opened. By noon he had arranged for the purchase of the house. The deed was made out in the name of Lilian Oakes.

With the house situation settled for the time being, Lilian turned her thoughts to a second art show. As it happened the show scheduled for the gallery had been cancelled, which made space for Lilian, but the opening was only two weeks away. She contacted three picture framers and learned they were booked solid for months ahead. Ready-made frames would have to do. She took a bus into town, looked at ready-made frames. She wrote a note to the shop owners and asked if she could borrow frames for her show in return for the free advertising. The answer was no.

Sarah, having been tied up on a time-consuming case, had neglected Lilian in recent weeks, and late one evening while driving by she noticed that Lilian's light in the workroom was still on. Her rapping at the window alerted the dog, which in turn alerted Lilian. As always Lilian's face lit up at the sight of her friend. She ran out and opened the door and pulled her friend inside with a hug, careful to keep her charcoal-stained fingers away from Sarah's coat.

"So, tell me what you've been doing." Lilian signalled.

"Busy. Night and day. This case is driving me crazy. But it's fascinating at the same time."

Lilian watched as her friend talked and talked. Then Sarah stopped. "But I came here to find out how you are doing?"

Lilian took her hand and led her into the work room. She showed her latest work. She also showed her the brochures and pointed out the date for the showing.

"Looks like you're almost ready," Sarah said.

"Only the framing." Lilian wrote. "Wish I could do my own framing."

"There must be somebody."

"I can cut glass and handle the matting, but the framing...you need special tools."

"Who do I know that's a carpenter?" Sarah said, "A cabinet maker... and gazing at two of Lilian's crowd pictures, said: "Who's the dude?"

Lilian looked at her questioningly. Sarah walked over to the largest of the canvas and pointed to Leroy. Then she pointed to him again, surrounded by children. And again, seated across the kitchen table. Lilian's face reddened. "A friend," she wrote. Then she brightened. "He's a carpenter, a builder."

"So why don't you ask him?"

"I don't know."

"At least, if he can't do it himself, he may be able to give you a name. Do you have his address? I'll go by there and leave a note on his door."

Lilian wrote a note, made her request, signed her name and then under it she drew a quick sketch of her dog in a pleading stance. As Sarah drove by Leroy's she spotted him just pulling in the driveway. He was instantly recognizable from Lilian's drawings. She pulled in and stopped behind the pickup.

"Excuse me," Sarah said as she climbed out of the car, "are you Leroy Martin?"

"Yes." Leroy studied the tall, slim, smartly-dressed woman before him.

"I'm Sarah Whitmore, a friend of Lilian Oakes."

"Yes?"

"She asked me to leave this note in your mailbox, but since you're here I'll give it to you directly."

"Thank you."

"Well, I'll be going then. I'm sure she'd like to hear from you as soon as possible."

"It's a little late now," said Leroy looking at his watch, "10:45. I'll go over first thing in the morning."

"Great, I'll tell her tonight."

"But she's deaf."

"E-mail. I'll send her a note on the e-mail. She always checks it before she goes to bed."

"Well, thanks for your trouble. I appreciate this."

Sarah waved goodnight, got back in her car and drove home where she quickly typed an e-mail to Lilian on her ever-running computer.

As good as his word, Leroy showed up at 7:00 a.m. Lilian motioned him in and pointed to the coffee pot. Then she described what she needed. "No problem," he said. "I've got most of the tools with me."

"There are more in the shed," she wrote. Together they walked out to Nedra's shop. Dust and dirt filmed everything. This was one space Lilian hadn't spent much time in. Lilian showed him a brochure of frames she had acquired and pointed out those she thought would complement her art. Then she wrote, "Are you sure you have time for this?"

Leroy smiled. "You've maybe saved my sanity. I need a project. My mother's getting on my nerves. Look, I'll have to go to the lumber yard and I need to go home and collect a couple of saws and a work table. Plus we'll need stain and varnish. I'll be back in a couple of hours."

When Leroy returned, he backed the pickup in next to the shed door. Inside he found Lilian working with the shop-vac, moving things around, making space for him to work. He watched her for a few seconds. She had a trim figure, undisguised by the old paint-splattered shirt he'd seen her working in before. He noticed her light brown hair tied into some kind of knot at the back. Then she turned and saw him. Her face was smudged and flushed. When she smiled her whole face lit up.

She pulled her note pad out of her pocket. "I appreciate this, Leroy. I really do."

"Look, here is some moulding, and metal strips, probably some kind of alloy. Maybe you'd like some made of this?" Leroy brushed the dust off the strips, which were in perfect condition, just as Mark Lawson had left them more than 20 years earlier.

Lilian smiled and nodded. Then she turned and walked back into the house. The dog followed her. A few minutes later she returned with an armload of paintings. Leroy had lined up his saw blades, plugged in his electric tools, arranged his finer tools on a tray, and begun taking measurements. Lilian leaned the paintings against the wall, then pulled out her notepad. "Like a surgeon." she wrote, nodding at the tray of tools.

Leroy laughed and went back to his task. Several times throughout the morning Lilian peeked in to see how he was doing. Twice he had saws going. He was wearing eye-protecting goggles and something that looked like white ear-muffs. She returned to the house, made two or three sketches of him working, then took a cup of coffee out. At noon she made them sandwiches.

After lunch Leroy got up, stretched, and walked around the room. He spotted the open sketch pad and saw himself in goggles and ear protectors. He grinned, and shook his head in delight. Then he walked into her workroom and studied the two crowd pictures. He recognized Sarah immediately. He spotted the waitress at Tim Hortons, and other familiar faces. Then he recognized himself, with a rueful look, studying the rest of the crowd. As he looked at the painting he had a feeling for a second or two that the people painted were actually moving around. He felt the hair raise on the back of his neck. Another face stood out from the crowd. It had an otherworldly aura about it.

"Who is this?"

Lilian shrugged. "Not sure. I've seen her somewhere, maybe in a dream."

"You are really, really good."

"Thank you."

Leroy worked until 5:30, then went to the house to tell Lilian he was going. He stopped by his mother's, showered, changed his clothes and drove to the AA meeting.

Over the next week Leroy worked at the picture framing. He enjoyed the task. He built shipping containers for the pictures as well. Through the pictures he began to see the world Lilian lived in, to see it through her eyes. Life, vibrancy, movement were all there. Passion, hope, despair. He found one that looked like Lilian as a young girl and stopped to study it for a while.

Lilian walked into the shed holding a cup of coffee for him. She watched him gazing at a picture, then leaned in to see which one it was.

"This is you," Leroy said, taking the coffee.

Lilian shook her head, no.

"Looks like you, a lot like you. A sister? Cousin?"

"No."

Leroy continued gazing at it. "No, not you. A daughter?"

"A painting," Lilian wrote.

"She looks so familiar to me. Something around the eyes, the way she is standing....I know, she reminds me of my daughter..." He turned to look at Lilian, but she had gone back to the house. He put the painting aside, apart from the others, and went on with his work.

In the afternoon Sarah Whitmore stopped by. She saw Leroy in the shop and greeted him as she walked by. He returned her wave.

"How are you progressing?"

"Getting there, I think."

"Oh, these look wonderful, Lilian must be so pleased."

"I think so." Then Leroy held up the painting of the girl. "Oh by the way, do you know who this is?"

Sarah studied the painting: "Looks a lot like Lilian...looks a lot like you."

Leroy held the painting out again. "Funny."

"What's funny?"

"Well, I don't know. Every one of these pieces draws you in. Sometimes I'm not sure really what I'm looking at, but I do know how they make me feel."

"I know what you mean. Lilian definitely has a talent for getting to the heart of her subjects. Well, I must dash, I want to see her for a few minutes and I'm running late."

"All that running around will get to you, you know."

"That's what my Dad says. See you."

In the house Lilian turned to her friend with a hug, then riffled through a pack of recipe cards, held one up. On it, she'd written: "Tell me everything."

"I'm working on an adoption case. It's very hard. The birth mother wants the child. The adoptive parents have had it for a year. They don't want to part with it. It is so hard to know what to do. Anyway, I'm busy looking for precedents. Studying cases. What I'd really like to find is stats about adopted children. I'd like to know if they have been interviewed, studied, or if anybody knows just how well adoptions work. It would have to be better for some than for others. Each child and parent would have a different relationship. And there is the old question, can the birth mother give the child more than the adoptive mother? What is more important, blood or money? If the birth mother, as in this case, has no money, no job, no husband, no visible means of support, what can she give this child?

"Also, since she is so young, if she keeps the child, what does she know about nurturing? What about her own needs? She hasn't finished high school yet. Should a child raise a child?...but, hey, you didn't want to hear all this."

Lilian nodded yes.

"Well, as I was saying, the birth mother has nothing to offer except her mother love. Is that enough to sustain a new life? In this case, the adoptive parents do have money. They both have careers. He is a professor and she teaches grade school. She is 28, he is 36. They waited until they got established before trying to have children. Then she discovered that she had a cyst on her ovary, which turned out to be malignant. This was followed by a hysterectomy. So adoption is her only option. The money they have already put out on this one-year-old child boggles the mind."

Lilian wrote: "Is there any way they could share? Visiting rights for the birth mother?"

"Well, that's possible. But unlikely to work. The girl lives in Toronto. They live in New Brunswick."

After Sarah left Lilian went out to see how Leroy was doing. A glance at his work and she wrote: "Wonderful. The frames are worth more than the paintings."

"Oh, I wouldn't say that." Lilian could see he was pleased.

The next week Lilian's show would start. Meanwhile Lilian ran from workroom to shop, changing her mind and re-changing it on what to show. There would be space for 50 paintings. She had to choose among 150. Leroy simply kept showing up, calmly working away producing new frames and shipping containers. He could see Lilian was having a difficult time making up her mind. Once when she brushed past him, he turned and caught her arm and said: "Look, these will all sell sooner or later."

"But I need 50," Lilian wrote.

"Well, what about a variety?" Leroy picked up the frame he was working on and fitted it to a painting. "Say, this pen and ink, some of those done with charcoal, some oils and some acrylics? These crowd pictures, definitely. And some of the pastoral scenes. Oh, and this one." Lilian looked at the drawing Leroy was holding up. Leroy was watching her. A rainbow of emotion filtered across her face. She looked at him, and then shook her head.

"Who is it, by the way? Looks so familiar." But Lilian had turned her back without hearing his question. Leroy went on working.

Despite Lilian's obvious anxiety about the upcoming show, Leroy found he was comfortable in her company. He knew nothing of art. Yet he felt the power of her work and sensed it was good. He tried to imagine what it must be like to live in a silent world, a world without music, a world where no birds sang. It must have been miserable for her as a child. She would have missed so much.

Then he began thinking about all the time and the opportunities he had wasted. He could have done better, got a decent education. Actually he had made money in spite of himself. If he had studied he could have gone on to become an architect, to design buildings himself, instead of always hiring it done. Then he shook himself. "Okay Leroy Martin. Enough of the pity party already. The past is past. Let's see what you can do with today."

In the days after the art show Lilian felt a letdown. All the energy that had gone into the show was one cause. Also the success of the show itself was overwhelming. She immediately made a cheque out to Leroy Martin, not only to cover the original $10,000 loan, but to cover his work on the picture frames and shipping crates. Along with the cheques, she passed him a letter in which she wrote:

"None of this would have been possible without your help. I could never have been ready in time. I hope you will continue to come by. It has been good having you around the place. You and Sarah have become my first real friends."

Leroy was touched. "I'd like that," he said, then looking at the cheques, he added: "There's no rush on this, you know."

"I like to keep things straight," Lilian wrote. "Lets me concentrate on other things."

"What will you do now?"

"More drawing, likely. Also, I want to use the computer more. It has been such a help."

"Maybe I should try to get on line."

"Why not?"

Before Leroy left he packed his tools and put everything back in the shed, then swept the floor and went over it all with the shop-vac. The place hadn't looked so good since Mark Lawson worked in it. Leroy also looked at Mark's tools. Very good quality.

Lilian spent a couple of days wandering and resting, feeling melancholy. Somewhere in the back of her mind was the hope that her daughter might have got in contact, but then why should she? A chance in a million. If she was still alive and in this country. To get her mind off that, she decided spring cleaning was in order.

She pulled down the curtains and scrubbed the small bedroom from top to bottom, cleaned the windows then polished the fine wood floors. Next she went to her work room. Nedra Hanning's partially finished quilt, still on its frame, she lugged to the shed. Then boxing her art supplies, she set them in the hall, along with the easel. Then the work room was thoroughly cleaned. A closet which had been filled with junk and books was turned into a supply cupboard. Those rooms set to rights, she began on the livingroom. Down came the drapes, the pictures, the books. She removed two old soiled chairs and a couch that had been in the house since the 1950s. She painted the ceiling and the walls. Then she took out several tables which cluttered the room. She pulled up the rugs and threw them outside, then set to scraping down the lovely hardwood floor to the bare wood. After that she layered on several coats of varathane, carefully sanding between each coat, then finally going over the whole floor with steel wool. When she finished, it felt as silky as the lovely cupboards and shelves constructed by Mark Lawson, the original builder.

While the floor dried, Lilian poked her head into the room a number of times and each time she was struck by the beauty of the bare room. The woodwork, natural wood that had darkened to a warm coppery gold over the years, pleased her as did the magnificent windows which allowed the widest possible view. The well-constructed cupboards and shelves were an added bonus.

She went on through the hall and the kitchen, emptying drawers. She measured the floor in the kitchen and ordered a piece of cushion floor and glue from Sears, then laid the floor herself. The cupboards she scoured.

As the days grew warmer she began to work outside. She refinished two small end-tables and chest of drawers, which had been in the living room. She wasn't sure that she wanted the chest of drawers in that room. In fact, she couldn't make up her mind about the end-tables either. Instead she got busy in the garden.

She created flower beds and planted shrubs. Then looked out one morning to see the dog busy digging up the bulbs. She chastised the dog, then looked for and found a small fence which she placed around the beds. She also planted two pine trees at the end of the lot.

As a break from her manual labours Lilian went into the house, washed her hands, made coffee and sat down at the computer to check for messages. Quite often there was a cheery note from Sarah. One day she was surprised to find one from Leroy. So, he'd bought a computer. Good for him.

Lilian went at it methodically, taking all the tours, studying the tutoring programs, and becoming adept at the Internet. She was thrilled to find sites where art, the art of the masters in museums and galleries all over Europe, could be seen. However, after downloading one picture, she realized she would need newer and faster equipment if she was going to learn more about those riches.

Still, each day she worked at it a little bit. Then one day she came across a site, called "people search." She opened it, and found a site where adopted children were looking for their birth parents. She tried to log on, but discovered the site had moved. While she waited for the machine to grind its way to the new site, there was a power surge and the computer went black. Throughout the afternoon she kept checking the machine but she couldn't seem to get back to that spot.

When Sarah came by later that day to tie up some legal matters concerning the house sale, insurance, etc., Lilian sought her advice on a new computer. Together they picked out a machine with a 21" monitor, a scanner and all the other bells and whistles. Sarah also explained how Lilian could set up an account and sell her paintings through the Internet.

"Marvellous." Lilian wrote. "Marvellous. Thank you. Now, what are you doing with your life?"

"So busy. I've been so busy."

"No boyfriend?"

"No." Sarah hesitated, then added, "Well, not really." Lilian studied Sarah's face.

"Someone you like?"

"Yes. But he's married."

"That's bad."

"Yes. I don't have much time to think about it really. Which is probably a good thing. But what about you? Aren't you lonely? Wouldn't you like to have someone?" Lilian did not answer but her face took on that pensive look Sarah had come to recognize. "There is someone, but you don't want to talk about it."

Lilian shook her head, then wrote, "maybe sometime."

"Maybe sometime. Okay. Whenever you're ready."

"Thank you, my friend."

"So how are you making out?" Leroy asked. He'd been driving by and spotted Lilian working in the flower beds. As he drove in the yard she looked up and smiled. She was glad to see him, he could tell. She beckoned him in. Automatically she filled the kettle and set out two cups. Then she walked in to the hall and checked the computer, which she had left on. Leroy watched her, thinking as always what youth and strength there was in that slim, supple figure. She could be 18 instead of 40. Suddenly he saw Lilian's expression change. Something had got her exercised. He walked in to look at the computer to see what was bothering her. Lilian held up her hand for him to wait. Then she pulled a sheet of photos from the printer. Leroy, hearing the kettle start to whistle, had gone back to the kitchen where he found a pot and a coffee filter, spooned in the ground coffee and was pouring water over it when Lilian returned. Something was up.

"What has happened?" Lilian studied his face for several moments. Then having made a decision, she pulled out her note pad. "Leroy, I have to tell you something."

"Go ahead. I'm listening."

She pushed the printed-out pictures towards him. Leroy looked at the first one. It was a two-year old, looked a lot like his daughter. Then a picture of a teenager. That one was easy. "You?"

Lilian shook her head.

"Then who?"

"That time in the gravel pit. I got pregnant."

Leroy's coffee slopped back into his cup. "No."

"Yes. A baby girl. My parents had it adopted."

"Oh my God. And you think this has something to do with that baby? Of course it does, the pictures you drew. Sarah noticed it. Said the child in the painting looked a lot like me. I thought it was a relative of yours. Well it was. Yes. Oh, Lilian, I'm so sorry."

"I want to see her."

"Where is she?"

"Toronto."

"Does she know she was adopted? When's the last time you saw her?"

"February 6, 1974."

"1974. Not since she was born? How did you know what she looked like as a young girl, a teenager?"

Lilian made a motion which Leroy read as "in my heart and head."

"I have to see her. She is sick."

"Sick? How do you know?"

Lilian pulled out the last series of paintings she had done. What Leroy saw was a skeletal frame in the middle of a hospital bed.

"Would you like me to take you to Toronto?"

Lilian nodded yes.

"When? Now? Today?" Lillian kept nodding her head.

"What about the dog? No. I know, I'll take it over to Mother's. She won't be happy, but she'll look after it. I'll pack a bag and be right back."

Leroy found the dog's kibble, dish and a leash and boosted the dog up into the pickup. The dog braced its feet and began to whine. "Come on, beast, up you go."

"Well, what am I supposed to do with that?" his mother whined.

"Feed it two cups of kibble twice a day and fill its water dish. I'll tether it outside the garage door so it can get in out of the rain. All you have to do is remember to feed it. Of course, you could also walk it, or ask one of the kids next door."

"Well, I suppose."

"See you Ma, be back in a few days."

"Well, I must say you're the one for taking off in a hurry. I wanted..."

But Leroy was tossing his suitcase into the back of the pickup and pulling down the door. When he got back to Lilian's she was standing at the gate. He put her case in the back.

"Okay, ready?" Leroy asked. Lilian nodded.

"We're off then."

Just past Riviere-du-Loup they made a pit stop, and past Montreal, they stopped for a late dinner. Every minute she sat in the cab, Lilian leaned forward as if that would make them get there quicker. Leroy badly needed a nap, but he kept driving. He turned to Lilian, touched her arm and pointed to the back seat. "There's room for you to stretch out there." Lilian shook her head.

At Cornwall, he had to pull over. He climbed into the back, saying, "wake me in half an hour." Lilian nodded. Twenty minutes later Leroy came awake. He heard steps passing near the truck. He sat up and looked around. It was Lilian walking towards him. She had gone in and bought them coffee. While they gassed up, he used the washroom, and they were on their way.

There was so much on his mind and so much he wanted to say to Lilian and he didn't know how to say it. What was his place in this drama? Where did he fit? What was his duty? The person they were going to see was a stranger to him. Hell, he was almost a stranger to his own son, who had grown up in his own home. Of course, Leroy had been too much into the sauce to know just what the boy needed. He wondered if he should try to find him, look him up while he was in Toronto. What if this whole damn thing was a hoax? He glanced over at Lilian, still straining at the windshield. "Okay, Lord, one day at a time. I'll take it as it comes. I'll remember that nothing's going to happen that you and me together can't handle." Leroy kept repeating the thought, mumbling the words to himself....you and me together...you and I. "Oh, God, well, I need help now. I need all the help you've got to spare. And, please dear God, let this not be a hoax. I've caused this woman enough pain already. She doesn't deserve it."

At the hospice, a nurse's aid came into Natalie's room. She gazed at the skeleton before her, and sighed. Then, having some spare time, she decided to turn Natalie, to rest the paper-thin flesh of her hip and shoulder. As she started to work, she noticed the mottling colour of her legs. She hoped that Natalie wouldn't die on her shift. Glancing at the clock, she read 4:24 a.m. and wrote up her report. When the nurse checked on Natalie at 7 a.m., Natalie's breathing was slow and shallow. Natalie's friend Brenda had asked to be called. The nurse went out to the desk and made the call.

Twenty minutes later, alone in her room Natalie stopped breathing. The narcotic having slowed her central nervous system, her lungs filled with fluid. Dimly she felt the presence of a woman with her arms wrapped around her breast. In a pickup, coming closer and closer down the highway. Her mother. Her birth mother was coming to look after the children. Now she could go.

Brenda shook her son Paul. "Yeah, Ma, whassup?"
"I'm going to the hospice. You stay here with the kids, ya hear?"
"But I can't, I gotta ball game."
"Paul, Natalie may be dying. I have to go, and you have to get the others up and stay with the twins. I'll be back as soon as I can. Get up now. Please."
"Yes, Ma. Whatever."
"Now."
"Okay, okay, I'm coming." Paul sat up. Brenda had called a cab. She only had $20. She hoped it would be enough. How she would get home, she had no idea.

Brenda rushed into the hospice and up the stairs. The nurse met her in the door and shook her head. "She's gone?" Brenda asked.
"Just now. Very peacefully. You may sit with her for a while if you like."

Brenda walked in to the room and took a chair beside the bed. She didn't feel like crying. The sadness was deeper than that. She lightly touched the skeletal corpse. Then her eye caught the picture printed off her son's computer. She stared at the picture for a while. "Yes," she thought, "that's how you looked, Natalie. Goodbye, dear friend."

"So, what happens now?" Brenda asked the nurse.
Well, the body goes to the crematorium.
"Who pays for that?"
"She has no family, you say?"
"She was adopted. Hasn't seen or spoken to the adoptive parents in years."
"Well, the city will take care of it. You could arrange a memorial service if you like. Some people do that. Invite her friends and all."
"Thank you."

Brenda, with just enough change for the streetcar, ran to catch it. Only after she was seated did she think. "Oh, God. The twins."

Leroy glanced over at Lilian. She wasn't exactly crying, but she was experiencing some terrible emotion. He patted her arm. She bounced across the seat and cuddled down under his arm. She was shaking. He held her with one arm and continued to drive.

At 10:30 a.m. they were bypassing Newcastle. "Not long now," Leroy said.

Lilian nodded. She wasn't sitting on the edge of the seat any more, but she was alert to what was going on around them.

"Ever been to Toronto before?"

Lilian shook her head.

"What's the address again?"

Lilian passed him the notebook.

"Sackville. We'll turn down the Don Valley, get off the Bloor exit. Shouldn't be too hard to find."

Leroy drove down Parliament and east on Spruce Street. He couldn't get on to Sackville, so they locked the truck and left it on a side street. Together they walked the footpath until they got to Sackville. While looking for the address, they saw a woman hurrying towards them. "Wait, wait," she called.

Leroy stopped and then Lilian stopped. The woman spoke to her: "You are Lilian?"

Lilian nodded.

"I'm Brenda. I recognized the NB license plates. I'm the one who sent you the e-mail. Well, rather my son did."

Lilian searched her face. Leroy explained: "She'd deaf-mute, but she can read lips."

"Yes? Oh God. Well, we're right here. Come inside."

Leroy and Lilian followed Brenda into a townhouse on Sackville. It was bare of furniture but cluttered with children's toys.

Brenda sat down, then she faced Lilian. "You're Natalie's birth mother?"

Lilian nodded.

"There's no easy way to say this. Natalie died this morning."

Lilian nodded again. Leroy, standing helplessly by, put his arm around Lilian.

"She died peacefully. She was only really sick for the last few months."

"How did she die?" Leroy asked.

"AIDS. Oh, this is so hard. Natalie wasn't very happy with her adopted parents. She was wilful, and wild, and they were very strict. We don't know how she got it...but she stayed clean while she was carrying the twins."

"Twins?" Leroy said. "You say she had twins? Where are they now?"

Brenda got up and lumbered in to the den. "Paul, bring out the children."

In a few minutes, a teenaged boy appeared carrying a pair of squirming toddlers, with chocolate pudding-smudged faces.

Lilian, with a tiny animal sound, ran towards him. Leroy stood like a stone. The girl twin hung onto the neck of the teenager. The little boy opened his arms towards Lilian.

"Zach's a little slow, doesn't talk," said Brenda, "but Zoe does. She's just shy at the moment."

Leroy watched the drama unfolding. "What plans did she make for the children?"

"She didn't. She thought she would get better. She did before. I've had so much on my mind. She made me promise to take care of them. But I already have three of my own and I'm living on assistance."

"You said the boy is slow. How do you mean?"

"He doesn't talk."

"Could he be deaf like Lilian?"

"I never thought of that." Brenda and Leroy watched Zach with both arms wound tight around Lilian's neck. Lilian then reached an arm out to Zoe, and Zoe, having given careful consideration to the matter, went to her.

Leroy watched them for a minute more. Then he said: "Look, you're going to need a little time. I'll go get us some rooms at the Chelsea, and we can figure out what we are going to do from there."

"Okay, you go ahead," Brenda said. "I'll make us some tea."

After two hours, the twins were sleepy. Lilian helped to tuck them in. Then, taking out her pad, she held a conversation with Brenda. She learned that the apartment Natalie had lived in had been sub-let but that her things were in storage. Having established that nobody in the welfare system had been notified about the children, she asked what the legal ramifications were. Brenda did not know. Natalie had worked and paid for their keep until the last few months.

It came on early evening and still Leroy did not return.

"That's a man for you," Brenda said. "Can't believe a damn word they say."

Lilian shook her head. "Something's wrong. He'll be back."

At midnight Brenda said, "Look, you can sleep on the couch. It isn't very comfortable. Or, wait a minute, I have a roll-away, if you'd like to sleep in with the twins. I'll take my two youngest in with me. Lilian nodded and thanked her.

On her way by the computer, Lilian asked if she could use it to e-mail her friend in New Brunswick.

"Be my guest," Brenda said.

Lilian sent an e-mail to Sarah Whitmore. "I need your help," she wrote, then outlined the situation.

She was still awake when dawn arrived, and with it the first gurgling sounds of the toddlers. Lilian sprang up and changed the babies, then took them down to the kitchen. Paul was already up. He put out some bowls, milk and cereal. "Help yourself. Ma will be down in a while."

Leroy awoke on the sand near the boardwalk, his head hammering like a dozen woodpeckers. He spit out a mouthful of sand. Then he sat up, checked his pockets. Empty, except for the truck keys and a hotel room card. Where the hell was he? Toronto? That looks like Lake Ontario. He needed to urinate. Getting to his feet, he moved along until he came to the washrooms, but they were closed and locked. He turned his back to the early morning traffic and urinated into the sand. Then just as he zipped he saw a woman with a large dog on a leash walking his way. He turned and walked back towards the car park. Sure enough, there was the truck, still sitting where he'd left it.

Instead of getting in the truck, Leroy walked past it to the fountain. But that had been turned off. He thought he was sober enough to drive, but he knew he'd never pass a breathalyser. His last memory was of drinking beer at the Edison with his youngest son. He remembered the boy telling him he was no good, that Leroy had been a miserable father, and that he had nothing to live for. He remembered getting angry with the boy and taking a swipe at him. And then the boy walking off. He remembered walking into the LCBO and buying two quarts of whisky, and then getting in the pickup and driving to the Chelsea Hotel and booking in. After that there was a blank. He walked from one end of the boardwalk to the other, feeling all the usual burden of guilt and fiery shame. He'd been dry nearly two years. He thought he'd had it licked. But he knew better. Once a drunk, always a drunk. What's more, what he really needed more than anything else right this minute was a drink. But the liquor stores wouldn't open for several more hours. And, oh, God, what about Lilian? He'd just left her in that rathole down on Sackville. Just walked out on her. Oh, God, what must she think? What was he to do? Walk out into the lake?

No. Lilian was depending on him. After all, he was the cause of this whole mess. He had to go back and look after things.

Still feeling dreadful, Leroy unlocked the pickup and got in. Then, he looked in the glove compartment. He was lucky. In his drunkenness he must have stuffed his wallet in there before going down to the beach. His wallet contained a receipt for his hotel room, No. 865. Who says the good Lord doesn't look after fools and drunks? On his way back along Queen Street he stopped at a Tim Hortons and bought a large coffee with cream and lots of sugar. He thought about eating a muffin, but his stomach revolted. Back in the pickup he drove carefully west. He went past Sackville and Parliament and Church and then turned north and west to the Chelsea where he parked in the underground parking and took the elevator to the eighth floor.

In the suite he stripped his clothes off and got in the shower, then carefully shaved. Then, since it was 8:00 a.m. he figured with the kids in the house, everybody would be up at Sackville. Taking a deep breath, he called Brenda's and asked her to give Lilian a message. He had a couple of matters to attend to, and he would be there at 10:00 a.m. Brenda said she would pass on the message.

He called his daughter but got the answering machine, so he said he would try and reach her later. He called the hospice where Natalie had died and after several more calls he had made arrangements to pay for the cremation and to have Natalie's ashes shipped east. It wasn't much to do for the daughter he'd never seen, but it would be important to Lilian and he felt a desperate need to redeem himself. Then he went downstairs and into the dining room where he choked down some toast and several more cups of coffee. It was time to face Lilian.

Lilian took the twins out of their high chairs, wiped their faces and set them down on the floor. Then she washed the breakfast dishes and set them to drain on the counter. Three more children arrived, and the din finally brought Brenda out. The children were having a great time making saucy remarks behind Lilian's back. Now and then she would turn around, look at their faces and smile. She knew what they'd been up to. But it didn't matter.

"Well, the twins have sure taken to you," Brenda said, as she watched Lilian at the sink with Zach holding one leg and Zoe seated on the mat beside her. Lilian nodded.

"Did you find anything to eat?"

"Not hungry. I fed the twins. The others had cereal."

As soon as Brenda got her coffee in front of her and lit a cigarette, Lilian said: "I want to pay you for looking after the twins. It can't have been easy stretching the dollars."

"You can say that again. But you seem to be all right financially."

"Now, yes." Lilian wrote. "But only during the last year, since I've sold some paintings."

"What did you do before that?"

"Took care of my parents."

"And when they died, you inherited?"

"No. My brother did. Everything, including money my parents received from the government for my handicap. I never knew."

"So how did you manage."

"I found a wonderful lawyer."

"Pah. Ain't no such animal."

Lilian smiled. "Oh yes. A smart lawyer, and a friend."

"And Leroy? Just a friend?"

"Yes." Then Lilian wrote: "Brenda, I want to take the twins home with me. I need them. They need me."

Brenda studied the woman intently. She could definitely give them more than any foster home. Brenda had seen too many children that had been moved from foster home to foster home, and Zach would need special understanding. Lilian seemed the perfect person to give it. It was an answer to a prayer, if she'd believed in prayer.

"When do you want to take them?"

"As soon as Leroy gets here."

"You sound pretty sure he'll come back."

Lilian nodded. Just then the doorbell rang. Brenda got up to answer. "Ah, it's you. Lilian said you'd be back."

"Where are they?"

"In the kitchen. Come on through."

It didn't take long to bundle up the twins and pack their few belongings. Brenda also gave Lilian all the snapshots she had of Natalie, and Lilian promised to have them copied and sent back. They also stopped and picked up Natalie's things from storage. At Whitby they stopped at a mall, and while the twins sat in the truck with Leroy, Lilian picked up disposable diapers, T-shirts, shorts, another blanket and some plastic toys.

Near Kingston Leroy stopped to nap, while Lilian took the twins for a picnic and a run. She would also have to get shoes, running shoes, pairs and pairs of shoes. Meanwhile the day was warm and the toddlers had a wonderful time running and sitting, chasing butterflies and exploring daisies. After a couple of hours, when the children had become tired, Lilian returned to the truck to find Leroy stirring. They fuelled up and were on their way. From there on they stopped only to get gas, food and coffee.

As he drove along, Leroy glanced from time to time at Lilian and the twins. She had never seemed so animated. Yet now and then, when the twins were sleeping, the grief for the daughter she'd lost was plain and palpable. He reached over and pulled her close to him. Words were such useless things. After a while, he cupped her chin in his palm and turned her face to him. Then he told her: "I've arranged for Natalie's ashes to be sent back to you in Cedar Springs. We'll find a plot and give her a proper burial somewhere near."

"Thank you," Lilian signed. Then the tears poured silently down her face.

On they drove through the night. Usually Leroy did his best thinking while driving. But this time the thoughts swirled around and around. He had thought he had the alcohol beaten, but had learned that his recovery was merely a respite. He'd been lucky not to have been hurt. He had been rolled on the beach. All the spare bills and change were taken. It was a good thing he'd locked his wallet in the truck. Fortunately the thief didn't bother with his keys.

But where did he fit in with Lilian and the twins? Did he want to fit in? After all, he had just shucked all the responsibility of his company, had decided to change his life, live less stressfully. And he'd been such a no-good father the first time around. Was he likely be a no-good undependable grandfather? Would it be better not to get involved with them?

Hardly had the thought expressed itself in his mind when Zoe stood up in the back seat, leaned forward and put both arms around his neck.

Driving into Cedar Springs, Leroy said: "Look, what if I picked up a couple of foam mattresses? Those would do until you get proper beds."

"Good idea. That way they can't fall out." Lilian wrote. "Also we need groceries."

"Right," Leroy said, then pulled in to the Atlantic Superstore. "You go on in. I'll stay here with the kids. Do you have enough money?"

"Yes."

By the time Lilian got back 20 minutes later, Zach was standing glued to the window. Zoe was checking out the stubble on Leroy's face. It looked as if Lilian had bought out half the store. Leroy wound the windows down and locked the twins in, long enough to open the back of the truck. Then they were on their way. He dropped off Lilian and the children and went on to find foam mattresses. While in the furniture section of the store, he looked at the cribs and beds and decided he could make something better. Then he recalled one more thing he had to do, run by his mother's and pick up the dog. He had to put the dog in the cab because of the foam mattresses and stuff in the back. He rolled down the passenger window and the dog put his head out. Leroy would have to take the truck in and have it washed and vacuumed out.

Back at Lilian's he let the dog out and started bringing things into the house. The dog bounded in to Lilian. She jumped and turned around. She'd forgotten all about the dog. Then the dog dropped down and walked over to check out the twins. Zoe pulled her hands back, but Zach's face lit up. He stood up and put his arms around the dog's neck. Another friend.

During the next hour, Lilian was busy putting things out of reach of the twins. She hadn't realized how fast they could move, or how curious they would be. She shut the door of her workroom. The safest place was the living room, since there was nothing in it but a chair. In the bathroom and the kitchen she removed all cleaners from under the sinks. The first time Leroy came over, she would ask him to put locks on the doors. High up.

That night as she fed the children, Zoe looked up at a drawing on the wall. "Mama," she said, pointing. It was a sketch Lilian had made before moving into the house. A thrill of excitement ran through her. Somehow she had seen Natalie at different stages of her life. Then she recalled the last one she had done of the skeletal form curled in the foetal position on a hospital bed. She sighed. Zoe pushed Zach. He turned around, then looked where Zoe was pointing. The little boy looked at the sketch a long time. "Mama," Zoe said again. Zach shook his head, then turned to Lilian and smiled.

The next few weeks were busy for Lilian. There was so much to learn about the needs of the children. She had discovered that Zach was deaf. She knew there were schools for deaf children, and she would find out what to do about that. Meanwhile, she had studied sign language and taught Zoe and Zach as she went along. The only time she sketched was when the children were sleeping. She sketched them at every turn. Quite often Zach would run into her arms and demand to be held. Zoe always followed him. And so she spend a lot of time simply holding the children. Leroy came by twice to take her shopping. The children sat in the pickup with him while she bought food and supplies. The only time he saw her flustered was when she brought shoes out to the pickup for the children to try on. The children preferred being barefoot. In the end Leroy took Zach and bought him a pair of boots identical to his own, and then got him some running shoes. Zoe demanded the same and got it.

Leroy watched Lilian with the children. If it was possible, she was looking younger every day. It was hard to believe she was 41. He saw the joy and love between her and the children and in a way, he felt left out. Meanwhile, he put off building the house on the hill. Instead he built beds for the twins. He built rocking horses. Zoe made a lot of him when he came to the house. Zach clung to Lilian.

One morning Leroy coaxed the children outside. He had built a small tractor. Zach looked at it, but Zoe immediately climbed on. Leroy took a long pole and while Zoe steered he pushed the tractor with an expandable aluminium extension pole. Zoe was delighted. Another day he came with a small cart. By then Zoe had learned to pedal the tractor herself. That morning he attached the cart to the tractor and set Zach in the cart. Zoe pulled him around the yard. Then she got off the tractor and turned to Zach and signed: "Now you." Zach climbed on the tractor and began to pedal, his little face scrunched with the effort. Having made a couple of rounds, he motioned for Zoe to get in the cart. Through the window Lilian watched. The beatific smile on Zach's face was wonderful. She grabbed her sketch pad.

Another day Leroy showed up with with a big grin on his face. After greetings and hugs from the children, he said to Lilian, "I brought you something."

"What?"

"Come out to the truck and see."

In the back of the pickup were two identical captain's beds. They were beautifully made of maple and oak with a satin finish, and had deep drawers underneath. At the top of each bed was a small wooden plaque carved with the names: Zoe and Zachry.

"Beautiful," Lilian gestured. "Thank you."

"Okay, Ma'am, where do you want them?"

"The small bedroom. I'll move my bed into my workroom."

Half an hour later they had the beds set up in the small bedroom. The children placed their toys in the drawers under their own beds. Lilian made up the new beds and placed a small faded, braided rug between them. That was all the furniture needed. The closet contained built-in cupboards and drawers where the childrens' clothes were stored.

That night after the twins were settled down, the dog took up his station on the faded braided rug. Lilian checked her e-mail to find a message from Sarah. She had tracked down Natalie's adoptive parents and she had spoken to the husband. They had not known of Natalie's death. However, he explained that his wife had been ill and they could not accept the burden of Natalie's children. Sarah had assured them that the children would be fine, but she required the adoption papers, birth-certificate for Natalie, etc., before she could process the papers. He said they had tossed everything out, but that the papers were registered in Toronto. It would take a little time. Sarah had also asked if he would sign a paper approving of Lilian as guardian of the children. He had agreed.

Lilian breathed a sign of relief. Only a few more days.

Driving home to his mother's, Leroy found himself whistling. Lilian had liked the beds. It was fun watching the twins and holding them. He liked being around Lilian. You had to admit it was a little strange. A silent woman. But he could read her face now, and understand her gestures. She could read his lips.

"You're in a good mood, Leroy," said his mother.

"'Believe I am, yes."

"What's brought this on? You're not drinking, are you?"

"No, ma. Not drinkin'. But I got a surprise for you."

"I hate surprises."

"You might like this one."

"Well, I don't know...."

"Sit down, Ma. I got something to show you." Leroy pulled out one of Lilian's sketches of the twins. "Meet your great grandchildren."

"Leroy, whatever are you talking about?" Mrs. Martin said, picking up the sketches and adjusting her glasses. "Great grandchildren, indeed!

First time I've heard of it. Why wasn't I told?"

"I just found out myself a little while back. It's kind of complicated..."

Leroy told his mother the whole story.

"And they're here in Cedar Springs, you say?"

"Yes."

"Well, when do I get to meet them? This new family?"

"I'll arrange it."

"I need to get my hair done, first."

"I'll take you to the beauty parlour, but I don't think the twins will care." Surprised and relieved at his mother's reaction, Leroy walked around the table and gave her a kiss on the forehead.

After supper Leroy sat down at the table and wrote a letter to Lilian. It wasn't exactly a love letter, but it spelled out his feelings, and it asked her to marry him. They got along well, he wrote. They were good for each other. They could help each other. And the twins needed them both. If she would give him a chance, he would do everything in his power to make her happy. If she felt her house was too small, he would build them another. A big house with lots of room for the twins to grow up in. He'd already found some land she might like to see. She didn't have to answer right away. But would she think about it? He placed the letter in his shirt pocket. He would deliver it the following day.

ISBN 155212813-X

9 781552 128138